# A W⌐        IN STONE

EDITED BY GRAEME FRIEDMAN & ROY BLUMENTHAL

# *A Writer in Stone*

SOUTH AFRICAN WRITERS CELEBRATE
THE 70TH BIRTHDAY OF LIONEL ABRAHAMS

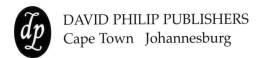

DAVID PHILIP PUBLISHERS
Cape Town   Johannesburg

TO TRACEY, MY LOVE
— GF

TO SAM, TESSA AND LANCE BLUMENTHAL, MY FAMILY
— RB

First published in 1998 in Southern Africa by David Philip Publishers (Pty) Ltd, 208 Werdmuller Centre, Newry Street, Claremont 7800 South Africa

ISBN 0 86486 428 0

Printed by ABC Press (Pty) Ltd, 21 Kinghall Avenue, Epping, 7460, Cape Town

# CONTENTS

Es'kia Mphahlele  *Foreword*  viii
Graeme Friedman & Roy Blumenthal  *Introduction*  x

Mark Gevisser  *No Special Cases: A Profile of Lionel Abrahams*  1
Jane Fox  *Ode for Felix  The Grampus  The Dancer*  13
Zachariah Rapola  *The Contact*  15
Julia Cumes  *Split*  20
E M Macphail  *Ugogo*  22
Kaizer M Nyatsumba  *Lost Pride*  26
Douglas Reid Skinner  *The Conversation*  27
Tony Ullyatt  *Love's Austere and Lonely Offices*  28
Ethelwyn Rebelo  *Man-spirit*  29
Lionel Murcott  *Two Faces*  35
Douglas Livingstone  *Spinal Column  Giovanni Jacopo Meditates (On Uprightness)*  36
Barney Simon  *Monologue for Vanessa*  37
Anne Kellas  *The Brother I Never Knew*  40
Robert Royston  *Two-headed History Lesson*  41
Michael Gardiner  *Lionel and the Renoster*  43
Njabulo S Ndebele  *'I Hid My Love in a Sewage . . .'*  50
David Medalie  *Crowd Control*  52
Eva Bezwoda  *'There is Blood on the Street . . .'  "I Never Promised You a Rose Garden . . ."*  61
Ivan Vladislavić  *A Science of Fragments*  62
Leon Joffe  *'Will I Still Remember Your Face . . .'*  69
Sipho Sepamla  *Dear Lovely  Da Same, Da Same*  70
Debby Lapidos  *Small Talk in Hillbrow*  72
Catherine Stewart  *Looking*  75
Nadine Gordimer  *Once Upon a Time*  76
David Farrell  *The Snowman's Heart*  82
Paul Christelis  *Rabbit Season*  83

Sandra Lee Braude  *The Course*  87
Riva Rubin  *My Friend as She Waits*  88
Lilian Simon  *The Darkness*  89
Marc Glaser  *Now Like a Kite*  93
Maja Kriel  *Berth*  94
Wopko Jensma  *Spanner in the What? Works*  96
Peter Wilhelm  *Zeke in Yugoslavia*  98
Christopher Hope  *Kobus Le Grange Marais*  106
Nat Nakasa  *A Native of Nowhere*  108
Graeme Friedman  *The Beggar in the Bookshop*  111
Seitlhamo Motsapi  *Missa Joe  Sol/o*  119
Shirley Eskapa  Between the Sheets  120
Eleanor Anderson  *A Lady Aged Seventy-Nine Offers a Roborant Word to a Friend Turning Fifty  Fingertips  My One Regret  Late Thoughts  A Spokesman for the Clinic  Froze*  124
Modikwe Dikobe  *The Marabi Dance*  126
Ahmed Essop  *The Sacrifice*  130
Herman Charles Bosman  *The Traitor's Wife*  134
Robert Greig  T*he Sheep-farmer's Wife  Monsters*  139
Roy Blumenthal  *Tattoos are Forever*  141
Walter Saunders  *The Start of the Journey*  145
Oswald Joseph Mtshali  *A Brazier in the Street*  149
Rose Zwi  *Oaxaca, Mexico*  150
Guy Butler  *Myths*  155
Don Maclennan  *Thought and Language*  157
Frances Hunter  *Dreamwriting*  158
Gus Ferguson  *Carpe Diem Limerick*  159
Benjamin Molefi  *Sleeping in the Church*  161
Patrick Cullinan  *A Boy's Own Adventure*  163
Abram Hlabatau  *June '76*  170
Jonathan Morgan  *TeNinEightNooit*  171
Floss M Jay  *Today*  182
Farouk Asvat  *To the Quintessence of Clay*  183
Rose Moss  *The Widow's Widow*  184
Arik Shimansky  *A Good Season for Dying  A Poem in Real Time*  190
Alistair Dredge  *Wanted: One Housekeeper*  191
Pnina Fenster  *The Killling of Cowboy Kate*  192
Tatamkhulu Afrika  *Skull*  196
Mongane Wally Serote  *For Don M. – Banned  City Johannesburg  What's Wrong with People?*  198
Jillian Becker  *A Cry in the Daytime*  200

Ruth Miller  *Milkman   Rat*  206
Es'kia Mphahlele  *Dinku Dikae's Terror*  208
Mike Alfred  *I'll Never Be   Soon I'll Be History*  215
Hugh Lewin  *Wagon-wheels   Hearing in Alex*  217
Stephen Watson  *A Farewell*  220
Cuz Jeppe  *A Pleasure Disallowed*  221
Francis Faller  *Evening with a Bachelor Friend*  223
Yvonne Kemp  *Abide with Me*  224
Geoffrey Haresnape  *Expedition*  230
Hillary Hamburger  *Reality is the Richest Source: An Interview with a
   Friend*  232

*Acknowledgements*  245
*Contributors*  247

# ES'KIA MPHAHLELE

## *Foreword*

What a range of contributors, all coming to pay homage to Lionel Abrahams at his Rivonia farmhouse. A celebration of a life devoted to South African literature. Short stories, poems, essays, vignettes, notes about Abrahams's influence on the careers of these writers. All these and others feature in this tribute.

Gevisser's profile, Gardiner's essay and Hamburger's interview reveal not only the nature of Abrahams's profound influence on South African literature, but also this poet–novelist–essayist's thoughts, arguments, protestations and fusses. Abrahams: sometimes the orthodox liberal who declined involvement in the larger political issues or causes, but often the open-minded writer who did not attempt to seek facile answers for his inner uncertainties.

'As much a literary figure as a littérateur', is Mark Gevisser's view of Abrahams. In the latter role – the littérateur – Abrahams has been like a bird-watcher: a finely tuned ear for listening, a highly sensitized observer, reader. He has seen unfold before him one literary wave after another in this country, corresponding to the waves of a people's consciousness, bringing with them divergent concerns and therefore themes and therefore idioms.

Here, as the galaxy in the contents pages shows, is presented enduring literature reflecting a many-sided world, or even constellations of worlds. Now you imagine you're hearing a chorus of voices, then you realize how dissonant the compositions are in relation to one another. Then again you discern a unifying principle. One which yesterday could be easily identified as banner-flying, axe-to-grind polemics or incantations, even at their least banal, turns out today to be a commitment to life and the art and craft of the written word.

Nothing here approximating a shrine waiting for us as supplicants, no liturgy being chanted, no high priest – all of which would flatten the literature into ritual clichés. Rather the compositions represent a myriad points of light that will not disappear, daytime or night time.

Which says the obvious: that each artist carries his or her own instrument, tuned in his or her own way.

From what we have heard and read about Lionel Abrahams's literary commitment, we trust that this anthology will mean to him what it means to each individual artist who is represented here: a tribute worthy of Abrahams's notion of the value of life, of what he stands for, as a writer and as a human being among humans.

*Lebowakgomo, February 1998*

# GRAEME FRIEDMAN & ROY BLUMENTHAL

## Introduction

### THE RELATIONSHIP MAN

> I open to the writer in the sand,
> the carpenter of metaphor, washer of feet,
> the teacher, the healer, the wit,
> the queller of shoals and winds,
> the feeder, the yarner, the relationship-man
>    *– Lionel Abrahams, from 'The Writer in Sand'*

We're writing this introduction in a farmhouse retreat on the banks of the Vaal River, outside Parys. The others – five adults and six kids – are all asleep. It's dark, and crickets are shrieking down at the river. Somebody's snoring.

We've been remembering the moment when we told Lionel about our idea for his seventieth birthday present. Lionel Abrahams is a gleeful sort of chap. He hauled himself upright in his chair, straining his neck forward, waiting like a baby bird for food. His mouth gaped, then pulled into a smile of sheer delight. "Well . . ." he said. "Tell! Tell!"

And when we told him about this book – a book featuring writers who regard him as their mentor, others he has influenced, his old friends – he smiled so broadly, and grunted with such satisfaction, that we thought he might fly from his wheelchair.

With his delight resonating, we sent word out: "If Lionel Abrahams has in some important way influenced you in your literary career, please send us a selection of what you regard to be your best work." We wanted poems, short stories, and novel extracts, pieces that by their excellence alone would salute him. A celebration of writing.

The response was overwhelming. We were delighted but not sur-prised. He is, after all, a man who has spent the last fifty years or so fostering relationships with his fellow writers. We see him as a 'relationship-man', a man who values the meeting of minds, the joy of interaction. In our search through the published works of some of the authors featured in this volume, we lost track of the number of books and poems dedicated to him.

His influence has spread beyond relationships. The books he has brought into our world, the keen critical voice he has raised above the din: these all come together to allow the academic, Michael Gardiner, to credit Lionel as 'the most influential person in South African literary history'.

He has changed the course of literature – more than once. He published Mongane Wally Serote's *Yakhal'inkomo* and Oswald Mtshali's *Sounds of a Cowhide Drum*, first works for both these poets which 'would later be acclaimed', writes Patrick Cullinan, 'as heralding the "renascence" of black poetry'.

He played an important role in steering Modikwe Dikobe's *The Marabi Dance* towards publication. It, too, has become a South African classic.

Two years after Herman Charles Bosman died, Lionel began editing his uncollected work. Several volumes were published, and Bosman's popular revival was underway.

Lionel's collection of Ruth Miller's work has helped to ensure her place as one of South Africa's foremost poets.

Through Renoster Books, the publishing company Lionel ran with Robert Royston and Eva Bezwoda, and later, Bateleur Press, which he ran with Patrick Cullinan, more than twenty titles were published. These were first books for many of these writers.

Lionel's literary journals provided a platform for writers to show their work. *The Purple Renoster* (1956–1972) was a pioneer journal. Gardiner's essay on page 43 explores its impact on the literary landscape. Lionel's next journal was *Sesame* (1982–1992), which has recently been resurrected on the internet under the banner of *Electronic Sesame*. Lionel has also sat on the editorial boards of *The Bloody Horse* and *Quarry*.

In the literary landscape, sand blows away; stones stay behind. These books and journals are what we see as the enduring evidence of Lionel's influence.

Lionel's attention to relationships has created a living web of influence stretching across place and time.

We received submissions from all over South Africa, as well as the United States, Israel, England, Australia and France. There are people who have been in his workshops, or have been privately tutored by him, whose children are now becoming writers. Julia Cumes is one such literary 'grandchild'. When she was growing up, Lionel used her parents' home as a venue for his workshops. She cites him as 'bringing writing into my world, giving the act of creative writing a special value'.

Which leads us to those writers' workshops. Lionel has run his workshops at various places in Johannesburg for well over twenty years: Alexandra, Wits University, the Johannesburg Art Foundation, and now every Monday night at his home in Rivonia. He provides a space for people to read their work and get honest responses, not only from him, but from each other.

Hillary Hamburger's interview with Lionel closes this collection. In it, Lionel laments the fact that for some time he did not understand that many of his students were hoping for a therapeutic group. We don't think this should be lamented. Of course, many of us write in order to relieve our tormented souls – or at the least, mild neuroses – but his is a writer's group, and as such his skills as a writer's psychologist are superb: he is a great practitioner of the art of interpretation. He does it with an understanding of unconscious process and intent, and a feeling of compassion. He takes each writer seriously. Highly skilled writers and 'wannabe' authors and poets all get the same level of highly focused interest from him. He helps people to feel confident enough to think of themselves as writers. Many of the stories and poems included here come out of these workshops.

A typical workshop: Ten writers in a room. Lionel sits at the head of the table, his right arm poised on its armrest. Someone's poem deposited before him prompts the arduous journey his hand must make in order to grasp and position the page. He has been spastic since birth, and a back operation years ago has left him in some pain and with reduced motor co-ordination. Yet that stiff, jerky movement of his extended thumb and forefinger is sure: the page is taken. The poet reads. And Lionel listens with a fierce and churning concentration. And often he is moved.

In his own writing, he leads by example. Reality and his own experience count for everything – something suggested to him by Bosman. Torment and triumph run through his four poetry collections – *Thresholds of Tolerance*, *Journal of a New Man*, *The Writer in Sand*, and *A Dead Tree Full of Live Birds* – and his 'novel in 18 stories', *The Celibacy of Felix Greenspan*. His authority as a critic and essayist comes from his raw honesty.

In the profile which opens this book, Mark Gevisser examines Lionel's political sensibilities. He puts it this way: '[Lionel] has taken on, in the literary world, a perhaps more difficult persona, one of a self-confessed curmudgeon; the cranky old liberal firing fusillades against a New Order in which language and reason and standards are under perpetual threat.' Lionel's stance has brought conflict from the left (the PEN controversies, in particular) and the right (security-police attention).

More than anything – whether one agrees with his utterances or not – the thread that we discover as we look into his doings is one of fierce individualism. He spoke out on behalf of those fellow writers silenced by apartheid forces. But he never seemed to do this from a sense of himself as a politician or activist. His motivation came from an attachment to people as opposed to ideology.

There seems to be a tension within his personality: the humanist Lionel – the relationship-man – is at times over-run by the Lionel who is a stickler for his sense of moral detail, his adherence to standards. This is why he might now attack the same people he spoke up for in years past, given enough provocation.

But it is not Lionel the political commentator we are honouring here. It is Lionel the mentor and teacher. Even those who have been in conflict with him over political issues happily agreed to be included in these pages, such has been his overall good influence on their careers.

Ten years ago Patrick Cullinan brought us a collection of Lionel's writing – his prose, poetry and critical essays – in *Lionel Abrahams: A Reader*. Others, too, have honoured him. He has been awarded two honorary doctorates (from the Universities of the Witwatersrand and Natal). And he has won several literary awards, including the Olive Schreiner Prize (which he shared with Sipho Sepamla).

This book recognizes that Lionel's work extends far beyond his own œuvre. Half of the contributors have won literary awards. Many of the Sanlam Prize-winners for the last ten years appear in these pages. But there are also names you won't recognize. Almost half of the pieces are being published here for the first time.

A thread of conflict between intellect and the heart tugs its way through the book. Leon Joffe's profound and personal sadness in 'Will I Still Remember Your Face' contrasts with the bleak numbness of the protagonist in Peter Wilhelm's 'Zeke in Yugoslavia'. Kaizer Nyatsumba shows us someone who mourns his 'Lost Pride': he is a 'civilized' African in exile, passion has been traded in for a well-mannered reserve.

Debbie Lapidos makes her debut with the seductively sharp and funny 'Small Talk in Hillbrow', her street-side commentary slicing away at desire and prejudice. Christopher Hope – no stranger to the world's bookshelves – gives us a different humour with the savage satire of 'Kobus Le Grange Marais'. We find in Eleanor Anderson a Dorothy Parker-like wit, always prepared to dig away at the unmentionable.

Alienation is another theme. Zachariah Rapola's protagonist in 'Contact' sits alone in a crowded bar 'contemplating contact' with the only other outsider in the place. The story makes a striking comment on the shakiness of South African youth.

There is a lot of maturity at work. Where we encounter politics, it is neither gratuitous nor unidimensional. The pieces are not driven by ideology alone, but by each writer's sense of the personal – mirroring a principle so important to Lionel. The trap of didacticism is avoided in different ways. Nat Nakasa's piece – so funny, so sad, so full of talent – fills the reader with such a sense of loss. Only a few months later he was to kill himself in exile in New York. Hugh Lewin, in dealing with a stark political reality in his poems, renders them with enormous compassion. Like the other offerings dealing with memory and social amnesia, these poems show us how much more we can learn – emotionally – from literature and art than from academic tracts.

Some writers offer us protagonists with twisted minds. The extract from Paul Christelis's *Rabbit Season* shows us a disturbing helix of hunter and hunted. The heroine in Yvonne Kemp's 'Abide With Me' proffers her pain and liberation in a startlingly dislocated way.

No doubt we've left out writers who should be included here. And there may be some we are unaware of. Others we have had to omit due to space considerations. A few submissions reached us too late for inclusion.

When you've finished this book, there's more to be found in a special edition of *Electronic Sesame* on the internet. It is intended as an accompaniment to this volume, and includes some of those pieces we didn't have space for, and others written especially for the online publication.

Back in the Parys farmhouse, it's time to call it a night. Graeme jams shut the covers of the two lever-arch files containing the submissions. David, his son, comes down the unfamiliar passage in his Power Ranger pyjamas, rubbing his eyes.

"Do you know what, Roy?" says David.

Roy stops typing on his notebook computer. "What's that, Davey?"

And David says:
"The moon goes down,
the stars change into the clouds,
the sun comes up,
then it was morning."
A midnight poem from a four-year-old. It makes us think of Lionel's influence. Of how it has entered into the lives and homes of so many. Of how it will go beyond this generation into the next.

*Parys, January 1998*

# MARK GEVISSER

## a profile of Lionel Abrahams

### NO SPECIAL CASES

There is something transformative about a first encounter with Lionel Abrahams. At the outset, it is hard not to be overwhelmed by his extreme physical dysfunction: even the slightest manipulations – the scratching of a forehead, the minuscule movements required to shift his mechanized wheelchair, the enunciation of a response – require such effort that you are not sure how he will make it through the interview. You struggle to understand; you are frequently thrown off the course of an idea by his contortions.

But ineluctably, the dynamics begin to change. It's not just that you begin to become more familiar with his lexicon of staccato gestures, facial grimaces and slurred vowel-sounds. It's that he entices you so fully, through his communicative powers, into the world of his intellect, his book-filled study, that you buy into its own set of coordinates: before you know it, he has extended the walls of his world to encompass you. A few hours later (it's never less than a few hours), you go back out into the ambulatory workaday world and realize that it, rather than Lionel Abrahams, is different, strangely deficient. And you're incomparably richer for the insights you have just gained.

A student of Abrahams explains his potency thus: "His mind is so powerful, that he is able to use it to make you forget how useless his body is." After a few hours with him, I felt the relationship between his body and his mind to be, in a way, less complicated. He was born with a severe neurological condition, a type of palsy known as 'Jewish Tortion Dystonia'. But unlike many disabled people, he does not attempt to perform the impossible conjuring trick of pretending his body isn't there. It *is* there, in a very matter-of-fact, unprecious, and unself-pitying way. Sometimes it needs help, other times it will manage fine by itself, as long as you exercise a bit of patience.

In *The Celibacy of Felix Greenspan,* Abrahams's compelling autobiographical novel, the disabled young protagonist is seduced by the notion, supplied to him by a master at the home he lives in, that he can put 'Mind over Matter'. So entirely does Felix embrace his master's mystical, proto-Louise-Hayes-ish notions of 'the power of positive thinking' that he stops himself just moments before trying to swim across a dam – a test that would surely have killed him.

Felix's next mentor, based strongly on the character of Herman Charles Bosman (who was to exert a profound influence on Abrahams's life as his creative writing teacher) gives him the far more workable idea that he can move toward the achievement of creative – and physical – potency through willing his mind to engage with matter, with the world, rather than forcing it, impossibly, to transcend it.

In a poem called 'Meditation with a Cat', Abrahams describes, with loving precision, the movements of the animal: 'She unfolds her curious elastic ease/ through the rich space of the room,/ tensed by suspicion,/ sprung by the cunning lust to kill,/ testing the limits of the moment . . .' And then, a whiplash turnaround: '. . . the moment she, after all, is gaoled in.' Gaoled, because 'her motions, her motives/ are less hers/ than mine./ Perception and concept and design/ are the space wherein I'm free.'

It's the expression of an intense, almost swaggering poetic bravado: the cat only moves, dear reader, because I make her move for you. She is sensation alone, mechanical, gaoled by my plans for her, by the moment of the poem. I might not be able to move my own body, but I can perceive and conceive and design *her* movement – and that's how *I* can be free. Somewhat reminiscent of Yeats's 'Lapis Lazuli'.

How well Abrahams understands the power of 'Mind over Matter'. But his triumph is in how fully he took Bosman's lessons to heart, in that he has put his difficult body so successfully into the world. He has single-mindedly gone about accumulating the experience he requires as writer – from eating fruit to travelling the world to having sex to engaging with politics and with the city he lives in – as if there were not so strong a barrier in his way. He has not retreated into cerebral celibacy. In fact, it is hard not to be struck by just how physically charged he is: he glows.

Certainly, a lot of his poetry is cerebral or polemical, but much else is devoted to sensuality and sentiment. His love-poems to his wife Jane Fox are, to my mind, among the best of that genre written in South Africa – I'd rank them up there with those of his arch-adversary in the cultural wars, Jeremy Cronin. Both, for all their polemical soap-boxing, can write about love, and sex, in a way that gives flesh to

Abrahams's defining credo: that interpersonal relationships, rather than political processes, have the power to change the world.

Unlike the South African 'greats' who have made it into the planetary canon – Gordimer, Coetzee, Fugard – Abrahams's own literary output has been slender: four volumes of poetry, one novel. In fact, he published his first book only when he was fifty. Perhaps, he volunteers with a chuckle, this is because he hasn't been "ruthless" enough in protecting his own time. The result: his influence, as a publisher, teacher, editor and proponent of South African literature has been profound.

He is that rare thing indeed in South African culture: a literary figure as much as he is a littérateur. He has a generous knack for immortalising his mentors: he is significantly responsible for the popular revival of Herman Charles Bosman, and he spent years arranging publication for a comprehensive collection of the poetry of his other great teacher, Ruth Miller. His literary magazine, *The Purple Renoster*, defined both quality and vanguardism in South African literature through the 1960s. His publication, in the early 70s, of the first, soul-searing volumes of poetry by Oswald Mtshali and Wally Serote are among the most significant milestones in the development of contemporary South African literature. As this very anthology testifies, his career has touched almost every single significant South African writer of the past half-century, from Guy Butler to Zacharia Rapola.

We sit now, on the eve of his seventieth birthday, in the study of the rambling old Rivonia farmhouse he shares with Jane, to whom he has been married for the last fifteen years. She too is a writer – she assisted him in the editing of his literary magazine, *Sesame*, and she is a regular in his Monday night writing workshops. Abrahams does not hide the scars of a difficult life, but now there is something quite comfortable, almost sated, in his manner. His home with Jane is *gemütlich*, easy with itself. It has, about it, neither the self-conscious clutter that proclaims 'intellectual' nor the self-conscious aestheticism that proclaims 'connoisseur'.

I ask him what it was about Bosman's ideas that gave him so compelling an antidote to the 'Mind over Matter' credo supplied by his first mentor. "What was it?" he echoes, in his manner of repeating a question so that he can turn it inside-out, as if to expose its less immediately apparent implications to the light of day. "What was it? It had to do with his vision of art, art in the world, and one's possible relation to art. It had to do with connection, art as means of entering into a relationship with strangers, across space and across time . . ."

There is a mysticism to this response, a lack of the usual cloudless acuity, that points to the effect Bosman had on his young protégé, an effect so profound that language eludes him when he tries to explain Bosman's role in his life. Even Abrahams, for whom language is reason itself, must concede that there are certain topics – salvation, for one – that are mercifully beyond its grasp.

Above Abrahams's desk is a huge blow-up of a newspaper photo of his mentor. A jaunty Bosman strides down a Johannesburg street with a woman on each arm above the caption, 'Herman Charles Bosman with his two wives.' Abrahams obviously loves the raffish boulevardier in Bosman, loves the mischief-maker and the dissident, and has modelled for himself a similar role in literary society. Bosman remains his guide in many ways – from the importance of having a sense of 'place' in Johannesburg, to the notion, that Abrahams often expounds, of 'aesthetic patriotism', a belief in rigorous standards that would enable an indigenous South African literature to become world-class.

When Abrahams published his first short story in *Trek* in the late 1940s, Bosman (who incidentally was *Trek's* literary editor) wrote him a letter, congratulating him as 'the Pauline Smith of Johannesburg'. "By that," Abrahams explains, "he was pointing to my particular identification with a locality."

No South African writer's identification with this city is stronger. "He was the pivot," says writer and critic Stephen Gray, "of a glorious school of Johannesburg writing that took hold around him in the 1960s; people like Lionel and Barney Simon were pioneers of the Golden City vernacular; theirs was a gritty suburban realism."

When I read Abrahams's writings about the city into which I was born – the Jewish Johannesburg of the 60s – I feel an almost inexplicable longing for a place I never knew. Part of this is because I have always felt that I was born into an environment that was shutting down, closing up, after the effusion of the 50s, due to the stranglehold of Verwoerdian apartheid. Abrahams – perhaps because of his idiosyncratic relationship to politics – has shown me another side: he writes approvingly of how his friend the poet David Wright saw the Johannesburg of the 60s, 'with its new publishers, new theatres, new literary magazines, new sorts of encounters between white and newly visible black writers resulting in new possibilities and perplexities [as] something of a vibrant centre.'

But Abrahams's writing about my home town provokes in me so

intense a longing primarily because of something more profound: his acute understanding of how this perpetually self-imploding, self-reinventing city of ours relates to memory and amnesia. This is an understanding enhanced, no doubt, by the ironic fact that his father was a demolition contractor responsible for pulling down much of Johannesburg's history: 'Memory', he writes in his magnificent 'The Fall of van Eck House', 'takes root only half in the folds of the brain:/ half's in the concrete streets we have lived along./ Implosion, abrupt negation, amputates flesh of dreams./ van Eck House – I'd hardly been aware/ it bore this newer name: of I.'

There is, says his old friend and editor, Patrick Cullinan, a core of mischief to Abrahams's personality. "When I first met Lionel, I'd find it difficult to be in public with him. I'd always feel so bad for him. But then Barney Simon [one of Abrahams's closest friends] said something to me I have never forgotten: 'Don't ever forget that Lionel is the one who is amused. He's looking, and laughing at them a lot harder than they're laughing at him.'"

In *Celibacy*, the young Felix overcomes the terrible ostracism he experiences at the home (not least for being a smart-alecky Jewboy in a very Afrikaans environment during the war years) by inventing the character of Professor Mac-U-Laff, a stand-up comic routine in which Felix 'makes you laff', gets the other kids slapping their sides by parodying himself and playing the court jester.

Abrahams the chortling jester – which is how his friends know him: head thrown back in gleeful mirth – is not a figure with which the public is familiar. He has taken on, in the literary world, a perhaps more difficult persona, one of a self-confessed curmudgeon; the cranky old liberal firing fusillades against a New Order in which language and reason and standards are under perpetual threat. But this, believes Cullinan, also has a fair dollop of self-parody in it. "Sometimes," he says, "it's as if Lionel is playing it up a little bit, the elderly man of letters tut-tutting."

"Let's put it this way," says Jane Fox. "Lionel has no problem being combative. He'll fight for something he believes in. 'Letting off his popgun,' he calls it."

Here, for example, is Abrahams in the mid-80s, decrying the 'death' of English: 'As we rush toward [the new dispensation], the anticipatory excitement in many takes the form of an appetite for demolition. The coming new man is not allowed to have anything in common with us, is not conceived of as having any use for our proven values and proven structures. Out they must go! Down they must go! Épater les bourgeois! Whee! I believe this negative radicalism is strictly limited in its thinking and promises us a dull, impoverished mental world with less language and therefore less freedom than ever.'

Ten years later, does he feel this prophecy to be accurate? "It's not as bad as all that," he chuckles. "Perhaps I wouldn't put it so strongly. There are a number of people holding on to what is right." The laughter stops. He is dead-serious now. "But I'm far from altogether happy. In the field of language and literature, authority has become very timid. One of the swearwords of the day is prescriptiveness, and as a result linguistic imprecision is not so much tolerated as embraced as the norm."

With this he launches into a tirade against the use of expressions such as 'job situation' rather than 'job', 'problem area' rather than 'problem', 'life-styles' rather than 'life', 'intelligence levels' rather than 'intelligence'. "To me it suggests that among the movers and makers, there is a defensiveness, a preference for vagueness, to obfuscate the fact that they can't deliver on promises."

This is classic, curmudgeonly Abrahams. I too am irritated by the reign of jargonish sociospeak over governance. But if a bit of linguistic sloppiness is the by-product of democracy, as opposed to the extreme linguistic precision of apartheid with its taxonomy of rules and fixed locations, then I'll put up with it. Why can't Abrahams?

"He has become," explains his friend, the writer Peter Wilhelm, "something of an icon of classic liberalism. What seems to annoy him more than anything else is the breakdown of language, which he sees as the breakdown of rationalism, because he identifies the coherent use of language with the power of reason itself. Bad art or bad language, in that light, represents bad thinking, and out of bad thinking you get social dislocation, random murders, genocide. . ."

Part of what appears, incorrectly, to be orneriness stems from a distaste for anything faddish or fashionable. One of his oldest friends, the writer Rose Moss, remembers that, at Wits University in the 1950s, "people would go off to the Treason Trial to see what was happening, but Lionel would have nothing to do with it. In fact he was disdainful of it. His sense was that a lot of people were being opportunistic; they were interested in showing their moral superiority, not in public action rooted in their own experience."

This anti-faddishness sometimes seems to lead Abrahams to throw the baby of a just cause out with the bathwater of its less virtuous proponents; another example of this is his almost bilious dislike of literary theory, which he believes constitutes – along with political correctness – the very direst threat to art.

Ask Abrahams who impresses him in contemporary South African literature and he'll respond, "Coetzee, Coetzee, Coetzee, both in fiction and in criticism." JM Coetzee returns the compliment: "Lionel Abrahams has been a reliable and fairly rocklike presence on the South African critical/reviewing scene for a couple of decades. He is an old-fashioned critic of the FR Leavis or Lionel Trilling type, but there's nothing wrong with that. He is an acute reader, with generous sympathies – an unusual combination."

Abrahams's critical perspective combines a transcendental mysticism about art received from Eliot via Bosman ('between us [the reader and the poet], by some damned miracle,/ the poem takes place') with a staunch positivism that embraces set standards and values and decries the relativism of cultural studies. 'Ironically,' he has written, 'in dismissing the received standards of literary excellence as merely a Eurocentric cultural convention, [. . .] white critics [of the left] were in effect saying to the black newcomers to the disciplines of print: "The best is not expected of you; the best is not for your enjoyment." '

This is why he refused to class the 'ritualized slogans, jeers and exhortations' of oral struggle-verse as 'poetry', why he wrote, about *Staffrider*, that 'I began to find the magazine largely unreadable. Its openness was of a different sort from what the first issue had led me to expect. It was open to expressions of the people's voice to the extent that other voices seemed to be crowded out. What to me was so disappointing in the populist utterance is that it drew so little on actual experience and so much on politically sanctioned, flattened, smoothed and simplified notions of what experience was supposed to be. The tone was shrill but the content often had the paradoxical blandness of stereotype and cliché.'

Abrahams struggles, perpetually, with how to be an 'individualist' voice in 'collectivist' Africa. 'How', he asks in a recent column in *Sidelines*, 'am I to proceed with my life as a South African if, for instance, individualism and "western" logic are somehow inherently wrong, at any rate un-African?'

He mistrusts politics precisely because of its 'flattening' collectivity. "I'm no kind of political activist," he tells me. "I'm no kind of political apologist. I don't bend my abilities to anybody's purpose. I don't let anyone engage me. Which is not to say," he adds with a characteristic undercutting smile (a physical signification of ambivalence and contradiction one does not often pick up in his polemical writing), "that I can't be seduced!"

He is inherently conservative. He was only really roused into rage at the excesses of Verwoerdian apartheid when the government passed its infamous 'gagging' clause, silencing 102 writers – many of whom were not even communists – in 1966. He wrote in his diary (published later in Patrick Cullinan's collection, *Lionel Abrahams: A Reader*) at the time: 'My willingness to trust the Nationalists' fundamental good intentions in a situation of extraordinary complexity, my desire to see them given a chance to put their solution to the test, are knocked awry by this reminder that they go in abject terror of the mere words of their critics. [. . .] Perhaps the militant liberals are right. Perhaps it has to be war . . .'

When they were at university, says Rose Moss, "Lionel just didn't believe that politics was that important, because of his credo about literature, which is that you solve things through personal interaction. He saw communication through literature as the medium through which good things happen; not politics."

Because of this overarching credo, Abrahams was initially optimistic, in the late 1970s, about the formation of PEN (Johannesburg), a meeting place of writers that worked as a sort of encounter-group across the races and organized township poetry readings. He joined PEN and was elected onto its large executive committee.

But his political coming of age – and his ultimate, rather bitter, fall from innocence – was the fractious dissolution of the organization a few years later. He experienced – and articulated publicly – a sense of dismay when black writers, supported by white leftists in a dilemma, insisted on closing up shop because political imperatives made it difficult for them to continue working with some whites while there was a struggle to be waged against others.

One of Abrahams's major involvements was the editing of Modikwe Dikobe's rough diamond of a novel, *The Marabi Dance*, a project that took the better part of a decade. He was accused of interfering unduly, as editor, with Dikobe's own writing and sensibilities. The issue raises all the most complicated questions about race and patronage in South Africa. Abrahams rejects the accusation out of hand: "It was as though," he told me once, "it was a dirty window we cleaned up a bit. We might have replaced a pane or two, but we did not ever interfere with the author's intention. Every single idea in the book is his and his alone."

Njabulo Ndebele is one of the black writers with whom Abrahams clashed in those years – although the two have always had a strong mutual respect. "I have been," says Ndebele now, "impressed by one thing in Lionel Abrahams: the consistent thread, in his thinking, of the importance of the humanizing values of literature, and that these values can only be achieved through a rigorous attention to the exacting demands of making art. To many on the left, such a position elicited a great deal of impatience. Lionel's positions may be irritating, but impossible to ignore, and you grudgingly accede to them!"

Ndebele offers himself as an example: "As a young man I submitted a poem to him for publication, and he rejected it, because he didn't think it was good enough. I was outraged! And I penned a longwinded response, deploying politics and social context in my defence. Now, of course, I see that Lionel represents an abiding core of value which one appreciates – about innovation, about being skilled, about putting stress on learning and excellence. I see that he is a symbol of lasting value, and I appreciate the courage with which he took those positions when it was difficult to take them."

Nonetheless, Ndebele feels that there is also "a core of innocence, a certain lack of understanding" in Abrahams's positions: "Man, how could someone not understand that the poetry of wild gesture and stance-taking in the 70s and 80s was imperative?"

In perhaps his most compelling articulation of the liberal position in post-apartheid South Africa – the 1995 Hoernlé Memorial Lecture he delivered to the SA Institute of Race Relations – Abrahams makes a distinction between the Jeremiahs of South African literature, 'dominated by an idea of South Africa in a state of political and moral sickness' (Gordimer, Fugard, Brink, Coetzee, Ndebele, Breytenbach, Hope), and the Isaiahs, whose 'visionary patriotism [. . .] inspire[s] transformation, growth, flight' (Paton, Small, Mphahlele, Schreiner, Smuts).

At the end of the lecture he recites his familiar litany of the decline of our civilization: 'We are living in an avalanche of change. Many of the changes cause me pain. The order of my world is threatened. Security, convenience and pleasantness are less to be counted on. I have to witness insulting, wasteful, self-destructive savagery, and remind myself that trash on the streets is less terrible than blood on the streets [. . .] I have to wait while the exasperated, the disappointed, the misled try their hand at fulfilling the symbolism of President Mandela's inauguration by overhauling everything – even the hospitals that succour their own people, even the museums, libraries and universities that give the nation some means of mastery over time and brute circumstance – remaking all in the image of Africa.'

Jeremiad though this may sound, he lands up identifying himself, unexpectedly, with Isaiah: 'Sorrowfully, critically, but without paralyzing anger, fear or disgust, I have to endure and survive all this – in the words of Isaiah, to hide myself "as it were for a little moment, until the indignation be overpast" – if I am to embrace our African destiny.' Abrahams occupies a unique position in South African intellectual consciousness: he holds within him both the exuberant Isaiad hope of a Bosman and the measured Jeremiad scepticism of a Coetzee.

There is a clue, perhaps, to Abrahams's polemical intolerance of any position other than one that adheres to cast-iron standards of aesthetic value, in something else he said when delivering that Hoernlé Lecture: he made what he called the 'brutal but necessary remark' that, 'in the arts, as I see it, the deserving case – the poor widow, the paralyzed beggar, the child of the oppressed, the hero of the struggle, the survivor of genocide – has no special claim. Genius, talent, meaningful accomplishment, the aesthetic transmutation of experience, are the only justifications.'

To many, Abrahams would seem, by virtue of his physical incapacity, just such a 'deserving case'. And yet he has made it, as a writer, through no special privileges, no affirmative action, but by dint of his own talent, hard work and perseverance. There's more than a little of a 'pull yourself up by your bootstraps' intonation to his polemic.

'My Skin . . .', writes Abrahams in a recent poem called 'Flesh', '. . . is no safe place./ The walls of my house contain/ sufficient travail,/ the floor lies ready to bruise me,/ beat out my breath. Health, safety,/ time for work are not vouchsafed./ I must carve them out of each slippery/ hard-textured day, must grapple/ with the knotted minutes for those luxuries:/ my bare subsistence, a glint of meaning./ This is why, for all I have heard,/ I remain, you could say, aloof;/ in practical terms, you could say,/ ignorant of the struggle.'

It's hard to take Abrahams's protestations of disengagement – of 'ignorance' and 'aloofness' – seriously. His friend, the writer Ivan Vladislavić sees him as "the model of a literary life, precisely because he represents the possibility of a life in books, without withdrawing from the world. He insists on a public life."

As Abrahams puts it, his "thoroughgoing honesty" (in one poem he parodies himself as 'honest Abe whoring with facts') impels him to lay bare the contradictory tensions of his life and work: the tension between the self-involvement he requires to keep his own house – the house of his body – intact, and the public engagement he needs to exercise his credo of communication; the tension between cast-iron aesthetic and moral values, and the more shifting exigencies of life and politics; the tension between the attraction of putting 'Mind over Matter' and the realization that he must engage with 'Matter' if he is to write.

In person, he is very comfortable with the irreconcilability of these tensions, and with the articulation of self-doubts. Unprompted, he itemizes these for me: that he is a bad liberal because he is impatient and intolerant, that he has not read enough, that "there are times when I talk as though I know, even when I don't", that he is not always "brave enough" to possess the "thoroughgoing honesty" so central to his beliefs.

I am astonished when he goes on to tell me, following the Monday night writing workshop I attended, that he fears he performed only at around 35 per cent. "Oh come on Lionel," Jane interjects. "I think you're being hard on yourself! I'd put it at 45 per cent." I sat through the four-hour session, somewhat agape, watching a performance that I would have put somewhere up around 100 per cent. His criticism was unerringly accurate, and almost aphoristic in its acuteness. Most remarkable was to see, in practice, what I had often been told of – his ability to understand the writer's intention and to help the writer achieve this intention, even when he's not always in sympathy with it.

On the Monday night I attended, twenty or so people clustered, in pools of lamplight, around a long table in the Abrahams's living-room. They ranged in age from early 20s to 70s, and took turns to read their offerings, in prose or verse. "Delicious!" one older woman said after someone's recital of a poem – and the gathering around a dining-table did make it seem, at times, like a feast of language; a careful feast, for Abrahams is no voluptuary, and the environment he engenders is more workmanlike than precious.

Abrahams encourages people to write from their own experience, and although this is the most helpful way to teach the craft, it does sometimes result in a walled-in generic suburbia that seems to be floating atop, rather than engaging with, the kind of South African experience about which Bosman was so passionate. This can be seen most clearly in *Sesame*, which, despite being a child of the turbulent 1980s, is devoid of the formal and spiritual adventure of *The Purple Renoster* that preceded it. If this is true, Abrahams allows, perhaps it is because *Sesame* was receptive to the kind of individualistic approach to writing that more boisterous publications, like *Staffrider*, eschewed.

At the workshop I attended there were only two contributions which so much as nodded at the transition we are living through. There was, though, mercifully little of the pseudo-therapy that plagues writing workshops and specifically autobiographical work, and although there was some platitudinous affirmation, there was just as much bracing, on-the-ball critical comment: Abrahams has encouraged a culture of honest generosity. Some students take much pleasure in sparring with him, as does he with them. Others hang on his every word, beaming in his beneficence, or even his opprobrium. "Thankyou! Thankyou!" said one, after he had cut her to ribbons.

On guruness, Lionel Abrahams has this to say: "I have been presented as an establishment figure, as though I were part of an important institution. In a way I wish I were. I'd be better off than I am now. I'm usually aware of how fortunate I've been, in terms of friendship and creativity. But I haven't worked out a way of getting fat. I've just gone about my life, doing what I feel I must and can, as the demand arises, and the demand is as likely to be an internal as an external one. If the results add up to a particular position of guruhood, well, that has never been aimed at. It exists as a nice kind of accident."

*three poems*

## ODE FOR FELIX

Ho Ho, a friend
I've found a friend
and what a friend is he!
With graceful beard and gentle eye
right merrily bent on me.

A mossy cardigan hangs round
his small and skinny bod;
an elf he seems
but what a bloke –
a huge enormous gorgeous bloke
a mighty magic spelling bloke –
a sort of ink-stained god.

With ginger pop and liquorice
he weaves a crafty net.
An unsuspecting maiden, I
all smitten in his web do lie:
"Dear spider," is my happy cry
"I'm jolly glad we met."

## THE GRAMPUS

The first day of the Second World War
my father, wearing his maroon bathing suit
with its drooping shoulder straps which bared
most of his eggshell chest to the north wind,
stood shivering in the sea, knees white as water,

waiting for the humping peril of the next wave.
It swelled, reared, gathered itself at the crest,
began its crashing glassy roll, and he
calm as a fish, raised his arms and dived
through it as if it were nothing.

                                        Afterwards

in the dark sandy hut he quivered and shook,
scrubbed himself with a holey towel
thin as a sheet, fingers and feet
blue as a rescued corpse, groaned,
blew out his cheeks, spluttered and hissed.
"Why do you make such a noise?" I said.
"Because I'm a GRAMPUS," he said, "I'm
SNORTING like a GRAMPUS." Then my mother
packed his suitcase, and he had to go.


## THE DANCER

Balance is a matter of bracing –
no careless poise for him.
Each journey's end's a climax
of chameleon grips on
                chairbacks
                        doorknobs
                                people:
a snail adventure
        from bed to chair
                from chair to desk
                        from desk to bed
not undertaken lightly.

Installed, he grows in his chair
like a neat plant in a pot
sprouting wisdom and wisecracks.

So rooted he seems
yet friends and lovers know
how joyously he dances.

# ZACHARIAH RAPOLA

## *a story*

### THE CONTACT

I am tormented by the seat I am sitting on. It pricks and jabs my buttocks, which have grown flabbier through lack of exercise – they haven't been caressed or squeezed by a woman's hands for eighteen months. They are sore from the strain of the bar stool. Yaa! I am sitting in a tavern.

In the chaos of the bar I am the only odd party. My state of quietness unsettles me. Around me bodies collide, sway and jostle.

"I swear, s'true's God . . ."

"Ya! That was the best funeral in years."

"Outie! Never seen so baya mooi gesigs in one service."

Sis! Heartless moron.

"Boy – that was the mother of all fashion parades."

Sis! Soulless pig.

My head goes into a tail-spin as I try to keep track of the speakers; muffled, shrill and croaking voices desperate for attention. They invade and possess reluctant ears. At the height of the mood, everything has lost its meaning. Noses lurch about, scouting and fishing for virgin air, contaminating it before they reach their intended recipients. Women's perfume and men's after-shave vie for the aromatic trophy. Each body is striving to stamp its individuality by wearing the most expensive.

"S'true's God . . . this beer tastes like a virgin's navel sweat." I look at the speaker. Like me he is apart, isolated. He gives a wink at my buying his supposed scientific discovery. Then it dawns on me that his speech was not intended for me, but rather for a bunch of thirteen- and fourteen-year-old girls sitting not far from us. An observant eye can see the tennis balls tucked underneath their bras.

And I am sitting contemplating contact.

He is like me. Yet at the same time I feel different from him. Not only him, but the entire bar crowd. A friend once described me as stand-offish. But I don't agree. It is just that I have always felt excluded. Even from that embracing generic term: male.

This is confirmed by the beer glass in front of me. I note that the froth at its base has been there for the past thirty minutes. It refuses to dry. Soon I will be thrown out for inhibiting business.

Then this man, sitting alone, will be reduced to one of a kind.

Still, I realize that sitting here with an empty glass is the only strategy left to attract attention to myself. Maybe somebody will offer to buy me another glass. Maybe some curious woman will offer to share her beer or hot-stuff glass with me. Then maybe intimate dialogue will follow. The kind that leads to a romantic escapade. Maybe then, who knows, one potential buttock-squeezer will be secured.

But first I need to come to terms with the strange feelings that are becoming a common feature in my life. How come I am always confused about who I am? How come even my sweat doesn't dry? The beer takes effect. My head starts swerving. Maybe I am another person, like an actor, an impostor or impersonator. Temporarily cast in the role of portraying another person. Suppose I am a woman trapped in a man's body, or a white person trapped in a black skin. Or maybe even an animal condemned to eternal affliction in a human body. Suppose all these supposes are true.

The dizziness comes again. I clasp my head in my palms. That makes me feel better. Steadier. Then loneliness seizes me. I jerk up and rush to the dance floor. I plunge myself into the den of lahlaumlenze, swaying bodies. The smell of sweat and foul breath assails me. But I dive lower. Hypnotised by the gravitational pull of swaying hips, swinging breasts, gyrating pelvic bones, twisting limbs and flailing arms. Above this, a blaring fusion of African, reggae and rap music. A relentless tempo. I go back to my seat.

And I am sitting contemplating contact.

"S'true's God, I swear. The police arrested him at a pharmacist . . ."

"Eii son! The Safe, was it . . .?"

"Listen man! E gashu ba ebambe with packets of condoms . . ."

"Condoms!"

"Condoms!"

"The latest make. The ones the TV and radio say they feel just like a part of your body. And he was already trying on one when security found him." Everybody doubles up with laughter.

Just then I turn to find him looking at me. I start fumbling around. His eyes soften their stare. A smile spreads over his face. Familiarity has now descended on us.

He then takes a marathon final swig of his draught. The 'khmmhhh-kmmhhh' that accompanies it is drowned by the music and shrill voices engaged in intense competition.

It seems that the internal dam caused by that gulp has given him pluck and courage. For I see him stand. Eyes fixed on me. They are not his, but those of the intoxicated seducer in him. His walk to my side of the tavern is slow and shaky.

"Hhh-y-yoo . . . knoooow . . . whaaaaat? A-aa . . . I li-yke yu."

He flops on the stool next to mine, his neck straining to support the weight of his beer-soaked brains. He beckons a service-girl.

And I sit there watching him.

He is in his early thirties. He has a likeable face. The sort of face that mothers would trust their daughters with.

His draught is delivered. The pretty service-girl gives him a sweet smile; he does not notice. He lifts the draught to his mouth. His throat sluices the liquid down. In frantic movements it is sucked down his gullet. It strikes me that the city engineers probably studied and modelled the sewerage system on the alimentary canal.

I pull my eyes from his stomach, where they had followed the beer on its journey. I notice that under the pretext of drunkenness his eyes have been stripping me. I hastily pull my lumber-jacket to hide myself. This does not distract him though. He continues peeling me naked with his hungry eyes. He does not notice Damaria. She is the new resident waitress-cum-escort girl. She decides to perch herself on his lap.

"Hii-gh sweetie."

"Futsek!" he barks at her.

She jumps up, pauses a moment, looking at him with shock. She slithers away. She is not bad, this Damaria. She is about seventeen. A new extra service the tavern owner has added for the overall comfort of his clients.

"I don't like them bitches."

I am shocked by his language. This can't be justified merely on account of the beer. I realise that his speech wasn't laboured at all. I smile and meet his wink. Conversation becomes easier.

"But listen to this," he almost pleads, "it started . . . I can't remember . . . I thought it was a passing childhood activity. But my sister ended up with isikhwelo. Even after she got a steady boyfriend, she still came after me."

"Didn't you, I mean, your mother or father, say a thing?"

"Those! It was worse, bra. Bathe uk'khala a ko size, you know that, man. It was better with nobody knowing. Then she started with her heavy drinking and bringing condoms as well. I was sort of grateful of that. But then there were times she would vomit on the bed. S'true broer, uk'khala a ko size. And she said, if I refused, she would tell everybody. Just think of it – a laaitikie like me – my friends at school and those in the neighbourhood talking about it."

"What happened?"

"My mother and father! A hostel was better, broer. It was indoda eyaz'phekela, an orphanage, a harem, confinement in a solitary cell amid squabbles, sulkings and perpetual frowns. With father having his pots at one side of the kitchen, and mother having her own at the other side . . ."

I look deep in his eyes, somehow thinking I might encounter the actor in him again. But no, he is serious.

"One day it had to happen . . ."

"What?" I ask. He raises his eyes and looks at me. Slowly I see his right hand stretching to my face. His hand, dabbed in sweat, starts caressing me.

While listening to the feel of his hand, I start thinking about our discussion – no, not that – our consultation. No, not that either. It is a proposition. The opening and pouring out of one strafed solitary soul to another.

Is this what women have to endure? This well-rehearsed and perfected epic detour that men bombard them with. Which is sealed with a shy, blushing, *Okay Sello, let's give it a try.* Or an assertive care-less-not-what-you-think, *Agg! Shame Thato, you don't even feature in my nightmares.*

Poor boy. This makes me feel superior to him. The kind of superiority vegetarians exhibit toward carnivores. This is contrasted by the panic I start feeling. I also feel an urge to come closer to him.

I notice that the noise around us has subsided. I look around and find that most of the patrons have left. The ones who remain are either too drunk to drive or have been left behind by their partners. Most of them are now sprawled and scattered around like rags. Their earlier festive mood is gone. Here and there I see moths. They are exhausted from having fluttered their wings for most of the night. They are now slithering and fluttering on the floor. Damaria, where is she? Probably somebody has secured her services, purchased a revisit to the crevice that leads to fleeting tranquillity.

He and I are the only ones who are alert. The pressure of our interview has probably played a part in that. The need to bring the matter to its conclusion is pressing. His eyes stare unblinkingly into mine, probing for an answer.

Then he stands and beckons me to follow him. I can feel excitement and expectation rising in me. We reach the toilet. He starts rubbing and nuzzling himself against me, kissing and twitching, his breath heaving and rapid.

And I am standing contemplating contact.

His stubble and skin feel like sandpaper on my face. His hands hustle for my chest. Encountering little warmth, they slide down. I recoil as his tongue seeks mine, but his passion is too overbearing for him to notice this.

His urgency has taken possession of his actions. An entranced zombie, fumbling; a hypnotised child, groping forward, beside himself. Striving to reach a point. Striving to grasp reassurance and comfort. Then I see the foetus in him, clinging to the mother for nourishment. Clinging and refusing to let go of the umbilical cord.

This makes me understand why midwives play the role of butchers. By severing the cord. Not so much to free the newborn, but to free the mother from the clinging, selfish infant. And I wonder if I will be able to give such comfort and nourishment as he now demands. Maybe we are not one of a kind. And I wonder if my hardened masculinity will be able to give that vestige of sensuality he is groping for. It might be that it is only by copulating with a woman that a man re-experiences that elusive warmth and comfort only the womb can provide.

Then the sun sets for him. A potential off-spring is flushed down the toilet.

# JULIA CUMES

## *a poem*

*Lionel's friendship with my parents pre-dates my birth and I remember him as a benevolent, gentle, and revered presence in our home. Our house was the venue for some of the creative writing groups that centred themselves around him, and these brought writing into my world, giving the act of creative writing a special value. My one and only experience – when I was fourteen – of reading something I had written to the group, and having it critiqued, was daunting, to say the least. The group's response must have been given with care, since writing has continued to be a friend, and a source of great joy to me.*

### SPLIT

Outside my ballet class, the street is a clean, black tongue.
Cars are parked close as teeth – just enough space
between chrome to avoid the scrape of blue on fuchsia,

silver on teal. I'm waiting for a ride home.
Inside, girls split their milky limbs;
backs arc the perfect curve

of fountains. I see their arms swish chiffon,
hair curled into jewels, mouths plush satin. Comparing waists,
they are duplicated everywhere; the room opens

infinitely on itself, the silver patina unfolding a thousand doors, pianos,
necks whose cords undulate in creamy hues.
I watch them with one eye on the street;

my mother doesn't like to wait. A man runs down the black macadam,
his feet beat in time to jetés, sissones. Between the sweep
of an arabesque and a pirouette, he's down,

the two cops bucking to keep his face against tar. One screams
"Your pass, your fucking pass," thrusts a hand into pockets.
The other kicks.

An allegro straddles the air; sinewed limbs
slice the mirror into triangles, squares.

From under the man's head,
the flow is a ribbon spiraling
on asphalt – velvet and vermilion.

# E M MACPHAIL

## *a story*

## UGOGO

In less than a week Lydia will be leaving for the States. There is always so much to think about before she goes. This time she must not forget the lotion that the chemist guarantees will fix even foreign mosquitoes. Of course she has already bought the Marmite, the Anchovette and Mrs Ball's Blatjang. In the last few months hardly a day passes without her going to search for cotton underwear and real-wool jerseys for her grandchildren. She will leave the chocolate to the last minute to be sure that it is fresh. It wouldn't do for the narrow slabs in the green silver-paper wrapping with the words Peppermint Crisp in red and black to turn grey. But that had only happened once, even though she had kept it in the fridge. And it hadn't tasted any different. It was because she had bought two dozen slabs as soon as she returned in case the Greek on the corner should be out of stock when she was about to leave the next time.

Lydia lives to the north-east of Johannesburg in a block of flats – one of many – where none are higher than five storeys. Killarney is an island surrounded by mansions with gardens in which roses, fruit trees and green lawns flourish. In spring the warm dry winds blow the scent of the flowering syringa trees in Lydia's direction. Standing at her bedroom window while doing her breathing exercises, she is able to see the brick-red tiled roofs of the double-storeyed houses, the new brilliance of oaks and camphor trees and the pink and white mist of fruit blossom. She is always glad to return home and, most of all, she enjoys the first few days. No matter how well her trip has gone nor how many people she has met, those first days at home are the best. Before she returns Tryphinia will have come in to air the flat, to polish the furniture and silver. She will have cleaned the windows. Surrounded by her belongings it doesn't take Lydia long to adjust. The radio tells her how empty the dams are. She will read about the latest bank robbery while drinking her early-morning tea in bed. Tryphinia will give her the news about school boycotts and unrest in the townships. Lydia will tell herself that the more things change the more they stay the same. As soon as she is dressed she will ask Tryphinia for the shopping list and she will take the lift to the automatic lock-up basement garage. Then, before unlocking her car, she will stand back for a moment to admire it. They bought it the year her husband died and it looks as well cared for as when he was alive. A Mercedes doesn't date, the garage man says. The Germans know how to make cars, which is why Mercs and BMWs are the ones most often stolen. But he will add that Lydia, like other old ladies, doesn't go out at night and her car is safe enough in the lock-up basement garage. When she leaves for the States the mechanic comes to disconnect the battery and drain the radiator. Before she returns he makes it ready for her to drive. He is very dependable.

Lydia's one son lives in Philadelphia, the other in Boston and they hardly ever see or even phone each other because they don't have the time. Both will ask her if the Merc is being properly looked after and both will say that it is a very reliable car that will never let her down. They will not listen to what she has to say about the insurance, the licence, the maintenance, the price of petrol and the senselessness of keeping a car she hardly ever uses.

Today Lydia drives the Merc down the side road. She leaves it under the trees where there is plenty of shade and it isn't far to the bus stop. The two schoolboys who are always there, waiting to carry parcels, go to the shops for soda water and newspapers, or clean cars, will look after it for her. They know she will give them R5 and for that they will clean it as well. Of course she does not pay them until she has made sure that the hub-caps and windscreen wipers are all still in place. She tells them they have no business to boycott school but they laugh and say that the school is no good. Unless Lydia wants the car cleaned she never leaves it with them for the whole day.

She catches sight of the bus and knows that if she climbs on quickly the young man standing next to her will help her to the stairs. She likes to sit on top and look into the gardens on Oxford Road. When she returns later she prefers the long side seat near the driver where she can see the passengers as they leave the crowded bus.

She has been going to the same hairdressing shop in Hillbrow for twenty years and nowhere else has she found anyone who will make the narrow little waves with the tight curls that she likes. Also they don't mind touching up the front and the roots instead of insisting on a full tint. She wants to look nice because she has been invited. It's always like that before she leaves. There are so many who want to see her and she always promises to post their letters as soon as she arrives. But parcels are out.

Every time she has her hair done there is a different girl but she always does what Lydia asks. Afterwards she sits on the bench in Edith Cavell Street and waits for the four o'clock bus. There is so much in Hillbrow to remind her of when she and her husband first came to South Africa. There is the bookshop where they did most of their reading. On the corner is the café where you could get proper coffee and they would listen in to the discussions which helped them to improve their English. From where she sits she can see the building at the far end of the street where they lived and she taught French and German. She notices that washing is now allowed to be hung on the balconies. After she has been sitting there for a while she sees the same light-green car with a dented boot and buckled bumper drive past again. And then again for the third time. There are four young black men in it. When it stops, one gets out and comes over to where she is sitting. His black hair is brushed upward into a flat platform on top. She moves her handbag to her right side so that he can sit down.

"What are you reading, gogo?" he asks.

"It's just a magazine," Lydia says.

"You are not reading *The Weekly Mail*?"

"No," she says. "I read that at home."

"So you are reading about our struggle?"

"Oh yes," Lydia says, "I have read all about it."

"And what are you going to do about our struggle, gogo?" he asks.

Lydia smiles at him as if he has made a joke. "Oh I am too old. Even you call me granny. My sons must help with the struggle."

"It is better," he says.

The light-green car returns and waits across the street on the side reserved for bus traffic. Then another young man gets out of the car and comes over to the bench. He sits down on the other side of Lydia. He is very drunk. He puts out his hand to her which she shakes with her left one because she is holding her handbag with the other.

"You are always shaking hands with the left hand?" he asks.

"Oh yes. Please excuse me. You see I am left-handed," Lydia smiles.

She thinks she hears him say something about bad luck. Then he moves nearer to her and asks, "Can I kiss you, gogo?"

With hardly any hesitation Lydia puts out her cheek to him.

"Yes. Certainly," she says.

The two young men sit on for a while. Then both, at the same moment, stand up and walk across to the light-green car waiting on the other side of Edith Cavell Street.

The schoolboys tell Lydia that the Merc is now very clean. They point out that the hub-caps and windscreen wipers are still present. She has already told the garage man which day she is leaving and he will collect the car keys from Tryphinia after she has left. She has asked him if the car is using oil because that is what her sons will ask her. She supposes there will be the usual arguments. As always, they will both insist that she does not sell the car. She knows better than to tell them she would rather take the bus. The year she told them that, there was such a row, first in Philadelphia, later in Boston. They both said that she could afford it and neither of them wanted to hear from others that their mother didn't even have a car. Lydia had said that was rubbish because buses and sometimes a taxi still cost and the flat was enough already. She could have found a much cheaper place in not such an upmarket area but no, her sons would not hear of it. They wanted her to have the best. She must stay in the same locality as the other parents who had also sold their big houses when their children went away.

Tryphinia makes tea for Lydia. There is the Kugelhof cake which she does so well and Lydia cuts a good slice of it. Of course she will not say anything about the green car to her sons. It would not be good for them. But she tells Tryphinia and asks her what she thinks about it. Tryphinia says it seems to her that perhaps the young men are missing their granny.

# KAIZER M NYATSUMBA

## *a poem*

*I used to be a contributor to* Sesame, *and Lionel was always the dedicated editor – he went through a poem or a short story with a fine comb, and copiously made notes before returning a submission to its author for re-working. Not only is he a doyen of South African literature, but he has also helped many a beginning writer.*

**LOST PRIDE**
*for Imani Dancers, whose performance at Denison University inspired me*

Back home
   in Africa
   we sing 'civilized' songs
   we sing soul-operating
   jazz
   heart-probing soul
   and conscience-searching reggae
We sing all these things
   and marry them with *mbaqanga*
   and *isicathamiya*
   and be happy

They, too, sing
   here in America
   they sing something different
   they sing traditional music
   veritable African music
   and African dance
and I am abashed
   for I, being African
   can no longer do all these things
   for I am 'civilized'.

# DOUGLAS REID SKINNER

*a poem*

**THE CONVERSATION**
*– Cedarberg Mountains, 1988*

If the geese are still out feeding on the pond,
and sheets of rain have not yet begun falling,
and the sky is dark and uncertain to the viewer,
clouds hide bare peaks at the valley's end;

and the white water-flowers aren't yet a feast
nor the sighing pine trees smoke and fire,
and swirls of dust still careen up suddenly on
the winding road down which they disappear;

and the course of conversation in the kitchen
doesn't take into account such phenomena,
but instead is concerned with History's horrors
– women, Owen, slaves, child-labour, Simone Weil –

they'll go on sailing on the darkening mirror
that possesses in itself the sky's sheer mind,
while the keys, cups and books lying on the table
will remain forever unmoved by insight;

and those people who sit up talking until late,
who discuss ideas, and consider and remember,
later listen, before sleep, to the rain close over
Mars rising in the east, and the geese as they

squawk and swagger, going back to shelter.

# TONY ULLYATT

## *a poem*

*Lionel was one of the first editors to accept and publish my poetry in the old Sesame – and one of the first to provide me with feedback on the texts he rejected. Uncomfortable though those comments felt on a first reading, they got to the very heart of the shortcomings in the writing. If, over the years since then, my poetry has improved in any significant way, it has done so only to the extent that I have been able to build on Lionel's wonderful insights.*

### LOVE'S AUSTERE AND LONELY OFFICES

One of the boys in our school dormitory
was the archetypal pain-in-the-arse:
you know the type – looking down at their feet
whenever they have to venture down steps,
wearing a cotton vest to stave off chills
which threaten their lives, summer and winter.

He ran away from school right after lunch
on one of those quite ordinary days.
He has never been found, although some think
he will return. I'd like to believe them
but the cynic in me wants to point out
the many subtle ways death can muster.

Still, to make certain the neighbours see
the implicit trust she has in her son,
his mother washes his vests every Monday,
just in case he should return and need one.

# ETHELWYN REBELO

## *a story*

### MAN-SPIRIT

My mother refuses to colour the grey away from her hair. She still wears it long, in a ponytail down her back. She is thin and drapes her body with loose, coloured robes. Each garment is connected to a different activity: her green lace for gardening, her brown cotton for baking, her red silk for company, and her yellow muslin for sleep. "Your mother is weird," I am told by some. Others, the kind who look more closely before making pronouncements, find her beautiful. Those who learn to know her, fall in love with her. This is because my mother is a magician, a weaver of spells, woven with the taste and texture of her food.

I help her in the kitchen. Only I am left. Although she did not make it easy for her children to leave her, my sisters have long gone from the house. Perhaps if my father had not died, things would have been different, but my mother viewed our needs for independence as abandonment. My sisters were all stronger than me, and their boyfriends helped them to stand up to her. I was the youngest and her favourite and this made me more vulnerable. I have never been able to leave her in the past and now, because of Ayanda, I will not leave her in the future.

I no longer complain about my situation. I too know now what it is like to love a man and to be loved by him. At first, apart from my mother, no one else knew of his existence. Then I made a terrible mistake, an error of judgement resulting in our separation from each other. But, before that, I can assure you he was always beside me.

You may be wondering how we met? He came to me, seemingly out of the blue, as I lay down for an afternoon nap. But he did not come completely. It was as if he wished to reveal himself to me gradually. At first it was only his touch, petal-light, that I felt, each day as I curled, wide awake, on my bed. I would feel his caress move slowly from my toes, up my calves and thighs and onto my abdomen. From there he would reach for my breasts, shoulders and neck until I was paralysed with pleasure.

Later, he showed me his face, brown, with dark eyes, delicate nostrils, a crown of beads around his forehead, and a small beard. Then I heard him whisper his name, "Ayanda." Finally, one night, he presented me with his entire figure, tall, with copper bracelets embracing well-shaped arms, an African David. His skin was soft, the colour of milk chocolate, tender beneath my lips as I kissed him all over his face, his shoulders, his chest – in the moonlight.

Conscious of his presence beside me, I would assist my mother with her work in the kitchen where she created her magic. Shortbread, infused with spices, to help with sleep, vanilla-sugared cake for depression, rum biscuits to calm, chocolates for excitement or heavy work, cannabis stew to relax inhibition – these were my favourites.

I also started work as an 'escort lady' at Giorgio's Hotel, an activity I never discussed with my mother. If she asked where I was going, I would always say that I was waitressing. I viewed it as a temporary measure aimed at getting a decent amount of money.

Our house was in a bad state of disrepair. The paint was peeling, the panes were rusted, the floorboards cracked. Our furniture was worn. None of these defects troubled the old woman. Provided she could cook, bake and garden; as long as her recipe books were intact and I was still there, nothing could touch her. But I noticed the expressions on the faces of people who came to buy food and herbal remedies. So, I went to work and when I came home, I took to browsing through pamphlets and brochures advertising furniture. To sleep in a double-bed manufactured from clean pine, with new duvets and cushions, to entertain in a sun-filled room with matching settee and armchairs, would be to live in paradise. I longed to appropriate these objects for myself. How delightful to feel Ayanda's gentle stroke caress my body as it lay engulfed in the luxury provided by Lubners, Joshua Doore, or the OK Bazaars.

Steven, my boss at the hotel, told me that my best asset was my personality. I think he meant that I was friendly, and that I quickly put my customers at ease.

They were just bodies of different shape and pigment to me. I did not really concern myself with them. All I ever thought about was my man-spirit. I smiled and they would think I was smiling at them. My ecstasy amazed and delighted. They believed it was in response to their touch. One of the men, short, freckle-faced, I forget his name, joked that since I enjoyed it so much, perhaps I should be paying him, instead of him paying me.

In the beginning of course, some thought that I was talented at faking it. But there are some things that are difficult to contrive: the juices between my thighs, tears of pleasure and release. Beside, below, or on top of me, they were, however, merely a small diversion in my awareness of him, much like a fly may momentarily distract one's attention. Only he was real to me, the customers, nothing more than reflections on water, small waves concealing the life beneath the surface. In the depths of my stream of consciousness, he and I swam, passionately and alone.

At first, I wished to know more about him, to learn where he came from, to understand why he had come to join me, but he never explained. Once I asked, "You are the spirit of a Xhosa warrior, aren't you?" He did not reply, his touch breezed past my cheek. Strange to say, with time, it no longer mattered who he was or from where. Perhaps it was because I realized he was a creature, in some way, of my mother's magic.

Not that our times together were filled always with questions or sensuous experiences. We shared a great deal of humour with each other too. For example, he seemed to find men with fat backsides bouncing up and down particularly funny, or else, I remember a lawyer with particularly thin legs beneath a bulging, square body, eliciting peals of laughter from him which only I could hear – thank heavens.

He was also protective of me. I only had to look appealingly at him if I thought a particular customer could turn out to be nasty and he would bash them over the head so that they suddenly developed an excruciating headache and they were no trouble to me at all.

As I did not tire easily, I believe I made more money than any of the other girls. We were able to buy furniture. A new pine double-bed replaced my rusting, iron, single one, and a stained-glass lamp-shade covered the lone bulb hanging from the ceiling in my bedroom. For my mother, there was a microwave oven.

"My fairy daughter, my sweet goblin child is clever and good to me," she sang, and he smiled.

I lived a relatively calm and happy life, not like my workmates. Most of them were heavy on drugs, their lives a process of stumbling on from day to day as prostitutes only to finance their weekly or daily supplies of Mandrax, heroin or whatever.

When they fought, it often became ugly with physical violence. One woman persuaded her boyfriend to break the nose of a rival whom she accused of stealing 'crack' from her. For this reason, I tried to maintain what I hoped was a 'spaced-out' civility with most people, pretending that the far-away look in my eyes was due to an illegal substance rather than to my desire to keep my distance. If I had seemed to adopt a remote manner out of choice, they might have accused me of being proud and I would have made enemies.

Steve's wife, known as 'Times' (short for 'Sunday Times'), appeared to be a friend, so I let down my guard a little with her. I was told once that she was jealous of me because I was more popular than her, but I experienced her as kind and considerate, if a little nosy. The good aspect of her nosiness was that she was able to convey useful gossip to us about certain of the clients. These were generally bits of scandal she interrogated out of her husband – scandal that was important to us. For example, it was a matter of survival to know that George Oosthuizen was quick with his fists and that Naidoo was connected to some very dangerous people. In turn, Steve also learned that Colette was increasing her cocaine intake, that Martine was in heavy debt with the drug peddlers, that Thandi had insulted a customer, and so on. For this reason, many of the girls did not really like her, although, as the boss's wife, she was treated with caution.

Times's real name was Debbie, 'Deb' to her face. In truth, she seemed to have a good heart. Her husband was quite willing to use his fists on us at any time and she regularly interceded on our behalf. I liked her and forgave her for keeping him well informed of all our faults and foibles.

He never learned, however, that with her long blonde hair and baby face, she slept around at times for pleasure. Steve was one of those men who did not mind if his wife slept with another man, provided he got paid for it. Knowledge of her 'freebies' would have enraged him. I and the others all kept quiet about it, fearing his anger which became generalized and haphazard when aroused.

One evening, Times tried to persuade Steve to attend Alcoholics Anonymous. "You're getting to be a drunkard like my uncle John," she screamed.

"Why are you suddenly so worried about it?" he yelled back. I kept still, a statue in the corner of the faded, red velvet room. Clearly, chairs would soon be smashed, skin bruised. I also wondered why she was suddenly so worried about it and suspected that it had to do with her wanting to spend more time with her less commercial sexual interests.

As I had expected, the fight culminated with her receiving a swollen right eye. Her mouth too, was cut and sticky with blood. I suggested that she accompany me home where I would dress her wounds and feed her. It would also give Steve time to cool off. My mother had several times indicated a desire to meet some of my friends and I asked that she pretend to be a fellow waitress.

"We can't walk alone at night," she protested, "we might get mugged."

"It'll be fine," I reassured her, knowing that Ayanda was close by. "I do it all the time."

My mother was delighted at the unexpected company and rushed to change into her red silk. After ministering to my friend's injuries, I began to warm up some stew. Mulled wine was simmering on the stove and peaches in brandy were ready for dessert.

"You are a very special woman," my mother told Times.

"Me?"

"Yes, I can see that you could be a great actress."

"How can you see such a thing?"

"Oh, it's the emotion in your eyes, the expressive way in which you move your hands."

"I used to be very good at it at school."

My mother smiled.

With dinner we became more talkative and intimate.

"Are you involved with anyone?" Times asked me after her second helping of dessert.

"Ayanda," I laughed.

"Who is Ayanda?"

"He's right here, standing by the door. You cannot see him." I explained. "He is my love." Then I told her about his caress, about his skin, the crown of beads on his forehead, his protection of me, about our jokes, about everything.

She began to giggle uncontrollably and when she had quietened down, she decided it was time to return home to her husband.

"Don't forget what I've told you," my mother shouted after her. "You are very special."

At work the next day, Steve screamed that my drug-taking should not interfere with my work. He would have punched me in the face had Ayanda not made him catch his foot in the carpet and trip.

I have wondered whether Times really understood what she was doing to me, whether she purposefully wished to hurt me. Perhaps she believed she was being a good friend.

She made me lose him. She told everyone I was crazy and forced me to hospital where they stuck needles in my arm and fed me tablets that drove him away. As always, he tried to protect me, to save us. The sister kept dropping her equipment, the doctor had a severe attack of sneezing. But we were outnumbered.

Now I am in mourning. I dress in black, think of my man-spirit and pray to be reunited with him.

I talk to my mother about my many memories: of lying down in the afternoons for a nap, waiting for his whisper, of his smiling presence in the kitchen while we baked. I remember how sensitive he was, what a good listener, what a wit.

She was told, in the hospital, about the true nature of my work. Happily for me, it did not surprise her and she was less upset about it than I had expected her to be. In fact she has said very little about it. We speak mostly of Ayanda.

"I will bring him back, just give me time."

"You are the best mother in the whole world."

"Well, rather Ayanda than someone who might take you away from me." She kissed me gently on my forehead.

I pray that she succeeds. I beseech that she finds the power. She will try, I know, she needs me to help her with her magic, her baking and the cooking of her cannabis stews. It is important to her that I am happy and energetic rather than immobile with misery.

Until then, I think and dream of his whisper, of his touch and I plan my revenge. It does not matter whether Times realizes the enormity of what she has done to me or not. The dragon within me is awake. She has injured me grievously and someone needs to teach her that interference is well and good, but that there are limits to it.

So, with my mother's assistance, she will receive a cake, overflowing with pecan nuts, almonds and sugared fruit. She will not know that it is a truth cake, a delectable cinnamon-flavoured masterpiece – which will force her to confess to Steve about her 'freebies'.

# LIONEL MURCOTT

*a poem*

**TWO FACES**

She shows me her old face, aged about sixteen,
in a big photograph. I would not have known her: pensive,
dark eyes slanted away from the camera,
full young flesh; no, not pensive – a weight
of unhappiness fleshing the jaw, opaque and slack
with the inability to focus an anger
which she no doubt can scarcely dare to name.

And her new face, perhaps forty, across the table,
translucent with indignation over the family
that bound that girl, this woman: telling
of the injustices, the shameful fear
of shame, of truth, the failure to see her separateness.
Her face is quickened, focussed; and yes, pretty:

I want to be kissing this woman after dinner.

# DOUGLAS LIVINGSTONE

## *two poems*

### SPINAL COLUMN

The first sputnik blipped above me
where I worked twelve metres down
at the jaws of dam construction
in an outraged Zambezi;
hearing the broadcast about it
that evening, recalled a light
cord tied at my back which strung
the man groping in mud
to sometime starmen, knotted
under my ancient aqualung.

### GIOVANNI JACOPO MEDITATES
### (ON UPRIGHTNESS)

Best is the Joy of finding yourself
Concupiscently Erect;
Then there's the Joy of finding yourself
Politically Incorrect.

# BARNEY SIMON

## *a story*

**MONOLOGUE FOR VANESSA**

I live in a building which has nineteen flats, all with bathrooms, but not all with kitchens. I have a kitchen and a bathroom. The bathroom was painted orange and black by the people before me. I live on the second floor opposite to an office building and its garages. My flat is usually very dusty, because the telephone exchange is being built next door. It is also very noisy during the day, sometimes even on Sundays. I greet four people in the building; I know the names of three of them, but not of the woman who polishes her door-knob.

I keep a bottle of gin and two bottles of Paarl Perlé. My flat is serviced by a thirty-eight-year-old Venda, called Phineas. He drinks my gin. He used to dilute it, but he doesn't bother any more. I have never spoken to him about it. He rules the building. He cleans my floor with a feather duster. During the winter, he sells coal so that there is often not enough for the boiler. Sometimes he disappears during the weekend and we only have cold water.

One night a drunken woman knocked on my door and complained to me that he had taken her handbag which contained her money and her pass. She said that he would not give it to her until she slept with him. I went to Phineas's room with her. Phineas and another man who said he was her cousin, laughed at her. While I spoke to them, she took her handbag and left. Later, I heard her voice upstairs again.

The following Sunday I heard heavy footsteps on the stair. I saw a black woman run screaming down the road, chased by a black man. Her breasts were bare. Soon after, Phineas knocked on my door and asked my boyfriend and me for help. He said he had found a white man having sex with his girlfriend. We went upstairs to his room. A white man holding an umbrella was ducking in a corner. Phineas and another black man started spitting at him, hitting him, insulting him. The police came. The white man said that he had been on his way home from a church meeting when a woman asked him for help. She said that Phineas had taken her handbag. When he went upstairs, he was attacked and the woman disappeared. The police did not believe him. He had no jacket and she had no blouse. The police took statements from everybody and went away.

Many people in the building have missed tape-recorders, clothes and liquor, and blame Phineas for their loss. The maids of the building claim to have seen him selling clothes and coal to the construction workers next door. This seems likely. He earns a very small salary, and could not otherwise afford the liquor he drinks.

I don't want people to watch me from the office-block opposite. Sometimes the lights in the passage don't work. I listen to footsteps outside. Sometimes I put paper in the keyhole. If there was a fire, I would take my jewellery and my photograph albums and my sheepskin coat, and an Israeli Coca Cola bottle my father once gave me. I am not Jewish. The flat is cheap. I stay here because it saves me money and because I hate moving. Sometimes in the evening it is beautiful. The traffic slows down and the sky, with the shadows of buildings and their lights, is very beautiful.

The other day, twelve black men were shot dead in a mine. I know from what I have read and from what people have told me that they come from places where they earn very little money. That they have families there. I have read that they were angry because they did not get rises when other men did. I know they didn't have trade unions to argue for them. I know that their need is terrible, and that they don't have much hope, and that they must have been very angry. I think that the police were very scared when they shot them. I wondered what would happen in Soweto and the world. I saw that the Stock Market went down and then came up again when not a lot was said or done. I read that a lot of shares were bought in London and New York. The *Rand Daily Mail* said on its front page, beside descriptions of the damage, that they were the first to bring news of the tragedy to their readers.

I'm not sure what I feel now. Sometimes I understand things, and sometimes I can't even think. Sometimes I am scared and sometimes I can't really say what I think is dangerous. I know terrible things happen all over the world all the time. I know that when it gets a little more terrible, people protest, but that also passes into part of the world's everyday. I know that I can't feel for long – that I don't even remember for long.

I know my life is strange. I don't want people to watch me from opposite. I put paper in my keyhole. But Phineas, whose life frightens me more than anybody I know, has a key to my flat. He uses my bath and my deodorant. Once I came home early and met him leaving my flat with a woman. He is not afraid to take what he wants. I am grateful that he does not choose to take too much and that he does not choose to harm me.

My work doesn't really interest me, but it's all right and it buys me things and permits me to save. I don't play sport. I see films, and sometimes plays. I go on holidays, to South West, to Durban, to Cape Town. I want to go overseas and I will go by plane. I know that there are hijackers, and that one day, people will be prepared to die in order to bring danger to South Africans. They might one day plant a bomb that will kill me. I understand that. But they don't threaten my world. It is my world that threatens me. Actually, I don't mind anything. I don't mind dying, I just don't want to be helpless.

# ANNE KELLAS

*a poem*

## THE BROTHER I NEVER KNEW

Mother what is this place?
A memory garden.
But what is this place?
A memory garden.
What is this place?

They sell chrysanthemums of perfect dimensions
behind the wire swing door.
I don't tell my mother I'm suffocating,
hear the bees scream,
I want the empty sunlight outside,
the ordinary street,
the old-fashioned bus-shelter
shaped like half an eggshell.

I forget about the place until she takes me back again;
I remember the little stone angels
and the mute granite slabs that stare
like so many blind eyes to the east,
I forget until she takes me back again,
eventually I forget I ever asked
what is this place
and I forget that it's a memory garden.

# ROBERT ROYSTON

## *a poem*

*From my first meeting with Lionel I was struck by his attitude to literature as something alive and thrilling. He communicated this powerfully, along with his sense that new writing was somehow part of the benign and exciting wave of human and humane progress which could only be temporarily halted by authoritarian regimes. Lionel cherishes new talent and, being a special person himself, has a rare ability to make others feel creative and special.*

### TWO-HEADED HISTORY LESSON

His first head glowed with the thought:
Ten years
Divided by wheat
Equals the prince.

His second head's brain
Was a bulge of frozen smoke.
This head's body was a secondhand jacket,
Fire-stitched.

(The first head pondered.)

Pale fingers had plucked the second head's heart
From the bloodropes of a cheyenne squaw.

(The first head replotted the battle.)

The second head's unmatching bones
Were selected from the earth's lost property office.
It's knees quailed.

(The first head considered the repeating rifle.)

The second head's pulse was staccato.
It heard pipes snap, filled with human juice.

(The first head heard the clock tick.)

The second head's eyes were those of a man
Left for dead
Who rises suddenly in the smoke
And looks around.

(The first head, reaching chapter eleven,
Shouted "no".)

The second head shouted no.
But out of its mouth came "boom".
Its hair vanished up an invisible chimney.
Medals and dive-bombers
Hooked starry furry and horned
Flags
Rained from its mouth.

The other head, suddenly calm,
Swelled with the thought:
Small towns divided by the cold
Equals the peace.

Its brother head answered in screeches,
Left a trail of mine fields
As it walked away.

# MICHAEL GARDINER

## *a critical appraisal*

### LIONEL AND THE *RENOSTER*: EDITOR AND CRITIC

*van Renosters gepraat: is jy 'n suid-AFRIKANER?*
Wopko Jensma: 'Ja Baas'

There is no question about the central importance of *The Purple Renoster* in the recent history of South African literature.

Beginning as a production by a small group of friends and associates in 1956, *The Purple Renoster* carried the work of approximately one hundred contributors in its twelve issues, the last of which appeared in 1972.

The single constant in the *Renoster*'s episodic history is the owner and editor, Lionel Abrahams. Though assisted and supported by friends, Lionel directed his magazine throughout its life.[1] Reviewers, once commissioned, were free to express their own opinions, but the poems, short stories and essays were selected for publication by Lionel. And he was sure about what was worth publishing, despite his declaration in the first issue that he would be 'passive about standards'.[2] Lionel's 1980 gloss is that by 'standards' he meant 'objective criteria supposed to be universally valid', and that by 'passive' he meant that the criteria used for judging whether to include a piece or not would be 'essentially subjective': 'I would proceed on the faith that what engaged me was likely to engage others . . . and that in setting a level of literary quality for the magazine I would not be guided by theories or ideals but be led by the actual writings that came to hand.'[3]

Implicit in so potent a definition of passivity is the determination in Lionel never to predetermine conditions for writers. As he reminded me recently in discussion, for him, freedom of expression is not an 'issue' but an essential condition for writers. His unswerving conviction on this matter is essential for an understanding of his editorship.[4]

Well over half of those people published in *The Purple Renoster* have contributed in significant ways to the growth of South African literature. At the time of their publication in the *Renoster*, only people such as Bosman, Guy Butler, Ruth Miller, Sydney Clouts and Douglas Livingstone possibly could be regarded as established literary figures. As Lionel has pointed out, the *Renoster* introduced to South African readers the names of Riva Rubin (Lador), Rose Moss (Rappoport), David Farrell, Jillian Becker, Eva Bezwoda (Royston), Robert Royston, Yvonne Burgess, Wally Serote, Arthur Nortje, Jeni Couzyn, Rose Zwi, Ahmed Essop, Sinclair Beiles and, with *The Classic*, Oswald Mtshali.[5]

*Renoster* contributors subsequently acted as editors of at least six magazines: *Bolt, The Classic, Contrast, The English Academy Review, Ophir* and *Snarl*. This is less a testament to the smallness of the South African literary world than a comment on the interventionist energy which the *Renoster*'s presence attracted and encouraged. Contributors have also drawn increasing attention to South African literature in English through the subsequent publication of collections of poetry, short stories, novels, essays and plays as well as by compiling and editing anthologies: Jean Marquard, Njabulo Ndebele, Sheila Fugard, Margaret Allonby, Stephen Gray, Ruth Keech, Es'kia Mphahlele, ZB Molefe, Walter Saunders, Geoffrey Haresnape, Don Maclennan, Peter Horn, Wopko Jensma and Barney Simon. This list is not exhaustive.

Still others have participated in conferences, become involved in political movements and churches, influenced school, college and university syllabi and have worked as journalists and reviewers, arguing in their many ways for appropriate attention to South African writing.

It is true that when *The Purple Renoster* first appeared, there was no other magazine devoted to South African literature in English. But by 1965, other magazines had come into existence[6] which together made possible the remarkable upsurge in the publication of poetry in particular, an upsurge which culminated in an irrevocable shift in the centre of gravity of South African literature – not only in English – marked by the publication by Renoster Books (co-owned by Lionel Abrahams, Eva Bezwoda and Robert Royston)[7] of Mtshali's *Sounds of a Cowhide Drum* in 1971 and Serote's *Yakhal'inkomo* in 1972.

A further distinguishing feature of the *Renoster* was its intention to combine the publication of poetry, prose, drama and essays, with critical commentary on contemporary publications and an historical account of South African English literature. Even though the latter aim was never realised, the intended combination of literary activities and attention to their historical context is what universities have sought to achieve only recently through the formation of Departments of African Literature, African Studies, Cultural Studies and the like. But by insisting upon the validity of the subjective and the individual, and by working mainly with the physical reality of submitted material, Lionel resisted all attempts to institutionalize *The Purple Renoster*. That trust in his own judgement and in the material which was available has been vindicated to a remarkable extent.

It is therefore impossible to discuss *The Purple Renoster* without discussing Lionel's role as editor, literary mentor and as the central figure in those groups of people who sustained him and were sustained by his sagacity and passion. Ten years after the closure of the *Renoster*, he launched *Sesame* and so continued that sort of focus for writers. In addition to his editing and compiling for publication the work of others, his extensive and continuous engagement with material submitted to him for commentary and response, as well as his active literary and cultural friendships, Lionel continues to meet regularly with groups of writers. His tenacity, his blessed longevity and his delight in the literary have made him the most influential person in South African literary history.

Now this is not achieved only by receptive passivity. Though never a crusader, Lionel translated his sense of the literary through *The Purple Renoster* into two major directions: 'a capacity to find a proud, celebratory pleasure in the discovery of new talent'[8] and in his editorials, reviews and essays. This is not to forget his own poetry, short stories and novel. But the *Renoster* was never really a medium for them. The first of these directions has been intimated by the lists of the names of contributors to *The Purple Renoster*. What they went on to do and become, and their place in the history of literatures is part of a larger discussion which would lead us away from the focus upon the magazine in this brief account. However, it is necessary to draw attention to the quality of the graphic work which also distinguished *The Purple Renoster*. Lionel describes himself as "lucky" in obtaining the services of Carolyn Seawright, Miriam Friedland (Stern), Wopko Jensma, Arthur Goldreich, Harold Rubin, Nils Burwitz and Anne Sassoon, among others. But their contributions are as striking as the literary material published, and are indicative of the degree to which people of such abilities knew that their work would be taken seriously by association with *The Purple Renoster*.

Lionel's editorials, reviews and essays reveal in other ways his distinctive concerns. All the issues except 3, 10 and 11 carried editorials, and the 'little tradition of joking editorials'[9] came to an end in issue number 5 when one hundred and two South Africans had been 'named' as communists and so gagged from writing and publishing. Lionel wrote:

'By our compliance in any connection, with the prohibition against publishing the words of the 102, we have made this magazine, like every publication in this country, a vehicle of the minister's implicit contempt.' (p 2)

The minister was BJ Vorster and the year was 1963. In that same issue, five poems by Dennis Brutus, without attribution, were published immediately after the editorial, as a demonstration of how the gag could be circumvented and as a challenge to the authorities to prosecute.

When Lewis Nkosi suggested, from abroad, after the proscription of the works of forty-six exiles, that *The Classic* and other South African literary magazines should respond by closing down, Lionel wrote an editorial, 'Edenvale, Terezin and Silence',[10] in which he referred to children's suffering in a township, the performance of Verdi's *Requiem* by inmates of the Nazi transit camp for artists, and Nkosi's suggestion.

He wrote the following:

'The suggestion is an affront. If we go silent voluntarily, it must only be for the extreme reason that we have given over our lives to the direct or indirect alleviation of our Edenvales, only because we have nothing left over for art, only because we have become too busy to speak. The deliberate silence of political gesture, cultural boycott, dissociation or protest, does violence against the spirit, no less than the silence imposed by intimidation, censorship, or the law of the gag.' (p 4)

Writing in 1980, Lionel observed: 'My editorial . . . was an attempt both to acknowledge and to refute the challenge – which could be seen as the attack from the left, whereas my protests in the previous editorials had been against the assault from the right by authorities.'[11]

I believe that it would have been wrong for literary magazines to close down. But I supported the cultural boycott as I supported the sports boycott and the imposition of sanctions against the government of this country then. The characterization of Nkosi's suggestion as 'an affront' and as 'the attack from the left' seems an over-reaction of an inflexible kind. But it would be a mistake to simplify Lionel's position here. He invokes the response of the Jewish musicians to inevitable extermination by the Nazis as an instance of artists doing what they do and do best. There is no equivalence being drawn between Nazism and apartheid. In other words, Lionel asserts again and again that the practice of art is subservient to no other human activity or necessity.

In *Renoster 2*, writing under the pseudonym Libra, Lionel responded to the deaths of Roy Campbell, Jochem van Bruggen and CM van den Heever by commenting on their authenticity as South African writers, a concern consistent with his observation that, 'What there was in the way of policy [for the *Renoster*] to begin with was my own application of Bosman's marriage of aestheticism and patriotism:'[12]

'Precisely because we are, in the most important way – Europeans – any of us who have absorbed any real feeling for the arts, no matter what our skin colour, we don't need to go so emphatically troubling the world about that side of things. Our schools and universities and libraries will look after that. We are also, all of us who live here, again, no matter what our skin colour, Africans. And in this age of jet-propelled Comets, concrete pavements and condemned game reserves it is not Europe that threatens to elude us, but Africa.' (p 44)

One's unease about what 'Africa' means here – is it non-technological or obscured by technology? – is deepened when the discussion goes on to say:

'And this is where van den Heever, van Bruggen and the couple of handfuls of truly indigenous writers like them – in Afrikaans, English and the Bantu languages – come in. They can restore to us our sensible, as opposed to intellectual, awareness of Africa . . . Through them it is still possible to make contact with the soil.' (p 44)

Lionel is on tricky, if not treacherous ground here. This is an example of one of his rare forays into territory where he is less than usually sure. When political issues came to him – in the form of Special Branch (Security Police) raids, the prohibition of writing by 'named' and exiled people, banning and censorship – then he dealt with them directly, vehemently and courageously. But he eschewed engagement with larger political events (which so marked the *Renoster*'s time-span) and said, in 1980: 'As to politics, I was both ignorant and un-interested,'[13] and in the same article: 'But the influence of both George Gemmell and Bosman in their different ways had helped to anaesthetise me to the effect of public events' (p 39). Even by the mid-1960s, when Lionel had developed a lively interest in public events,[14] he steered clear of engaging with them through *The Purple Renoster*. My guess (or intuitive feeling) is that whereas he had good reason to trust his own judgement in selecting material to publish in the *Renoster*, he had the good sense to keep the magazine free from what he personally was not as deeply sure about.

The aestheticism which Lionel derived and adapted from Bosman is illustrated by his review of Guy Butler's edition of the *South African Book of Verse*,[15] in which he accurately and discerningly distinguishes the few viable poems from the preponderance of versified dross. In so doing, Lionel states with great clarity an attitude to the writing of poetry propagated by Christina van Heyningen at the universities of Stellenbosch, Witwatersrand and Natal:

'But strong emotions [. . .] lead poets to poetry. Then why is this particular emotion, of concern about race-oppression in South Africa, different? Because it is too particular and at the same time quite impersonal. It is both private and public in the wrong ways: for it is based on one's private agreement with certain temporarily public opinions (the correctness of which I am not questioning). [. . .] But when the poet treats of ideas that are public but not universal, or at least traditional, he must, before he can express anything else, move men into the primary assent that makes those ideas viable. Anything short of that is an economy of mental and emotional energy that suits journalists and tendentious novelists but ruins poets. For it is an indulgence in borrowed ideas, an exploitation of ready-made feelings.' (p 34)

In responding to these views, one should keep in mind that the examples Lionel had to hand demonstrated entirely the incapacity of those poets to deal with 'race-oppression'. But not all poetry fails in these ways. One only has to read Lionel's review of Serote's *Tsetlo*[16] to recognize that matters of race, class and experience are among the factors absent from the argument provoked by Butler's selection. But is it not refreshing, at the same time, to encounter critical commentary which declares its position as openly as this does? Here there is no evasiveness, no glancing over theoretical shoulders nor any obfuscation.

In his strange and sad essay, 'Credo Post Mortem',[17] Lionel explores questions of sanity, madness and faith in relation to humanity, producing a magazine and the process of legacy. The essay is a gloomy struggle between doom-laden sentiments and rational efforts to assert the creative and life-bearing. The reference to legacy (in Lionel's view made possible by speech) was what caught my attention, for it brings a further dimension of Lionel and *The Purple Renoster* to mind.

Lionel has understood himself to be a legatee. As both European and African, as Jewish, as recipient of the philosophies of Gemmell and Bosman: these influences he has acknowledged in numbers of places. And he is more than only those constituents, for his chief delight has been in what he received from people as editor, adviser, critic and reader. And as a legatee, Lionel has translated himself into a legator, issuing *The Purple Renoster* to thirty-nine subscribers but hundreds of readers and, with the publication of the collections by Mtshali and Serote, making poetry available to thousands of buyers. And, again, there are his own collections of poetry, his essays and his novel, his editions of Bosman and further benefactions. That small knit of people who produced *The Purple Renoster* initially has increased into many threads in the fabric of South African cultural history.

In 'Credo Post Mortem', Lionel said:

'The madness that sustains the production of a magazine such as mine takes the form of a faith, concerning the inter-relation between literary expression and human reality.' (p 6)

The cadences of that sentence are Bosman's; the sentiments are purely those of Lionel Abrahams.

---

NOTES

1. Lionel Abrahams: '*The Purple Renoster*: An Adolescence'. *English in Africa*, vol 7, no 2, September 1980, p 36. Hereafter, Abrahams.
2. *The Purple Renoster 1*, 1956, p 3.
3. Abrahams, pp 33–34.
4. Editorials, reviews and essays in *The Purple Renoster*, amplified by the essays in Patrick Cullinan (ed), 1988. *Lionel Abrahams: A Reader*. Johannesburg: Ad. Donker. Hereafter, Cullinan.
5. Abrahams, p 46.
6. See *English in Africa*, vol 7, no 2, September 1980.
7. See Abrahams, pp 46–48, and Cullinan, pp 311–317.
8. Abrahams, p 33.
9. Ibid., p 40.
10. *The Purple Renoster 7*, 1967, pp 3–4.
11. Abrahams, p 45.
12. Ibid., pp 35–36.
13. Ibid., p 36.
14. 'From a South African Diary', in Cullinan, pp 146–188.
15. 'This Hurts Me More Than You', *The Purple Renoster 4*, 1960, pp 30–38.
16. 'Political Vision of a Poet', in Cullinan, pp 208–209.
17. *The Purple Renoster 11*, 1972, pp 6–7.

# NJABULO S NDEBELE

*a poem*

**'I HID MY LOVE IN A SEWAGE . . .'**

I hid my love in a sewage
Of a city; and when it was decayed,
I returned:
I returned to the old lands,
The old lands
Where old men old women
Laugh all day
Until their lungs are as dry as dust:
Where old men and old women
Talk all day
About the weather, about proverbs, about fields . . .
About trivial things:
Where they talk all day
About trivial things . . .

There was I in the wilderness,
Outlandish years dull
Like the rings of a rusted bell.
I stood aloof when the cows
Spread their moo across the rural greens,
I was king,
I was king of the bees,
I ruled over the honey,
I ruled over the milk pail
Full of white bubbles.

Ha! Ha! I held my hollow belly
In laughter when a hen dropped an egg.
My arms akimbo,

I knew the secrets of the world,
I knew the secret pleasures,
The better pleasures,
And God, let me lie on the grass
At the entrance of life – unwanted life.

Below the bottom of life,
My love lay drowned in the stench,
Of course I knew it
I knew my love was dead;
But oh no, let me lie unbothered
On the grass at the entrance of life,
Let me break the bonds that make me me,
Let me drift in the wilderness of callousness,
Let me drift an unidentified soul . . .

And when the fumes of decayed love
Were unfurled unto the winds,
And they covered the plains and the greens,
And their rot chewed by the trees,
And their rot sung
By choirs of drunken birds,
I knew I had lost;
God, I knew I had lost;
O who am I? Who am I?
I am the hoof that once
Grazed in silence upon the grass,
But now rings like a bell on tarred streets.

*a story*

## CROWD CONTROL

Harold hated the middle of summer – not for what it was, but for what it brought. As the month of December approached, he would begin to brace himself for six or seven weeks of torment. He knew that the holiday crowds benefited the city economically; he knew that every restaurant-owner, every proprietor of a guest-house, everyone who had a stall at a flea market must welcome the pleasure-seekers and their money. At a level within himself where there was pragmatism and common sense – a sort of mezzanine level, full of light and plastic plants – Harold could accept that, as a resident of Cape Town, there should be some kind of welcome within him too.

But at another level, deep in the basement of his heart, Harold felt all the anxieties of one entering a torture chamber. For those weeks of high summer there would be no hope of tranquillity within him, no space in his fretful unease for himself, just as there was virtually no space for him on the street, on the pavement, on the promenade in Sea Point, where he liked to walk in the afternoon, or in the restaurant where he liked to eat twice a week. Soon they would be here, those for whom pleasure was a ruthless ambition, greedy for sun and fun, pushing at him and past him with all the terrible chauvinism of young flesh.

He would not leave the city during those months, even though there was no practical reason why he should not do so, for he was retired and could afford to take a holiday in a less popular part of the world. But he would not, for that would be like surrendering to the marauders. And so there was nothing for him to do but to retreat within his resentment; and to wait; and to hate. He indulged to the full his hatred of the crowds – of their shoving, their shouting, their hooting, their demanding anonymity. And why should he not hate, after all, seeing that he never did anything with his hatred? To hate and not to harm: what could possibly be wrong with that? And the hatred of those who were anonymous was such a vague, diffused kind of hatred, for all its keenness; it could not reach them in the least.

Once he was in his flat, he could block out the sight of the crowds, although he could not avoid entirely the sound of them. From the street below, he could hear the heedless noises that they made as they annexed for their pleasure even that time which has been called the small hours of the morning, but which, in their hands, was now grown large and brash. Harold could see the sea from his flat: the setting sun was a presence in his sitting-room. He would watch, a respectful onlooker, as it performed its quiet and solitary ablutions in the Atlantic every afternoon. But now the ritual brought him no pleasure, for that same sun had spent the day pleasing the crowds on the beaches, pandering to them like a courtesan; and now, tainted with their satisfaction, it sank into the sea, leaving the hot, fuzzy night to indulge them in its absence.

At the level within himself where he could be sternly rational, Harold knew that he was over-reacting, yet he seemed unable to stop himself. It was the same as his morbid anxieties about the population explosion. Ever since he was a child, Harold had been terrified of the population explosion. He used to lie awake at night, torturing himself with scenarios of ghastly claustrophobia. The earth had become a catacomb into which the living hordes were thrust. He would have to share a room with eleven others. He would have to live in a broom cupboard. He would have to be put down when he reached forty years of age because there was no more air or food for him. No one cared who or what he was, only that he breathed and ate, and that was unforgivable.

When he spoke soberly to himself, he knew that there was nothing to fear. The population explosion was a receding threat. Affluent countries had falling birth rates; in some cases, deaths exceeded births. The solution was obvious: improve the conditions of people's lives and the babies would stop coming. And if the world could not heed the simple lesson, what was it to him? He would be dead long before the situation could ever begin to affect him.

But in the murkier regions where his fear lay, the possibility of the world's controlling its spawning meant nothing. Harold thought of places he had never been to, never would visit: Bangladesh, for instance; or Ethiopia. When he lay awake at night, he would think of Bangladesh and Ethiopia. He didn't know what to do about them. He saw dirty furrows and water thick as pus. Wailing babies appeared, born out of the yellow water itself, born with pot bellies and wizened faces, wave upon wave of them, murderous, dying babies. And he hated them so. He hated their rapaciousness and their terrible feebleness that nothing could oppose. And he hated Mother Theresa, who nursed them instead of giving them condoms. And he wondered where one could hide from these malnutrants. There is not enough to go around, he thought: if some have, others must do without. He would not give what he had to them, for they were insatiable and their need was like a void: they would not even notice that anything had been given to them, while he would be left with nothing.

To try and calm himself down, he would think of uninhabited places: of a vast savannah where the horizon was farther away than it had ever been, so far that even the clouds could not reach it. No human figure appeared here to disturb the wave-like motion of the grass. This was the unpopulated world that came before – the clean world; or perhaps it was the depopulated world that comes after – the cleansed world. He longed for that world, even if it meant that he could not be a part of it. And he felt vaguely that he was not alone in wishing for it; that there must have been others, especially in this crowded century, who had longed for it too. He did not know who they were, yet he felt a vague sense of kinship with these people.

He spent as much time as he could in his flat, waiting for the acute period of high summer to pass. When he was forced to go out, he tried always to lessen the ordeal of the crowded streets by spending time in the Sea Point library. He found the muffled noises and the discreet librarians soothing. The only drawback to the library was that he was inclined to meet Bennie there. He had known the man for thirty years. The fact that they had nothing at all in common was known only to him; Bennie had remained quite unaware of this fact for three decades. Invariably Bennie spoke too loudly, greeted too effusively, said too much – about his wife, his five children, his eighteen grandchildren. He recommended books that held no interest for Harold: after all these years, Bennie had still not realized how far apart their sensibilities lay. When he was there, Harold would choose his books hurriedly; otherwise, he would spend hours in the library, browsing contentedly, almost forgetting the horrors that awaited him as soon as he stepped outside.

Last summer he had found another haven – an antique shop which he came across one day in a quiet side street. It was called *Exclusive Cape Antiques*. Inside the shop it was cool and dark. A ceiling fan sifted the air unobtrusively, while a grandfather clock, refusing to be hurried, admonished the cowed hours. He began to look forward to his visits. He felt reassured by the sedateness of the shop, by its unruffled air. It was a reticent place; that was what he liked best. More often than not, he bought nothing. Even if no new artefacts had come in since he was last there, he didn't care. He was happy to look again at what he had already admired.

The proprietor, an elderly woman, surveyed all with a stately air. One or two customers would come in – discerning people who knew what they wanted, knew far more about antiques than Harold did, if the truth be told, but what did it matter? He was beginning to learn. As his confidence grew, he bought something every now and then, but always something small, for there was no room in his flat for anything large. Although he loved the old wooden furniture – some of it more than two hundred years old: the country cupboards made of kiaat or cedarwood, the half-moon tables made of stinkwood with yellow-wood inlay, the stinkwood display cabinets – he would have had nowhere to put any of it. There was no point making his flat cluttered. But a silver snuff box or sauce ladle, a crystal decanter, six sherry glasses – these things would not rob him of his space. He bought them slowly, savouring the pleasure of the acquisition, making one purchase every few weeks.

The elderly proprietor, as she grew accustomed to seeing him in the shop, became friendlier and, eventually, quite chatty. She told him that she and her husband started the shop more than forty years ago, when they came out from Europe. She extended a beringed hand. "I am Mrs Frank," she said. Harold shook her hand. The abatement of her stern manner gratified him. Mrs Frank seemed to him to be like one of those severe headmistresses whose crusty exterior hides a rough kindness; the sort of person of whom people always say afterwards that her bark was worse than her bite.

What pleased him too was that, after this, she took a greater interest in his purchases, telling him that what he had bought was rare; it was unusual; very few were ever made; very few still existed. As he fought his way home through the crowds that moved as if with one mind to the video stores, the hamburger stands, the ice-cream vendors, leaving polystyrene cups strewn behind them, he felt grateful that there was still such precious singularity in the world.

Some of Mrs Frank's clients had been buying from her for decades, she told him: she had very loyal customers, very loyal. Harold felt that their loyalty was being offered to him, so that he could partake of it too. He was being invited to begin his own long relationship with

*Exclusive Cape Antiques.* "Anything you want, you tell me," said the old woman. "I get it for you. You just tell me." There was nothing that Harold wanted in particular, but her assumption that he was a serious collector of antiques flattered him; so, after much thought, he told her that he wanted a gold fob-chain. "No problem," she replied, "I can get it for you." And within three weeks he had it.

It was like being admitted to an elite club. What was needed in order to become a member was the ability to appreciate what the shop had to offer, to see that there had been occasions in the past when prescient individuals had stood back from the remorseless welter of the world, and that what was sold in the shop was the stuff of that momentous pause. Let the lemmings run, Harold thought; let them run past me and leave me behind.

Mrs Frank began increasingly to confide in Harold. He felt honoured, as if the privilege of her conversation were in itself one of the precious items on offer in the shop. He learned that she had managed the shop alone for eight years and presumed that this was because her husband was dead. She told him, however, that her husband was still alive, although gravely ill with emphysema. He lay at home, tended by a full-time nurse, unable to do without his oxygen canisters. After that, Harold felt obliged to enquire after her husband every time he came into the shop. She would sigh and shake her head. "He is not good. How can he be good?" she would say; but he could see that she was pleased by the enquiry.

"Do you have any children?" he asked her once after the routine enquiry about her husband. "Will there be anyone to see to the shop when you are gone?"

"We have no children," she said. "And what about you? Do you have any?"

"No."

"Then we are the same. We are the last of our breed."

"Well, at least we have not added to the population explosion," Harold said, smiling.

"No, that is not us," she said. "We do not do that. We never have. It is them." She indicated the street outside. "It is them. The Africans. They have babies like rabbits. Like flies. It is a big problem."

Something struck Harold about the shop one day, something that, oddly, he had not noticed on all his previous visits. He waited until Mrs Frank had finished dealing with a customer, so that he could ask her about it. "Tell me," he said, "why do you stock South African antiques? Why not European antiques? I would have thought, in view of your background . . ."

"No," she said, before he had finished the sentence. "No, my husband and I were not interested in that. Europe is finished. Finished. South Africa is our home. It has been good to us. Although we deal with old things, we cannot live in the past."

Harold found these sentiments surprising. He had thought of Mrs Frank as a sort of displaced European aristocrat, a remnant of a stately, pre-war Europe that was now gone. He had taken for granted in her a nostalgia, a measure of scorn for the newness of South Africa. But this was not the case. "There is history here too," she said. "Look at the beautiful things in this shop. They show us that the past is here also. South Africa is a young country, but it is an old country too. We have never felt that we did not have a place here or that we do not belong. We are happy to die here."

"I'm pleased to hear it," said Harold. He thought about what she had said for some time. That night he held the fob-chain in his hand and thought, "This is what has been salvaged. This is the precious thing that lies amidst the dross. It is here, if only I can keep finding it and never lose sight of it. That is what she is trying to tell me."

When he went to the shop a few days later, he could scarcely believe what he saw. All the shop windows were broken, the pavements were covered in glass, and policemen were sifting through the debris. Mrs Frank stood in the street, agitated and breathless, her usual composure wholly abandoned. "Look at this!" she shouted, as soon as she saw Harold. "Look! Look what they have done!"

"Who?" he asked. "Who has done this?"

"They go past," she said. "They are singing and making a noise. Then they smash the windows, they take things from the shop, some of them they smash, they just throw them down in the street."

"Who?" he asked. "Who?"

But Mrs Frank ignored his question. She told someone else how the windows had been broken, how the precious goods had been vandalized. "This is what will destroy this country," she said, waving her arms wildly. "No one can control them. They move in groups like animals and then they become like animals."

Harold eventually managed to establish what had happened. A group of striking workers had gone past the shop, chanting slogans and singing. No one seemed to know who they were: someone said they were refuse collectors, but someone else insisted that it was the postal workers who were on strike. There was even the unlikely suggestion that they were all messengers-of-court. They turned off the main street, using the side street as a short cut to the foreshore; and then, suddenly, no one seemed to know why, they had attacked Mrs Frank's shop. In five minutes the damage was done and they moved off.

"Never have we had any problems," Mrs Frank was telling the people who gathered in the street to look at the devastation. "In forty years we have had no problems. We make no trouble, we have no trouble. Now it starts. These things that they have broken, they cannot be replaced. Never. They are one of a kind. Now it starts. This is the beginning, but I can see the end. Better that we die now, my husband and me."

She protested that she did not want to leave the shop, but, eventually, someone persuaded her to get into a car and she was driven away. The shards of glass on the pavement were being swept up. Harold felt that there was no longer any point in staying there. In the rather hysterical response of Mrs Frank there was, he felt, some truth. It did feel like the beginning of the end, but he could not say of what.

He went to the library, needing to feel that one of his havens was still available to him. He prayed that Bennie would not be there, but, of course, there he was, beaming broadly and pressing a book on him. He tried to resist, but Bennie was persistent and Harold, still shaken by what he had seen at the shop, felt that it was easier to give in than stand and argue. He scarcely listened to what Bennie was saying about it. As he made his escape, however, he heard him say, "You'll find it fascinating – even you, a lapsed Jew."

"I'm not a lapsed Jew," he said. "I'm a non-religious Jew."

"I'm joking," Bennie shouted from across the street. "Can't you take a joke?"

That night Harold struggled to get to sleep. When he did sleep, he was afflicted by nightmares. In one of them the babies from Bangladesh and Ethiopia appeared, but this time they were here, in Cape Town. They were as scrawny as ever, but for once they were not simply lying around, weak and dying. They ran, quick as monkeys. He followed them down the streets, knowing, with a morbid certainty, that they were heading for *Exclusive Cape Antiques*. Sure enough, they swarmed into the shop and he followed them in, unable to break away. They paid him no attention, yet they held him in thrall. He could hear their screeches of delight as they held the trinkets up to the light, before they dropped and smashed everything. They climbed onto the furniture and excreted all over it. He wondered how they managed to produce excrement in such vast quantities, seeing as they had not eaten anything since they were born. He felt he had to find Mrs Frank, to protect her from them, but he could not see her anywhere. He grew more frantic and then he awoke.

It was four in the morning and there was no chance now of falling asleep again. There was drunken shouting coming up from the street below. He went to get something to drink. On his way back from the kitchen, he saw the books he had brought from the library on the dining-room table. He looked at them again and then, idly, he picked up the one that Bennie had urged him to take and began to glance through it. To his surprise, he did not find it boring at all. It was a book written by a Jewish doctor from Johannesburg. The doctor was an amateur historian. He had become interested in what had happened to the Nazis and Nazi collaborators who fled Europe at the end of the War. Whereas it was widely known that a large number of them had made their way to South America, the doctor sought to show in his book that it was less well known, but nonetheless the case, that a substantial number had come to southern Africa too: to South West Africa in particular, but also to South Africa. The doctor had done a great deal of careful research and Harold found the argument wholly credible. He became engrossed in the book.

What the doctor's discoveries meant was that these people had been living hidden amongst them all the time. They had slipped undetected into the general population and were protected by the mass of humankind which, despite its reputation, is a great deal less curious than one would think. No one had paused to single them out, but this is what the doctor now did. At the back of the book he included in an appendix what was, perhaps, the most interesting part of his enquiry – certainly, it was the most tangible. He listed alphabetically the names of those individuals whom he had managed to identify, specifying what they had done during the War and adding whatever information he had regarding what had happened to them since they came to southern Africa. Many of them, of course, were dead. A surprisingly large percentage, however, were still alive. Harold ran his eye down the list. The words 'living at present in Cape Town' caught his attention and he paused to read the entry. The man's name was Wilhelm Franz. He was one of those who, from the autumn of 1941 onwards, supervised the deportation of German Jews from metropolitan Germany to Polish and Soviet ghettoes in the east. These Jews were crowded into goods or cattle wagons and many did not survive the journey. Wilhelm Franz, Harold read, had been the proprietor for over forty years of an antique shop called *Exclusive Cape Antiques*.

He put the book down on the table and walked to the window. The street below was quite still now; even the late-night revellers had fallen silent at last. The sun had not yet risen, although there was a tell-tale pinkness in the east. The sky and the sea had the world to themselves.

# EVA BEZWODA

## *two poems*

### 'THERE IS BLOOD ON THE STREET . . .'

There is blood on the street.
A man fell from a window.
We shake red hands.
At the end of a thought
Comes a little fullstop of blood
A simple alphabet,
Red dots, question marks, a name.
We exchange looks
With eyes that have a red streak
In the corner.

### "I NEVER PROMISED YOU A ROSE GARDEN . . ."

"I never promised you a rose garden"
Liar. You did.
A garden of marbled roses
And stony angles.
Petals and holy eyes turned upwards.
You promised the endless white roses,
The timeless drip of rain, rain,
On stone. Liar.
The earth is cracking through the marble
Worms live on the roses.

# IVAN VLADISLAVIĆ

## *a story*

*Dear Lionel*

*Nearly twenty years have passed since I belonged to 'the group', that writing circle at whose still centre you stand. The members would take turns to host the gathering, and so we were always on the move from Yeoville to Brixton to Braamfontein and back again. But, for me at least, our headquarters, our high command, was the island at the end of Fifth Street where you lived and worked. Although you have long since moved to the foreign territory of Rivonia, I confess that in my imagination you are still in your old den, and I cannot drop down the hill towards Orange Grove without picturing you there, in the little suburb of Victoria, and feeling better. I find an explanation for this in your poem 'Views and Sites', where you write about your own attachment to certain unlikely places in the city. You ask:*

> *Or is it where a topsoil of memory*
> *has been allowed to form*
> *that one feels a little more*
> *alive, a little more at home?*

*I was a relative newcomer to Joburg in the late seventies, and the writing group helped me to make a place for myself here. There were practical things to be learnt in that company: the discipline of regular work, the give and take of criticism, the knowledge that sometimes the only way to improve a piece of writing is to pour the reader another glass of wine. Thanks to you, I published my first stories, and was encouraged to put a collection together. In time it became possible to think of myself as a writer (in the privacy of my own home, at least).*

*Lionel, you are a great conjuror of possibility. In the light of your particular magic, it becomes possible, for instance, to think clearly, to feel strongly, even to think clearly and feel strongly at the same time. And, always, to write. More precisely, to pursue a writing life, to live by writing. In your own work you achieve the impossible: love for this tawdry city, these 'too changeable streets'. You keep alive the memory of your own Johburg – watermarked with that surprising 'h' – and so it stays alive in us, even as 'the old skyline comes down'. Your map of Johburg, which I take gratefully as a map of your heart and mind, has helped me to find my way.*

*Thank you, and happy birthday.*
*Ivan*

## A SCIENCE OF FRAGMENTS
*In memory of Lulu Davis*

> *Fragments neither close*
> *nor open meaning:*
> *they may mean anything except*
> *wholeness, except certainty.*
> Lionel Abrahams

### AN UNPOSTED LETTER

On the day of her death he sat down to write and took her death, or rather his grief, as theme. He found disturbing the haste with which he needed to convert grief into fiction. Yet he admitted that his grief, her death, became more believable with every word he set down. He read the words over as if he had chanced upon them in the flyleaf of a borrowed book. He was moved to tears by his own face, in a mirror.

On the day of her funeral he rewrote the piece three times and typed it up. It hardly filled a page. Rereading it, moved once again to tears, he found an error, and had to type it over. It had to be perfect.

He unpinned two paper figures, a dancer and a sleeper, from his notice-board and folded them in his page. Now that it was folded into quarters the page became a letter. He sealed it in an envelope and put it in his pocket.

It was late. He dressed hurriedly, and while he was dressing he realized that he intended to post his letter in her grave. It amazed him that this had been his intention all along.

The need to post the letter stayed with him, a voice speaking softly in his pocket, as he walked with the other mourners to the open grave.

In the end, he did not post the letter. A spadeful of sand came to seem the adequate gesture, a sheet of white paper an affront. But another consideration urged restraint: he had become too attached to his own words to part with them.

# FRUIT

She props herself in a fork of the apricot-tree and picks fruit. She is a lilac shadow in the quiet green heart of the tree. In her hands the apricots are succulent suns. She bites into them gleefully and spits out the pips.

He sits on the verandah in an armchair and watches her out of the corner of his eye.

She picks five apricots and drops them in the lap of her lilac dress. Then she discovers that she needs both hands for climbing. So she eats two of the apricots, stores three in her mouth, and climbs down. The hem of her dress snags on a branch and the cloth tears.

She goes to where he is sitting. Her cheeks bulge with fruit. He stifles laughter.

An indistinct fanfare from her full mouth, and then her lips open slowly and she pops the apricots out one by one. She does this with a flourish, like a magician, but he is reminded of a fish; a bird regurgitating from its crop; an insect laying eggs. He looks at the fruit, shiny with spit, in his hand.

It hurts her that he goes to wash the fruit under the garden tap, but she says nothing.

## VERSIONS OF HIMSELF

Once, at an exhibition, he bought a photograph she had taken: 'The Waiting Room'. A cardboard box full of chaos and decay. A looming matchbox. Two giant moths. Mulberry leaves as tall as trees, uprooted. Silkworm cocoons stuck to the grey walls. Silkworm droppings. Pink scented sweets. Bones. Electric flex. A crashed dove. A die toppling onto its lucky face. A dead pig. Five plastic people on a bench (from l. to r.):

The watcher
holds an object in his lap and looks into it, rather than at it: a book, a crystal ball, a mirror, a reliquary.

The lovers,
man and woman, their heads resting together, their hands meshed, inanimate. Her eyes are closed. Or perhaps they are simply lowered to look at his hand.

The listener
holds an object to his ear: a telephone, a shell, a bloody rag.

The other man,
the dark one, cut off by the edge of the photograph, in shadow, his head down, his hands hidden. Below the brim of his hat a face without features.

## CONVERSATION

With the dawn a grey chill came into the room. He reached for the bottle and she suddenly burst out: "I used to like your hands but I've changed my mind. They're the hands of a clerk."

He replied, trying to be cruel, "You have the hands of a plumber."

Her head jerked, as if he had struck her, but she laughed. She clapped her workman's hands, full of scratches, the nails chipped and rimmed with black, and she snorted with delight.

## BROKEN MIRROR

*In the Cavalier Bar at the Flashback Hotel he turned an empty glass in a pool of its sweat on the counter. On the back of a Laughing Cavalier serviette he wrote:*

*'You crossed the border. You came to rest in a homeland of deaf earth and dumb stone. Now and always, you are travelling on a foreign passport.'*

*He asked the barman for the date and wrote it next to the laughing face. The ink ran. He put the serviette in his pocket.*

*Meanwhile, she floated in the immense calm beyond the waves. She opened the valve in one of her water-wings and it jetted stale air below the surface. She puttered in circles, on her back, looking up at the circling clouds.*

*Under one arm she carried a story, her own, missing a chapter or two, wrapped in bright yellow oilskin and tied up with string. The story refused to sink. She forced it under, boiling bubbles as if it were drowning, but it twisted out of her hands and bobbed stubbornly to the air.*

*She swam back to the shore, towing the bright package behind her.*

*In the margin of the sea, in large letters, he wrote:*

*'Forgive me my story, as I forgive you yours.'*

*He sat down to watch the sea erase his message. But the tide was going out and*

*'Forgive me my story'*

*persisted. He had to cross it out himself with the palm of his hand.*

*No one saw him leave. While her eyes were closed he walked out in the sun-
shine at Jan Smuts airport, his head turned purposefully away, his collar up.
He phoned the Flashback from a booth. Reception said the number rang and
rang.*

*In the gardens then, in a childhood place, in the beautiful gardens of the
Flashback Hotel, her veins slow with sleep, one leg drawn up, her bones heavy
with words, her eyes wide open and dark, she curled at last into cactus-
needle, leaf-vein, moss, lichen, loam.*

## CONVERSATION

She said, "I have the mind of a forty-year-old divorcee in the body of
a sixteen-year-old schoolgirl."

He replied, "Or vice versa."

She did not hear, or pretended not to. She looked at the grey morning behind the window-panes. The look on her face was so unexpected that he almost laughed: a jaded, adult expression, signifying world-
liness, cynicism, regret.

## VERSIONS OF HERSELF

Once, for his birthday, she gave him the fragments of an animated film
she had made. A cardboard box spilled out the bits and pieces of a
puzzled world: paper people, two inches tall, wax-crayon rainbows,
trees, hungry eyes and mouths.

There were hundreds of versions of the heroine, herself, each dif-
fering slightly from the next.

For an evening he amused himself, hunting out the figures that
could be placed one after the other to build the raising of a hand, a
single step, a leap over an obstacle, a pirouette. Then he put the box
in a drawer.

Years later he came across the box when he was tidying up. He kept
two versions of the heroine and threw the rest away. He pinned the
two survivors to the notice-board above his desk:

The dancer

wears a tattered lilac frock. She stands on one foot, her other leg
drawn up almost to her chest, her arms stretched for balance. Her hair
explodes over her shoulders. Startled eyes, two full stops, are the only
features of her face.

The sleeper

wears the same frock, lies on her side, one knee drawn up and hugged. Her hair pours over a turned shoulder and obscures her face, which she presses into a pillow of earth. Just visible, one heavy-lidded eye, shaped like a comma, closed.

## CROSSING

They waded into the waves to cool their feet, and he scared himself with a joke about sharks. Then the word 'shark' kept circling under the conversation. They walked on in silence towards the wreck.

The wreck, when they reached it, disappointed him. From miles away it had promised to be a monument, something magnificently wasted. From close it was merely metal, dead, rotting into rock. Even the gulls left it alone.

She was more than satisfied. She wanted to swim across to the wreck. She said it was an island worth exploring. He dissuaded her, mentioned sharks again, pointed out the cross-current, threatened to go home.

They climbed up to the dunes, where they had imagined shade. But as he lowered himself onto the sand, the dune shifted with his weight and slid into heat.

She settled down and slept. The sun put a gloss of sweat on her skin, a hot fluff on her shoulders. He came close and watched her sleeping face. This crossing held no dangers. This space could be bridged by a hand or a word. An image slid out of the blue: a finger stirring chips of shell to catch the light. He drew back, unaccountably afraid, spilling sand around him.

She dreamt (she said, when she awoke) that she braved the crossing. The sea was wild. She was washed, exhausted, swallowing salt-water, into the hold. A shaft of light showed her a ladder, but high and out of reach. She scrabbled against the sheer walls and tore her palms on rust. She went under once, twice. Then a wave lifted her gently, as if she was a child, and guided her hands to the rungs. She climbed up to the deck and was saved.

## DEBRIS

In the waiting room, in the shadows, the dark man speaks:

if I should stay up all night with a lucky-packet watch on my wrist, in the dawn, in the corner of a room, in the mysterious symmetry of wall meeting wall, if I should lie on my back with the curtains open wide, in Braamfontein, the sky, from my dirty window, the Hillbrow Tower with a polka-dot bow-tie, a bruised sky full of blood, in salmon, puce, cerise, peach, apricot, plum, a thorn-tree, the musical fountains at Wemmer Pan, a papier-mâché Drommedaris, a fibre-glass Van Riebeeck, the gilt-edged dumps, the laundromat in Pretoria Street, dirty linen dancing in the suds, in the butchery at the Restless Supermarket, a butcher with three fingers and a bloody Band-aid, if I should smell salt, tea-rose, turpentine, if I should see, in the rearview mirror, rows of mielies arrive-depart-arrive, in a telephone booth, if I should open at random to a name, to a number, in the pages of a notebook bound in black, with a red spine, on the last page, or the first, in a margin, if I should hear in the ribcage of the hardest word its soft heart beat

## ECHO

On the anniversary of her death, his grief, he takes two versions of her, a dancer and a sleeper, from their shroud. He can no longer remember why he chose these two from among the hundreds. He pins them up, pushing the pins carefully into the familiar wounds.

# LEON JOFFE

## *a poem*

### 'WILL I STILL REMEMBER YOUR FACE . . .'

Will I still remember your face when it is crooked and trying
To speak but there are no words; will I still recall
Your eager warm body when it starts to fall
At every step, when there is no more bluff or lying?
Will I still be able to hold your face in my hands and smile
And mean it; or will your hurt and pain and rage and dying
Kill the love in my eyes?

Will I still remember your laughter long after it has grown
Silent, along with your hope, along with your dreams?
Will there still be a future for 'us', or will 'us', as it seems
Now to me, mean nothing: me always angry and you always down,
And what then? What then? Will I still be able to touch
Your hand, your arm, your neck, your blouse, your gown
And you quiet and expectant?

Will you still know who I am? Will you ask my help, or throw
Yourself around from chair to chair, hating me for being sane
And watching you with beaten eyes? Or will you beat me again
And again, your fists futile on my chest, or will you go
Away, or fall from some terrible height
When I stop watching you for a minute? And who will know
Whether you meant it?

I have one small photograph I will hide from others, to feel
In the dead of those times, when I, a disbeliever, kneel.
I will kiss your paper smile, and smile at your eye's laughter
And laugh at those dreams you had for us, after
All of the long years had passed, and we could be alone.
And I will love you again, before my heart turns to stone,
I will love you always while you're still my own.

## *two poems*

### DEAR LOVELY

My heart cough little bit
Minute I touch touch for you
This here and that there
Oh my mostest beautifullest

How I was being born
And you was born or coming front or back
Just the devil can know
Oh my number one thing

But you must listen here:
Is one thing I never ask it:
Apologies to be poor
So now
I buy you for most all
A first-class train
Complete of head-rest
And cushions and all
And everything

We go Cape Town to Cairo
On a lovers' walk
Me and you just
Oh my sweetest dear lovely

How now you feel?

## DA SAME, DA SAME

I doesn't care of you black
I doesn't care of you white
I doesn't care of you India
I doesn't care of you kleeling
if sometimes you Saus Afrika
you gotta big terrible terrible
somewheres in yourselves
because why
for sure you doesn't look anader man in da eye

I mean for sure now
all da peoples is make like God
sometimes you wanna knows how I meaning for
is simples
da God I knows for sure
He make avarybudy wit' one heart

for sure now dis heart go-go da same
dats for meaning to say
one man no diflent to anader
so now
you see a big terrible terrible stand here
how one man make anader man feel
da pain he doesn't feel hisself
for sure now dats da whole point

sometime you wanna know how I meaning for
is simples
when da nail of da t'orn tree
scratch little bit little bit of da skin
I doesn't care of say black
I doesn't care of say white
I doesn't care of say India
I doesn't care of say kleeling
I mean for sure da skin
only one t'ing come for sure
and da one t'ing for sure is red blood
dats for sure da same da same
for avarybudy.

# DEBBY LAPIDOS

*a story*

## SMALL TALK IN HILLBROW

"I'm married now," Barbara tells me. She sits down and lights her cigarette. She looks around the café afterwards as if to see who is in her audience.

"Oh that's nice," I say.

"To a decent oke," she adds.

"That's nice. What does he do?"

"Actually he's an engineer."

"Oh, where does he work?"

"Nowhere at the moment."

Her hair is no longer the bright red that it was in summer but a fading blonde with grey roots. She continually brushes an imaginary strand away from her face. An eyebrow with a kink in it straggles out of place. Around us the air is steamy with cigarettes and cooking and in the background Jim Morrison is dwelling on his usual subject matter. "Your ballroom days are over, baby," he sings.

"He's not wrong about that," Barbara says, tuning in.

The waiter stands at our table with writing pad and pen. His belt is made of pink and blue plastic and his bleached hair is trimmed and styled into a side flick to show his earring to its best advantage. "What'll it be, girls?" he asks.

"Two coffees please."

"White?"

We nod. He minces off moving his hips to the beat of the music.

"Ag shame," says Barbara, staring after him.

"So, tell me more about your husband," I say.

"Not much to tell. I met him at the bar in the Huguenot. We live in the Huguenot. His name is Heinrich and he's sixty years old, thirty more than me. By Hillbrow standards he's a catch."

I laugh. "Why's he a catch?"

"Lots of reasons. One, he's white. Two, he's not a criminal or a moffie. Three, he's got enough money to live."

"Okay. He's a good choice."

"But not perfect," she says.

"What do you mean?"

"Well, he *is* German."

"I can hear by his name."

"But not all hairless and pasty like some of them are."

"That's good," I say.

Jim Morrison is crooning over the speakers.

"*Actually,*" Barbara says, tuning in again, "I'm depressed."

"Why?" I ask. "Your life's coming together."

"Ja, you're right. I don't know why. Maybe it's the general vibe."

We sit silently while she considers. "Everyone looks like they've got AIDS," she says and points to a regular wearing sunglasses who sits alone at a corner table.

"I'm sure he's just thin," I offer.

"No, I know that one. He's on first name terms with half the prossies in Hillbrow. That means four hundred of them."

"Why four hundred?" I ask.

"That's according to this magazine article I saw."

"Oh," I say.

"Ja, there's eight hundred in all so then half is four hundred . . . and you know what I mean 'on first name terms'?"

"Ja. But still Barbara, they say it's not easy to get AIDS from women."

"I'm not so sure," she says, "these women are vrot."

The sliding door squeaks open and a draught of cold air blasts in with a man wearing shorts and a t-shirt. It looks as if saliva is running from his bottom lip. And he's shivering.

"Shame," says Barbara, "you see that oke?"

"Ja," I say.

"He arrived here a week ago and they mugged him when he was walking in Berea with his suitcases on his first day. That's all they left him with. The clothes on his back."

"Ja, muggers can spot a foreigner a mile away."

"He's lucky to be alive, never mind."

"Ja," I say.

"There's blood on the streets, it's up to my knees," sings Jim.

"You know that Greek oke?" Barbara asks.

"No," I say. "Which Greek oke?"

"You know, that fat one? Dimitri? Well, anyway, it's not important 'cos they killed him last week outside his garage."

"Who's they?" I ask.

"Some blacks."

"Shame," we both say.

"Terrible what happens here," I say.

"He was such a good oke," says Barbara.

The air smells like an English breakfast. A fight is in progress outside and Indian men run past the window holding guns and clubs.

"It reminds me of my dream the other night," says Barbara. "Except I had blacks with pangas in it and they were in Abel Road."

"Ja, it *is* similar," I say.

"Ja. I keep having those sort of dreams. The other night I dreamed I was mugged."

"It's a sign of the times," I say.

A lot of police are outside now. One of the Indians is hurt and lying on the pavement while a crowd gathers around.

"Heinrich wants to get a rottweiler but I don't think it's fair to the dog to live in a hotel room."

"I agree with you but a big dog *is* the answer."

"Oh look!" She points at the table near the door. "There's some friends of Heinrich. I'm just going to say hello."

"Okay."

A table of gays beside me cackle and purr. A glamorous man who looks continental sits in the corner.

# CATHERINE STEWART

*a poem*

## LOOKING

"You look beautiful"
she said
"tall and confident in those greens and browns and that coat"

"like a model"
she said
"beautiful" she said.

"It's easy to look like a model" I said.
"All a model does
is look." You

touch. You taste.
I smell you. I hear. You
have tried me now. My look

dribbles from your chin
onto your scarf
spoiling
your look
for all those other lips
gnashing

to taste you up to their eyes.

# NADINE GORDIMER

## *a story*

*Many years past, a young man wrote a story entitled 'Down Upon The Green Grass'. It was delicately but supremely evocative of the perceptions of a child-hood: the character's particular one, and that of more general experience. The character upon the Zoo Lake grass grew up, with the unfolding and develop-ment of his author's talent, to become Felix Greenspan, a personality as unforgettable as any icon in JD Salinger's fiction. Lionel Abrahams's fiction and poetry have pursued a path through the dark forest of our selfhood, leav-ing for the reader a trail not of crumbs but of illuminating words. On a story-teller's birthday, another story-teller offers another story, of a childhood which, in the passage of time and history, became very different from that which was captured beautifully at the Zoo Lake long ago.*

### ONCE UPON A TIME

Someone has written to ask me to contribute to an anthology of stories for children. I reply that I don't write children's stories; and he writes back that at a recent congress/book fair/seminar a certain novelist said every writer ought to write at least one story for children. I think of sending a postcard saying I don't accept that I 'ought' to write any-thing.

And then last night I woke up – or rather was wakened without knowing what had roused me.

A voice in the echo-chamber of the subconscious?

A sound.

A creaking of the kind made by the weight carried by one foot after another along a wooden floor. I listened. I felt the apertures of my ears distend with concentration. Again: the creaking. I was waiting for it; waiting to hear if it indicated that feet were moving from room to room, coming up the passage – to my door. I have no burglar bars, no gun under the pillow, but I have the same fears as people who do take these precautions, and my windowpanes are thin as rime, could shatter like a wineglass. A woman was murdered (how do they put it) in broad daylight in a house two blocks away, last year, and the fierce dogs who guarded an old widower and his collection of antique clocks were strangled before he was knifed by a casual labourer he had dismissed without pay.

I was staring at the door, making it out in my mind rather than seeing it in the dark. I lay quite still – a victim already – but the arrhythmia of my heart was fleeing, knocking this way and that against its body-cage. How finely tuned the senses are, just out of rest, sleep! I could never listen intently as that in the distractions of the day; I was reading every faintest sound, identifying and classifying its possible threat.

But I learned that I was to be neither threatened nor spared. There was no human weight pressing on the boards, the creaking was a buckling, an epicentre of stress. I was in it. The house that surrounds me while I sleep is built on undermined ground; far beneath my bed, the floor, the house's foundations, the stopes and passages of gold mines have hollowed the rock, and when some face trembles, detaches and falls, three thousand feet below, the whole house shifts slightly, bringing uneasy strain to the balance and counterbalance of brick, cement, wood and glass that hold it as a structure around me. The misbeats of my heart tailed off like the last muffled flourishes on one of the wooden xylophones made by the Chopi and Tsonga migrant miners who might have been down there, under me in the earth at that moment. The stope where the fall was could have been disused, dripping water from its ruptured veins; or men might now be interred there in the most profound of tombs.

I couldn't find a position in which my mind would let go of my body – release me to sleep again. So I began to tell myself a story; a bedtime story.

In a house, in a suburb, in a city, there were a man and his wife who loved each other very much and were living happily ever after. They had a little boy, and they loved him very much. They had a cat and a dog that the little boy loved very much. They had a car and a caravan trailer for holidays, and a swimming-pool which was fenced so that the little boy and his playmates would not fall in and drown. They had a housemaid who was absolutely trustworthy and an itinerant gardener who was highly recommended by the neighbours. For when they began to live happily ever after they were warned, by that wise old witch, the husband's mother, not to take on anyone off the street.

They were inscribed in a medical benefit society, their pet dog was licensed, they were insured against fire, flood damage and theft, and subscribed to the local Neighbourhood Watch, which supplied them with a plaque for their gates lettered YOU HAVE BEEN WARNED over the silhouette of a would-be intruder. He was masked; it could not be said if he was black or white, and therefore proved the property owner was no racist.

It was not possible to insure the house, the swimming-pool or the car against riot damage. There were riots, but these were outside the city, where people of another colour were quartered. These people were not allowed into the suburb except as reliable housemaids and gardeners, so there was nothing to fear, the husband told the wife. Yet she was afraid that some day such people might come up the street and tear off the plaque YOU HAVE BEEN WARNED and open the gates and stream in . . . Nonsense, my dear, said the husband, there are police and soldiers and tear-gas and guns to keep them away. But to please her – for he loved her very much and buses were being burned, cars stoned, and schoolchildren shot by the police in those quarters out of sight and hearing of the suburb – he had electronically controlled gates fitted. Anyone who pulled off the sign YOU HAVE BEEN WARNED and tried to open the gates would have to announce his intentions by pressing a button and speaking into a receiver relayed to the house. The little boy was fascinated by the device and used it as a walkie-talkie in cops-and-robbers play with his small friends.

The riots were suppressed, but there were many burglaries in the suburb and somebody's trusted housemaid was tied up and shut in a cupboard by thieves while she was in charge of her employers' house. The trusted housemaid of the man and wife and little boy was so upset by this misfortune befalling a friend, left, as she herself often was, with responsibility for the possessions of the man and his wife and the little boy, that she implored her employers to have burglar bars attached to the doors and windows of the house, and an alarm system installed. The wife said, She is right, let us take heed of her advice. So from every window and door in the house where they were living happily ever after they now saw the trees and sky through bars, and when the little boy's pet cat tried to climb in by the fanlight to keep him company in his little bed at night, as it customarily had done, it set off the alarm keening through the house.

The alarm was often answered – it seemed – by other burglar alarms, in other houses, that had been triggered by pet cats or nibbling mice. The alarms called to one another across the gardens in shrills and bleats and wails that everyone soon became accustomed to, so that the din roused the inhabitants of the suburb no more than the croak of frogs and musical grating of cicadas' legs. Under cover of the electronic harpies' discourse intruders sawed the iron bars and broke into homes, taking away hi-fi equipment, television sets, cassette players, cameras and radios, jewellery and clothing, and sometimes were hungry enough to devour everything in the refrigerator or paused audaciously to drink the whisky in the cabinets or patio bars. Insurance companies paid no compensation for single malt, a loss made keener by the property owner's knowledge that the thieves wouldn't even have been able to appreciate what it was they were drinking.

Then the time came when many of the people who were not trusted housemaids and gardeners hung about the suburb because they were unemployed. Some importuned for a job: weeding or painting a roof; anything, baas, madam. But the man and his wife remembered the warning about taking on anyone off the street. Some drank liquor and fouled the street with discarded bottles. Some begged, waiting for the man or his wife to drive the car out of the electronically operated gates. They sat about with their feet in the gutters, under the jacaranda trees that made a green tunnel of the street – for it was a beautiful suburb, spoilt only by their presence – and sometimes they fell asleep lying right before the gates in the midday sun. The wife could never see anyone go hungry. She sent the trusted housemaid out with bread and tea, but the trusted housemaid said these were loafers and tsotsis, who would come and tie her up and shut her in a cupboard. The husband said, She's right. Take heed of her advice. You only encourage them with your bread and tea. They are looking for their chance . . . And he brought the little boy's tricycle from the garden into the house every night, because if the house was surely secure, once locked and with the alarm set, someone might still be able to climb over the wall or the electronically closed gates into the garden.

You are right, said the wife, then the wall should be higher. And the wise old witch, the husband's mother, paid for the extra bricks as her Christmas present to her son and his wife – the little boy got a Space Man outfit and a book of fairy tales.

But every week there were more reports of intrusion: in broad daylight and the dead of night, in the early hours of the morning, and even in the lovely summer twilight – a certain family was at dinner while the bedrooms were being ransacked upstairs. The man and his wife, talking of the latest armed robbery in the suburb, were distracted by the sight of the little boy's pet cat effortlessly arriving over the seven-foot wall, descending first with a rapid bracing of extended forepaws down on the sheer vertical surface, and then a graceful launch, landing with swishing tail within the property. The whitewashed wall was marked with the cat's comings and goings; and on the street side of the wall there were larger red-earth smudges that could have been made by the kind of broken running shoes, seen on the feet of unemployed loiterers, that had no innocent destination.

When the man and wife and little boy took the pet dog for its walk round the neighbourhood streets they no longer paused to admire this show of roses or that perfect lawn; these were hidden behind an array of different varieties of security fences, walls and devices. The man, wife, little boy and dog passed a remarkable choice: there was the low-cost option of pieces of broken glass embedded in cement along the top of walls, there were iron grilles ending in lance-points, there were attempts at reconciling the aesthetics of prison architecture with the Spanish Villa style (spikes painted pink) and with the plaster urns of neo-classical façades (twelve-inch pikes finned like zigzags of lightning and painted pure white). Some walls had a small board affixed, giving the name and telephone number of the firm responsible for the installation of the devices. While the little boy and the pet dog raced ahead, the husband and wife found themselves comparing the possible effectiveness of each style against its appearance; and after several weeks when they paused before this barricade or that without needing to speak, both came out with the conclusion that only one was worth considering. It was the ugliest but the most honest in its suggestion of the pure concentration-camp style, no frills, all evident efficacy. Placed the length of walls, it consisted of a continuous coil of stiff and shining metal serrated into jagged blades, so that there would be no way of climbing over it and no way through its tunnel without getting entangled in its fangs. There would be no way out, only a struggle getting bloodier and bloodier, a deeper and sharper hooking and tearing of flesh. The wife shuddered to look at it. You're right, said the husband, anyone would think twice . . . And they took heed of the advice on a small board fixed to the wall: Consult DRAGON'S TEETH The People For Total Security.

Next day a gang of workmen came and stretched the razor-bladed coils all round the walls of the house where the husband and wife and little boy and pet dog and cat were living happily ever after. The sunlight flashed and slashed, off the serrations, the cornice of razor thorns encircled the home, shining. The husband said, Never mind. It will weather. The wife said, You're wrong. They guarantee it's rust-proof. And she waited until the little boy had run off to play before she said, I hope the cat will take heed . . . The husband said, Don't worry, my dear, cats always look before they leap. And it was true that from that day on the cat slept in the little boy's bed and kept to the garden, never risking a try at breaching security.

One evening, the mother read the little boy to sleep with a fairy story from the book the wise old witch had given him at Christmas. Next day he pretended to be the Prince who braves the terrible thicket of thorns to enter the palace and kiss the Sleeping Beauty back to life: he dragged a ladder to the wall, the shining coiled tunnel was just wide enough for his little body to creep in, and with the first fixing of its razor-teeth in his knees and hands and head he screamed and struggled deeper into its tangle. The trusted housemaid and the itinerant gardener, whose 'day' it was, came running, the first to see and to scream with him, and the itinerant gardener tore his hands trying to get at the little boy. Then the man and his wife burst wildly into the garden and for some reason (the cat, probably) the alarm set up wailing against the screams while the bleeding mass of the little boy was hacked out of the security coil with saws, wire-cutters, choppers, and they carried it – the man, the wife, the hysterical trusted housemaid and the weeping gardener – into the house.

# DAVID FARRELL

*a poem*

## THE SNOWMAN'S HEART

1

Pinched in the ribs of a punishing winter
nerve can break on its fault line of memory
recoiling muscle draw mouth into pock
set the back in implacable squint. I didn't feel
the frost that crabbed her as she budded
in my tangled bed; didn't spot it
squeeze her till she split.

2

The suburb lies stunned under a week of snow;
only I am standing, hanged by my own erection
in a chilled kitchen, knocking back orange juice
hearing my heart chatter like an old fridge
seeing strangled muscles surface rigid
in a shoal of burst veins.

3

On a late February morning thaw drops like a leopard
shocks of grass are gouged from the snow
as I burrow back into winter. All night
I am borne away from her; in sleep
I am two men who wrestle, teeth cramped,
muscles locked, for right of passage.

4

At 3 am I kneel to cramp in this frozen fortress.
Fire melts my spine where you left my back bare.

# PAUL CHRISTELIS

## *an extract from the novel*

**RABBIT SEASON**

We're driving to the Drakensberg where we're to spend the weekend with friends of Jan, Albert and Lilian Sosostris. Jan and Lilian worked together at *Cosmopolitan* co-ordinating the fashion pages. Albert spends his time being wealthy in semi-retirement at the age of thirty-five.

"He's your kind of guy," Jan tells me as we travel into an oncoming thunderstorm.

"What's my kind of guy?"

"You know . . . defined. Very . . . sort of . . . defined."

The outline of mountain against sky, clear in the early part of the journey, is now blurred by the sheets of storm. Jan thrusts her arm out of the window, spreads her fingers against the wind. Soon, bits of rain are flying about in the car, smacking her softly in the face.

We turn into a driveway over which hangs a sign reading 'Wonderland'. We drive along a narrow track for about a kilometre and then, after a bend, a sprawling lawn appears sprinkled with little concrete figures. At the far end of the lawn, two figures begin to move. They walk over to the car to greet us.

"Janny!" shouts Albert.

"Al, baby!" They fall into a shared energy. Lilian is close behind, holding a kitten, waiting her turn. She and Jan embrace, the kitten disappearing between their stomachs. Jan turns to introduce me. "The new beau," she says, hand on my shoulder. I've never heard her say that before. I shake hands with Albert and Lilian. They smile and say how welcome I am, how they've been dying to meet me.

"I've been dying too," I say.

"What?" says Jan.

"I've been dying . . . to meet you too," and they laugh and offer to take our bags, but we've only brought one, so I get it from the boot and we all walk up to the house which looks as if it's balancing on the edge of the mountain, a deep valley draped below it.

Jan and I are shown to a guest room on the second floor. It has a country feel to it, lots of wood and flowers. There are two single beds separated by a reading-desk, little parcels of toiletries and hand-towels on each bed, accompanied by notes saying 'With wishes for a warm stay, Al and Lil'.

"The beds aren't together," I point out.

"So? We'll just take out the table and push them together."

"For how long did you say you've known Albert?"

"Seven, eight years."

"He likes you."

"We don't have that kind of relationship."

I unpack my stuff. Two changes of clothes, toothbrush and a book on the life and times of Bugs Bunny. I'm up to the part where the author analyses the rabbit's best performances. One of my favourites, 'What's Opera, Doc?' features Elmer Fudd singing 'Return My Love', an aria based on the 'Pilgrim's Chorus' from Wagner's *Tannhauser*. Bugs plays the hapless rabbit once again stalked by the comically demented Fudd. He stretches himself in the role, flirting with androgyny, spoofing operatics, dancing circles round Fudd's diminutive Viking. The final scene in which Elmer commissions a natural catastrophe to wipe out Bugs must rate as one of the most sublime in cartoon history. In the aftermath of the destruction, Elmer, noticing that Bugs is dead, laments his actions in a painfully remorseful lyric, "What have I done? I've killed the wabbit! Poor little bunny! Poor little wabbit!" Jan comes up from behind me, kisses the back of my neck.

"We're having rabbit for dinner," she says. "Lil's a magnificent cook."

Jan helps Lil prepare dinner while Albert and I take a walk in the garden. It's dark already, but shafts of spot-light criss-cross the lawn, illuminating the concrete figures.

"Those ones are all gnomes," Albert says, pointing to a clump near the deep end of the swimming-pool. "Lil loves gnomes. The rest are mine." He shows me his favourites. The Cheshire Cat. The Queen of Hearts. Mock Turtle. "I want to collect the whole series," he says.

"Jan tells me you work with computers."

"Used to. Got in and made a killing. Now I've got the money for the things that are really important."

"Such as?"

"You know, I want to create things," he says. "I get such a thrill from making something out of nothing." He shows me another figure.

"It's got no face," I say.

"I tried sculpting this one myself, but when I got near the end, I just couldn't get it right, so I left it." I lean down and brush my fingers over the blank surface as if to fill in the features of a face.

"The face is the hardest part," he says, taking a cigarette from his shirt pocket and putting it in his mouth, "especially when you're used to computer screens." He lights the cigarette, then offers me one. His face is now lit by the lawn lights and the faint tip of the cigarette. "Eyes are shit-difficult. You wouldn't think so."

"Eyes reveal the truth," I say. "That's why they're so hard."

He thinks about this, inhaling deeply. "Jan's eyes! Beautiful, huh!"

"Making things is scary," I say.

"Mmm," he says, his attention relocating to the verandah where Lil stands, calling us in to dinner.

The rabbit in tarragon is followed by an almond blancmange and, later, coffee and liqueurs. Albert's good at making Jan laugh, stories about his fishing trips. Lil and I chat about life in the mountains.

"I work from home," she says, "but I go into the office once or twice a week. We aren't city people at all." Her kitten meows at her feet. She picks him up and feeds him her finger.

"Don't the two of you get lonely here," I ask.

"It's so peaceful," she says. "And there's so much to keep us occupied." She takes the kitten's head in her hands, brings him up to her lips, and kisses him.

"You planning on having children?" I ask.

She puts the kitten on her lap. "We can't have children. We're thinking of adopting."

"'Sosostris'," I say, changing topics, "is a very exotic name."

"It's Greek."

"'Madame Sosostris, famous clairvoyante,
   Had a bad cold, nevertheless
   Is known to be the wisest woman in Europe'."

"What's that?" she asks giggling.

"Poetry."

"Oh. That's interesting. You read poetry?"

"My mother taught it at university. Our house was full of poetry."

"That's lovely!" she says. "A house full of poetry. Does she still teach?"

"She's in hospital."

"I'm . . . sorry to hear that."

"To hear what?" asks Albert.

"His mother," says Lil. "She's in hospital."

"Anything serious?" he asks.

"Cancer. Final stages."

Jan looks at me, startled.

"Is it operable?" asks Lil.

"No. It's the end."

"That's too bad."

"She's got no more hair."

"Shame," says Lil.

"Jan," says Albert. "You okay?"

"I'm just tired," she says. "I'm going to go up to bed, if that's okay with you."

When I get upstairs, Jan is in the bathroom, naked, washing off her make-up. "What on earth possessed you to make up such a story?" she says.

"They don't have to know the truth."

"What's wrong with telling them about the accident? I don't understand . . ."

"It was just a story. A story I made up. If I had told them the truth, that would also have been a story. That's all they want to hear. A good story." I start laughing.

"It's not funny," she says.

"When you say it over and over again, it sounds ridiculous," I say. "Story, story, story, story, story, story, story . . ."

"Stop it!" she yells. "You're making me scared!" She's leaning over the basin, her breasts moist from the water's steam, drops forming on her nipples. I stand behind her, watching our blurred faces in the steamed mirror. My hand moves from her thigh to her pubic hair. My fingers play with it, stretching the hairs as far as they can go, then releasing them.

"Ouch!" she says.

"Did that hurt?"

"No."

I start rubbing and she moves her legs apart. I put my middle finger in my mouth and then insert it between her legs. She arches her back, her breasts thrust forward.

"You . . . you haven't lied to me, have you?"

I pull my finger in and out, rhythmically.

# SANDRA LEE BRAUDE

## *a poem*

### THE COURSE

It's twice now
I have served
my heart
upon a platter –
and twice
you have rejected.
It seems you have a distaste
for the bleeding part.
Ah well,
the deed is done.

I still have strength
to stand apart
and think upon the matter,
perhaps to staunch
the pain;
I may yet bravely join
the empty crowds again.

# RIVA RUBIN

## *a poem*

*Lionel, beloved friend, mentor of my youth, is one of the compass points of my life. Despite the fact that we have lived so far apart for so long our dialogue has never been broken.*

**MY FRIEND AS SHE WAITS**

My friend lies with her grandchild on the bed,
they watch the light in the afternoon as it seeps
towards them along the walls.

My friend has been given her death like a garment,
a woven caftan, sensuous and severe, with deep
sleeves full of shadows.

My friend has planed the bones of her forehead,
flared her nostrils, rounded her eyes to meet
in beauty whoever calls.

# LILIAN SIMON

## *a story*

### THE DARKNESS

Even though his eyes were again red and watery, my father took me
to school on my first day. We had to wait in a queue and when our
turn came, my father let a woman go in before him with her child
because she said she had a bus to catch. When he did get to the secretary's door he knocked and wouldn't open it until she called, "Come
in!" Once inside her office he waited for her to ask him to sit down
before taking a seat.

He looked at the form she gave him, took off his glasses, wiped
them with the little cloth from inside their case, then pressed a hand-
kerchief against each eye in turn. He winced and his face was very
pale. The secretary stared at him then turned to answer the telephone.

"What's the matter, Daddy?" I asked.

"Nothing, my girl, don't worry. You know my eyes always give me
a bit of trouble. I'll have to go to the doctor – the eye-specialist – when
I've finished registering you here."

"You're not going to the shop?"

"No, I'll have to open up late today."

He never closed the shop. How many times did I hear my mother
shout, "That bloody shop is the most important thing in your life and
you don't even make any money out of it."

"Daddy, you shouldn't have taken me to school today. Why didn't
Mommy?"

"She wasn't feeling well. She said she was going to stay in bed."

He finished filling in the form, waited for the secretary to put down
the phone, then handed it in to her and thanked her.

"Your daughter can wait outside my office," she told him. "Just now
there'll be other children there as well and the Grade One teacher will
come and fetch them."

When we came out of the office a bell rang. I watched children in uniform hurrying past. They knew where they were going and they were with their friends. How would I know what to do? Maybe the teacher wouldn't like me . . . Maybe I would hate school.

"Don't be frightened," my father said when he left me. "You're going to be the cleverest girl in the class."

I watched him limp off, his short body almost bursting out of his dark, shiny suit and the back of his neck bulging over his shirt-collar. As he walked out of the door he put on the old grey hat I'd seen him brushing that morning. I wished that he didn't have to work so hard in his shop.

My mother said he needed a rest when I asked why he was always tired when he came home. He told me he'd like to go to the Game Reserve. He'd heard all about it from some of his customers. "They say the lions lie right next to the road." The only time he'd ever been on holiday was during his honeymoon when he and my mother went to Parys for four days. She said they travelled by train because he couldn't take her on his bicycle in her going-away outfit. She had to explain what a 'going-away outfit' was.

All that day I was very busy at school. A fat teacher who smiled a lot, gave out slates with hard grey pencils that squeaked as we wrote 'a' for 'apple' and 'b' for 'bat'. After that we drew pictures and then we played games.

"Be a bunny," teacher said and we hopped up and down the field. "Now you're all birdies," and flip-flop we flew.

Then it was rest time in the classroom and teacher said we must close our eyes and pretend we were lying on the sand next to the sea. I'd never been to the sea so I thought about lying on the lawn at the Krugersdorp swimming-bath.

Even though I was so busy I kept worrying about my father. The last time he had trouble with his eyes the doctor just gave him medicine but maybe he would put him into hospital now. Would he have to have an operation like my mother after she went to see a specialist? I was afraid to go home after school and find out.

"What did the doctor say about Daddy's eyes?" I asked her when I came home. She wasn't in bed. She was sitting on the verandah with a book in her hand.

"I haven't seen him. He didn't come home for lunch."

We didn't have a phone then so I couldn't find out if he was at the shop. I ran to him when he came in at half-past six, his eyes still red.

"Daddy, what did the doctor say?"

"He says I've got something called 'glaucoma'."

"Glaucoma!" my mother shouted but I didn't know what the word meant.

"Yes, that's what I've got. The doctor says he sees it sometimes in people who come from Lithuania."

"But you were only twelve when you came to South Africa," my mother said.

"I know, but that's what I've got." He took a little bottle out of his pocket. "I must keep putting in these drops . . ." He turned to me. "Will you remind me?"

"Of course, Daddy . . . Will your eyes get better quickly?"

The hand holding the bottle shook a little. "Well, it's not something that can come altogether all right."

"Oh but Daddy, your eyes can't stay so funny."

"They won't always be so red but I can't really stop with the drops even when they're better. I've just got to be careful, that's all."

"Yes, you have to be very careful," my mother said, and she closed her mouth so tightly that I could see a white line just above the top lip.

That night I went to bed early but I couldn't fall asleep. When I got up to fetch a glass of water from the kitchen, my parents were still sitting in the lounge. I heard them talking as I passed the half-open door so I stopped to listen, standing with my bare feet on the floorboards.

"People sometimes live for a long time with it," my mother said. "And they don't always go blind."

"Yes, I know." My father's words came out very slowly. "And I've got a very good doctor. He really looks after me. But I've got to be so careful." He didn't speak for a moment. My feet felt very cold as I waited and the cold went right inside me when he continued. "They say people who can't see, can hear better than anybody else. I suppose sounds are louder when everything is dark. It must be terrible to look into darkness always."

"God forbid!" my mother said.

Those drops became part of my father. At night I saw the bottle standing on the shelf in the large cold bathroom that served a family of five always in a rush. When I went to the shop they were on a table in the little room at the back. They stood next to his tin of instant coffee and the bottle of milk that served his cat as well as himself. Sometimes the cat jumped onto the table and I was afraid he would knock over the little bottle of eye-drops.

When I was in Matric, I came into the bathroom one night to find my father scrabbling in the medicine-cupboard. "What are you looking for, Dad?" I asked.

"My eye-drops . . . I can't find them anywhere."

We emptied out the little cupboard and put everything back, then we tiptoed into his bedroom, trying not to wake my mother while we looked through an assortment of bottles on the dressing-table. She did wake and asked, "Can't you let a person sleep?"

The drops were not on the dressing-table nor were they in the kitchen. "I must have left them in the shop," my father said. He took out his pocket-watch on its long chain – a customer had paid an account with it. "Hmm! Too late to catch a bus. I'll have to walk there."

"I'll come with you, Dad. There's no school tomorrow."

The wind howled around us as we took a short-cut through the veld and over the vlei across the spruit, where the mosquitoes sang as we approached. Then we drew near the cemetery where tall tree-shapes sprang up out of the darkness. The wind jibbered through those trees and even with my father next to me I was afraid.

He was walking more and more slowly, dragging his left leg heavily and his breathing was laboured; sometimes it came out in a kind of whistle. I was glad when we reached the shop soon after the cemetery.

The little bottle of eye-drops was standing in its usual place in the room at the back.

He never left those drops behind again. He didn't forget them even when he suffered a heart attack. I was grown up then and my mother had become a semi-invalid.

"I must take my drops to the hospital," he said as I packed his suit-case while my mother sat holding her head. "I can't go one day without them." His voice was hoarse and whispery, his face yellow and shrunken. Every now and then he grimaced, his hands and shoulders stiffened and his jaws clamped down over grinding teeth.

I put the drops into a toilet bag which I placed on top of his pyjamas. He couldn't speak when I showed him where they were, just nodded.

He was bent almost double as he hobbled with me to the lift. He let me in first, then just as I was about to press the button for ground-floor, he saw two women approaching. He went out of the lift and stood, still bent, with his hat in one hand while he held the door open for them with the other.

# MARC GLASER

*a poem*

**NOW LIKE A KITE**

now like a kite in my former days
have I not seen flight flimsy and impractical as air
and parleyed with the dead folk who are washed white-clean
    by death
and bartered at the chess board
where the knight and queen caress
and visited old men in homes of death
with death played catch-me-quick
and catch-me-death
and lifted up in chimneys high
as burnt parched cellophane into sky
and mingled softly with the fluff
and cotton wool of clouds and bluff?

# MAJA KRIEL

## *a story*

*I dedicated my anthology of short stories to Lionel, calling him mentor and magus. As mentor his door was always open, his telephone unattached to any blocking device. Lionel was there. He was immediately accessible for conversation, serious or trivial advice, help with spelling or punctuation. With his writing group, he presided over those long, sometimes self-indulgent Monday nights with great generosity and concentration, his ear fine-tuned to shape and form and pattern. Like a doctor he would make his diagnosis, prescribe prolonged treatment or a stitch or two and a bandage. Sometimes the medicine was addictive. But unlike medical practice, even when the illness was malignant, the therapy was always benign and healing.*

*But it was as magus that the alchemy happened. How does one analyze the nature of his influence or its entrance into the intractable loops of the imagination? It was subtle and patient, probably as unconscious to him as to the receiver: a particular interest, a belief, the expectation and recognition of value. In today's vocabulary it would be called empowerment. Perhaps his influence was the expression of a special faculty. One can call it a certain kind of love.*

### BERTH

Amy knew that Josh would come home to do his dying, the same as he came home at night to do his sleeping. That is what home is for. He did his living elsewhere.

Every night of his life he would prepare for the morning: put out a pair of socks, a vest, underpants and a shirt. He would lay them out tenderly, freshly ironed, to wear the next day. The suit would be lying on the chair, ready to step into. In the morning she would hear the click of the latch as he opened the front door and then the slam as the door closed behind him. Twelve hours later he would return with the newspaper and his briefcase. Tired. After supper he would prepare his clothes for the morning again.

And now he has come home for good. Unfit for anything else. He asks for ice cream: "Ice cream. Ice cream." Eats it, leaving smears on his moustache. Sometimes he forgets to wear his trousers. Home for good. Sent home to do his dying.

Now she does the talking. She speaks for him. And dresses herself brightly. She will be vivid for them both, then it will not be noticed that he wears a hat to hide his bald pate, even though sometimes it falls off or he removes it to scratch his head. She will be funny. Make him laugh. They buy him pills for the pain, and the chemist asks: "What do you want them for?" He says, "Just a little cancer." And they laugh and laugh.

If he is to die, then let him die well. She will help him.

She walks him slowly through the garden to show him the flowers, leading him by the hand.

"You're a good woman," he tells her.

That is not what she wanted to be.

She buys him a gold wedding ring.

He never wore one.

# WOPKO JENSMA

## *a poem*

### SPANNER IN THE WHAT? WORKS

i was born 26 july 1939 in ventersdorp
i found myself in a situation

i was born 26 july 1939 in sophiatown
i found myself in a situation

i was born 26 july 1939 in district six
i found myself in a situation

i was born 26 july 1939 in welkom
i found myself in a situation

now, when my mind started to tick
i noticed other humans like me
shaped like me: ears eyes
hair legs arms etc . . . (i checked)
we all cast in the same shackles:
flesh mind feeling smell sight etc . . .

date today is 5 april 1975 i live
at 23 mountain drive derdepoort
phone number: 821-646, post box 26285
i still find myself in a situation

i possess a typewriter and paper
i possess tools to profess i am artist
i possess books, clothes to dress
my flesh; my fingerprint of identity
i do not possess this land, a car

much cash or other valuables

i brought three kids into this world
(as far as i know)
i prefer a private to a public life
(i feel allowed to say)
i suffer from schizophrenia
(they tell me)
I'll die, i suppose, of lung cancer
(if i read the ads correctly)

i hope to live to the age of sixty
i hope to leave some evidence
that i inhabited this world
that i sensed my situation
that i created something
out of my situation
out of my life
that i lived
as human
alive
i

i died 26 july 1999 on the costa del sol
i found myself in a situation

i died 26 july 1999 in the grasslands
i found myself in a situation

i died 26 july 1999 in the kgalagadi
i found myself in a situation

i died 26 july 1999 in an argument
i found myself in a situation

# PETER WILHELM

## *a story*

### ZEKE IN YUGOSLAVIA

1

Noon in Sarajevo. Our little company has been summarily dumped, exhausted and mapless, in a central square that seems to be a market of some kind. Men and women swarm about with their jabbering ethnicities and presumptions; they speak a mélange of tongues, Serbo-Croat I'm told, unknown to us.

We find a café, a table, food, drink. The food looks like blackened eyes of goats in a pungent sauce. God help me: I feel a surge of nostalgia for the native eating shops of home. I am supposed to be on a diplomatic mission, but no one knows to whom I have to speak: they stare at me with terrified eyes. Their war is coming back.

I have a strong sense of the East, those pungent scents of sweat and spice; but there is no collective impact of intellectualism, as in Russia, where some worker presumptively hooks his face into yours to seek a dialogue on cosmology, sex, life after death, political change. These people are skittish: and no wonder.

Not a day passes without regret that I accepted this venture. Whatever the original intent – socialist friendship, I reckon – events occur too rapidly to validate that promise. We are passed recklessly from one confused official to another, their command of English degenerating with their anxiety. Nothing will come of this.

I keep telling myself it cannot go on much longer, that I will be recalled home for the negotiations – surely I can be of some use there rather than here on the margin of a dark, unknown hinterland of terror? But night after night we end up in some filthy hotel, some spot on the map that seems far from any exit to home.

Looking at these miserable people, I keep thinking: Our war is over.

We've done this already. Why don't you drink in that lesson instead of beer and slivovitz and make your peace? The world doesn't want your war, not this late in this awful century.

But I cannot speak to them. I am cut off, and from my colleagues. Alone among them I represent what I suppose one must call the new order at home and so they regard me with caution, the worst of them with a lickspittle fear. It's as if they believe I'm a spy observing their behaviour: yet if they decided simply to go out and get drunk, I would race them to the bar.

2

The Iraqi boy in Sarajevo was a dental student. On the slimy grey flag-stones outside the Imperial Mosque on the left bank of the Miljacka River he flashed his ugly teeth in happy surprise to learn we were from South Africa. "Mandela! Mandela!" he kept saying, exposing the turrets, trenches and battlements of his horrid teeth. How disconcert-ing to discover such young ruined faces when you have been told that health care is universal! It is as if, with the abolition of beauty contests, beauty itself disappeared.

We heard him out through the wretched membrane of translation. He was, it seemed, eager to find in us sympathy for his dream of returning to fight for Saddam against the Americans. The Gulf War was about to occur. It still seems so close, yet the years flit like days and we must soon enter the next millennium. That war was long won and lost, the boy reduced to a fine ash somewhere on the road to Baghdad, I dare say. Still, I sympathised: it is terrible to be a stranger far from home. Such forlorn childishness.

The impact of a mosque can be of austere and intractable divinity. The men at prayer, numberless and remote in their holy declination, present a distinct, enviable focus of blinding yet alternate vision. Yet in the Imperial Mosque the bare expanse of the interior was somehow low, low in the sense one encounters in Orthodox churches – a stooped, even cramped architecture of piety which requires a shriv-elled saint's hand in a glass box.

Perhaps we will keep such relics of our saints one day, once passion is gone and our condition has smoothed out, become mundane. I will suggest we do not put heroes in glass boxes for the inspection of the populace; there is always a depressive aura, and always a revolting scent of physical decay: as if belief itself were in decay, mouldering like common flesh.

The missionaries who bent our ancestors to their faith will have done well if this reverential fate – the worship of corruption – is averted. Trust rather in vodka, the black market, repetitive fucking, and the gun. That seems to be what's on offer: who will salvage the ruins of socialism?

Beauty contests – I know you will think me obsessive – are being reinstated in once-socialist nations. In the heart of Mother Russia there is a Miss KGB: Katya Mayorova, happily introduced to visitors at Moscow Directorate's Dzerhinsky Square. She is very beautiful and has perfect teeth. According to a report, 'Her skill in kicking an enemy's head with her foot emphasises her maidenly charms. Her bullet-proof jacket must be worn with the elegance of a long-legged Cardin model.'

In roach-infested hotels where the waiters get their small-arms training at night, I lie back and think of Miss KGB, flower of our century.

Onward then! On to the eight-hour orgasm!

3

The Iraqi boy had come to pray and be inspired. His arms were brown and frail in the autumn sun. We left him in the mosque – the other believer there an old, veiled woman, tears erupting from her yellow face – and walked beside the Miljacka to the Princip Bridge. We crossed to the right bank where a museum holds memorabilia of the conspirators of 1914 – those prophets of Greater Serbia, cleansing themselves in blood for the greater bloodletting to come. In the concrete pavement at the entrance are set two footprints marking the place where Gavrilo Princip shot the Archduke Franz Ferdinand and his wife on 28 June that year, and began a war.

I stood in those steps, facing the crazed street.

Here in Sarajevo, Princip is a great romantic hero. His Byronesque portrait distils a resemblance to the Iraqi boy outside the mosque: the eyes both frightened and spurred on by an idea beyond his life. When some young comrades burnt an equally young American girl to death in Guguletu, they had that look. You could say they had the eyes of our time.

But what happened in Flanders has been forgotten in Sarajevo, a grimy, clanking city in a valley amid the breathtaking greensward mountains of Yugoslavia. We drove all day on a bus from Belgrade and saw industrial desolation in which people revert to the most ancient forms of labour. Soot-blackened women in drab headcloths stoop in the hard fields with hoes and shovels. Soon, at gunpoint, they will dig graves for their men and then for themselves and their children.

Alas for the philosophy that has placed them in those postures: it was a dream-like aberration, a yearning for an elemental continuity to supersede the tragic isolation of self-consciousness and death and which is aflame for justice in the earthly kingdom. Yet it has condemned the wretched survivors to the most primitive life you might find this side of Mars. It was too good for this world. Now the filth, the litter, the half-folk who live in bins and eat rubbish, clawing for air.

The levelling impulse – if that is what it is – produces a marvellous incantatory rhetoric; later come the heads on pikes, the burnt children. And even the paradisal division of labour between the sexes reduces, as we should know by now, to a feminism as abstract as visions of animal rights. The beasts of the field will have no rights until we cease to eat them.

As news of the stunning emptiness that awaits us spreads – like the microwave background radiation of the Big Bang, thinning out over aeons, but discernible – fear and corruption rave at the door. In a villa overlooking Lake Bled in Slovenia, Marshal Tito ordered the monastery bells on a little island silenced in the afternoons while he slumbered in Alpine serenity. Now that he is dead, and long dead, rotten, the silence endures. There are no bells on the water.

Soon the components of his earthly kingdom will descend into civil war. That was where we came in.

4

Rationalists like to point to the great deflations of history: how Man once considered himself the centre of a universe of one sun and one moon and a sprinkling of stars and planets. Then it was asserted that the sun was the centre. Then came the discovery of the wider galaxy, within which the number of stars is millions or billions – astronomical rubbish. Nor should our home galaxy be considered unique; there are plenty more wherever they came from. We were crushed to a speck in a vast, expanding cosmos.

And now new theories posit an even greater, perhaps an ultimate deflation. The whole universe, with its expansion and physical laws, may be nothing but a bubble in a sea of cosmic foam, gusting from the great Void.

Well. What is one to make of that? As much or little as ever one did: I suspect it grew bigger the more we looked.

5

Our translator, Ivana, was once a beauty queen! She confessed this to me last night and for the first time I took her in, inhaled her: her flaming hair falling over dark eyes and the pale skin stretched just a little too tight. I did not ask what year it was, when she won, or even whether she won at all or was a runner-up, Number 2 or 3 or 4. Nor what land it was in. Yugoslavia is not one land.

6

Tito's grave in Belgrade is approached up a green pathway flanked by soldiers in purple. They look like soldiers from another century, when dash and flair counted above camouflage, before the era of the machine-gun and the five-day artillery barrage. The wind in the trees rustles with peacefulness and the pilgrims are sombre. Looking down to the leaden confluence of the Danube and the Sava, a great centre of Europe, Tito's spirit seems everywhere and nowhere, like God.

Our guide, Filip, whispers his heresies: the great leader, he says, was a Croatian; yet here he is, buried in Serbia. Filip is bitter. His father was a Chetnik, a royalist, and while packed off to a concentration camp by the Germans, the communists turned him into a horribly grinning skeleton, and he died. The bright sun masks the mass graves of a thousand years.

There is no Yugoslavia, Filip informs me. There is Serbia, Croatia, Bosnia-Hercegovina, Slovenia, Montenegro, Macedonia. And so on. I've heard it all: riots, unrest, factionalism, Catholic against Orthodox against Muslim. The Germans killed most of the Jews.

On the bus in the countryside, Filip, happy in the back with a beer, derides those we pass. "Look! A one-legged Bosnian dwarf! A Bosnian kaffir! Shoot him in the street." He has learnt the word from one of us but pronounces it 'caffre'. "Look – a one-legged Bosnian caffre!" Ivana huddles in silence behind her hair. Each day she grows older; her lipstick is scribbled all over her face by a shaking hand.

There is something unsaid between Filip and Ivana. They are from different lands.

Staring at the white stone of Tito's mausoleum, one wonders if this monolithic, inhuman being is at rest. There is a smell of shit. It is possible to see the mobs ascending this hillside one day to smash at the rock and pluck him out into the vivid Serbian air to answer the questions posed by history. They would rise up in Novi Belgrade, those tracts of mass housing so easily shattered by earthquakes, expanses of shoddy development that ran out of the Treasury until the system itself was bankrupt and all that was left was slogans, posters, the huge features of the founding fathers.

On the wall of the PLO consulate in Maputo – a few blocks from the Polana Hotel which faces onto the litter of the Avenida Julius Nyerere – one can remark the difference between pictorial representations of Yasser Arafat (a glowing, vivid, optimistic vision) and photographs of the leader: ugly, small and unmanly. And the city is unclean: cleanliness and paint are bourgeois, or there is no foreign exchange for them.

Belgrade is like that. And everywhere, with the imaginative impact of slime, the people's art. Looking at one or another titanic representation of Lenin or Stalin or Tito or Machel, I see the same abominable representations as the photographic sweetness of British royalty. All defects are magnified by the magnification of the people's art.

Someone, one day, will hold my views against me.

## 7

In the room next to mine Filip and Ivana scream. Is it abuse? I cannot say; they are impenetrable to me. Whatever I have told them of my own country and its travails cannot have registered: they are consumed by their own present, the foreshadowing of war, death made manifest. Their high voices are like grinding steel in my brain: I have heard such voices before. I have heard myself like that.

When they are silent I cannot but believe they are making love, pouring into each other each defeat and hope that has brought them into the room together, and the nullity of what awaits.

## 8

South of Dubrovnik – down the winding intricacies of the Kotor Fjord – the sea is like mercury. From the glazed windows of the bus, or standing on a stony ledge high above the utterly still surface of the Adriatic, the water has a dark, blank appearance: yet it has a frosting of hard light. The limestone mountains are precipitous. The road traverses gusts of pale stone, frozen in light that cools to violet at the seaside, with beaches like grey clipped fingernails lying in shadow, deserted at noon.

Inland, the mountains are high and recessed and the deep rivers in the ravines give them a romantic, abyssal look. Along the coast the cypress groves of cemeteries mark the entrances and exits from the villages.

In Dubrovnik the resort hotels are cut into hillsides. They cradle the view of the bay and the waterways down which the cruise liners parade with their deliberate boast of affluence, out there where the warships will patrol. The water is so dark, heavy and saline, that it is frightening to swim in it. Yet I did, I felt I must.

Unnaturally buoyant, I crawled out to a bobbing red globe that helped to mark a region of safety. Thick leaden ropes are strung in chains across an acre of sea in front of our hotel.

Kick down under the slow waves, and it's ink-dark and fearsome; up into the brilliant air, and grey rocks seethe in water like giant skulls.

Ivana swims with me. I feel her body in the water. Miss Yugoslavia.

This is Ulysses' sea. The old, hard light of the Adriatic accommodates a wandering and homesick spirit. One settlement we saw – the modern villas impacted by the light, driven down upon more ancient foundations – was called in the demotic, 'The place where the sea captains built houses for their whores.'

Did the news of their hopeless infidelity reach home? Did the tumult of home, the sound of breaking stone, reach them in their exile? The palace coups, shifting tides of influence and opinion? On the bus with Filip and Ivana we heard as little about our home as one such as I, whose love is wilderness and whirling birds in a great blue sky, might hear of Yugoslavia. To them, my puzzled reveries were incomprehensible; they listened out of puzzlement, aware only of each other.

And the further we went, mountain or coast, the less I understood. On the bus, as the days and the beers progressed, one heard Filip's monotonous, emphatic abuse of those we passed: his 'caffres', his others. He became a drunken lout and Ivana sat as far from him as she could; her eyes were bruised, though whether that was from tears or blows I could not say. Whatever had occurred between them was past; it had been fleeting, evanescent as a dream of prosperity beyond history.

Did they have a sense – like mine – of the pillars of comprehension eroding; of ancient grassy ruins appearing behind the blueglass façades of modernism? Of the sound of the wind more dreadful than silence sweeping the colonnades of dispossession and a kind of

Mesopotamian solicitude of desert and the forgetting of things?

Up and down the Dalmatian coast we wandered, waiting to be recalled. I grew weary of Filip, slurred and blackened by facing the sun. I saw Ivana look at me and look away. Sometimes I thought of the Iraqi boy, the boy in Sarajevo, seeking to leave the alien Slavic animosities for his own exploding land, for his lonely, fiery death on the road to Baghdad.

9

And when we were called back, we went.

## KOBUS LE GRANGE MARAIS

He sways on his stool in the Station Bar and calls for a short white wine
And knocks it back and sheds a tear and damns the party line,
And talks to himself and blocks his ears when the tired old locos shunt:
"Way back in '48, we said, die koelie uit die land
And kaffer op sy plek, we said, the poor white wants his share:
They put me in my place, all right," said Kobus Le Grange Marais.

"I was all my life a railwayman, all my life a Boer,
And there's none unkinder than a man's own kind, I tell you that for sure;
I fought in the O.B. till I was caught and I sweated my guts in a camp
For the bombs I threw and the bridges I blew and here's what I get for thanks;
The turning wheels took off my legs and I'm not going anywhere
But downhill all the way from here," said Kobus Le Grange Marais.

"My pension held up far worse than my legs, so I went to the dominee:
A bed in the garage will do, I said. 'Man, where's your pride?' says he.
He wanted to pray but I turned to go when the police decided to raid,
They took him away in the big grey van and came back for the kaffer maid.
I have an idea he did a lot more than park his Ford in there,
Or so the Women's Federasie said," said Kobus Le Grange Marais.

"O it was dop and dam and a willing girl when we were young and green,
But Jewish money and the easy life are the ruin of the Boereseun,
He disappears into the ladies' bars and is never seen again
Where women flash their thighs at you and drink beside the men,
And sits with moffies and piepiejollers and primps his nice long hair:
You'd take him for an Englishman," said Kobus Le Grange Marais.

"The meddling ghost of Reverend Philip, he haunts us once more –

His face is pressed to the window-pane, his knock rattles the door;
From Slagtersnek to Sonderwater he smears the Boers' good name;
And God is still a rooinek God, kommandant of Koffiefontein:
If what I hear about heaven is true, it's a racially mixed affair;
In which case, ons gaan kak da' bo," said Kobus Le Grange Marais.

"The times are as cruel as the big steel wheels that carried my legs away;
Oudstryders like me are out on our necks and stink like scum on a vlei;
And white man puts the white man down, the volk are led astray;
There'll be weeping in Weenen once again, no keeping the impis at bay;
And tears will stream from the stony eyes of Oom Paul in Pretoria Square:
He knows we'll all be poor whites soon," said Kobus Le Grange Marais.

He sways on his stool in the Station Bar and calls for a short white wine
And knocks it back and sheds a tear and damns the party line,
And talks to himself and blocks his ears when the tired old locos shunt:
"Way back in '48, we said, die koelie uit die land
And kaffer op sy plek, we said, the poor white wants his share:
They put me in my place, all right," said Kobus Le Grange Marais.

# NAT NAKASA

## *a slice of autobiography*

### A NATIVE OF NOWHERE

Some time next week, with my exit permit in my bag, I shall cross the borders of the Republic and immediately part company with my South African citizenship. I shall be doing what some of my friends have called, 'taking a grave step'.

For my part, there is nothing grave about it. You needn't even be brave to take the 'step'. It is enough to be young, reckless and ready to squander and gamble your youth away. You may, I dare say, even find the whole business exciting.

According to reliable sources, I shall be classed as a prohibited immigrant if I ever try to return to South Africa. What this means is that self-confessed Europeans are in a position to declare me, an African, a prohibited immigrant, bang on African soil. Nothing intrigues me more.

And the story does not end there. Once out I shall apparently become a stateless person, a wanderer, unless I can find a country to take me in. And that is what I have been trying to achieve in the past few days. I cannot enter America on an exit permit even though I have a scholarship to take up in that country. The Americans will let me in only on a valid passport from a country that is prepared to have me when I leave America.

Apparently, there can be no question of getting the Americans to depart from this, their official policy, unless, perhaps, I moved into the US as a Cuban refugee. For I have read about many Cuban citizens who left their country for the US in that way. But I have ruled this out as something too involved to try. Meanwhile, I have thought of becoming a Zambian, a Nigerian, or a Malawian. But these countries have no embassies in South Africa, so getting their travel documents would take ages.

My best bet may well be to embrace the Jewish faith and procure

Israeli citizenship. But again that has its own complications. As an Israeli I may automatically be prohibited entry into Egypt. I may be barred from going to report on any Pan-African conferences that may be held in Cairo in the future.

On the other hand, should I become an Egyptian, I may be expected to declare war on all my Jewish friends – and, Heaven knows, there are many of them. Besides, I don't think I have ever seen an Egyptian, and I have no idea of Egyptian life.

There is some hope, however, that my problems may be solved by the good old Scandinavian countries. I may become the first Scandinavian Pondo in history.

A black viking! Imagine it!

Finally, if all this doesn't work out, I may be compelled to become a Russian. In this way I might even crash into the limelight as an international statesman. After all, the Russians are known to be very keen on backing an African as the next President of the United Nations. Instead of scouring Africa for a candidate, the Russians might start backing their own African – me.

Having achieved that status, there would be nothing to stop me from rising to the highest office in Russia itself. Who knows? I may wind up as the Prime Minister of the Soviet Union. After all, Dr Verwoerd was born in Holland and he became the Prime Minister of die Republiek van Suid-Afrika.

If I should feel homesick while ruling Russia, I could pass a few laws to South-Africanise Russia a little. The first step would be to introduce influx control in Moscow. Get all the native Russians to carry passes and start endorsing them in and out of town. There are enough African and Indian students studying in Russia nowadays to help me carry out my plan. Apartheid all over again! This time with the Russians at the receiving end. Admittedly, this may be described as Afro-Asian minority rule. Others will call it baasskap. But we would call it parallel development, or black leadership with justice.

We could introduce the exit-permit system to cut down on the numbers of Russians in the place. At the same time we could bring in millions of Indians and Africans from Bombay, Calcutta, Umtata and Zululand on an immigration scheme – just as South Africa brings in white immigrants by the thousand every month.

We would have to scrap Communism from the start. In fact, I would import South Africa's Suppression of Communism Act lock, stock and barrel. Communism would be an enemy number one. Anybody who opposed my apartheid policies too much would wind up banned or detained.

Unfortunately, all these are mere dreams. For the time being, my future lies in a number of diplomatic bags. Various consuls are trying to see what can be done for me. I hope, when I write next week, it will be as a former South African. As far as I can, I shall try not to interfere with your domestic affairs, let alone meddle with your white or non-white politics.

# GRAEME FRIEDMAN

## *a story*

*Monday 6:30 pm. Lionel's Workshop. I'm going to read the first few pages of a short story that has silent movies as its theme. I'm a little nervous because in the beginning I hold back on characterization of the narrator in favour of a slightly surreal picture – which I hope will set the mood for the silent movie theme – of a young schoolgirl walking the streets of Hillbrow.*

*My turn to read comes round. When I'm finished Lionel throws back his head jerkily. I've come to know and welcome the gesture. It's one of recognition: something in the material has moved him. "Ah!" he says, "now that's a beginning!"*

*It's these moments when I know, sometimes from something he says, sometimes from the look in his eye, or one of those twitchy smiles of his, that he has understood my intention and feels I've delivered it with authority.*

*At other times it's not affirmation at all, but a gentle criticism, one always respectful of my identity as a writer. "Too intellectual", "it's overwritten", or "the idea has remained in your head, you've not shown the reader enough".*

*It's these moments that have fed me, that have fostered in me a sense of being a writer.*

## THE BEGGAR IN THE BOOKSHOP

The day I fled the country I went to my father's bookshop in Commissioner Street, just up the road from John Vorster Square. He was sorting through a new consignment and he looked up, alerted by the *bing-bong* of the electronic door chime.

"Robert, glad you came. Help me stack these will you? Here, that lot in antiquity, the others in the English lit section."

I picked up one of the books he'd indicated. "What about this one?" It was Douglas Bader's biography, *Reach for the Sky*.

"Ah, let's see. Humour?"

You had to know my father to understand the joke. It was a standing joke, so to speak. My father and his veteran buddies used to make fun of Bader, of the fuss he made of being able to walk after he'd lost his legs. The joke was that, while he'd lost his right leg up to the thigh, he'd only lost the lower portion of his left. It was easy to walk if you still had one knee joint.

I was seven or eight when I first noticed, really noticed, that Dad was different. We were over at friends. The kids were in the water, along with a couple of the adults, and Dad decided to jump in. There were some people there who'd never met him before, and they stared when he appeared for his swim. He walked to the pool on his hands, his lower body – what was left of it – thrust forward for balance, the stumps of his thighs poking out of his shorts. Manipulating himself like a gymnast on a pommel horse, the muscles of his upper arms pumped up, he brought himself to the water's edge, then lowered himself in. It was all deep-end to him. A five-year-old stood taller than he did. Seeing him through the trying-not-to-look eyes of those strangers, I thought, he's different, he's not like everybody else's dad. He has no legs.

We were stacking in adjacent rows, opposite each other, so that every now and then, over the shadowed edges of the books' spines, I caught sight of his face, on the tip of his nose the reading glasses that would hang on his chest whenever he didn't need them. His neatly combed black hair – slicked down with Brylcreem – the cropped pilot's moustache, thin lips. Those pale eyes. Before losing his legs he would've been shorter than the height I'd grown to, but he'd had the prosthetics people add a few inches.

"I'm leaving tonight," I said.

"So you're actually going, are you?"

"Yes. I don't have much choice, do I?"

"Crap, Robert. You have all the choice in the world. You can do what all the other boys are doing."

Some of the other boys were going to university to avoid the army. But Dad wouldn't hear of that. Country first, yourself second, was his last word on the subject. Without his financial support, it wasn't possible.

We finished our piles and I followed him to the front where the boxes of new books lay. His style of mobility required an effort which he almost masked by the rhythm he managed to inject into it. Without knee joints, with your prostheses strapped to your thigh stumps, you have only your hips to walk with, you must swing the entire leg apparatus from just that one joint. Douglas Bader had his left knee, which meant that he had two joints to work with, and had to control only the mechanical ankle.

My dad walked by kicking each stump upward. The knee would bend automatically. Then he kicked the stump downward, landing on his foot. Without ankle and toe muscles to spring him off, he had to push his upper body over his legs, which he did by leaning forward, unbalancing himself so that his torso weight carried him over the leg that was placed in front, then using his momentum to keep walking. Kick the stump forward, then downward, like the cracking of a whip.

Dad had refused to use a walking-stick at home or at work, where the evenness of the floor was predictable and there were surfaces to hold onto. Outside, an unevenness on a pavement could up-end him.

We got to the front as an old man on crutches came shuffling in through the door. "I haven't eaten in two days, baas. Baas, I can't work, baas. Look here." The beggar gestured to his stump. He was wearing someone's old army browns, grimy, knotted below the amputated thigh. "Please, baas, only fifty cents for some bread."

"What rot!" My father growled. "Get a job! If I can work with no legs, you can work with one!" He snatched one of the beggar's crutches from him, leaving the old man wobbling in the doorway, and landed a smart blow against each of his own prostheses. Dad enjoyed the look on people's faces when something heavy came down on those legs. He used to do that when I'd displeased him as a kid. I'd be hovering just out of reach, and he'd pull his belt out of the loops of his pants and whack it against himself. His pants would begin to slip down, revealing his underpants and the elaborate set of straps and corsetry that fastened his legs to him.

In the bookshop that day, with the old man still teetering on his good leg, my father tossed the crutch back at him. It struck the doorframe and clattered to the ground. I picked it up, reached out to steady the old man, and helped him out of the shop.

"Here," I said, giving him the coins in my pocket.

"Thank you, kleinbaas," he said.

I watched him shifting away, the knot of trouser leg swinging to his slow shuffle.

"Don't pity them, boy! You do that and they'll never stand on their own two feet."

"That old guy doesn't have two feet, Dad."

"And what do I have? Three?"

"We've been educated, Dad. If you don't have that, all you can do is physical things."

"Rubbish! I get around this shop, don't I? Who the hell do you think packs all these books?" I knew how chafed his thighs got. When I was younger I'd watch him rub cream on them. "In any case, do you think he really means all that baas nonsense? Huh! He's working us. It's these stupid ideas of yours, Robert. This country's given you everything you've got. You're being a damn ingrate."

"I – I'm not."

"Crap! We fought Hitler to keep this country free!" He slapped his legs. "I've earned the right to give you what I have. And now you're kicking me in the teeth. Christ, I was so sure you'd see sense. Told your mother, even. You're my son after all, Goddammit!" He shook his head. "To think that a Fourie man would refuse to serve. You've brought shame on the family, Robert. I'm ashamed of you!" I thought he was going to reach for his belt, but he just stood there shaking his head.

I didn't know how to say to him: Dad, you taught me this. You taught me to stand up for my beliefs. You're the one who's famous for having guts and glory. You're the one who flew Marylands on daylight raids on the harbour at Benghazi and then, in a plane so badly shot-up it should've fallen into the sea, managed to limp your way hundreds of miles through thick cloud with ice forming on the wings to a crash-landing at Sidi Barrani. You brought your crew home, only you left your legs in that desert. And then, barely two weeks later, told General Smuts when he bent over to pin that medal to your chest, "My friends were always on at me to lose some weight. So I did. Thirty-five pounds. All in the legs."

I struggled with my feelings, but only mumbled, "Goodbye, Dad," and walked out of the shop. I didn't want him to see a Fourie man crying.

Later, Mom took me to the airport, reassuring me all the way that they wouldn't stop me at passport control, and that Dad would still talk to me.

"He'll calm down," she said. "It's just the shock of your leaving, that's all. He's going to miss you terribly, you know."

"He has a funny way of showing it."

"He just can't be soft, that's all. You mean everything to him."

I took my seat on the plane, in my bag a little money she'd managed to save and the number of a conscientious objectors' group in London.

It was after the war – don't ask which one, as far as Dad was concerned there was only one war – after he'd learned to walk again, that he opened his bookshop. He'd had to move a few times. They kept tearing down the buildings. The last place he'd taken about twenty years ago. He accumulated more and more stock, until the shelves and aisles were overburdened. You'd walk down the rows between shelves sagging under the weight of the books, then come across a pile on the floor you'd need to step over because in that corner of the shop the stacks were so close together. If two people were there at once, one would have to retreat into the slightly broader main aisle for the other to get past. Occasionally he'd have to deal with a health inspector whom he'd need to sweet-talk in order not to get the place condemned as a fire hazard.

After I left during the State of Emergency in '85 my contact with him was limited to a footnote at the ends of my letters to Mom. In December 1989 I got my first letter from him. Mom had passed away. He'd already buried her. "You weren't going to come anyway," he wrote.

I did go back. In '97. We could finally afford a holiday. No, that's not the reason. A few years before, when it was safe for us to return, my wife said to me, "Go! See your father. We'll be fine."

"It's too expensive," I told her. "We can't afford it." But we both knew it was an excuse. I couldn't go back. I wasn't ready. I'd have to face him without the comforting buffer of my mother. I'd have to face her awful absence.

When we got to Jo'burg I left Felicity and the kids at the hotel and drove the hired car into town. I'd written to tell Dad I was coming. What if he hadn't got the letter? I should have phoned. The streets had changed. On the way I passed a new Hyatt and a new Hilton. Vendors on the pavements, trellis tables loaded with leather goods, children's toys, African art. Posters on poles advertised an upcoming rugby test, the arrival of Alvin Ailey. People hovered about stopped cars at the traffic lights.

You could do your shopping from your car: clothes hangers, window shields, driver-friendly notebooks. A man in a clown outfit handed me a leaflet for a new townhouse development. SECURE, SAFE SURROUNDINGS, it read. At each light, open hands insistent at closed windows and blinkered faces. The playing fields were being levelled: here were *white* beggars. And then there were the ghostly thieves. Which ones were they? This tummy-rubbing child moving hungrily between the vehicles? Or that man with the misspelt plea on his piece of cardboard? I'd been warned. Keep your windows closed, doors locked. Don't leave any bags or valuables in sight.

In town I drove into a parking lot a couple of streets up from the shop and paid the attendant. Walking along I suddenly thought, what if he's moved again? Maybe they've torn the building down. And then: what if he's died and nobody knew to inform me. I didn't recognise many of the shops. I passed some vendors cooking boerewors and mielies on open drums, turned a corner and there was the familiar façade.

He looked up from his book, slipped his reading glasses off his nose. They dropped onto his chest.

"Hullo, Dad."

"Ah, so you've arrived, have you?"

"Yes. Got here this morning."

"And your wife?" He looked behind me, toward the door. "And the children?"

"They're at the hotel. Resting."

"Yes, I suppose they must be tired. It's a long flight. How old are they now?"

"Marie's six and Damon's four."

"Ah, yes, that's right. You named the girl after your mother. Marie would've liked that. I must take you to see her grave. You've not been there yet, have you?"

"No. I came straight here."

"Good. We can go later. Her flowers need changing."

"Flowers?"

"I take her flowers every week. Roses, usually. They were her favourites."

"How," I said, " – how've you been?" I stuck my hand out to shake his.

"Hell," he said, pulling himself up. Chairs were another challenge for him. No knee joints to take the weight. Steadying himself on a nearby counter, or table, or armrest, he had to push with great force, and then make sure he didn't topple over. He took my hand and pulled me towards him. He'd never hugged me in his life.

I let go. "You seem a little . . ."

"Shorter?" he said.

"Yes."

"I am. Had the height adjusted. Makes it easier. Muscle strain, something in the back. I'm getting older."

He'd re-arranged the shop. The counter had been moved to one side, up against the window, and in its place was an arrangement of two worn-out easy chairs and a small table with coffee, sugar, milk powder, and a kettle on a tray. He'd moved the stacks around too.

"I see you've moved War up here," I said. "Thought you always said you had to have something lighter in the front."

"Doesn't matter now. No-one comes in any more."

"What do you mean, no-one?"

"Oh, one, maybe two people a week."

"And you stay open for them? To sell one or two books a week?"

"Open at 8:00, close at 5:00. Been doing it for fifty years. I'm not about to stop now."

He began walking down the row. I noticed that he was using a walking stick. He reached the sink at the back of the shop and, steadying himself on a nearby shelf, turned around, two coffee mugs in his hand.

"What's this?" I was pointing to a clutch of objects – small animal parts, feathers, a leather pouch – next to the cash register on the counter.

"Good-luck muti," he said. "To keep the place safe."

"You were attacked?"

"No." He laughed. "I've got the muti."

While he was busy making the coffee I strolled down the aisles. At the back of the shop, where the stacks for Law and Philosophy used to be, was a metal bunk bed, neatly made-up. Next to the bed, on a small table made from a pile of *Encyclopaedia Britannicas*, was a reading lamp, and in the corner, a heater.

"Dad!" I called out. "Are you sleeping here? What about the house? You've still got it haven't you? Dad?"

"Of course I've still got it," he called back. "The car, too. You're talking about the bed? It's for an old army comrade."

"Oh," I said, more to the rows of books separating us than to him. I went back to the front and pointed at the chairs. "That's what these are for?"

"What? Oh, yes. More comfortable."

"And that's why War's up here now?"

"Ja. Easier to get to when we're arguing a point. Like this morning. We were talking about the numbers of black servicemen Up North. Native Military Corps, Cape Corps together. I said it couldn't have been more than a few thousand, he said more than fifteen . . . He was right."

"*He* was right?"

"Yes. And you know what?" Dad began to laugh. "He even has more leg joints than Douglas Bader. You'll have coffee?"

"Yes, please. Milk, no sugar."

"Cremora okay for you?"

"Sure."

He turned his back and began making the coffee. I wandered down the aisles again, looking for the children's section. I was going to ask Dad if I could take some books back for the kids.

The door chime rang. What did he mean no-one came any more? I hadn't been in the shop ten minutes and there was a customer.

"So you've got them?" Dad's voice.

"Ja," came a black man's reply, "they wanted thirteen rands. For two packets of biscuits!"

"Up North they cost nothing."

"Yes," said the black man. "But before Tripoli there were shortages."

"Only for you lot."

"Ja! That's true."

I came from behind a stack to see the smile on Dad's face. "Arthur," he said to the black man, "this is Robert, my son. He's arrived."

"Ah, the son! Robert, it is a long time your father and I have waited to see you again."

"Do I know you?"

He came towards me, the yaw of an artificial limb in his step. "What do you think?" He rapped his knuckles against his leg. "No more crutches, kleinbaas."

# SEITLHAMO MOTSAPI

## *a poem*

### SOL/O

my love
there are no accidents
in war – no kisses
on the belligerent lips of crocodiles
no loves greener than
the dancing hearts of children
no reveller jollier than the worm
in columbus's boiling head

there are no songs beautifuller
than the stern indifference of the hills
there are no flowers more clamorous
than the seas of children
home in my little heart

i tell u this
as the sun recedes
into the quaking pinstripe
of my warriors
grinning & vulgar in their muddied dreams
of power

i tell u this love
because the roads
have become hostile

# SHIRLEY ESKAPA

## *a story*

### BETWEEN THE SHEETS

I always long for winter. Transvaal summers are too hot and last too long. I like the look as much as the feel of long hair, and in the summer my neck sweats and glues my hair. I am not one for the outdoor life, and although our swimming-pool looks as merciful as a bowl of crushed ice, I never so much as wet a toe, not even on the sunniest day.

The bite of a winter's night is precious to me. With arms and shoulders covered I am sheltered. Soft flannel sheets which look and feel like blotting-paper draw out and absorb the day's accumulated dying; the cradle of the pillows consoles, like a caress against a breast. Inside the sheets I feel supreme relief.

In the outward sense, I do not live alone. I have a husband to share my bed, and to share the days, at the time I want to tell you about, my son Justin, who was then aged three, and inside me, growing without the least of my help, another child. I feared the loneliness. When the child had spurned and left the womb, I would be bereft.

My husband did not find the light disturbing, and while he slept I read. The fragile sighs of the child did not break my compulsive drive across the pages. I read on and on and on. I devoured books and often could recall nothing of them. Even the presence of a separate life breathing only my breath could not take or break or mute the call of my own future death. Under the shallow milk of my pallid daily conversations depth existed only in the books. There I submerged.

At about two in the morning, when the too-short winter night was coldest, sleep entered. It would take me a few moments to get warm as I moved into my twined posture (remembered from the womb?) before sleep, my restored amniotic fluid would embrace me, cover all of me, would carry me to safety, absolute safety, sublime safety.

For a moment – on *that* night – I was dropped from sleep into consciousness. I thought I had kicked a book off the bed, and then sleep drew me back in again. Once again I was dropped, the lights flashed on. I sat up and screamed. I dug my elbow into my husband's ribs. He sat up and screamed.

"Shhh! Shhh!" They were holding their hands to their mouths, "Shhh! Shhh!" They were moving towards us on shoeless feet, the axes over their shoulders glinting lavishly in the electric lights. Their clothes were black, their foreheads and chins were hidden behind black balaclavas, their hands were black. They were shadowless. They came slowly, tortuously, like three moving sculptures. A charred triumph stared from black eyes.

One halted at the foot of the bed, moved his axe fractionally forward. The other two slowly, noiselessly, marched on, divided, came either side of the bed, stopped.

I screamed again. The axe nearest me moved slowly downward to rest against my neck. (I almost wrote 'nest': the axe had the shape of a bird on the wing.) Afterwards my neck was slightly grazed. "Shhh! Shhh! Shut up or we'll kill you." I held still. But wouldn't we be killed anyway?

"We want your gun, give us your gun or we'll kill you!" They flung my pillows to the carpet where they lay like crumpled angels. There was no gun in the bedroom. They were moving about.

"Money." The one nearest me said.

"In my bag," I could make my voice answer.

One of the others flung the bag. He snatched it. Only silver coins. (I have never kept my money in a purse. It is scattered. I abhor order.)

"But this is only silver." Shifting his axe to his left shoulder.

"I can't take your bus fare!" (Pronounced 'fay-er'.)

"Please, take it . . ."

They were wrenching down suitcases, he turned to help. Afterwards he came back and scooped the silver coins into his hands.

"My wife is pregnant." My husband said again and again: "My wife is pregnant!" Mad to say it. So what? They were pregnant with death . . . What were they saying? What were they arguing about in their black language?

Silence. Two of them advancing towards me. Time slipped away from my mind, it was static time in a dream. I knew what was happening only, not what might happen . . . Two left hands removed blankets. The edge of the axe came nearer. Sharpened and knife-thin. My woollen nightgown untangled as it was raised. Very gently raised. A fleeting hand examined. I felt the hand. A bulging hardened belly. The nightgown was lowered. *Such tenderness.*

One of them axed the telephone. He had padded himself against the cold. He swayed, like a golliwog dancing. He slashed the phone straight and crooked. Quick blows. Always vicious. When the phone disintegrated into tiny pieces he turned on the tray of tea-cups.

The noise. Suddenly there was Justin blinking into the room. I . . . I'd forgotten his existence till he stumbled through the door. Death was all I'd been thinking of, my death, I'd been fearing a slow death, an arm severed, a leg, a slow butchering. The terror not death itself, but the long route it would take before arriving. But Justin standing under the arch of axes had released me from my terror. The three of us in the bed seemed safer.

A strange trustingness. I felt a complicity flowing through the six of us – (uniting us?) – we were all in something together. I was the soldier, arms raised in surrender. I was the patient dependent on the psychiatrist. The world was shut out. At the pitch of our lifelong conditioning – fear, distrust, permanent emergency – the trust had been born. There is something unwholesome in the kind of trust the psychiatrist wants. But ours that night had an honesty, like the trust between a prostitute and her client: a deal would be done. They're saving my life, I felt, saving it. You trust the man you think has the choice of your life or your death.

But the pulse of trust was strongest that hour, when it was born.

"Would you mind leaving me with one suit? I won't be able to go to work." My husband smiled.

We grew the capillaries of friendship that night, a secondary friend-ship, like the secondary circulation they say an injured heart has to grow . . .

They picked up the suitcases. My guardian, the one who said 'fay-er' for 'fare', stopped at the door. "I'm sorry, Ma'am."

They were gone and our calm with them. The gun was in another room. My husband leaped, ran for it. I heard its firing, his most horri-ble screams for help. They must have been lying in wait for him. They must have been hacking him to death.

"Come," I dragged Justin. "They are killing Daddy. We must go and get killed too!"

"No! No!"

But it was we who had broken faith, lied and tricked them: white erasing black again . . . They'd believed us when we said there was no gun. We had a second telephone downstairs. When they were caught it was said the punishment for armed attack would be death. I was ill. I went to a nursing home. But I was tangled in all the cycles of hate.

"Kaffirs, they'll swing for this," I heard again and again. "Death is too good for them . . ." A few friends and some strangers asked what being raped was like . . . But for me, blackness darkened reality, pardoned, and transmuted guilt into innocence. When I said I would kill anyone, even *you*, if my child was starving and I couldn't get work because of a piece of paper, they thought I was deranged, and said so, at the trial.

They began to hate me, too.

And now, you see, the ten-year sentence is almost over. As I said, we broke faith, we fooled them, and I wait now as I have been waiting for ten years.

Sleep no longer nourishes or carries me. For ten years I have dreamt that I am at a tea party in a little thatched summer house at the bottom of my mother's garden, swinging upside-down from a rope, and in my hand I have an axe, and with each swing, with a deft flick of the wrist I randomly sever whatever head falls within my range, like a golf club cracking a ball.

I am addicted to sleep.

# ELEANOR ANDERSON

## *six poems*

### A LADY AGED SEVENTY-NINE OFFERS A ROBORANT WORD TO A FRIEND TURNING FIFTY

Dry that tear, my dear, resist this rue,
Everything'll be okay, I promise you,
Believe me, I was old once too.

### FINGERTIPS

bad bad part of town,
strolling young men, glancing.
rush on my errand from my locked car
rush back,
keys wink at me behind the glass,
my groan is a small howl.
a man beside me. "problem?"
from his pocket he draws wire
sleight-of-hands it,
bows me into my car, strolls, not glancing.
my R20 note trembles at my fingertips.

### MY ONE REGRET

Inadequate it's made me feel, and embarrassed,
that all my life I never once was sexually harassed.

## LATE THOUGHTS

Gravely short of love and money, I said,
"I will end it all, me and my frustration."
But it was not until after I'd jumped
that I realised the gravity of my situation.


## A SPOKESMAN FOR THE CLINIC

Their wounds are so horrendous, yet their deaths so drab.
That I must try, and once more try, to understand
What need it is that makes them fling their lives
In their Creator's face.
They keep us busy! and my staff get scared,
But still give all they've got to give.
So one drab morning recently I quit my desk
To go and plant some poppies in a sheltered place,
And I prefer to think that some of them will live.


## FROZE

One blazing day when time flowed slow
into the dam of love I dipped my toe.
It froze.
Then wham! So did all my toes.

# MODIKWE DIKOBE

## *an extract from the novel*

### THE MARABI DANCE

Mr Tereplasky arrived at his office earlier than usual and demanded to see the foreman as promptly as possible.

The phone rang: "Rooiveldt Dairies."

"I have received your account for more milk than you delivered. I rang your clerk last week to say that milk deliveries had been very irregular and late, arriving after my husband and children had left for work and school . . ."

The caller banged the receiver down.

"Hello? Is that the Rooiveldt Dairies? This is the Braamfontein Station. Your men have left two four-gallon cans of milk on the station last night."

Mr Tereplasky flung himself out of the office.

The telephone rang again.

He ran back and picked up the receiver. "Rooiveldt Dairies."

A hoarse voice gurgled some incomprehensible words: "Dit is Marshall Square," and changed into English. "The Rooiveldt Dairies trolley cart has collided with a municipal bus and we had to shoot one of the horses because its leg was broken."

"Rambuck! Rambuck!" Tereplasky ran again out of the office as if stung by a bee. "You have ruined me! Thirty years of hard work has gone to hell in two weeks . . ."

Mr Rambuck had not yet heard that the trolley had collided with a bus and a horse had been shot, nor did he know about the milk cans left at the station.

"Hy is mal," he thought.

"Mr Rambuck, you made me get rid of July. And now I can see the reason. He understood the work better than you. And you felt that you could not be under a black man. I was a fool to listen to your advice. I am giving you one month's notice."

Mr Tereplasky took over the work which had been done by Rambuck: checking the milk at the station, filling bottles, going over the customers' list with the men who did the rounds, instructing the clerk to issue notices to all the customers asking them to notify the office immediately of late deliveries. To satisfy himself he even stuck postage stamps on the letters and went himself to the post office to fetch the post. If there were any returned letters from customers who had moved he searched for their new addresses. He stood at the stable door to see that the horses were properly fed and brushed. In the evenings, after work, he took home all the account books and statements and got his wife and daughter to go through them and put aside any queries to take to the auditors.

Mr Rambuck was given the duties of seeing that the compound was kept clean and that there were no flies to be seen in the dairy premises. "If he does not like the work, he can leave before his notice month expires. I have had enough of him since he got rid of my father's old boy."

Mr Tereplasky often came home exhausted.

"You are going to ruin your health, Lazar. Why don't you get July back? It won't cost you anything to say: 'I am sorry old man – come and work. I will pay you more money.' Or to treat him as a human being and give him due respect."

"What respect must I give him? Do you mean I must call him 'mister'?"

"Why not?" interjected his wife. "If you feel too proud to call him 'mister' then call him Mabongo and stop calling any of the men 'boys'."

"Have you become a friend of the Natives?"

"Lazar! We must learn to respect them so that we can live in peace with them."

"Alright Hannah. I'll get Mabongo tonight."

He got into his car and drove to the Dairy which was situated to the south of Johannesburg, in the working class area. When he arrived he called to one of his employees: "Frans, get into the car. I must get Mabongo tonight." He drove back in the direction from which he had come – towards the northern area which was largely a middle-class area except for Doornfontein which was a 'black spot'.

It was between nine and ten when the car's lights shone into the Molefe Yard where Mabongo lived. After ascertaining the number, which was painted on a corrugated iron gate, Frans got out of the car to ask a woman who was still cooking outside if Mabongo still lived there.

"Go round to Angle Road," she told him, "the yard is full of mud and the baas will spoil his trousers."

By swerving the car towards the east, then turning slightly to the south Mr Tereplasky and Frans reached the Angle Road entrance.

Mabongo had seen the headlights and knew that it was his employer's car.

"My baas is coming."

"You say your baas is coming and do nothing to get maime and tlokoalatsela? You stand there like a fool!"

Mathloare took out the herbs and urged her husband to prepare himself as Ndala had directed.

Frans again got out of the car and went to knock at the main door. On receiving no answer he walked into the dark passage and knocked on the door of the Mabongos' room.

"Tsena," called Mrs Mabongo. "Hau! Hau! Where do you come from late?"

"I have come with the baas. He wants Mabongo to come and work now."

Mr Tereplasky, after waiting some time in the car, got out and called to July. He came into the dimly lit room saying: "Come Mr Mabongo, I am sorry. Come to work and I will pay you more money and you will never be sacked again. Come now, don't be a woman."

During this discourse Mabongo stood erect and looked his former employer straight in the face. He kept pushing out his breath which had the smell of the piece of molomo monate.

"Are these your two wives?" asked Mr Tereplasky and then fixed his eyes on Martha and thought to himself what a beautiful wife Mabongo had.

"No, it is my child."

"Then she must come and work for the missus."

"I am a singer," replied Martha in perfect English.

"Then you are no good to work in kitchens."

"I do any kind of work. I am only engaged at this time because there is going to be a competition and I must practise hard in order to win the prize."

"How old are you?"

Martha fumbled on her fingers: "Sixteen."

"You look too big for sixteen. I thought you were twenty-two or more."

Turning to Mabongo, Mr Tereplasky again appealed to him to

return to work.

"Tsamac le lekgoa le – go with the white man," shouted Mabongo's wife as he pretended to be unwilling to go with his former employer. So Mabongo gave in.

"I have sacked Rambuck," Mr Tereplasky told him as they drove back to the dairy. "He told me lies about you: that you bewitched the horses so that they could not be handled by the other boys."

Mabongo blushed and thought of the root still in his mouth and suspected that his employer may have noticed the black stuff on his eyelids.

"I have lost a lot of money in the two weeks you were away. Your favourite mare has been shot by the police because its leg was broken in an accident; milk has been left on the station and gone sour and the customers have refused to pay their accounts because their milk has not been delivered. The missus will be glad that you have come back."

"My cousin is a great doctor," Mabongo said to himself.

The car left the main route to the south and went through dimly lighted streets, passing houses where windows and doors appeared to be well secured against intruders.

Mr Tereplasky noticed for the first time the contrast between the southern and northern areas: "Bright lights there and windows big enough to allow light through and a night watchman to see that nobody comes to the house . . ."

Mabongo wasted no time when they got to the dairy. He went to the stable, at first feeling sad at the loss of Molly, his favourite mare. But the other horse, Jim, stamped its hooves and snorted in joy at seeing its old friend again. The new horse, still unnamed, looked blankly at the stranger who had entered the stable. After patting Jim, Mabongo moved to the new horse and stretched out his hand as if in salutation. The horse answered by rearing and stamping the ground.

"Medrai!" He called its name aloud and the horse pricked up its ears.

# AHMED ESSOP

## *a story*

## THE SACRIFICE

When Zahid reached the age of eight years his father decided that he would sacrifice a lamb during the festival of Eid. So Zahid and his two friends, Afzal and Bilal, went with his father in a hired truck into the country and bought a lamb from a farmer. On the way back to Fordsburg the three boys sat at the back of the truck and put their arms around the lamb. They tied the lamb to a pole in the yard in Terrace Road where they lived, and scattered hay which the farmer had given them for the lamb to feed and lie on.

As the festival of Eid was two weeks away the lamb became a pet to the boys and they called it Snow. They and the other children in the yard loved to caress its wool, give it water, sit beside it, and even talk to it. At times Zahid untied the lamb and ran about with it in the yard and along the pavement in the street, with the other children following in glee. The three boys were very excited about their gentle pet and washed it and made its wool gleam by brushing it. They then decided that their pet needed green grass. They saw a house in Mint Road, one of the few in Fordsburg, which had a patch of lawn in front of the porch. They knocked at the door, and the householder, a tall man, came out.

"Can you give us some lawn when you cut it?" Zahid asked.

"Why do you need it?"

"We want to give it to our lamb."

"Lamb?"

"Yes, my father bought one for Eid."

"Well, why not bring the lamb here and it can eat the grass."

So the boys, with Zahid's father's consent, took the lamb to Mint Road where it grazed on the lawn. Zahid's father praised them for caring for the lamb. He said, "It's a creature of Allah and He will reward you for caring for it."

130 ✳

Solomon who lived in the yard said to the boys, "Zahid's father is going to offer the lamb as sacrifice. Do you know that the Lord sacrificed himself for mankind? You are too young to know about that. The Bible says Jesus was a lamb of God. You are doing good work by looking after it."

The children did not understand Solomon and ran with the lamb out of the yard into the street where soon every child wanted to touch it and play with it. The name Snow was joyfully and lovingly repeated many times.

When the festival of Eid neared, Zahid's father said that the time for sacrificing the lamb had come. Zahid asked his father what the word sacrifice meant.

"You are too small to understand fully, my son. When you are a man you will sacrifice your own lamb. There was a man called the Prophet Ebrahim and he was a holy man. When Allah asked him to sacrifice his son Ismail he was ready to obey. Then Allah ordered him to put a lamb in Ismail's place and the Prophet Ebrahim cut the animal. That is sacrifice."

"You mean you are going to cut Snow like the butcher?"

"Yes."

"But you can't."

"I must. We Muslims follow what the Prophet Ebrahim did. Then we will give the meat to people in the yard."

Zahid went out of doors with tears in his eyes. He went to the lamb and sat down beside it and caressed its head. The lamb looked at him and pressed its head closer to him. Then Bilal and Afzal came running towards him and said that they had seen a house with lawn in the back garden and had asked for permission from the lady of the house to bring their pet and the lady had agreed.

"It's no use," Zahid said. "My father says he is going to sacrifice Snow on Eid day."

"Sacrifice?"

"Yes." And he told them what his father had said.

The two boys sat next to the lamb and listened. The lamb looked up at their bewildered faces.

"Father says he is going to give the meat to everyone to eat."

"Eat our lamb?" Afzal asked.

"That's what father says."

The joy that the boys had derived from their lamb companion had endeared them to it and they could not understand why anyone should wish to kill their friend. After a while they went out of the yard into the street, saddened by the impending fate of their pet.

That night when his father went to the mosque, Zahid spoke to his mother, and pleaded that she speak to his father not to kill the lamb.

"The lamb has not harmed anyone, mother."

"Your father must do what he has to do. He didn't buy the lamb for you to play with."

"But how can he kill Snow?"

"We must sacrifice during Eid and feed the poor and hungry."

"But nobody is hungry here. We can buy meat from the butcher and give it."

"That is not the same."

"Why not? The butcher sells meat every day. I want to keep Snow."

"You don't understand. You will when you are bigger. Lambs are eaten every day for food and killed by butchers."

"The butchers have not played with the lambs."

"That doesn't matter. Lambs are made for eating."

"I don't want my pet to be eaten."

"Don't argue. We know what must be done."

"I won't . . ." he said, beginning to cry.

"You can cry as much as you like. Your father is going to cut the lamb."

On the morning of Eid Zahid's father told him to come with him to the mosque for prayers. When they returned his father said it was time to sacrifice the lamb. He went to the kitchen and took out from the dresser-drawer a large gleaming knife which had been specially bought for the occasion. He told his son, "I will let you hold the lamb's legs while I cut."

Zahid's father went outside, called Hajji Musa, the well-known faith-healer and demon exorciser, and Solomon to help him. Solomon tied the lamb's legs with a rope while Zahid's father and Hajji Musa held it. Then Solomon lifted the lamb and took it to the drain and placed its neck over the cement edge.

Zahid ran out of the yard, his two friends following him. When they were in the street they heard Snow cry out as the knife cut into its throat. The three boys put their fingers to their ears and tears filmed their eyes. They sat on the edge of the pavement for a long while and did not go into the yard.

When later they went in they saw the lamb, skinned, hanging from a cord under a rafter. The boys went to the corner where Snow used to be tied and swept the place as a last rite.

Zahid's father called the three boys and said that as soon as he had cut the lamb into pieces and made parcels they could distribute the meat to various families, including Afzal's and Bilal's. Quietly, the three friends slipped out of the yard. When Zahid's father could not find them he distributed the meat himself, keeping some of it for eating at home.

During the evening meal there was mutton curry on the table and Zahid sensed that his mother had cooked the meat of the lamb.

"I am not hungry," he said. "I will have bread and tea."

"You must eat some of the lamb we have sacrificed."

"That is my pet Snow."

"You must eat," his father said.

"I won't."

Zahid's father was not a violent man, but he lifted his hand and hit his son hard on his back.

Zahid cried out, jumped off his chair and ran out of the kitchen. His father said, "Where are you going?" following him.

Zahid went to his room and hid under his bed. His father and mother came into the room.

"He won't have any food tonight. That should be a lesson to him."

"He doesn't understand," his mother said.

"He must learn about sacrifice."

Zahid's father and mother returned to the dining table.

# HERMAN CHARLES BOSMAN

## *a story*

### THE TRAITOR'S WIFE

We did not like the sound of the wind that morning, as we cantered over a veld trail that we had made much use of, during the past year, when there were English forces in the neighbourhood.

The wind blew short wisps of yellow grass in quick flurries over the veld and the smoke from the fire in front of a row of kafir huts hung low in the air. From that we knew that the third winter of the Boer War was at hand. Our small group of burghers dismounted at the edge of a clump of camel-thorns to rest our horses.

"It's going to be an early winter," Jan Vermeulen said, and from force of habit he put his hand up to his throat in order to close his jacket collar over in front. We all laughed, then. We realized that Jan Vermeulen had forgotten how he had come to leave his jacket behind when the English had surprised us at the spruit a few days before. And instead of a jacket, he was now wearing a mealie sack with holes cut in it for his head and arms. You could not just close over in front of your throat, airily, the lapels cut in a grain bag.

"Anyway, Jan, you're all right for clothes," Kobus Ferreira said, "but look at me."

Kobus Ferreira was wearing a missionary's frock-coat that he had found outside Kronendal, where it had been hung on a clothes-line to air.

"This frock-coat is cut so tight across my middle and shoulders that I have to sit very stiff and awkward in my saddle, just like the missionary sits on a chair when he is visiting at a farmhouse," Kobus Ferreira added. "Several times my horse has taken me for an Englishman, in consequence of the way I sit. I am only afraid that when a bugle blows my horse will carry me over the rant into the English camp."

At Kobus Ferreira's remarks the early winter wind seemed to take on a keener edge.

For our thoughts went immediately to Leendert Roux, who had been with us on commando a long while and who had been spoken of as a likely man to be veldkornet – and who had gone out scouting, one night, and not come back with a report.

There were, of course, other Boers who had also joined the English. But there was not one of them that we had respected as much as we had done Leendert Roux.

Shortly afterwards we were on the move again.

In the late afternoon we emerged through the Crocodile Poort that brought us in sight of Leendert Roux's farmhouse. Next to the dam was a patch of mealies that Leendert Roux's wife had got the kafirs to cultivate.

"Anyway, we'll camp on Leendert Roux's farm and eat roast mealies, tonight," our veldkornet, Apie Theron, observed.

"Let us first rather burn his house down," Kobus Ferreira said. And in a strange way it seemed as though his violent language was not out of place, in a missionary's frock-coat. "I would like to roast mealies in the thatch of Leendert Roux's house."

Many of us were in agreement with Kobus.

But our veldkornet, Apie Theron, counselled us against that form of vengeance.

"Leendert Roux's having his wife and farmstead here will yet lead to his undoing," the veldkornet said. "One day he will risk coming out here on a visit, when he hasn't got Kitchener's whole army at his back. That will be when we will settle our reckoning with him."

We did not guess that that day would be soon.

The road we were following led past Leendert Roux's homestead. The noise of our horses' hoofs brought Leendert Roux's wife, Serfina, to the door. She stood in the open doorway and watched us riding by. Serfina was pretty, taller than most women, and slender, and there was no expression in her eyes that you could read, and her face was very white.

It was strange, I thought, as we rode past the homestead, that the sight of Serfina Roux did not fill us with bitterness.

Afterwards, when we had dismounted in the mealie-lands, Jan Vermeulen made a remark at which we laughed.

"For me it was the worst moment in the Boer War," Jan Vermeulen said. "Having to ride past a pretty girl, and me wearing just a sack. I was glad there was Kobus Ferreira's frock-coat for me to hide behind."

Jurie Bekker said there was something about Serfina Roux that reminded him of the Transvaal. He did not know how it was, but he repeated that, with the wind of early winter fluttering her dress about her ankles, that was how it seemed to him.

Then Kobus Ferreira said that he had wanted to shout out something to her when we rode past the door, to let Serfina know how we, who were fighting in the last ditch – and in unsuitable clothing – felt about the wife of a traitor. "But she stood there so still," Kobus Ferreira said, "that I just couldn't say anything. I felt I would like to visit her, even."

That remark of Kobus Ferreira's fitted in with his frock-coat also. It would not be the first time a man in ecclesiastical dress called on a woman while her husband was away.

Then, once again, a remark of Jan Vermeulen's made us realize that there was a war on. Jan Vermeulen had taken the mealie sack off his body and had threaded a length of baling-wire above the places where the holes were. He was now restoring the grain bag to the use it had been meant for, and I suppose that, in consequence, his views generally also got sensible.

"Just because Serfina Roux is pretty," Jan Vermeulen said, flinging mealie heads into the sack, "let us not forget who and what she is. Perhaps it is not safe for us to camp tonight on this farm. She is sure to be in touch with the English. She may tell them where we are. Especially now that we have taken her mealies."

But our veldkornet said that it wasn't important if the English knew where we were. Indeed, any kafir in the neighbourhood could go and report our position to them. But what did matter was that we should know where the English were. And he reminded us that in two years he had never made a serious mistake that way.

"What about the affair at the spruit, though?" Jan Vermeulen asked him. "And my pipe and tinder-box were in the jacket, too."

By sunset the wind had gone down. But there was a chill in the air. We had pitched our camp in the tamboekie grass on the far side of Leendert Roux's farm. And I was glad, lying in my blankets, to think that it was the turn of the veldkornet and Jurie Bekker to stand guard.

Far away a jackal howled. Then there was silence again. A little later the stillness was disturbed by sterner sounds of the veld at night. And those sounds did not come from very far away, either. They were sounds Jurie Bekker made – first, when he fell over a beacon, and then when he gave his opinion of Leendert Roux for setting up a beacon in the middle of a stretch of dubbeltjie thorns. The blankets felt very snug, pulled over my shoulders, when I reflected on those thorns.

And because I was young, there came into my thoughts, at Jurie Bekker's mention of Leendert Roux, the picture of Serfina as she had stood in front of her door.

The dream I had of Serfina Roux was that she came to me, tall and graceful, beside a white beacon on her husband's farm. It was that haunting kind of dream, in which you half know all the time, that you are dreaming. And she was very beautiful in my dream. And it was as though her hair was hanging half out of my dream and reaching down into the wind when she came closer to me. And I knew what she wanted to tell me. But I did not wish to hear it. I knew that if Serfina spoke that thing I would wake up from my dream. And in that moment, like it always happens in a dream, Serfina did speak.

"Opskud, kêrels!" I heard.

But it was not Serfina who gave that command. It was Apie Theron, the veldkornet. He came running into the camp with his rifle at the trail. And Serfina was gone. In a few minutes we had saddled our horses and were ready to gallop away. Many times during the past couple of years our scouts had roused us thus when an English column was approaching.

We were already in the saddle when Apie Theron let us know what was toward. He had received information, he said, that Leendert Roux had that very night ventured back to his homestead. If we hurried we might trap him in his own house. The veldkornet warned us to take no chances, reminding us that when Leendert Roux had still stood on our side he had been a fearless and resourceful fighter.

So we rode back during the night along the same way we had come in the afternoon. We tethered our horses in a clump of trees near the mealie-lands and started to surround the farmhouse. When we saw a figure running for the stable, at the side of the house, we realized that Leendert Roux had been almost too quick for us.

In the cold, thin wind that springs up just before the dawn we surprised Leendert Roux at the door of his stable. But when he made no resistance it was almost as though it was Leendert Roux who had taken us by surprise. Leendert Roux's calm acceptance of his fate made it seem almost as though he had never turned traitor, but that he was laying down his life for the Transvaal.

In answer to the veldkornet's question, Leendert Roux said that he would be glad if Kobus Ferreira – he having noticed that Kobus was wearing the frock-coat of a man of religion – would read Psalm 110 over his grave. He also said that he did not want his eyes bandaged.

And he asked to be allowed to say goodbye to his wife.

Serfina was sent for. At the side of the stable, in the wind of early morning, Leendert and Serfina Roux, husband and wife, bade each other farewell.

Serfina looked even more shadowy than she had done in my dream when she set off back to the homestead along the footpath through the thorns. The sun was just beginning to rise. And I understood how right Jurie Bekker had been when he said that she was just like the Transvaal, with the dawn wind fluttering her skirts about her ankles as it rippled the grass. And I remembered that it was the Boer women that kept on when their menfolk recoiled before the steepness of the Drakensberge and spoke of turning back.

I also thought of how strange it was that Serfina should have come walking over to our camp, in the middle of the night, just as she had done in my dream. But where my dream was different was that she had reported not to me but to our veldkornet where Leendert Roux was.

# ROBERT GREIG

## *two poems*

### THE SHEEP-FARMER'S WIFE

The sheep-farmer's wife,
with those adequate thighs,
brought jasmine smiling,
spoke of the Grahamstown school
of painters, their mauve hills,
bush clogging valleys, nude
skies and no people beneath.
One had been noted in Cape Town
and one would be made a professor
teaching realism to blacks,
a third sought to mount her.

The farm gave her plenty to do.
While the servant washed up,
she displayed her collection:
shelf upon shelf of portly blue
and pink jugs, brimming shadows.

### MONSTERS

I was Elvis, hair billowing, hips eloquent
of tumbled beds at ten years old.
Saw below rapturous faces, heard applause
that went improbably on, but left me
ranging camp, scavenging praise.

I passed a tent where the leaders sat,
half-broken voices deploying my days,
heard one, the son of a family friend:

"The way he yowled Love me Tender . . ."
I feigned illness, went quiet a year.

The same one, when plasters were fresh
off my legs, browning normal by the pool,
pushed me in. I could not swim:
wherever I rose, his fists were waiting.
Grownups extracted apologies; my defeat.

I distrust leaders still, will not sing.
Swimming, I'll wait till all have gone.
Yet when my baby is hooked by claws
of nightmares, I tell him hugs and kisses
can turn them to piebald pandas.

It's not so, and he knows.
If my horror and I should meet
I'd revive my roots of hate,
make him yowl and push him down,
grind a boot into his crown.

When I lay my baby down
he claims my thumb as talisman.
I can't follow tugs of sleep:
hope his light will dazzle monsters,
steady breathing lull them always.

# ROY BLUMENTHAL

## *an extract from the novel*

*My passion for writing developed when I tried to get my English teacher to submit poems of mine to the national schools' journal,* English Alive. *His constant refusal began my quest to prove to myself that I was a good writer. I began writing every night in a journal.*

*When I left school I bought an ancient typewriter through an advert in the Under R50 column in the* Star Classified. *I started submitting to literary journals. For three years, rejection after rejection came back, and many of the margin notes made by editors were mystifying to me. And infuriating. And often incoherent.*

*The only editor who seemed to have some insight was Lionel. One day he sent me an unacceptably incisive comment, and I blew up. I sent him a letter arguing that he'd missed the point. He promptly sent me a reply which I tore up in a fury. It said something like the following: 'By all means continue sending work to* Sesame. *But make your choice: if you want to argue, I'll simply return the rejected poems without comment, and you'll never know what I really think; or you can continue receiving my comments and possibly learn a thing or two.'*

*I decided that I'd rather get his criticism. After that I sent him a poem that he didn't send back. 'Surveillance as an Art Form' appeared in* Sesame 13 – *my first published poem.*

*Since I met Lionel about six years ago, I've been attending his workshop religiously. I don't always agree with him. We still argue. But he unerringly registers even the most obscure of my intentions.*

*I love it when he likes my work. And he spotted in some of my poems a style that he thought would make me a good prose writer – hence the piece you see here.*

## TATTOOS ARE FOREVER

"Shhhh!" whispered Donna.

Spider giggled. Leon pressed his ear to the kitchen door.

"Okay, hold me steady," she said. She raised her leg onto the counter top, below the wall-mounted crockery cabinet. Spider hesitated, then placed his hands on her hips. "Push," she said. He hoisted, and she stood up, her nose level with the top of the cupboard. He quickly moved his hands to her calves. "Yuck!" she said. "It's filthy up here!"

"What's up there?" said Leon.

"Ya," said Spider, "have you found anything?"

"Here's a spoon for you, Spider." She tossed a greasy spoon at his head, and he dodged. It hit the linoleum with a plastic thump. "Hold still, silly!" Her hand darted forward. "Yes! Got something!" She pulled a book from under the dust and grime. It was sticky and grey. She got down from the counter. "Leon, are you sure Mommy's still sleeping? Go check . . ."

He opened the kitchen door and tiptoed down the passage. As usual, the door was open just a crack. He listened carefully. A faint snore emerged every now and again, with a little whistling sound attached. He looked through the crack, and could just see an arm outside the covers, resting near the edge of the bed.

He went back to the kitchen. "She's sleeping. Snoring like anything."

Spider turned to Donna. "Let's go to *your* room."

She looked at the dirty book in her hand. "Okay."

Donna's room was the first door from the kitchen. Leon's came next, and Mrs Bosch's was last.

"Don't sit on the bed, sit on the floor." The two boys complied. She sat between them. "Leon, give me some of those." She pointed to a shell-covered box on the brown bedside table. Leon took a wad of the pink tissues and handed them to her.

The book was a thin softback with Christmas paper glued to it. Donna wiped the cover. As she rubbed, hordes of smiling, blue angels appeared, strumming gold harps.

"C'mon, Donna," said Spider, "let's see what it is."

"Shh!" She opened the book, blowing on the first page. Dust streamed away from her mouth, fanning into the sliver of sunlight edging through the curtains. The title was *Pussy Black* by Leonora Sutherfield. "Jees, this is old. Check at this." She pointed at the date.

1973. "We weren't even born yet." She closed the book, then let it fall open. The spine cracked as she held it up.

She read aloud, in a semi-whisper, ". . . the bed sighed under their dual weight, Fannela gasping in astonished delight. 'Oh,' she gasped, 'take me, oh take me, yes, yes!' Dean pulled his mouth from her wet nipple."

Leon giggled.

"Shut up," Donna said, and carried on reading. "He gazed hungrily into the languid pools of her amber eyes. 'I want you,' he said. 'Oh, fuck me, Dean, fuck me now!' Her back arched upward to meet his throbbing flesh, the lance of his manhood glistening near the rich black bush of her lush pussy. He pressed against her, and her desperate fingers guided him in. 'Yes!' she screamed, and a moan of pleasure enveloped their passion." Donna looked at Spider.

"Don't stop," he said. He stared at the page, his eyes held on the spot Donna's finger marked.

"Leon, what's that in your pants?" He moved his hands to cover his erection. She slapped at his crotch.

"Ow!" He poked her hard in the ribs. The book jolted in her hand. "Leave me alone! Why'd you do that!"

"Because you're disgusting."

"I'm not the one who was blushing, I saw you."

"Oh no I wasn't."

"Guys!" said Spider. "Calm down, quiet! Your mother will come. Carry on reading, Donna."

"Oh shit," she said. "You've broken it, Leon." The page she had been reading from had come adrift, was held into the spine by a few centimetres of paper at the bottom. "Now what are we going to do?"

A cough from down the passage. The three froze. "Donna?" Mrs Bosch's voice. "I'm sleeping here, don't you know? Are you making a noise in there?" Still in her room. "Tell Leon to bring me a glass of water, will you?"

"Yes Mommy," said Donna. "Go Leon, you heard her. Better hide this." She gave the book to Leon. "Spider, let's go to the kitchen."

Leon stood up, went to his room and pushed the book under the chest of drawers. He pushed a pair of shoes in front of it, just in case. He went to the kitchen, and found Donna and Spider talking about homework. They smiled at him, and he smiled back as he closed the tap. He had filled the glass to the brim.

"Leon . . . ? Where's my water, boy."

"Coming," he shouted, and started off down the passage.

He walked carefully, making sure that nothing would spill. The glass was so full the water bulged up over the edge. He got to the door. "Knock knock?" he said.

"Thank you my darling," said Mrs Bosch, "come in."

He tiptoed to her bedside, and started the slow process of placing the glass on the table.

"Don't be stupid! It's too full! Here give me that!" She thrust her hand at him, jolting his elbow. Water splashed over his legs. Some went on the bed.

"Sorry, I'm sorry, sorry," he said. He stood waving his arms about, trying to find something to wipe away the mess.

"You're useless." She sipped from the glass. "I said, you're useless. What are you?"

"I'm useless."

"I'm useless who?"

"I'm useless, Mommy."

"Go to the kitchen, my darling, Mommy's getting dressed." She pushed herself upright, heaving her legs over the edge of the bed. "Run along now."

# WALTER SAUNDERS

## *a poem*

**THE START OF THE JOURNEY**
*(for Lionel)*

1

we drove through the crush of hills
voices bellied to the engine's tread
Guy's photographic equipment on the carrier
Tancred's bombardon
the croquet set
(it was still a game)
Melisende's rosy-cheeked love-birds in a cage

drove through the pass's ambush
monstrous tracks
a tank in the embrace of liana and python root
armour caught by the blowpipe
Godfrey said

a lizard stuck its head through the eyeslit
Melisende shuddered
before us from a mopani tree
a parachute dangled its load

then the unwalled town

   this is where they found
   the lance-head rusted
   a holy relic said Godfrey

the square no longer a market-place
and in the execution pit
faces blown to hell

I painted it ten years before
and the famous writer said
that is atom man
I think you are going to be famous
Phillip
do you want to be famous?

outskirts again
reed huts a flattened mush
I didn't catch what Godfrey said
ancient cathedrals?
sub-economic housing?
trees again trees
Tancred cupped a hand over my ear and husked
the deathwatch beetle
no restoration now

even the inane smile of the forester
was filled with menace
and the beggar at the roadblock
held out a gloved hand
(Guy drove off with a roar
what did we have to give?)

2

the green sway
of abandoned canefields
(premonition of the sea)
they might as well have put a fire in
in the old style
Godfrey grinned
wild pig the master now
there was no holding him
razor strike at each cheek

then the crankshaft broke
and I remember Melisende's crazed weeping
a ghost carrying the cage
knowing she would have to let
the birds go

I could do with a shot of that
said Guy still cursing look he said
misery is my profession

> there was gossip at the Court
> and the King grew jealous

the King?

of Jerusalem

(Godfrey again
spinning a yarn)

stone wheel
a birdbath on its side
in caked black ashes
the red lines
of white ants on an axe-haft
and the sign
Paradise Valley
as though we'd stopped
a life or so ago

crocodile
slipping into the pool

in liquescent darkness
(angle $11°$)
a savage eye drawing a bead

3

in the end we knew how ridiculous we were
pink knees
soiled khaki
trying to hack our way

at evening dipping our billy-cans
in brackish water
lighting fires
where the rivers had retreated
using driftwood

grey figurine-twisted

    my father was a sculptor
    no
    my father was a shop steward
    and she the woman in the picture
    what a razzle my uncle used to say
    Melisende
    her dove-grey eye
    could carve you in two

look there
the pharos a gutted pile
and where we stumble now
the earth blackmails

    Godfrey claims he knows the lie
    (he has climbed the headland)

    that is where hundreds went down
    gold coins
    a peacock throne

wind's ratfoot in banana palm
shimmy of hourglass sand
chimeras
milk and honey
journey without end

    and this morning Tancred had a vision
    of the sea bone dry
    the sun a marlin
    hooked
    exploding its element

    Tancred

    petrified

the sea's bottom dried seaweed the pulse of rock

# OSWALD JOSEPH MTSHALI

*a poem*

## A BRAZIER IN THE STREET

Around the smoke-billowing brazier
huddled four urchins, smoking
cigarette stubs and swopping stories
like seamen telling tales over a bottle of rum.
    The wintry air nipped their navels
    as a calf would suck the nipple.
    Smoke, blowing into bleary eyes,
    and waving flames fashioned
    their bodies into crouching silhouettes.
One yawned –
and rubbed his sleep-laden eyes
and mumbled as if in a dream
"I once ate a loaf of bread with nothing . . . . . . . . . ."

Then a buxom woman, blanket
against the blistering chill,
came out of the house
and carried the red-hot brazier inside
to cook her supper.

And quicker than a rabid dog
leaps to swallow its tail,
the starless night gaped
and gulped down the foursome.

# ROSE ZWI

## *an extract from* Last Walk in Naryshkin Park

*Lionel is not only a close friend; he has also been the single most important influence in my writing career. It was he who gave the manuscript of* Another Year in Africa *to Patrick Cullinan, who subsequently published it at Bateleur Press in 1980. He played a similar role in the lives of many other writers, in the city, in the townships, and even farther afield, giving unstintingly of his time, dispensing criticism, advice and encouragement to anyone who asked for it. Lionel the poet, novelist, short-story writer, critic and essayist, might have written even more had he put his own work before the needs of others. In addition to this, his sanity, courage and clear moral stand on issues which confused many of us in the dark years preceding the new South Africa provided a guiding light to the perplexed. We celebrate his seventieth birthday and wish him many more healthy, productive years.*

### OAXACA, MEXICO

Bentze, Sheva's twin brother, had originally planned to go to the United States, not Mexico. By the time he was ready to depart, the immigration quota for Lithuanians had closed. Fascinated by the cornucopia-shaped landmass south of the United States, with the Pacific Ocean to the west and the Gulf of Mexico to the east, he noted the arbitrary line dividing the two countries: one continent, no seas to cross. He would start in Mexico and work his way north. Aquatic skills acquired in the River Shvete and the Sea of Azov, he said, had prepared him for crossing any river in the world, including the Rio Grande.

He might have become the first Jewish–Lithuanian wet-back in history. Instead, he remained in Oaxaca, a beautiful colonial town 450 kilometres south of Mexico City, which stands in a fertile valley, on a high plateau, surrounded by mountains. The weather is mild, he wrote home, and the natives are friendly. When he foolishly mentioned the black-eyed Spanish beauties of Oaxaca, his mother began a search for a bride, preferably a young Jewish orphan whose relatives (or lack of relatives) would not be a financial drain on him.

Gershon also fell in love with Oaxaca. Here he lost his urgency to create a better world; none could be more idyllic. He could understand why Cortes had chosen Oaxaca above all other places as his own province. The gold was in the long summer days, if not in the surrounding mountains. And the natives, as Bentze had written, were indeed friendly, the climate mild. Gershon learned Spanish quickly, made easy contact with the people, and enjoyed the spicy dishes and the new rhythm of life. Only in Berdyansk, his other Eden, had he felt so free. He assuaged his guilts by writing regularly to his mother, sending her a portion of his earnings, and putting aside what he could for sea fares. Life in Lithuania, his mother wrote, was more difficult than ever.

"Our neighbours don't know we're Jewish," Bentze told them soon after they arrived. "They think we're German."

Sheva's enthusiasm faltered. "Why pretend? Are they anti-Semitic?"

"They don't even know what Jews are."

"Are they Catholic?" Sheva persisted. In the shtetl the Catholic priests had stoked the incipient anti-Semitism of the peasants.

"Those who aren't pagan," Bentze admitted, "are Catholic."

"Then they know what Jews are. For this we had to travel in *d'rerd oifen dek*, to the rooftops of hell? We had enough Jew haters at home."

"Don't worry. The Mexicans are easy-going people. Everything is *mañana* and *siesta*." Bentze showed off his Spanish. "Nothing bothers them. Except the earthquakes . . ."

"Earthquakes?"

"Little tremors. They occur very seldom," he added quickly. "You get used to them."

"I want to go home," Sheva had wept that night and on many following nights. "Everything's so different, so strange. The people are too dark, their clothes are too bright, the food's too spicy, the climate's too hot. And I'll never learn their language."

She was lonely. The few Jews who lived in Oaxaca had integrated into Mexican life. Two of them had married local women, and the others no longer observed Jewish festivals, customs or rituals. Sheva lit candles every Friday night, kept a calendar of the Jewish holy days, and prepared special dishes associated with the festivals, just as she had done in the shtetl. The idea of eating pork or mixing meat dishes with milk dishes was abhorrent to her. The only time she ate meat was when Bentze, on a business trip to Mexico City, brought back a kosher chicken.

Gershon was often away from home. He and Bentze travelled to outlying villages, selling cloth and other manufactured articles, and bringing back village crafts and the black pottery for which Oaxaca was famous. They planned to rent a shop in town when they had saved enough money, and take turns to travel into the country.

Sheva hated to be left on her own, especially after she fell pregnant. The only neighbour with whom she had contact was their landlady Juanita, a jolly, middle-aged woman who lived on the same square as her tenants. Juanita took pity on Sheva. She taught her some basic Spanish, and took her to the market, where she persuaded Sheva to buy different kinds of fruit and vegetables. Under Juanita's tutelage, Sheva learned enough Spanish to conduct simple conversations with the stallkeepers and with her neighbours. She was beginning to settle in.

"When the tremors begin," Juanita told Sheva one day, performing appropriate actions, "stand under the lintel of the main doorway and wait for them to pass. Don't run outside. But don't worry. The big quakes don't come often."

They came one day when Gershon and Bentze were out of town. The floor seemed to tilt, furniture slid around, glasses and crockery crashed down from the shelves, and the windows rattled in their frames. Sheva was about seven months pregnant, alone at home, and she panicked. She ran into Juanita's house, and together they stood under the lintel, holding on to one another. For once, even Juanita was silenced. She clung to Sheva, releasing her only to cross herself. A great deal of damage was done to the town, particularly to the 200-year-old Catholic church opposite their house.

"If this can happen to the Catholics," she cried when Gershon returned home later that evening, "imagine what's in store for the Jews! I want to leave! I want to go home!"

This was 1928, and there was no question of going "home". The extreme Lithuanian nationalists had entrenched themselves in power, the rights of minority groups had been further eroded, and Leib, at one stage, had had to go into hiding. Gershon was putting money aside as fast as he could. He had to get his family out of Lithuania before Leib, hothead that he was, was sent into exile. Or worse.

As the time drew nearer for Sheva to give birth, Juanita took her to the only doctor in town, a heavy drinker. Juanita extracted a promise from him to remain sober until the baby was born. He kept his word until the pregnancy went two weeks beyond term. Hauled out of a bar by Juanita and Gershon, he could barely stand on his feet as he breathed tequila fumes over her. In vain she called for Mother and Home. Impatient with the pace of the birth, the doctor used forceps.

Sheva, at the end of the long, painful labour, looked at the bloodied face of the child whose forehead had been dented by the forceps, and cried, "It is better she should die than be an imbecile!" The birth trauma would be dredged up whenever I displayed what my mother considered aberrant behaviour. Her worst fears were realised when, in my teens, I joined a Zionist–Socialist movement and announced that I was going to live on a kibbutz.

As an infant, however, I had not shown any signs of brain damage. The only fair-skinned, blond, green-eyed child in the district, I became a favourite with the neighbours, who drew us into the community. Bentze's mail-order bride arrived soon afterwards from Lithuania, together with Sheva's younger brother Joel.

By this time Bentze and Gershon had opened a shop in the town, and Joel, after he had learned a little Spanish, travelled into the country-side. Sheva was beginning to enjoy life in Oaxaca when, one after-noon, she was woken from her siesta by the sound of shooting and shouting. Grabbing me from the cot, she rushed into the courtyard to find a crowd gathered around a grotesque papier-mâché figure of a man with an enormous nose and horns. The men were shooting into the air, yelling, and throwing up their sombreros. The women were ululating and shaking their fists at the papier-mâché figure.

"What's happening?" Sheva asked Juanita.

"Today we celebrate a great religious holiday," Juanita explained. "Today is the day we kill the Jews."

"Have you ever seen a Jew?" Sheva clutched me to her breast.

"God forbid!" Juanita crossed herself. "That," she pointed to the evil-looking figure at the centre of the incensed crowd, "is a Jew."

Gershon, finally, gave in to Sheva's pressure to leave Mexico. Not even Bentze's entreaties could persuade Sheva to remain in a country where Jews were shot in courtyards. First papier-mâché Jews, she said, then real ones. She wanted to go to South Africa where her mother, sister and two other brothers had settled.

So it was that three years after their arrival in Mexico, Bentze accompanied them to the port of Veracruz, where they embarked for South Africa. Gershon never ceased to hanker after Oaxaca. Worse: in order to make the move, he had used up the savings with which he meant to bring his family out of Lithuania.

We arrived in South Africa in 1930, in the middle of the Depression. Unable to find work in Johannesburg, Gershon took a job in Shabani, a small mining town in Rhodesia, where we lived for two years. Only then did he have enough money to open a barbershop in Johannesburg.

"How is it possible," Leib wrote, breaking his silence of several years, "to live in the *goldene medina*, the golden country, and not have enough money to send to your mother? You are no doubt supporting the whole of Sheva's family."

"On the contrary," Gershon replied. "It is only by living with them in a cramped little house, that we are able to make ends meet. The streets of Johannesburg, contrary to rumour, are not paved with gold. Last month I had to borrow money to pay the rent."

Most Jewish immigrants, he explained, had neither money nor language. They tried, with mixed success, to find a place for themselves in a society which divided English-speakers from Afrikaners, and the blacks from everyone else. "For once, the Jews are not at the bottom of the social pile. If you are white, you are automatically privileged. Jews react to this evil system in two ways: we can't solve everyone's problems; we can barely cope with our own. Or: this is how the Jews were treated for centuries; what can we do to alleviate the lot of the blacks?" Gershon did not say which option he had chosen. Leib would not have understood that his political beliefs had been compromised by his need to survive. Leib did not reply to his letter.

From his mother, Gershon received a letter with the words of "A Brivale di Mammen".

> *A brivale di mammen,*
> *Zolst du mayn kind nisht farzamen,*
> *Shrayb geshvind, liebes kind,*
> *Shenk ir di nechome.*
> *Di mamme vet dayn brivale lezn,*
> *Un zi vert genezn,*
> *Heilst ir shmerts, ir bitter herts,*
> *Erkvikst ir di neshome . . .*

Write a letter to your mother, grant her this comfort. Her bitter heart will be comforted, her pain assuaged, her soul refreshed.

The song concludes with the son receiving news of his mother's death. Her last request had been that he should say the prayer for the dead.

Gershon had no defence against this kind of letter. He had no money to send, nor much prospect of earning enough to bring them to South Africa. His letters, consequently, trickled down to one or two a year, with an occasional enclosure of a small sum of money. With the outbreak of war in 1939, it was already too late to write a letter to his mother, a *brivale di mammen*. It would soon be time to say the prayer for the dead.

# GUY BUTLER

*a poem*

## MYTHS

Alone one noon on a sheet of igneous rock
I smashed a five-foot cobra's head to pulp;
Then, lifting its cool still-squirming gold
In my sweating ten separate fingers, suddenly
Tall aloes were also standing there,
Lichens were mat-red patches on glinting boulders,
Clouds erupted white on the mountain's edge,
All, all insisting on being seen.
Familiar, and terribly strange, I felt the sun
Gauntlet my arms and cloak my growing shoulders.

Never quite the same again
Poplar, oak or pine, no, none
Of the multifarious shapes and scents that breed
About the homestead, below the dam, along the canal,
Or any place where a European,
Making the most of a fistful of water, splits
The brown and grey with wedges of daring green –
Known as invaders now, alien,
Like the sounds on my tongue, the pink on my skin;
And, like my heroes, Jason, David, Robin Hood,
Leaving tentative footprints on the sand between
The aloe and the rock, uncertain if this
Were part of their proper destiny. Reading
Keats's Lamia and Saint Agnes' Eve
Beneath a giant pear tree buzzing with bloom
I glanced at the galvanized windmill turning
Its iron sunflower under the white-hot sky
And wondered if a Grecian or Medieval dream

Could ever strike root away from our wedges of green,
Could ever belong down there
Where the level sheen on new lucerne stops short:
Where aloes and thorns thrust roughly out
Of the slate blue shales and purple dolerite.

Yet sometimes the ghosts that books had put in my brain
Would slip from their hiding behind my eyes
To take on flesh, the sometimes curious flesh
Of an African incarnation.

One winter dusk when the livid snow
On Swaershoek Pass went dull, and the grey
Ash-bushes grew dim in smudges of smoke,
I stopped at the outspan place to watch,
Intenser as the purple shades drew down,
A little fire leaping near a wagon,
Sending its acrid smoke into the homeless night.
Patient as despair, eyes closed, ugly,
The woman stretched small hands towards the flames;
But the man, back to an indigo boulder,
Face thrown up to the sky, was striking
Rivers of sorrow into the arid darkness
From the throat of a battered, cheap guitar.

It seemed that in an empty hell
Of darkness, cold and hunger, I had stumbled on
Eurydice, ragged, deaf forever,
Orpheus playing to beasts that would or could not hear,
Both eternally lost to news or rumours of spring.

# DON MACLENNAN

*a poem*

## THOUGHT AND LANGUAGE
*(for Lionel)*

*What oft was thought, but ne'er so well express'd.* – Pope

As a clumsy student I was stung
by this ingenious apothegm
telling me how pedestrian I was.

In '49 you clomped into the lecture hall
banging the doors of 215,
knocking the lecture benches
with your case, making a racket as you groped
for pen and paper
to scrawl what seemed to me
gangling illegibilities across a page.

Now I see you've got things straight.
Reading your poetry
I've begun to feel
deep stirrings in my hollow trunk,
bees summoned by the sun,
grumbling to knowledge of intention.

How did you get so far beyond
that polished, empty eloquence?
Doesn't the fact that you made honey
in your wrecked body
mean there are more truths
than those we merely suffer for?

# FRANCES HUNTER

*a poem*

## DREAMWRITING
*(Villanelle)*

The world is different in dead of night,
when truth is netted like a butterfly.
In dreams where poetry begins I write:

it seems as if I'm just a neophyte,
but surely my unconscious cannot lie.
The world is different in dead of night

and finally I nearly have it right
on why we yearn and suffer, live and die.
In dreams where poetry begins I write

and new-found meaning caught by ear and sight
may be a ground on which I can rely.
The world is different in dead of night,

when everything is clear and full of light
and essences I grasp could make one cry.
In dreams where poetry begins I write,

but when from sleep I wake, the words take flight:
I can't remember, even though I try.
The world is different in dead of night.
In dreams where poetry begins I write.

# GUS FERGUSON

## *two poems*

*How could I resist writing in praise of an editor who described one of my first published poems as 'delicious'? Among the qualities that I love and respect in Lionel, in his various guises as poet, essayist, publisher, novelist, mentor, critic and friend, are his gentleness that complements his fiercely uncompromising integrity which forces his critics to re-evaluate the moral power of liberalism, his genuine and articulate compassion, and his glorious sense of fun. This last quality is mostly manifest in private conversation (he desperately needs a Boswell) as a precise, deliberate and glittering wit and a delightfully sly, self-mocking humour. Glimpses of this appear often in his prose and now and then in his poetry – his humour is nicely caught in the brief poem, 'Pool', from* Journal of a New Man: *Where I'm deepest/ you may discern/ a few muddy secrets./ My surface contains/ the whole open sky.*

### CARPE DIEM
*for Lionel Abrahams*

A goldfish in a goldfish bowl
Surveyed the world outside
And felt completely in control
Of everything he spied.

Thought he: "I'm in my element,
My glass, a faithful lens
That shows a foggy firmament
That wobbles and distends.

"An ever-shifting universe
Of ectoplasmic forms
Beyond all known parameters
Of finite, fishy norms.

"And yet, this mystic interplay
Does serve me with such love
That I am blessèd everyday
With manna from above."

## LIMERICK

There once was a poet called: Gus
Who made an ecological fuss.
He'd rant and he'd rail
On the rights of the snail
'Til his lettuce cried: "What about us?!"

# BENJAMIN MOLEFI

*a poem*

## SLEEPING IN THE CHURCH

Depending on the tall grey building is no sin.
Yea, depending on it for security and shelter is no murder.
The hard cold floor being my Sealy Posturepedic mattress,
my arms are my pillow.

Through that window I sail like a snake,
a non-poisonous and undangerous snake,
a snake tamed by circumstances man-made.

Someone wanted me to live like a silly little rat,
that silly little rat which gives sleepers sleepless nights.
I wanted to live like a snail
which carries its own shelter and responsibilities.

I went to Ntate Sebutsa where he is a night-watchman,
asking him to allow me to take shelter in the building.
But he had no authority, so he sent me
to ask Mme Mmaselekane to permit me.
But because I was afraid to face Mme Mmaselekane,
as she was my guide, educationally and otherwise,
I decided to sail through the window unauthorised.

Through that window I have to sail in like a harmless snake.
Some tired nights my sleeping time gets to be late:
when I find people churching in the grey tall building
I have to join them like a church-goer.

Sometimes when the authorities were around
I sheltered myself with Ntate Manyika,

an old man who had no place to sleep
so he slept in the maroon truck, where I also
sometimes took shelter on cold or rainy nights.

The maroon truck moved to nowhere.
Now Ntate Manyika and I had no place to sleep.

Through that window I have to sail in like a snake.
Depending on the grey tall building is no sin,
but one day I shall live like a snail
which carries its own shelter and responsibilities.

# PATRICK CULLINAN

## *a passage from a work in progress*

*It would be just, I believe, and relevant, [. . .] to present the following two anecdotes [. . .].*

*The first concerns [some] conversations with David Wright, referred to in [Lionel's] essay 'Revenant to Eden'. In this piece Lionel talks of how he, spastic, communicates with David who is totally deaf. Lionel simply uses his typewriter to record his side of the conversation while David leans over him, waiting to reply. I am then brought into the account and described as 'growing lyrical with pleasure over the sheer richness of what was passing between himself and David' (using these same means to conduct our conversation). Absolutely true, but I must now add that the most memorable exchange of all was one where all three of us, David, Lionel and myself, sat drinking red wine and writing on slips of paper. Apart from laughter, few audible sounds or words were uttered. We communicated or 'communed' (Lionel's word) with enormous pleasure and, I believe, appreciable wit, in this manner. I refer not to an event of half an hour or so but to a long evening's discussion which ended after midnight. It was Lionel who provided the spark that set us so alight. But I see this occasion as just one of many happy days and nights inspired by Lionel's talk, those conversations on poetry and ballyhoo, personalities and pappadums, or whatever else has taken our fancy.*

*The second scene I recall, also with clarity and much joy, is set in Botswana. One day in the middle seventies Lionel and I decided we'd go and see Bessie Head in her village of Serowe. We thought it would be nice to have Bessie on our Bateleur Press list. As it happened we did not get to publish anything of hers; but it didn't matter – we both thoroughly enjoyed our stay in the presence of that dynamic personality.*

*We arrived at Serowe in the late afternoon. Bessie gave us tea and then sent us on to a local hotel, 'The co-op' she called it. When we got there my heart sank. It was set on a hillside and to reach the hotel reception a steep flight of stairs confronted us. It would be a major obstacle for Lionel to negotiate these steps, twice or more a day.*

*We made it somehow to the lobby at the top of the stairs. When we had booked in we found that there was yet another set of steps to climb to our bedroom. We were surrounded by friendly but highly inquisitive Botswana villagers and as soon as we set off to attempt the second flight it was as though a signal had been given. Spontaneously, two young men pushed from the crowd around us, gently seized Lionel under the arms and whisked him up the stairs to the door of the hut where we were to sleep.*

*After that we had only to appear at the top or bottom of the hotel and willing hands would grab this chuckling man of letters and transport him to his destination. What has stuck in my memory is not the bizarreness of the scene but the warmth and joy on all sides that those rides or flights up and down the stairs evoked. There was a kind of victory in the fun of it. It was a strange way to triumph but Lionel and the helping villagers were triumphant.*

*It is Lionel the communer I celebrate and salute.*

*– from the introduction to* Lionel Abrahams: A Reader

## A BOY'S OWN ADVENTURE

*(Tom is a nine-year-old schoolboy. He is at home for the winter holidays from his boarding-school in Johannesburg. The year is 1941.)*

His rides, often lasting whole mornings or afternoons, were a way of proving himself, of competing as best he could, in his circumstances, with the boy heroes of the Henty[1] novels. His resolution had been strongly reinforced when he became a Boy Scout[2] at the beginning of

---

[1] George Alfred Henty's books are scarcely heard of, and even more seldom read, these days. But in the 1940s, school libraries were full of his 'historical novels' for boys. They epitomised the British Imperial mission and its supposed virtues, even though the eighty-odd stories were set in vastly different historical times and places, from Carthage to Pretoria. But that didn't change the character of the boy hero – for indeed the same lad tended to turn up in each succeeding narrative – whether he was a Roman or an American: he was always manly, never lied, shunned introspection or an interest in the arts, and was always as boring as the preposterous English Public Schoolboy he was modelled on. Henty died on his yacht in 1902, just the right year for a doughty defender of the Empire to go.

[2] At this time it was official policy, as declared by Baden-Powell himself, that boys could only become Scouts after the age of eleven. The headmaster, however, believed that the war effort would be better served if the boys of his school were invested two years earlier, that is to say after their ninth birthday. An early knowledge of knots, stalking and Morse code would, the headmaster held, enable his pupils to resist the Fascist menace more readily. No one cared to disagree with him, especially as he claimed to have known 'old BP' (Baden-Powell) while beginning his career as a schoolmaster in England. And who was there to dispute either or any of his claims?

the school year. At his investiture he had promised to do his duty to God and the King and it was good to feel part of a world-wide brotherhood of loyal, brave and venturesome boys who had made the same commitment. Perhaps, Tom thought, the real heroes fighting 'up north', like his cousin Vyvyan, the fighter pilot, would also approve of his dedication.

But in order to match and prove his growing resolve to be a steadfast and plucky boy, Tom needed a challenge.

In widely separated places in the plantation there were prospecting pits sunk, as everybody knew, by order of old Sir William, his grandfather. This took place before the trees were planted, probably shortly after the end of the Boer War. It wasn't certain what he was looking for, perhaps he wanted more clay: some additional deposits for 'the works'. It was even possible he only wanted to know what lay beneath that portion of his rocky Transvaal veld. You never could tell with the old man.

The results of the drilling must have been disappointing because no development followed. The pits were fenced off with barbed wire, and the gum trees were planted around them. Only a few people now knew of them, giving them a glamour, a mystery which attracted Tom powerfully. He started to explore the holes from the surface. Around all of them, the encompassing fence had long since rusted and it was easy to get right to the edge and from there to look down into their depths.

Here lay Tom's hinterland, his underworld. Here was his challenge. He was going to explore one of the pits and if that went well he would explore them all. He knew it would be hard work getting up and down the shaft but he rejected the problem without further thought. It was not his body's strength that was in question, the real test was whether his pluck under danger would hold.

Tom chose the deepest pit he could find. It was all of twenty feet to the bottom and, should something go wrong once he was down there, it was probably out of sight and earshot from the nearest road. Another danger, so Tom had heard, was that wild animals, particularly snakes, often fell into the pits. To make sure on this last point, Tom examined the shaft at midday, when the force of sunlight penetrated and covered the floor of the hole. There was no movement down there, not even the least slither of a snake.

Without surprise, Tom did note once more that this shaft, like all the others in the forest, had a peculiarity. Peering down, he could see that over the years rain had eroded the deepest part, had eaten it away so that the lowest third or so had formed a bulb. It made the same shape as the test tube he used in Science at school: a straight shaft developing into a globe below.

The next morning, immediately after breakfast, he brought his bicycle out on to the kitchen lawn, pumped up both wheels, strapped on his sheath knife, tied a hank of rope to his belt and, with Bella bounding and barking alongside, was off down the dirt road to the forest.

Twenty minutes later Tom reached the pit. His skin was tingling from the rasp of the autumn morning air and from the excitement brimming in his chest. He began to prepare for the coming ordeal – and, as he set about it, he felt watched by many unseen but approving eyes. As he tied one end of the quarter-inch cord to a gum sapling, using a fisherman's knot, he could not stop the swank that moved into and with his fingers and which passed, so naturally, to each gesture following: the pace backward, the testing of the pressure on the line, the debonair wipe of sweat from his brow.

Even Bella seemed aware that something unusual and important was happening. She cocked her head at her master, whining uncertainly, and then gave a few tentative yaps. Tom knelt beside her, stroking her head and ears as he muttered, "Good girl, Bella. Good girl. Stay!" Finally, he tickled the underside of her chin, stood up and walked to the edge of the pit, paying out the rope until he could see it drop right down, plumb to the floor.

Slowly, grasping the line, one fist clasped close above the other, his tackies almost flat against the wall, Tom began his descent.

At first it seemed to be working. He edged down as slowly as he could, taking the strain on his arms, shuffling his feet against the moist side of the shaft. Then, as the rubber soles of his shoes began to slip, he lost control of his legs and was violently jerked upright, hanging, but bumping against the side. Desperately, he tried to get a purchase, to push his feet up against the wall once more, but now his fists were starting to lose their grip and he began to slither faster and faster towards the bottom. He hit the earth hard, crumpling onto his stomach, driving the breath from his lungs.

For a brief moment Tom blacked out, winded, unconsciously gasping, sobbing for air. Coming to, he felt an acute cold fill his body and he thought he was dying. In time, however, as he lay there, he heard his breath sawing in and out until, gradually, he began to feel it expel and suck in a nearly even rhythm.

He realised then that he was going to live.

Raising his head, Tom looked straight at a snake's head, an arm's length away, swaying just above the ground, the tongue flicking, dabbing delicately towards him. He sat up suddenly and the small brown creature slid sideways off into the farthest edge of the pit, where the underground globe had eroded most deeply, forming its darkest shadow.

As Tom knelt and then stood, he vomited a whole stomachful of mabela porridge onto the floor of the pit. Swaying slightly, staring at the mess at his feet before him, he felt a rush of fear, and with this came the blatant insight that he was 'a bloody stupid little boy'.

A-bloody-stupid-little-boy. And as the words redoubled and repeated in his head he could hear his father uttering and isolating each word, the scorn and chilled anger far worse than any beating. But above all he was scared. The snake was the least worry. As far as Tom could tell it wasn't even a poisonous one. The voice continued in his head: *Not a puffadder or mamba at all. You know those. Probably just a grass or mole snake. So forget it, forget that. Concentrate on now, what to do now. God help me, Gentle Jesus please help me! No. Calm down. Be a Scout, be a man, Be Prepared.[3] Don't panic! Get out of here – that's what the rope's for.*

The rope dangled before his eyes. Without thinking, he grabbed it with both fists. The pain was astonishing, as shocking and swift as a tooth being pulled. When he jerked his hands loose he was appalled to see that his palms were stripped to a sappy pulp of blood and flesh. The sight set him trembling uncontrollably: the cold he had felt earlier had returned. It seemed to be at once both a trigger and a response to his terror.

While he gazed at the blood dripping down his fingers, Tom slowly became aware of a noise that had been at the furthest reach of his hearing since he had landed on the floor of the pit. It was Bella howling: she was still on guard up there, twenty feet above him in the blessed sunlight and where the wind hissed through the leaves of gum-trees. He tried to cry out to her, to shout his joy that there was still this creature alive and close to him. But his voice had dwindled to a croak and it took two more attempts before his cries carried through to her. The howling stopped and then a furious tattoo of barks followed,

---

3 The Boy Scout motto was 'Be Prepared' or simply 'BP'. It is no coincidence that these were also the initial letters of Baden-Powell.

The Boy Scout Promise which had to be made in front of the whole troop went as follows:

'On my honour I promise that I will do my best –
To do my duty to God and the King.
To help other people at all times.
To obey the Scout Law.'

a doggy palaver of relief and frustration, confusion and joy.

'The situation was still desperate' – as Henty might have written – but as Bella's din continued to reverberate above him, Tom decided 'to make the best of the bad deal fate had dealt him. Summoning all the resources that a plucky spirit in a healthy body had given him, the stalwart lad determined to find a way out of this perilous dilemma.'

Well, at least the lad felt a little more cheerful. Unhappily, however, it soon became clear that there was, in fact, nothing he could do.

When planning the adventure, there were two factors that he had not taken into account. First of all, the rope was much too thin. It would have taken a trained gymnast or Indian rope-trick specialist to keep a grip on that meagre quarter-inch of sisal, whether going up or going down. Secondly, due to the eroding away of the wall, the final six to eight feet of the shaft provided no surface at all for a climber's feet to brace against.

Only one course of action remained open to him. He opened his mouth and yelled, "Help!"

The sun was much higher now, it was about eleven-thirty already, and now its light began to reach the hole and it became warmer. For the next half hour, sitting in the expanding patch of sunlight, Tom shouted as hard as he could, even though he knew his cries were muffled by the walls of the pit. He began to feel very tired, and even though the blood on his hands had encrusted, they still ached badly. His chest too, where he had struck the earth, was badly bruised and the sporadic shouting made it still more painful. Only Bella was able to keep up her continuous howling and barking.

And so it was that Tom suddenly realised that his dog was whining with pleasure and that there were voices above him and faces at the rim of the shaft, peering down at him. Voices descended, resonating slightly in the narrow space:

"Eh Baasie, u enzanjani Ia?"

"Hau, yena umtwana ga makuluskop!"

"Hay seuntjie, het jy daar ingeval of hoe?"

Tom waved his arms but stayed sitting where he was. He found it hard to concentrate on what they were saying. Moments later he saw a man shinning down a thick rope and then there was a deeply sunburned face, a white man squatting beside him and staring carefully at him.

"You's Mister Tony's boy, nay?"

Tom nodded, feeling more and more dazed. He felt the rope being passed under his shoulders and secured, then a shout and a jerk as he swung into the air.

When he woke the next morning Tom was in his own bed and Bella was nuzzling his pillow, trying to lick his face. His hands were swaddled in bandages and his chest was even more tightly bound in swathes of white cloth.

A movement on the other side of the bed drew his head round, as Mary bent down to embrace him. "My, you gave us such an awful fright – and if it hadn't been for Bella's barking and the men passing by . . ." was all she said.

"But who were the men, Mum?"

"The forestry team from the Works, old Labuschagne's span."

"And it was Bella that saved me?"

"Of course."

Tom sighed happily, smiled, but said nothing. How could he explain to his mother that he had just taken part in the perfect plucky-lad-rescued-by-loyal-dumb-friend story.

# ABRAM HLABATAU

*a poem*

## JUNE '76

The date matters not.
What matters are the events:
the sky was filled with black smoke.
White teargas kept people on track.
We were bullets
shot from the muzzle of the school.
My slate was smashed.
My face was wetted by tears, mucus and sweat.
My trousers were watered.
We were bullets
flying in all directions
but aiming at home.
When that target was hit
the bullet was kept for safety.
The date matters not.
I only knew what was happening
five years later.

# JONATHAN MORGAN

## *a story*

**TENINEIGHTNOOIT**

### 10

My rearview mirror gave me no warning of him, he just rattled past my side window, first the front wheels that came off some child's tri-cycle, then the back ones that had spokes and definitely had ball-bearings. There he was in a fucking go-cart overtaking me down Bezuidenhout.

Once he'd passed me I flicked my indicator, swung round him and sped onwards to my 2:30. On the dash's digital clock, two fluorescent dots flashed. When the one was on, the other was off. Okay, so the car really belonged to Harry Oppenheimer, if you want to be like that, but no-one could say I drove a skadonk. My iskorokoro days were over. I had to wear a suit and tie but I got to drive a 5-speed, 1800, out-of-the-box Honda Ballade. It was only on my way home that I realized exact-ly what it was I'd overtaken.

That same week, my boss, Barry Kiebel, calls me on the internal line. I tuck in my shirt, check my fly is up and make for his office. I have to squeeze past Alice his secretary, who's struggling to contain a three-metre fax from Singapore. I wonder if he wants to see me about the Rosebank deal. Maybe they signed last night. Even 0,001% x 12 000 square metres x R50 x 12 months is a win, especially for Barry. He gets a full 1% even though I've done all the work. Barry's not in his chair, he's standing where the window ought to be in this viewless cube. "Sorry Jim, head office has frozen your post."

### 9

I keep on thinking about it. I try to remember what kind of steering it had. If I go for a walk, I go down Bezuidenhout, if I drive, I go down

Bezuidenhout, but I never see him. I even set aside one day to find him and walk around asking domestic workers and watchmen and people in the park if they've seen him. One day I notice something under a Jacaranda tree outside a block of flats called Bobby Locke Place, near the water-tower. This time I stop and get out of my 'new' car which has no clock at all. I'm not wearing a shirt and with my flip-flops I kick the thing's tyres. It's covered in lilac petals I brush off with my hand to get a better look.

This isn't the machine that passed me doing 50-plus down Bezuidenhout. Its wheels are very small and all spokeless, as if they've come off a Checkers shopping trolley. The steering mechanism is more showy than functional. Instead of the usual wooden T-bar which is essentially a pivoting crucifix controlled by ropes, this one has an actual steering-column made out of a steel rod with an enamel dog's dish fastened to its end.

Some kids are hanging about. "Is the go-cart yours? . . . Is this yours?" The one little boy covers his eyes with his hands and giggles and the two little girls copy him. Is it this easy for a child to make difficult things go away? It's boiling down to a choice between my Zulu and their English but it turns out they only speak Portuguese. The oldest boy knows how to say 'sweet' in English and I walk over to the corner café and buy them a crunchie and a few chappies each. Outside the café stands an almost regular-looking Durban surfer type wearing Gotcha baggies and long sleeves. "S'cuse me sir, can you spare a rand for bread and milk."

I usually only get going around midday but the next morning I'm up and fully dressed by 9 am. Under the red-and-white seat I leave a note – 'If you know where the other fast go-cart is, contact me, 3 Diamond Court, Umhlazi Road, Yeoville. Reward offered!' – The kids are nowhere in sight. Maybe they're at crèche. I walk over to the café. When I'd bought them sweets, I'd noticed the newspapers were far from the counter. The owner of the Ace Café near my place is getting pissed off at me, scanning the job classifieds without buying. I support the changes and everything but affirmative action is beginning to get on my tits.

8

The best dice I remember, was the one down Atholl street which was Alan Levin's street and quite far from my house. It was a good street for dicing because, one, it was downhill all the way, two, it had no major turns, three, it wasn't too busy. It was a bad street for dicing because, one, it was downhill all the way and had too many stop streets, two, it didn't have enough turns to slow you down but that's what learning curves are.

At the top near Marc Myers's house, five Bata school shoes touch the tar. *10 – 9 – 8*. Even using both sides of the road there isn't enough space for all the carts. Marc's youngest sister Caron is down near the Jukskei river where Atholl road ends, holding a dishcloth. His middle sister Barbie, who I sort of smaak, is at the next stop street up, and his older sister Margot, with the orange hair, who's got the highest IQ in the school, is at the stop street nearest us.

In pole position is Marc's cart which is technically okay – his father's an engineer and has big bucks – but we know he won't win. *– 7 – 6 – 5*. Marc likes to keep his foot on the brake. Alan's dad isn't exactly short either. His cart has full-on bicycle wheels at the back, shiny new bolts, and the longest T-bar you can imagine. The whole thing is painted matt-black. Gary, who was later to die in his MG on the Durban road, has a small unimpressive-looking but fast machine. *– 4 – 3 – 2*. A lot of thought and time has gone into my cart. The wooden Coke box I sit in has an extremely low centre of gravity, the axles are threaded and greased right across. The ropes are nylon and all the woodwork is sandpapered for improved aerodynamics. And ever since my little sister Jones began walking, I've got spoked pram wheels, front and back. The other driver isn't even a contender, it's Gary's brother Craig, on one of those yellow-and-green plastic scooters you get at BP garages. *– 1*.

Marc's garden-boy Elias has to hold Marc's and Alan's and Gary's dogs 'cos they always follow us and cut us off. *– Zero!*

*Move over Craig! move over!* Where Atholl Road crosses Sally's Alley, which is where Margot is, we're all bunched up together, sort of neck and neck. We still haven't really picked up much speed. She doesn't whistle, which means there are no cars coming and we rattle past her. Here where the road dips a lot and Marc brakes, Alan and Gary and I pull ahead. Before we get to Barbie, who can't whistle, Marc chickens out. Gary's wheels are touching mine like in that Ben Hur chariot race at the bioscope. We are now passing Alan's house. I'm so low I can almost see under their white picket fence which passes me like a card trick in slow motion, slat by slat. I look down between my legs and I see my cart eating the line in the middle of the road.

I hear Barbie scream. I look up and she's hanging onto the stop sign with one hand, jumping up and down in her green Fairways school dress. All I hear is my name. Where the two roads meet, I ramp like Evel Knievel. As my front wheels take off, Alan's mom comes round the corner in her blue Valiant. I see the bottom of her exhaust pipe which nearly hits me on the side of my head. I hear her shouting and hooting as my back wheels land. Then the tar ends. Caron's waving the red chequered dishcloth in my face. "The winner! *You're the winner!* Where are all the others?" I prang into the long reeds near the river.

### 7

Two yellowbilled kites fly low over a mielie field, eyes peeled for rodents. Their deeply forked tails cast shadows like a pair of cursors moving across a computer screen. The male, who has a more rufous underpart, flies a metre below the female. Gary guns his bright red 1948 MG towards Durban. Next to him is Danielle. Her father owns a chain of hotels. They're both wearing Raybans. They see none of this. A crack in the windscreen beginning below the wipers grows each time an articulated truck barrels past them. Whoosh! Suddenly the male yellowbill is ripped out of the sky. His right wing catches a barbed wire fence. A herd of Brahman bulls graze in a field of lucerne. A woman harvests wild spinach morogo off the island in the middle of the road. Down Van Reenen's Pass the car in front of Gary stops suddenly. He brakes hard. His oxygen tanks and scuba stuff on the back window ledge fly forward and crash into his skull.

### 6

That Friday was a bad one. I got up at 7 to beat the queue to register for UIF. At the red robot at the corner of Rockey and Harrow I pull up beside a navy blue BMW. It's shiny enough for me to read, in its reflection, what is written on a cardboard sign around a man's neck. 'NO FOOD, NO JOB'. Nothing depresses me more than these guys. The curve of the BM's door and its tinted windows grotesquely distort the beggar's image. He walks up to his own reflection, rubs his stomach and mouths the words, "I'm hungry." It's a horror scene from a silent blue documentary I've watched before from behind tightly rolled up windows.

At the unemployment office I check in at a little counter with a glass window. It has two holes: one at the bottom, rectangular; the other is round, at mouth level. Out of the bottom one comes a little red vinyl disc with the number '138' on it as well as a lime-green form. Through the top hole, a woman's voice, "Take a seat on the bench and wait for your number."

I'd tried to get there early but 137 people are in front of me, sitting on low wooden benches, not much higher than the ones we used for gym in primary school. I sit down next to a man called Johannes Moloi. He used to work in the telephone department. Now he lives in an unused toilet in Park Station. I know this because I help him fill out his address on the form. On the way home, I get stuck in Albert Street and pay R100 to get towed back to Yeoville.

Friday nights at the Tandoor on Rockey Street are okay if there's a good band and you've got enough money for a few beers. Sitting around and clinging to the walls are all these desperately single people looking unapproachable. The band call themselves the Zap Dragons and act out a whole lot of shit rather than actually play music. Their lead singer wears tie-dyed long-johns, an electric guitar, and has green hair and a weak chin. Just before midnight I walk out and by twelve I'm back in my flat in Diamond Court, the same one I moved into the day I got out the army. Then it seemed bohemian. I run a bath – Diamond Court has the hottest water you've ever felt. An old man called Enoch shovels coal and fires up a huge rusty boiler in the basement every morning.

I'm driving down Bezuidenhout. A black guy in my old go-cart – with spoked wheels back and front – pulled by Alsatians in harnesses, tries to overtake me. I force him off the road. I get up and climb out of bed to splash cold water on my face. I haven't washed my sheets since December.

Early Saturday morning I'm up, make tea straight from the tap and walk down the road to the Bobby Locke flats to see if my note's been found. Neither the kids nor the go-cart are there. I then walk home up Bezuidenhout to see if I can't see the other go-cart. I ask a few people if they haven't seen it. I peer through an electronically controlled security gate into a driveway littered with scrap metal, and a huge Alsatian springs at me. I go see a doctor at the Gen and get a prescription for sleeping pills.

Behind the water tower there's this guy who fixes cars off the road in the veld near the ZCC temple. "Will you come have a look at my car?" He agrees to look for twenty bucks. We drive down to my flat in his Peugeot 404. His nephew, who is his apprentice, comes with him. I sit in the backseat. It has an armrest that folds down. He tells me he can get me a new clutch and put it in. "R1 100."

As I walk home, in my head I start writing a book complete with photos. 'Ten Sure-Clean Ways to Commit Suicide Within the Safety of Your Own Home'. Chapter 1: Suffocation. Chapter 2: Drugs. 3: Combinations (Drugs and Suffocation).

5

When my first unemployment cheque comes I walk down to Louis Botha Avenue and catch a bus to Norwood Hypermarket. Outside the main entrance where the trolleys are parked, next to a man with a white stick and a guitar, is a security guard with his guard dog. I notice the dog is breathing heavily. Its eyes are red slits, and little bubbles of white foam pop out of its nostrils. "Your dog is sick."

"It's not my dog. My dog is a very good dog. Now he is in Pretoria Pick 'n Pay."

From his uniform I see he works for Sting Security. I look up their number and phone them from the public phone just past the trolleys. Mrs Anderson answers and tells me her husband gets the dogs from some or other kennels. "Sting are responsible for the guards but not the dogs." She gives me the number of the kennels. A man answers and tells me his boss is not there.

I get a trolley and push it to the back of the store, to the hardware section. Into it I load a 3 metre length of 8 by 5 hardwood, two 2 metre lengths of 10 by 2 knotty pine, two reinforced steel threaded axles, a packet of nails and a ski rope. Along with a hammer and a saw it comes to over R300. I ask them to wrap it all up in black plastic. "We only deliver if it comes to over R500." I catch a taxi home.

On the staircase with all this stuff I pass the new girl who's just moved in to number 4.

"Hi."

"Hi."

I leave all the stuff in the plastic wrapping on the couch and sleep the whole afternoon. At 4pm the sound of a game wakes me up. I look out my bedroom window down on to yarmulkes and a bouncing basketball in the neighbour's yard. I have a shower and unwrap the plastic without breaking it. Past midnight Mr Cooper the caretaker knocks on my door. "I've had four complaints." There are only five other flats in the block. I wonder if the new girl complained. I stop using the hammer and make some sketches. Tomorrow I'll go look for wheels.

# 4

In a junk shop on Kitchener Avenue full of Dunlop Maxplys in wooden presses, ice skates and Mixmasters, I get directions to a second hand bicycle shop on Jules Street. Jules Street is pretty far south but turns out to be worth it. The bike shop also repairs lawnmowers. Behind the counter hangs a portrait of Basil Botha in a maroon school uniform. Next to this hang two framed Standard 8 certificates from Boksburg High School. He passed both Accountancy and Afrikaans (higher grade, over 70%).

I lie. "I'm making a go-cart for my nephew."

He takes me into the back room which is full of wheels and parts and lawnmowers and engines. "Do you want to put a motor on it?"

"No."

I walk out the shop with two pairs of excellent spoked wheels.

One night I'm lying in bed, thinking about a Vietnam movie – how a black guy in a trench injects air into his veins and pops his heart – and I hear what sounds like a power saw.

I make lots of little trips down Bezuidenhout Street to Bellevue Hardware. People get to know me. I spend a morning on the park bench with a little man called Paul Jakobs whose skin is the colour of apricots. He's got school blazers from eight different schools. Paul was born in Standerton and tells me he's walked to Cape Town and back more times than he can remember. "I remember Yeoville when it still had trams and long before that when it was farms." He loves wandering, he's a professional tramp. I see him looking for stuff in dustbins and asking white people for money. A piano teacher in Muller Street lets him stay in her back room. He's settling down. Paul's seen the go-cart but can't remember when or where. Maybe it was in 1943 when he first walked through Yeoville.

The girl from number 4 knocks on my door. She's wearing short mustard dungarees. "Can I use your phone?"

"It's been cut off."

"What are you making in your flat?"

I tell her I'm fixing things.

I collect up all my coke bottles and walk down to the Ace. The owner no longer minds if I don't buy the paper. Sometimes he laughs and winks at me when nothing is funny. I see that Marc, who now owns a chain of fast-food outlets, is advertising for managers. They pay two-and-a-half grand a month. In my lounge are four finished go-carts. The only thing Alan's needs is a coat of matt-black.

This will be my last unemployment cheque. I'm reading comics at the CNA and I see this Alternative Technology magazine with an article on pedal power. There's this whole rave about fossil fuels and saving the planet and what-what, but there's also this photo of an incredible three-wheeler-tricycle-type-rickshaw-contraption. In the photo is a Californian with a really long beard, half lying down, pedalling the three-wheeler with a canopy through a redwood forest. I tear out the page and stuff it into my shirt.

I wait in the queue outside the post office to use the phone. I've got my own Telkom phone card/foonkaart with a rhino on it. I could have chosen any of the big five. The whole place smells of piss. I pick up the receiver but I can't do it. Marc was a prick. If it wasn't for his old man he'd be nothing. That night I hear the power saw again. I wait for Cooper to complain. The sun wakes me up. There's still some Rice Crispies in the box, but there's no fucking milk. I stare at a rotten tomato sitting by itself in the 100-litre two-door fridge I bought last year from some people in Sandton who went to live in Canada. I slam the fridge door. "Fuck this, I'll phone him." I walk down Bezuidenhout to Rockey Street telling myself I won't get freaked by the Rastas who never remember I don't skyf. When they try sell me poisons, I just shrug and show them my elbows and palms. It feels like a very Jewish gesture. To be honest, I feel like shooting them. And the men at the robots. And the street kids. I bet they'd be happier. On the way to the phones I stop to play a few games of pinball. Nick, Renos's father, who owned the café, used to shout at Gary, "You brekke de glas you pay." Fuck that. I thump the glass. My favourite machine is Billy the Kid. I still have the moves. Usually his six guns blaze while I clock up free games. Today I TILT and TILT and TILT and TILT. Eight fucking rand. Shit. Time to do it, it's time to fucking do it.

The smell of filter coffee, fried eggs and Wachenheimer's kosher sausages waft out of the open glass windows of Cracker's Deli. I don't want to see anyone I know. I walk past the bank. Is that me, the thin oke with NEDBANK in his head?

It's almost time to buy a new telephone card.

His secretary answers. I ask to speak to him. Is it business or personal? Mr Myers's in a meeting, would I like to leave a message?

*Generic name – Fluoxetine.*
*Trade name – Prozac.*
*Description – Anti-depressant.*
*Special precautions – Do not drive a motor vehicle or operate machinery after ingesting.*
*Side effects – Tremors, impotence, diarrhea, insomnia, amnesia, constipation, dizziness, palpitations.*

The new girl is struggling to open her door. She's holding sheets of plywood and a packet from Bellevue Hardware. I help her with her things. She tells me she makes flying hippo mobiles.

"I'm Rita"

"Jim."

She has an old wood-and-glass sweet counter with hundreds of drawers full of fishing line, rivets, nails, tubes of paint, beads and marbles. There's no need for labels. You can see what's in each drawer through the glass. Nick had one like this in his café.

I need to lie down.

Bye.

Rest of the day, I don't get up.

Next day only to make tea.

I say get up and I say can't get up.

Get up just get up.

I knock on her door.

"Come in. Have you finished fixing?" Dozens of hippos hang from the pressed ceiling. If you pull the lead sinker they beat their wings.

I wonder what she knows. Short red hair and freckles. I think of joining the dots with a koki pen. My heart kind of gets an erection.

I say, "Come I'll show you what I made."

She leaves her door unclosed. We walk across the landing to number 3, past a dead pot plant.

I hope my key won't stick. I walk in front of her to my lounge.

"Woweee!"

I look at my flip flops.

"Four! Let's ride them." Her voice seems very loud.

They're not for riding.

Rita gets into mine. She keeps one foot on the Oregon pine floorboard and kickstarts herself. The wheels go round and she ends up in front of the TV. A red tilted head grins at me over a shoulder. I shrug.

"Okay. But only late tonight, after 12. At zero hundred hours."

She arcs two red eyebrows at me.

We pull the carts to the top of the hill. I let her use Gary's. The ZCC people are chanting and drumming and dancing. The wheels squish vrot Jacaranda flowers. Our shadows disappear under every street light. Neither of us touches the brakes. We pull sharply on our ropes at the bottom and broadslide into Rockey Street.

We're pulling the go-carts back to Diamond Court when the gang of ZCC men and women in green-and-white robes and crooked staffs and cow-hide drums pass us.

"Wanna come in for Horlicks?"

I take the folded picture of the rickshaw from the magazine out my pocket. "Will you help me build it?"

She won't let me use the go-carts for parts.

She loves Basil Botha's certificates. She calls Standard 8 his renaissance period.

We spend R170 which is nearly all her money.

The Yeoville police station is bombed. One night there's a thunderstorm. I wake up and run out onto the balcony naked, shouting, "Fuck this country, I can't take it anymore, can't you stop it? Please stop it!" She leads me back inside "It's only thunder, it's only thunder."

1

I'm pedalling the rickshaw down Bezuidenhout, reclining and looking up at the branches and the telephone wires. When I get to the library parking lot, there's this cop in his black leggings and white helmet. I can't believe what I'm seeing. This old man with a go-cart is getting a traffic ticket. I pull up beside them. The old man's wearing dark glasses fastened in the one hinge with copper telephone wire. His shirt has four giant yellow and black squares. His skin is black-black. His hair is almost as white as the cop's helmet. He's a bit gaunt but he stands well over six foot and has the body of a retired javelin thrower.

The cart is amazing. A cracked, beige, push-button telephone under the dash. The driver's seat is a piece of foam, upholstered in an old Mike's Kitchen plastic table cloth. A passenger seat, a running-board and seat belts, a rear-view mirror. At the back – next to one of those blue-and-white bumper stickers with the two doves that say I'M COMMITTED TO PEACE, ARE YOU? – he's sticky-taped a picture of Johnny Clegg and his wife. The cart's even got an old TJ number plate.

I get out of my machine. "What the hell are you doing giving this man a ticket ? He can't fucking afford it!" The cop looks up and winks at me. He jerks his thumb under his book of tickets at the old man. I'm standing between them. I look at the ticket. It's written in pencil.

*Name: ALFEUS MOHASANA*
*Registration number: TJ 43999*
*Amount of fine: R100*

Alfeus, in his shades held together with wire, next to his vehicle, reaches, proud as shit, for the official piece of pink paper. He takes it stoically, like a real South African motorist.

Then the cop looks at my contraption and says, "Do you okes know each other?"


Nooit

# FLOSS M JAY

*a poem*

## TODAY

Once up
and walking to another room
cold streams
of air
against my belly
and up my calves
sweep
the leprous mannikin
of my dreams
down
onto the carpet.

As he falls
his old skin dissolves
and sloughs off –
leaves him
naked
to the warm landscapes
of woken thought.

I pick up
the mannikin
and carry him into the kitchen
to have coffee
with me.

# FAROUK ASVAT

## *a poem*

### TO THE QUINTESSENCE OF CLAY[1]

I cannot show you
The spectral gardens
That were not meant for you
The signs that barred us from the world
I cannot show you the buckshot
That would have shattered your chest.

But can you see
The rusted chains
That lie in my heart
Like an anchor

That makes me want you
To stay free
Sailing as an atom and a light
Upon the winds of the universe.

But I know:
You will come
To partake in this laughter.

---

1 *'Man We did create from a quintessence (of clay) . . . then We made the sperm into a clot of congealed blood'. Quran s v 12–14 (MN 5.7.85 p 9)*

*'Who created man . . . out of a mere clot of congealed blood'. Quran s XCVI v 1–2*

## THE WIDOW'S WIDOW

As soon as the airline officials and I finished negotiating about my luggage, gone astray with my clothes for the wedding, I collected the rental car and drove to Hillary's house.

She hugged me, "Come into the kitchen. Are you parched? Flying turns me into yesterday's toast."

I laughed and we sat at the counter under her iron loop of copper pots and waited for the kettle to boil. Outside, chatter was filling the servants' rooms with a language I could not understand. It took me back to childhood when the sound of Magdalena talking with friends in the yard and my parents talking with friends in the house fused with everything else I did not know and could not imagine.

"I've got twenty lists." Hillary sounded overwhelmed by the detailed dovetailing the wedding demanded. She's never enjoyed the power of administrative accomplishment. I wanted to show her I understood why she was handling the logistics on her own. Henry had to be away negotiating and could not change the timetable, not even for his son's wedding. Not now, when the whole country was waiting for the move everyone expected. "The papers say De Klerk might release more prisoners before New Year." I was thinking of the most important prisoner, epitome of the change in my birth country.

Hillary's silence rebuked me for fishing. "I'll just tell the maid where to put the wedding flowers."

She went into the servants' yard and stood on the cement floor next to a cement sink. I could not hear what she said but I heard her maid answer, "Yes, Madam."

When she came back, I asked, "Where do you want me to stay?"

"We've been so busy we haven't had a chance to sell my mother's house. I hope you don't mind. The maid's still there looking after things."

As I nodded, the bridal pair splashed into the kitchen with hugs and exclamations.

"Your gifts could be anywhere," I told them. "With the rest of my luggage."

"But you're here. Tell us everything."

I was thinking how lucky they were to live at this moment when the whole country and the world would see a change momentous enough for myth. How lucky to share their day of joy with the joy I had been hearing on the news as, first one, then many prisoners were released and were met by singing and dancing. The last few months had been extraordinary – students put flowers in the barrels of guns in South Africa and crowds poured out of East Berlin. The land of my birth that had suffered so long, drought-stricken and ostracized, and the land of my parents' birth, also a prison, were full of people saying, "Freedom." They hugged strangers at the news. Every day anticipated the next with joy.

How lucky we were to have the wedding at a time that pinned our personal joy to joy in the world.

We didn't have much time to talk. Hillary needed to speak with her maid. I had to buy clothes, and to call Karen.

I drove to the dead woman's house through familiar streets lined with plane trees hardly changed since the afternoons I had walked under them to my music teacher's, the same dapple of leaves and sun, the same mottled trunks, the same brick houses behind them. My music teacher, about the same age as Hillary's mother, had probably died by now. She had fled Vienna just in time and her stories fused with those of my parents about the persecutions in Europe. In my mind, they fused with the lives of the servants I heard in the back yard.

The maid, wearing a pink apron, was expecting me. She introduced herself as Rosemary and showed me to the room where I would sleep in the dead woman's bed. That was the first time I saw the floor-to-ceiling cast-iron bars of a 'rape gate' between the entrance hall and the bedroom. At first I did not understand what it could be. Then the horror of the fear it revealed. How could things have gone so far that people would lock themselves into cages in their own homes. Would the country ever be able to recover from such insanity.

I did not believe any one wanted to rape Hillary's mother, though I knew that some places had come close to civil war.

"I've got to have a shower," I said.

"Would Madam like me to run a bath for her?" Rosemary asked.

The offer took me aback. Even in South Africa, I did not expect such services. I declined.

While I went off to the bathroom and dressed again in the clothes I had worn since London, she made tea, and when I came out, brought it to me on a tray and set it on a table between the two armchairs that filled the space between the widow's bed and the door.

Almost nothing in all my returns had reached into my memory with such dense eloquence as this tray I had not asked for, with its embroidered doily, teapot, milk, sugar, water, and a plate of Tennis biscuits. My mother would have received the same tray when she asked a servant for tea. On the verandahs of ocean hotels, on office desks and in the secluded space behind the shop counter where the owner has a chair, I had seen the same tray. When I visited Africans in their own homes and they wanted to do the proper thing, they would bring this tray. Pungent with familiarity, like the plane trees outside, it said, "Nothing's changed."

But everything had changed and was changing. I did not guess the extent of it until Rosemary asked, "Would Madam like me to stay?" I did not know what she meant, and she must have seen my confusion, "My madam used to ask me to stay and talk."

"Thank you, Rosemary. I can't talk now. I have to make a phone call, and then go out." I did not tell her my clothes had gone astray.

I drank the tea wondering what we could have to talk about. What did she and Hillary's mother talk about. Hillary? Perhaps Rosemary had children of her own and talked about them. Magdalena, who lived in my backyard when I was growing up, had two children in Bethel. They never visited, and she did not keep photos in her room on the soapbox covered with an embroidered doily like the one on the tea tray. She kept a saucer with a candle butt there and her Bible and a red cigarette tin that, she told me one day, held coupons for the burial insurance she was buying. Her children hardly existed in my imagination, although the husband who came to be with her every second weekend was a real person, and Magdalena sometimes took time to go to Bethel. Years after she died, I went to the location there, but no one knew anything about Magdalena or her children, and I drove away from the one-room mud houses, their rusting roofs held in place by big stones, knowing that I did not know anything of the life of the woman who had cared for me for eight years. All I knew was that she lived the way my grandparents had lived, needing permission for everything. But how it was without running water, how Magdalena pored over her Bible by candlelight while our house blazed with electricity, about that, I knew nothing at all.

Even the first time I did not accept Rosemary's invitation to talk I felt I was committing some wrong against her.

"How soon can you come?" Karen asked.

"I've got to buy clothes. The airline sent mine astray somewhere." I'd need a nap. "I'll take you out to dinner."

"Don't be silly, darling. We want you here."

At the shopping centre, guards stopped me to search my bag. Though everyone seemed to be carried away with talk of freedom, some things would remain. The inertia of institutions, the iron of habit, the mental cages and perhaps worse. The Reign of Terror in France followed a time when strangers hugged each other saying, "Freedom."

Authorized, I bought the necessities of life for the next few days and then, stupid with weariness, drove back to the dead woman's home.

Rosemary greeted me and offered me tea again, and talk again, and again I said no. "I didn't sleep last night and need to rest now."

Of course she couldn't imagine the exhausting flight. She had never been in a plane. She must have lived fixed as a tree in this place where she had worked years to serve a person, and now to guard furniture and empty rooms. With her presence alone.

I half slept, floating through images of the unchanged trees and brick houses, of Hillary talking irritably to her maid, and rumours that the day was at hand that would transform everything. Too soon, it was time to dress again.

Karen threw open the door and hugged me. Quickly, she led me to her living-room, filled with flowers as always. Her husband Edward had founded a kindergarten where he would accept a white child only if the parents sponsored a black child too. A few years later, he declined children from fashionable families, to favour children of domestic servants. They were on a picnic the day he died. A sudden storm had burst over the valley and he was running to scoop a child back to shelter in the farmhouse when a bolt of lightning found him, the tallest thing in a grass field.

Eight hours later, around midnight, her first night as his widow, Karen phoned me in America.

Those calls over continents and oceans and time zones – they're supposed to make it easier to be so far away, but they make it feel harder. When Karen phoned from Johannesburg to say, "Edward's dead," the sky darkened. It must have been my pupils contracting with pain, but I thought it was the whole world going dark, Africa impoverished when his light went out. Just three months ago.

I was finding it hard to be in the room without him. She saw me looking round, feeling him missing.

"Come on New Year's Eve," she said, "We always used to celebrate alone. But this year, I want a few friends who knew Edward. It's such a terrible holiday here, everyone drunk for days."

Karen grew up in Denmark, and her conversation keeps the habit of seeing South Africa as an alien place. I was with her once when we saw a policeman twice her size dragging an old man by the back of his jacket. She stepped in front of them and scolded the cop. He was so surprised at this blazing fairy of righteousness picking a quarrel with him that he loosed his grip on the jacket and listened, bemused, while his victim fled. I was amazed. I didn't know a born South African who'd have delivered such a spontaneous scolding. We were too trained to acquiesce. We did not know and could not imagine the decorum citizens in a free country expect. At the same time, Karen is passionately in love with Edward's country and filled their house with carvings and textiles that reveal her love. Now she is rooted in her past here, and will not live in Copenhagen again.

"I can't believe he's really dead. He comes to me at night, in my dreams. Every night he's with me."

As she was talking, Betty, her maid, came in, and I greeted her. She did not use the servile third person form to talk to me. We talked about Edward. "It'll never be the same," she said quietly.

She has been Karen's maid for thirty years. By now, they move with the same light, quick movements, and Betty knows exactly what needs to be done when Karen stages a party for parents and donors and they both prepare plates of finger food and edible flowers.

Betty served dinner and Karen and I talked.

I said, "It's so ironic, painful, that Edward isn't here to see the end of apartheid."

"Who knows what will take its place," she said. A sign of foreboding. I was taken aback. "Or if anything will change. Habits die hard."

After we'd been talking a while, she said she was tired, and we moved to her bedroom. She'd also had a rape gate installed when Edward died. Fear had found her after all.

I sat in the carved armchair he used to sit in when she wasn't feeling well but still wanted people around. Where I used to sit, she had a TV now. A salve for loneliness.

When I was too exhausted for more talk, she asked me to call Betty from the kitchen. "We watch TV together."

So Betty was one of the family now. No, she had served the dinner but did not eat it with us.

I found her in the kitchen ironing panties. Panties! Freedom takes learned skills. My mind flooded with thousands of habits and decisions that people here did not know and could not imagine. Like Karen's instant outrage at that bullying cop. Who, in a free world, would choose to iron panties? To compose that fussy tea tray? To speak the syntax of servility? The old laws might be about to die, but my first country looked likely to survive as a widow with gestures and postures locked in place.

When I came back to the dead woman's house there was light in the room in the back yard where Rosemary lived, but behind the house next door, the servants' rooms were bright and loud with music and the voices of men drinking. They were getting an early start on New Year.

Rosemary was not with them. She was alone, locked in place, waiting for me. She came out as I walked to the front door, "Did Madam have a good meal?" and walked in front of me to switch lights on so I need not go into dark rooms. I wondered what she did all day when there was no one to tend to, and what she would do when Hillary sold the house.

I let my shoulders droop and jaw go slack to show that I was too tired for tea or talk. This time she did not offer, but I knew the pattern. I was wronging her, or had wronged her sometime ago, long before I knew or could imagine.

# ARIK SHIMANSKY

## *two poems*

### A GOOD SEASON FOR DYING

On Sunday they told him that his kidneys had failed.
He sat on the wooden chair next to the window.
Flowers were budding on the tree outside,
the mad waltz of the bees.
He had read that a patient's chances of recovery are higher
if he sees trees from his hospital bed.

On Tuesday he couldn't get out of bed.
He lay listening to the rustle of trees,
the whisper of the breakers,
the rumours of his heart.
He could hear his daughters in the corridor.

### A POEM IN REAL TIME
*(for a writing workshop at 18:30)*

18:21
A poem in real time is like juggling three balls blind:
You can throw a ball in the air,
but can't know who it will hit,
where it will land.

18:23
Joshua is crying, he just vomited on his babygro,
sickly apricots, some Greek yoghurt and prunes.
Decibels later I can be creative again,
domestic art at its best.
    *19 January 1998 (18:27)*

# ALISTAIR DREDGE

*a poem*

**WANTED: ONE HOUSEKEEPER**

I am indeed a sight for sore eyes.
The days have settled on me like dust.
The rooms of my life have cluttered with incident.
My fridge has filled with smelly memories.
I wonder sometimes what colour the carpet was.

    Where to start? What first?
    What, in fact, to do?

    Hire someone?
    God might be up to the job,
    if He exerted Himself.

    God: Now there's an idea!
    Will all interested divinities kindly apply
    in writing, and supply references.

    Find a lover? I'm afraid
    one look would send her running for cleaner pastures.

I just can't eat memories fast enough;
the supply exceeds the demand.
More experiences? I think not:
they have to be stored somewhere.
And dusted.

# PNINA FENSTER

## *a story*

### THE KILLING OF COWBOY KATE

After about five minutes of examining my face in the mirror of the swimming-pool change-room, I realise precisely what I have to do next. Bleach my hair, Marilyn Monroe style. Kinky dip-curl over one eye. Peachy, pleated dresses. The corrupt, little-girl-lost look. Just a couple of hours at the hairdresser and I'd have a whole new image. Not that dressing like Cowboy Kate hasn't been fun. I mean, it's a no-lose situation – as far as the other women at the pool are concerned. Their Mickey Mouse t-shirts, pansy-printed pareos and straw hats versus my handtooled leather boots, tiny bikini bottom and plaited, black hair. I look like someone from a Peter Stuyvesant advert. At any rate – that's what Ud says. And if Ud wasn't wild for Cowboy Kate, I wouldn't be hanging around the pool bar of the Hotel Paradiso, waiting for him to buy me lunch.

"A kiss on the hand may be quite continental, but diamonds are a . . ." I croon to Ud. And it's all too obvious that even sighing over a city drainpipe, thighs akimbo, Marilyn has never been one of his fantasies. Perhaps I could try a variation on Cowboy Kate? Authentic Indian say, with turquoise beads and chamois fringing . . . But my instincts are taking me in another direction.

It always goes like this. In the beginning, men plummet abandoned and ardent into whatever my current phase is – forties peplums or crucifixes and lace, or mini-skirts and ballet shoes. Next thing I know, they don't even want me to bleach my hair – which is dangerous. Because I can find a man anywhere but when I feel that urge for a new hairstyle, there's no knowing where it will end. (The last time – which was corkscrew curls with red streaks – I got entangled in a ménage à trois. Six months later, I dyed my hair black – and found myself with Ud.) I don't need to keep photographs to keep track of the changes. I frequently find myself returning to the scene of the crime – arriving at

familiar gambling resorts or restaurants. But under altogether different circumstances – and with altogether different men.

Like the last time I was at Hotel Paradiso. Alexander was dark,
deeply spiritual and heavily into bondage. He'd been told by a famous
clairvoyant that he was fated to win a fortune on the very last night of
his holiday. So we spent our days drinking room-service champagne
cocktails, overtipping everyone and playing in the jacuzzi. I'd wrap
myself in black velvet. (I was heavily under the influence of Diana
Ross in those days.) And we'd go down for dinner. (He ordered me a
serving of every single dessert on the menu – just to taste.) Afterwards
he tied me to the bed, and we made love until it was time to go to the
casino. I didn't even notice that he was looking less and less like a winner.

It took three months of waitressing to help settle the debt. (The clairvoyant had an even rougher time.) And every time one of the steakhouse customers leered at me, I thought of Alexander steering a little
castle of casino chips in the direction of a croupier and telling her,
"This is for personnel."

It was round about then that I first saw Ud. He used to come to the
steakhouse all alone and pick fights with the other guys. Then he'd
buy drinks all round and watch me until everything started to dis-
solve. No talking, no band, no food, no customer's orders through the
service hatch from the kitchen. Just Ud's eyes. Then his mouth and
chest in the taxi back home. Waking up creased and crazy on the white
tiled floor of his entrance hall and starting all over again, thinking that
I'd really settle into this one.

But I'm not settling into Ud. I'm not the settling type. Six months
with anyone and things start to slip. Time to change my hairstyle,
cruise the one-arm-bandit freaks and the card players, set my mouth
just so.

I'll tell you exactly how it feels. It's like having a secret collection.
Like this person I heard of who hid in a corner of a bookshop. And cut
every penis out of a R300 tome on tribal customs. With a razor blade.
I'd never mutilate books, but I get a thrill when I imagine someone
going to the Milky Lane ice cream parlour for a celebratory snack –
pecan nut sundae with extra cream, say. And a pocket full of penises.

We're standing at the Mongolian Grill self-service buffet when Ud
turns philosophical.

"Of course, this whole place is the product of Apartheid," he says,
his hair still smelling of casino smoke. You can't help reflecting on
your principles when faced with a remark like that. (Especially when

you're ordering lunch under the noonday sun. And your stomach still filled with Bloody Marys and blackberry flapjacks from breakfast.)

Principles. That's the confusing thing.

For example I know of one couple who set off for one of these gambling weekends. On the way, they started arguing and took the wrong highway. Three hours later, they arrived at an hotel in an altogether different province. Irritable, red-eyed, chicken grease under their nails, coffee stains and crumbs all over the car seats. And the woman refused to book into the hotel. Because it had been built on sacred tribal burial ground.

Now I compare myself to her. And there's hardly any comfort in believing that Marilyn Monroe was probably more principled than Cowboy Kate. Here I am with Ud – a one-hundred-percent Aryan product. And while I wouldn't regard myself as Jewish any more, I can't help wondering what my childhood cheder teachers would say.

But by the time dinner rolls around, I've remembered just how easy it is to play your cards right. Right now, as Ud is caught in concentration at the blackjack table, I meet four, five, six, inviting glances. Then there are two offers of drinks. An invitation to dinner. And a note. Men, drinks, dinner – things just come to me. Say one of my boyfriends gives me a fistful of chips. I just close my eyes and the right number jumps out of my mouth. Lucky touch – that's what the croupiers are always telling me – lucky touch. Rooms are always filling with fresh bodies, clean shapes and new sizes. Between the folds of casino darkness, steamy and sin-soaked, I can see cigar butts, ice cubes and eyes. Between the whisky glasses and the fistfuls of chips, there are mouths to kiss – tickets to the next hotel.

And now there's only the sound of this new, this handsome stranger's car, on the cool, white road. And inside the car, the sound of his breathing, and the radio crackling with old love songs – tinny and magical. 'Cry Me a River' and 'Don't Get No Kick' and 'I Wanna Be Loved by You' and . . . The road is sealed tight inside the dry, blue sky. And way over, under a different piece of the same sky, Ud's still asleep. Perhaps he's dreaming of the freaks feeding the fruit machines. Or the dealers flipping cards slick and sweet onto green baize. Or roulette wheels whizzing and breathing. Dreaming of lucky numbers, and doubling down. Never dreaming that I'm halfway to another town with another image and another man and a purse full of his last night's winnings.

He doesn't know that I've killed Cowboy Kate, that I'm wrapping a yellow scarf around my head and practising my pout. And as he dreams thick and cloudy, I roll a joint and stroke this new, this handsome thigh. As soon as I've had my hair cut, I'm going to send Ud a postcard. Care of the Paradiso Hotel. I'll tell him to put some money on 17. Ever since I got into the car in the still, starry morning, 17 has been beating like tom-toms in my head. And I'm hardly ever wrong. I have a lucky touch, you know. That's what the croupiers are always saying.

*a poem*

## SKULL

I passed him,
not knowing him.
It had been more than twenty years.
But he spoke my name:
softly, and I turned.
The traffic fussed
past us at the crossing of the roads:
but his face was calm.
"How are you?" he asked,
his eyes intensely kind,
and gave me his hand.
It folded into mine like a woman's or a child's.
Had it always been so small?
I said I was fine, and he smiled,
his teeth the same
old toilet bowl's brown.
"Still two packs a day," I thought,
and shivered in his shoes.
We spoke of age.
He said he was seventytwo.
I said I was seventyfour:
added he was chicken to my fowl,
and the silly jest,
bearded as a baboon,
scampered round us,
slapping its sides,
leering like a loon.
He said he was waiting for 'them'
to fetch him with the car.

Family? Friends?
He did not say: did not once speak
of the olden times.
I watched his eyes,
fidgeted for the catch
that held his face in place,
wondered at the white-
of-egg translucence of his skin,
the imminence of its skull.
"You have grown thin," I said.
Again he smiled, nodded,
anchored still
in the amber of his calm,
old eyes bland
in their sockets' sullen holes.
"Cancer of the bowel," he said, and ran
with his floppy old man's shins
to the slowing-down car,
struggled himself in,
gently drew shut the door.
I looked to see
if he would raise a hand,
glance aside.
But the car passed
me with only shadows in its glass,
heading for where he had not said he stayed.

# MONGANE WALLY SEROTE

## *three poems*

### FOR DON M. – BANNED

it is a dry white season
dark leaves don't last, their brief lives dry out
and with a broken heart they dive down gently headed for the earth,
not even bleeding.
it is a dry white season brother,
only the trees know the pain as they still stand erect
dry like steel, their branches dry like wire,
indeed, it is a dry white season
but seasons come to pass.

### CITY JOHANNESBURG

This way I salute you:
My hand pulses to my back trousers pocket
Or into my inner jacket pocket
For my pass, my life,
Jo'burg City.
My hand like a starved snake rears my pockets
For my thin, ever lean wallet,
While my stomach groans a friendly smile to hunger,
Jo'burg City.
My stomach also devours coppers and papers
Don't you know?
Jo'burg City, I salute you;
When I run out, or roar in a bus to you,
I leave behind me, my love,
My comic houses and people, my dongas and my ever whirling dust,
My death,

That's so related to me as a wink to the eye.
Jo'burg City
I travel on your black and white and roboted roads,
Through your thick iron breath that you inhale,
At six in the morning and exhale from five noon.
Jo'burg City
That is the time when I come to you,
When your neon flowers flaunt from your electrical wind,
That is the time when I leave you,
When your neon flowers flaunt their way through the falling darkness
On your cement trees.
And as I go back, to my love,
My dongas, my dust, my people, my death,
Where death lurks in the dark like a blade in the flesh,
I can feel your roots, anchoring your might, my feebleness
In my flesh, in my mind, in my blood,
And everything about you says it,
That, that is all you need of me.
Jo'burg City, Johannesburg,
Listen when I tell you,
There is no fun, nothing, in it,
When you leave the women and men with such frozen expressions,
Expressions that have tears like furrows of soil erosion,
Jo'burg City, you are dry like death,
Jo'burg City, Johannesburg, Jo'burg City.


## WHAT'S WRONG WITH PEOPLE?

I saw a man
Come. Walk. Limp,
Fall.
Like a branch being sawn.

His eyes flickered like flame blown by wild wind.

People stood to look.
I was among them.

# JILLIAN BECKER

## *a story*

Lionel was my first attentive reader, my first constructive critic. I needed and sought his approval, and to my relief and joy he gave it. Our friendship, begun at university, flowered in the 1950s. I was writing my first book then, a series of lyrical short stories which were finally bound together under the title A Cry in the Daytime. As soon as each was finished I took it to Lionel and read it to him. We would sit in his book-filled room in his parents' house in Kensington, I'd read him the story, and he'd comment on it, always encouragingly.

He liked them. When he'd heard them all he sent them to William Plomer and asked for his advice as to who might publish the collection as a book. Plomer wrote back that these were not stories at all but 'mood pieces', and though he liked one of them, he doubted there was a market for that kind of writing. Lionel was as disappointed as I was. Before long, however, the book was accepted for publication by a small but well-established firm in London who was to issue it in conjunction with another publisher in Cape Town. Lionel was delighted at the news and said he would like to devote an entire issue of The Purple Renoster to the stories. I went to London and called on the publisher. He told me with devastating candour that while he was happy to publish the book, it would almost certainly be "one of the 8 000 which come out only to be instantly lost every year". I had no wish to publish a book straight into oblivion, so I said, "Thanks awfully but please don't trouble."

I wrote to Lionel to tell him what had happened. He said he still wanted the stories for his magazine. I was deeply grateful for his appreciation of the work, but it seemed to me that if it was not good enough for a moment of book-life in London, it could not be good enough for a moment of magazine-life in Johannesburg either. Lionel tried to persuade me to change my mind and I hated having to say no to him, but I stuck to my decision out of a mixture of pride and cowardice.

Subsequently – after my first novel The Keep had been published by Chatto & Windus in 1967 – some of those early stories appeared in various magazines, and one was chosen for South African Writing Today, Penguin

*Books, London, 1967, of which Lionel himself was co-editor. In response to the editors' invitation I had submitted a more recent story which Lionel had liked, but the other editor, Nadine Gordimer, had not. Then Lionel proposed that a story be selected from that first collection of mine, and they agreed on the inclusion of its eponymous piece. Later it was selected from the Penguin anthology by a literary agency in Bratislava to be translated into Slovak and broadcast on Czechoslovakian radio – the first foreign rights I ever sold. Here it is.*

## A CRY IN THE DAYTIME

Miss Griffith's head was round, and since her half-shut eyelids were as flimsy as though the air shone through them, it could have been the ring by means of which the finger of destiny swung her about. And out of her cage of bones came the thin high-piping voice of her, pecking about from note to note, never singing a whole song. She was my piano teacher, and her fingers were so bony she should not have needed her pencil to rap me over the knuckles. She was due to arrive at any moment, and I was expected to be at the piano, ready waiting, the sheets of music open on the stand, the lid awake, a chair placed for her at my side. Twice a week I wanted to put off her arrival for an age or two, and holding on to time with all my dread, moved down the stairs to the piano as slowly as I could. I looked long minutes at every picture sloping down the wall in stages like the stairs. The 'Cries of London'. They would have been as good as invisible from more than two feet away, so the stairway was the best place for them. Going down slowly, reading all the 'Cries', to keep from thinking of Miss Griffith, I thought about her hard and long. And I even decided her fate, her future, until I had worked her out of existence. I married her off. I married Miss Griffith the piano teacher to the old rag-and-bone man. For Miss Griffith's problem (which I shall describe), marriage, it seemed, was an old and tried solution, a traditional answer, on the authority of the story-books, of so many words and tales and admonishments and promises of heaven by parents and all our mentors, all our guides from pulling midwife to delving sexton.

"Will you buy my violets?" I read at the foot of one of the pictures.

But here I must explain my choice of the groom.

Thrice yearly, the old rag-and-bone man, the worst old man of all, came along our street yelling some noise that sounded like 'Aardeyaaaaha!' The octagonal wheels of his barrow punished the tar-mac, and the superstructure trembled and rocked towards the earth, groaning for death or abandonment. Within, the horrid rags were scattered over noisy, musty bottles. I never glimpsed any bones, but my certainty that he had collected a great many of them – femurs, tibias, skulls of thin men whose skin had been peeled as easily as that of a hot tomato, and half-gnawed marrow-bones snatched from the mouths of emaciated dogs in alleyways – added to my dread of him. At night, when I lay in the dark against the wall, I could hear through the bricks and the plaster a stealthy footstep on the carpet of the stairs, and it was the black-clad rag-and-bone man, coming with his sharp nails and his red eyes, mounting the long muffled staircase towards the nursery. At every moment I expected him to look round the nursery door. I listened for the footsteps, the occasional creak. But, happily, I would fall asleep before the step had reached the upper landing.

Now I knew that, on those three days each year when he came our way crying his cry, what he called for were buyers and sellers of his over-weathered wares. But none in our street ever – and I stood at the gate to watch – came running from the houses to deal with the shrivelled pedlar of decay. Yet three times every year he came, and cried his cry. Perhaps to cry was enough for him, to cry out so, and push the barrow so, and wane and wither year by year. But I, watching him that small way of his round, sensed for him an unfulfilment. Perhaps that was the demand he made upon me, and perhaps it was more than that, which was why he pursued me into the dark and all but into my dreams.

It was seldom enough that he, in the skin, pushed his barrow into my world. And yet at strange times he recurred. A piece of writing, half-finished under my mother's hand, would be put aside in favour of the croquet-mallet, but with a sigh for something unattained. And when she was gone to the green lawn, the rag-and-bone man came to the crack in the door. "Aaar!" I heard, and I moved away.

And none of Miss Griffith's days with us ever, as far as I can remember, coincided with a day of the rag-and-bone man. His cry never, in fact, atonally and intemporally, cut into the étude or the fugue, as she tapped her thick red pencil on the piano ledge, her green eyes hooded, her hands drawing the music into her rigid body, draining the instrument which would never, I regretfully found, run dry. Yet twice a week, it occurred to me now, she brought a reminder of the barrow man. For suddenly I understood that she was crying for something. At least her eyes were always wet and a little runny, and she kept them half-closed, as though to hold back secrets, but my mother knew them all, and told them all, if all were all indeed.

My mother called her 'Poor Bess'. And how that many-cornered body of a Bess had threshed about, as though to knock sparks off the sides of her life. But what she was yearning for, never happened. Much activity, though, had kept her yearning; activity at one or another time involved with nursing, Catholicism, philately, love, jewellery-making, a knitting circle for the merchant-marine, Christian Science, a brief biography of Paul Kruger, a medium, travel, a friendship with a Fabian, eurhythmics, water-colour painting, the Edinburgh festival twice running, correspondence with a lesser English critic, a concise explanation of the laws of Moses, Yoga and piano-teaching. There had been paraphernalia required and acquired during the pursuance of these enterprises. Somehow she had reduced them all (except the piano which would not be reduced) into musty things: tags of wool were souvenirs of the mufflers and balaclavas destined for the sailors; pieces of glass reminded her of nursing, beads and stones and metal of the jewel and Catholic days; paper of philately, painting, the Edinburgh Festival, the letter-writing, and the treaties with history. Perhaps there was a piece of bone to remind her of love. There was debris enough to dispose of if she would, but she crammed it all down somewhere in the thin yellow basket of her being. And still at every moment she was on the brink of miracle. The tidy sitting-room, to which I would consign her when she left our house, and which might have existed for all I know, was stocked out with crystal ball and Tarot packs, and a mass of manuscripts that worried at love, and bothered God, and flung Jesus with Moses into the boiling-pot.

This room, as I built it, was high above some narrow street. It was in a tower, and, like the Muezzin, out of it she cried, and another and another year was gone, leaving no gain behind. Except another pack of cards. And surely that is sad, to lean out of windows and wave and call – and the thunder's growl cannot be taken for an answer – to someone in the street, on a bridge, who will not turn or wave or shout through the same air of the same world. And yet she leans and calls, tired of the room behind her with the covered beds and the looking-glass, and all the souvenirs.

"Have you any old chairs to mend?" I bent to read.

Miss Griffith sighs and pulls down the window. She takes up her cards and begins to turn them over. A card she has not seen before astounds her, stops her, makes her exclaim.

"Here – what on earth is this? A man in tatters . . ."

I reached the bottom of the stairs, and there was the ring at the front door. I rushed to the piano, flung back the lid, propped up the music, and had her chair beside the stool before she entered the room.

She chirped "Good-morning," and nodded approval, and I looked at her longer than usual, scheming her wedding-dress. Concentrating on the scales, up and down, up and down, so tediously, I suspended her story. But then with the well-learnt piece and my dislike of it, I returned to the romance.

| | |
|---|---|
| *One* – two – three | *one* – two – three |
| *Wish* – that – that | *nast* – y – old |
| *Rag* – and – bone | *man* – two – would |
| *Take* – her – and | *keep* – her – and |
| *Stuff* – her – a | *way* – two – three |

Where were we? She in her tower, and he turning the corner of the narrow street, and crying his cry. She answers. Could she let down her hair? I made my diminuendo and my cadence *ppp*, and as she scolded looked at the tight little curls on her head, and decided no, she couldn't let down her hair. It wouldn't let down. I passed over the courtship which involved such unexpected difficulties, and on to the wedding.

She opened the book at the new piece. Clumsily I played the first bar. "Again," she said. I played the first bar and the second. "Again," she said. The first, second and third. It was like the House That Jack Built in reverse.

Meanwhile I dressed her in white and gave her arum lilies to hold. But I left him in his black rags. He was the man all tattered and torn who kissed the maiden all forlorn. And now I had them up before the cadaverous preacher, and they vowed.

To love. Miss Griffith had tried this once. Or over and over again. But it must be tried over and over again, said the cadaverous preacher.

To honour. She had honoured much and many. Until they had proved unsatisfying. Or unworthy, said the cadaverous preacher.

To obey. Can Miss Griffith obey anything but her own desire? – that yearning of hers? I asked the cadaverous preacher.

"This man is the answer to her yearning," he confirmed.

Well, the organ rolled – I was at the organ, playing the étude, the fingering wrong, and the sounds hurt Miss Griffith, as she drew them in through the trumpets of the lilies.

Arm-in-arm, out they go, *one*-two, *one*-two.

But already the man has lost his barrow. He has this cage of a wife hanging on his arm instead.

The happily-ever-after was about to begin when Miss Griffith gave her summing-up lecture and her usual adjurement to me to practise more diligently. I let them go on a honeymoon until the bride had gone out through the front door.

Now back in Miss Griffith's apartment, high in the tower, the bags are unpacked, and eternity has begun. Miss Griffith, or Mrs Rag-and-Bone, prepares the meals. And on Monday mornings she washes the shirts he has now to wear. He eats the food she cooks, and lies about in the clean shirts, and they live on her savings. He does not push his barrow, she does not teach me music any more. They both grow fat. They both become good-natured, even he, good-natured, no longer going at night with sinister intent to haunt the stairways and the landings, sigh and groan at the cracks of the doors. And Miss Griffith yearns no longer.

"A little more bubble-and-squeak, my dear?"

"Thank you, my dear."

For ever and ever.

Well, so there is no rag-and-bone man anymore. And there is no Miss Griffith. All that he was, all that she was, is changed, and they have gone away, out of my nights and my days, to float in a world that has no weather – so the story books have said, so the wedding-bells pretend.

I was nearly at the top of the stairs, when I paused a little breathless and read again (going very close) 'Will you buy my violets?' and strangely I thought of a grave being dug, and such a fear of forever possessed me, that I cried out silently in myself.

"No," I cried, but silently.

"No, no, no."

The story I had made was dead, and I interred its bones, covered them over out of sight, with a sense of the day, and the coming of days to own me still. With relief I reminded myself that even the dreadful was still ahead; pain, and its relief of pleasure; pleasure, and its relief of pain.

It was almost a prayer: that another day should bring back the lean and tattered cry of the rag-and-bone man; that Miss Griffith, even year after year, should ring at the door, rap with her long red pencil, turn the cards and curl her hair, and yearn like blazes without letting up. Miss Griffith yearning is Miss Griffith. Neither he nor she may grow fat. They must nibble and gnaw. Let the bones have no rest among the bright glass and the garments.

Ah! someone mounts the stairs. Let the morning come quickly.

Let the morning come, and the morning cries begin again.

# RUTH MILLER

## *two poems*

### MILKMAN

What does the milkman think of the light burning
When he deposits the bottle at three o'clock in the morning
(Neither of *us* waiting . . .)?
His footsteps heavy and informed with work; I reading
In the blare of the bedside lamp, longing to slip
Into milkwhite sleep, sure only of aloneness.
The dark milkman, unseen, black, unquiet
Stomps up the three steps, bashily places
Two fat pints in uncorseted bulges.
Later I hear him in a clink of neighbourly bottles.
I turn another page of the night's dark morning.

### RAT

I

I never saw the rats that trampled
The thin ceiling in the low room
Nightly, once it was wholly dark, feeling
Tentative scurries at first, and then a tumble
From wall to wall, a roll and rumble of claws
On the tight drumskin of my eyes
On the wide irises of my ears
And the fur of my skin.

'Wee, cowering beastie', soft and small
Under the sky, was no kind of kin
To big brother Rat in the roof in the gathering dark
Waiting for the pause in my breath, to start

Veering, like an armed man (no scurrying here,
No tiny feet tapping), but an iron clang
From wall to wall
Beating me in.

When I lay flat at last and wept
At the rats in my head, they repeated
The beating barrage and thud. It was I who crept
Like their brother mouse, cowering in its blood.

II
I am become a mouse in a field
Waiting the shear of the blade
In the sticky sun with the grass
Yielding under my thimble weight.

I am become a long whisker
Twitching, a face
Like a cut stone, a single muscle
Stiffening, awaiting the worst

Which is coming, surely,
Down the field of my days
Humming in the mouth of the wild
Buzzing in the clean swathe.

When you hold me in your hand
Tenderly, for an instant, before
I am flung on the stubbled ground –
I shall receive no comfort, Lord.

III
Tin disks upon the ropes
Moored in the disk of the sun.
Poison set, the sprung traps –
But the rats will come.

The armpits will blossom.
Death like a bee will hum
In each groin and bosom.

The rats are fat and warm,
They bide their time until
Without motive, or will,
They deliver us from harm.

# ES'KIA MPHAHLELE

## *an extract from* Down Second Avenue

### DINKU DIKAE'S TERROR

"You're coming tonight?" Rebone asked.

"Yes," I said.

We walked down Barber Street, from school.

"Hai, that new teacher gives too many notes."

"Well, we're no more in Standard Five, remember."

"So he must kill us and have no Standard Six any more!"

"I don't mind notes. Makes me feel bigger and still bigger with so many exercise books to carry."

"Look there!"

"What?"

"My father there in front of Fung Prak's shop. Somebody's stopped him. Let's go and see."

We found a white man in black uniform talking to Rebone's father, examining the horse as if he were looking for something in the hair, in the mane, under the tail, on the hoofs.

"It's not a policeman, Pa," I heard Rebone hiss out next to him. "It's not a policeman, Pa." Dinku Dikae might as well have been deaf. For the first time I saw a man tremble as the hawker did. He followed the white man round almost falling over him, but not saying a word. Rebone's face was one massive frown, and her attention was on the father all the time.

"Don't be afraid, Pa," she hissed. "He's a health inspector, not a policeman." Of course, he had been stopped several times before by health inspectors.

When the white man left, after saying brusquely, "All right," Dinku Dikae held on to the harnessing, like one about to faint.

"Let's go, Pa." She knew her father wouldn't work for the rest of the day after such an incident. They left Rebone holding the reins. I envied her holding the reins like that, so efficiently.

That afternoon and on into the night the picture of Dinku Dikae, trembling in the presence of the white inspector, could not leave me. Leaning against his strong horse, then moving to lean against the strong wheel and holding on to the spokes that radiated so much strength; then muttering something; then his broad back offset by the wasp-like frame of Rebone as the trolley's wheels gnashed their way down Second Avenue.

Now how come such a strong man with a heavy shoulder should fear a policeman or anybody or anything that suggested a policeman? I felt at once a close alliance with Rebone's father and a little awe for him. Yes, wasn't a policeman made to be feared – his handcuffs, big broad belt, truncheon, his heavy boots, his shining badge? Most of the police, even in our predominantly Sotho territory, were Zulus. They were tall, hefty, with large bellies, vast hips and buttocks and torn ear-lobes. The white police were only to be seen together with Africans when they came in for beer and tax and pass raids. We loved to imitate the Black policemen as they marched up Barber Street, truncheons pointed up, buttocks jutting out as they tried with little success to follow the commander's order, "Chest out and stomach in!" But we marched far behind them, tremulously.

I went to do school work with Rebone as usual. But the father was sullen and Rebone sad because of it.

"I treat my horse very well," Dinku Dikae said. "I treat him very well. What does the white man want now?" He looked at me as if I were involved, the way he was. "Police police police every time." He came to sit in front of me, wiping his forehead with the back of the hand. "I came here for peace and God knows I don't want dust in my path but where's peace to be found here?"

"He's *not* a policeman, Pa."

"Same to me look at it up or down the street when a white man looks for a fault it is to take you to the police." He paused. "She knows it but pretends not to." He was tacitly ordering me to listen. I did so willingly.

"Let me tell you something, son. We lived in Prospect Township in the Golden City. Three of us, me, Rebone and her mother. If you have never seen Prospect you don't know the world. You must sell beer to live or else work for a white man and why should I work for a white man when God has given me brains to work for myself. I made money enough to wash your body with. God forgive me I don't know but the police can make you wish and do things only the devil wants to do. Rebone's mother, God's woman, she died when Rebone was a child. I ran the long night to a hospital in Johannesburg for a doctor but I came back without a doctor and God be my witness I looked at her mother die, but I don't know how I could not do anything. A woman I called tried her best. She died, with the child, when the night died at one o'clock. I thought these eyes had seen enough darkness in the world until the Government of Johannesburg wanted to take away Prospect and build factories. Our people refused to move and God knows the police came in again and again and again more than ever before to throw out our beer. We cried and carried our arms on our heads and said Government of Johannesburg stop and the white police came again. I don't know but the Government is a strange person. We cried with tears and then we cried with anger and some of us foolish ones God knows I could never do such madness flung stones at the policemen. More of them came and shot bullets at us. A boy hardly your age comes out of the house next to us crying for help and a policeman points a gun his way and kills the child God is my witness while me and Rebone are looking through the window and see the gun smoke and the boy drop dead. Cold. Finished."

And at the last word the man flung his arms wide which he had been waving about to help along his narrative. Wide with the big tough hands open. So strong, so helpless.

"I wanted to take Rebone here away from Prospect from the Golden City for her to grow up good. I'm from Zeerust in the west in the land of Bafurutse but I don't know I can never go back there again with all the good land gone to the white man but now the famine is here and people don't buy much any more. There is a little money still only if you don't scratch backward like a hen so you see what you're working for. Now the police again and again and again."

People said Dinku Dikae was scared of the police because he must have killed somebody sometime in the past. Others said he had a chicken heart. Some said he would just drop dead one day from heart failure.

I wanted to go home immediately, but I was afraid and there was safety in Dinku Dikae's room. We couldn't do any work, Rebone and I, but I couldn't leave. There was a large bed along one wall, evidently the man's, and opposite was a narrower one, for Rebone. There were neat white quilts, the old-fashioned type with triangular patterns and visible cotton strands. A small table and four wooden chairs with high settles and iron wiring and bolts under the seats. Cooking was done outside, as in our home, on a brazier. He kept his vegetables covered with canvas in the trolley, but there were bags of potatoes behind the door. There was one window. A curtain hung on a sagging string in front of Dinku Dikae's bed and was slung up. Above Rebone's bed she pasted on the wall old bioscope placards, one showing Mae West in one of her seductive poses, hovering over the head of Frederic March on another placard. The male stared grimly out of the wall; the female looked like a mermaid that might have been forced to stand on its tail in an attempt to look more human. The placards reinforced my sense of safety. Luckily when I did go out, a bunch of people were leaving a house next to the Reverend M'kondo's, where, I remembered, a choir practice had been going on. A number of them were going my way.

Yes, fewer people were buying the miserable and depressed vegetables Dinku Dikae sold. Rebone left school in January of 1934; in the middle of the Standard Six year, the last primary school year. We were then sixteen. She had to help her father.

"Your father tells me you were at the Columbia last night?" I asked Rebone one Sunday morning.

"What's he telling you that for?" She looked daggers at me.

"They say they'll burn it one of these days so bad it is."

"What had you gone to do there yourself the other night?"

"Just to look, nothing more."

"I had a better reason. I was going to dance."

"Dance?" I gasped.

"Don't girls dance Marabi?" She was looking viciously casual.

"But at the Columbia! Didn't he want to kill you for it?"

"Hmm, he raved and raved and then he took his belt to beat me and I jumped over the table and on a chair, on the bed, and he couldn't get at me. Then he gave up. So funny now I remember it." She spoke with such animation that I couldn't help but laugh.

Marabastad was ablaze with talk of Rebone's having been to the Columbia. To dance! She even left school for the purpose . . . A girl that was bound to leave school, we knew it . . . She must have been going there long before now . . . Such a humble hardworking papa . . . It's a spear in his heart, this . . . Nurse a nettle and it scratches you in your late years . . . They say he's sickly already . . . It'll kill him, that's what . . . Children of the present generation . . . too clever if you ask me . . . What do you expect in a house without a woman? . . .

Rebone worked hard to help her father. But she went more frequently to the Columbia. "Business besides!" she said, which was a popular phrase for "let them mind their own business".

She tried once or twice to egg me on to the Columbia. I was afraid.

I knew I passionately wanted to go, not just to look, but also to dance with her. I dreamt it many nights. But I was afraid. Not simply of my grandmother: I could elude her. Not simply of what people might say: they would never stop saying anything anyhow. I loved Rebone all the more for the strength I did not have. Without even knowing it, I had stopped going to her home.

Moloi, the noisy, spirited boy next door saw it happen and he came and told us about it.

"Ma-Lebona finds her at the water tap. 'My child,' she says, 'daughter of Dinku Dikae, why don't you go back to school?'

"'Why?' Rebone asks her. You should have seen the girl you boys. She looked like our cat before the dog next door.

"'My child,' the old lady says, 'you're still too young for the whole of Marabastad to say so much evil about you. The things they say you do at the dance hall! They make one freeze with shame.'

"'Why don't you talk like this to your children, old mother? You couldn't keep your makoti[1] – two of them, and so you pick on me to give advice.'

"'Ao! my own children never spoke to me this way. Ao! my father will rise from his grave God's truth he will.'

"'Besides I'm not your child!'

"'Ao! See these grey hairs, child? You'll remember them till you die for insulting each one of them! I'll speak to your father about it.'

"'Yes, because you want him to marry you!'

"'Ao, ao, ao, ao, ao!' and the old lady clapped her hands as she spoke, calling Marabastad to come and see a miracle. 'You can't repeat those words, child!'

"You won't believe me, boys, but the girl dipped a small dish, small as my hand or yours, into her tin of water and splashed it into the old lady's face." Then Moloi laughed, and, as was his manner whenever he wanted to enjoy his laughter, pushed me away.

"What did Ma-Lebona say?" I asked.

"Say? You should ask me what she did."

"Yes?"

"She turned round and left, wiping her face with her clean apron full of pictures of flowers."

"That wasn't Ma-Lebona!" Danie said.

"Then it was you in women's dress."

"Ma-Lebona leave like that!" little Links said.

[1] Daughters-in-law

"Want to look for her in the drain then, under the tap?"

"Ag, stop your nonsense talk," I said, "I simply don't believe it."

Tongues got wagging. Rebone had poured water in Ma-Lebona's face. Rebone – yes. But Ma-Lebona? – no, a fly couldn't sit on her face!

"The little wasp!" Ma-Lebona kept hissing as she told grandmother and Aunt Dora. "That little wasp will bring home a load in her stomach at her age for poor Dinku Dikae to nurse or she'll drive him to the mad hospital. You hear me, Hibila and Dora, here – " She spat on her hand and pointed her finger to the sky. "As God's in the heavens I'll bite my elbow if she doesn't get a baby soon."

"No, don't say that. It's evil," grandmother said.

"I still say I'll bite my elbow."

I met Rebone often after that, but neither of us mentioned Ma-Lebona's name. She picked up a lover at the Columbia. It was common talk among the bigger patrons of the place. Fanyan, his name was. From the XY Ranch in Tenth Avenue. A handsome boy whose features cut like a razor-blade. I developed a consuming hatred of the boy. I gloried in the stories people passed round about Fanyan's wickedness. But I didn't have it in me to blame Rebone for her love affair.

Her father clearly didn't like it. His fellow-tenants told us that Fanyan and the Columbia were the cause of the continual use of the whip on Rebone and threats of greater violence from her father.

"Anybody who touches my girl is asking Bantule to invite him." That was Fanyan's signature tune which passed from tongue to tongue. Bantule was where the cemetery was. Whenever he and Rebone walked down Barber Street the boys in front of Abdool's shop whistled softly into their cupped hands. Fanyan walked like a hero, must have thought himself one.

The liquor squad were often plain-clothes men from the CID, whites and non-whites. They moved together on their raids. The uniformed police, all Africans, were under a white station commander and a few white sergeants. There were only two ways in which one could be escorted by a policeman to the police station. A man was either handcuffed and made to walk alongside a policeman, or handcuffed and walked down to the station by the scruff of the neck. The African police were brutal in their use of the baton. Times without number a man was walked down to the station bleeding like one who had fallen among mad dogs. The stock reply from the police when one wanted to argue against an arrest was: "You'll explain yourself to the white man," often to the accompaniment of a clout, a prod with a baton or a cuff with a large paw.

One of the liquor squad, a Black man, was popularly known as Makulu-Skop – Big Skull. His skull was unusually large, like a buffalo's. Grandmother often said, "Why don't you use the pot that's as big as Makulu-Skop's head?" meaning the largest pot with which it was necessary to cook only once at a time for the family. Soon the pot became known at home as 'makulu-skop'.

Makulu-Skop was a very energetic constable, more so than his white masters. He plundered mercilessly wherever he raided. He would disguise himself as a labourer and enter a house to buy beer. Instead of drinking he would arrest the man or woman of the house. At the mention of his name every drinking party broke up; beer was thrown out through the window; or it was returned to the pit in the yard or under the flooring boards; or poured into a pot on a stove. The name was relayed from house to house.

On a night in the middle of the week, when few people expect a beer raid, Makulu-Skop went round on a lone mission. Three men pounced on him and dragged him, blindfolded, to the plantation at the end of Second Avenue. His body was found hanging from a tree near the sewerage works.

# MIKE ALFRED

## *two poems*

*At the age of thirty-seven, more than twenty years ago, I was driven by an unsuspected demon to write what I thought was poetry. Over a period I assembled a collection, entered a competition, and was disappointed that my manuscript went totally unremarked. Eventually, common sense and curiosity overcame my injured ego and I sought critical advice.*

*From his leafy Orange Grove dwelling, Lionel Abrahams, after due consideration, responded to my collection thus: "I'll publish one." He also told me that my work would benefit by being written in complete, grammatical sentences and also, that brevity and less complexity would do me no harm.*

*He's always been tough with me, telling me directly what he's thought and felt about my work. He's done so with a caring humanity and psychological appreciation. Lionel has helped me feel worthwhile in bleak times. I whined about a review once. He said, "Mike, it's a jungle out there!" offering me reality's reflection and with it, so to speak, the sociology rather than the psychology of choosing to be a poet.*

## I'LL NEVER BE

No, I'll never be famous.
My less than voluminous
correspondence says: Thanks
for the socks. Congratulations
on your whatever. Please find
my cheque enclosed. Hardly
worth tucking away in an
attic or a bottom desk
drawer.

The famous seem to anticipate
the condition. Exercising their

gift of prescience, they conduct
a precocious correspondence
from an early age with natural
magpies. It smacks of some
arcane conspiracy. A gratuitous
stakeholding for the biography
industry. A symbiotic 'noblesse
oblige' we ordinary mortals
will never understand.


## SOON I'LL BE HISTORY

Soon, I'll be the one wearing
the old-fashioned suit in the
family photo, trying to hide my
ball-and-claw feet. Those luminous
condoms in the stud-box will keep
them guessing. Agatha Christie
notwithstanding, I'll be cobwebs
and defunct gadgets at the
back of cupboards, scratchy
music and books with yellowing
ideas. I'll be a bald Pirelli
awaiting the renaissance, a
Maginot-line of pillboxes, an
odiferous wardrobe of peacock
feathers, a salesroom of oh,
so many 'I wouldn't give it
houserooms!' People might
remember my sort, meandering
in museums on rainy
afternoons.

# HUGH LEWIN

## *two poems*

*I was sitting in exile in Harare, my account of my prison experiences*
(Bandiet) *banned in the very place it was meant for. I sent a few related*
*poems to Mike Gardiner, more for him to read than anything else. Mike sent*
*word back: 'Hang' would be published, by Lionel Abrahams. And it was.*
*Amazing. Somehow the thread I first picked up in Central Prison was com-*
*plete, the thread of reading Lionel's extracts from HC Bosman's* Cold Stone
Jug *for the first time while actually inside Cold Stone Jug. The thread that*
*has bound so much of South Africa together. Thank you.*


**WAGON-WHEELS**
*to Eli Weinberg*

After evening lock-up at the Fort
the bandiete would shout: "Wagon-wheels, Mr Weinberg!"
and Eli, communist and kantor, would pause
between the Internationale and Nkosi
to sing, shul-like,
for the motley murderers, rokers and rogues
and his awaiting-trial comrades,
sing
Wagon-wheels, wagon-wheels
Wagon-wheels carry me home
Wagon-wheels, carry me home.

And if you stopped a moment
on your way up Hospital Hill
into the rising hum of Hillbrow
you'd have heard it
only an echo perhaps
behind the walls and the double doors

hiding the nation's under-belly

Wagon-wheels, Mr Weinberg.

You won't hear it now.
Thirty years on the Fort still squats on Hospital Hill
where I'm propelled past by the evening traffic
past the door which spewed me into unimprisonment

and I can't help thinking of symbols
and the perpetuation of walls which stand still
ringing
with lost songs.


## HEARING IN ALEX
*Truth Commission, October 1996*

One witness
has a dark suit and waistcoat and a glove on his hand
to help with the arthritis – and a stick.
Thirty years before he didn't need a stick
to stir the streets, him and the other kids.
They picked him up, he said,
and roughed him up a bit in Alex
before taking him to Pretoria
– Kompol, the big house, their house,
with the warrens of offices like cells
in corridors where they do what they want –
and they start giving him the treatment,
pausing only to bring in another pick-up
(looking dazed) to watch,
while they batter him, and batter him, and batter him.
But I was lucky, he said, I shat myself
and they said: Yussus, maar die kaffir't gekak en – vat hom weg –
hy stink.
They start instead on the spectator. He is from Cape Town.
His name is Looksmart. By morning he's dead.

Another witness
tells how she heard about her teenage son;

how he'd been in the street with friends
when a passing hippo shot him
        – no sense to it, no reason –
then they collect him, she said, still alive
and batter his head against a rock.
Twenty years later, tall and high-pitched,
she spits fury
red-hot.
Maybe, she says, crumpling into her pain,
he'd still be here
if they hadn't hit his head against the rock.


Three witnesses together –
grannies, with doeks and darting eyes –
take it in turns to weep
as they tell of their children across the border in the safety
of Gaborone.
So many details: of the cars they took to get there,
the scenery along the way, all the details.
The soldiers, they explain, shot anything that moved
and raked the cupboard (where the overnight visitor hid)
tore even the cupboard to pieces, pieces, to pieces.
There was this large white sheet at the funeral, she said,
with all the names listed – and his wasn't there
wasn't there
wasn't there
but there, right at the bottom . . . ah, Joseph.


Afterwards, the hall echoes
with the laughter of kids in the square outside
and we sit
wondering about these lists of bodies
and mortuaries and more mortuaries
and coffins, coffins, coffins
bones, bones
and the glistening eyes of mothers
and survivors.
The evening shadows ring with the sounds of the children
and you have to think of tomorrow
and tomorrow
and tomorrow.

# STEPHEN WATSON

*a poem*

**A FAREWELL**

Port city, selfsame city, in all the promiscuity of summer,
with that scruffiness in your wind, salty on the leaves of shrubs,
with that sadness in your light once more, returning in the wind –
each year I add another word to the elements I've named before:
I call the light, last year windblown, now a laminate of salt;
each year I conjure colours – of amber, burnt sienna, earthy umber –
just to return to you your coastline, the khaki of a summer's day;
and the mountain by now afflicted as the moon has been by epithets,
the drab liturgy of suburbs that still eludes me like the dawns
when inland, against the light, far hills approach the harbour
and all along the skylines pines stand unaided, wordless, clear –
I've tried to name them all, and all the while in the good hope
that I could finally say goodbye at last, and not just learn again
through this love of love's frustration, the futility of words,
the unattainable peninsula that is this small corner of the world.

# CUZ JEPPE

## *a passage from a work in progress*

### A PLEASURE DISALLOWED

He still had time. Four months to put to sea. When he was on board the boat, he effectively put to sea every few hours, when he floated free as the tide came up. Maybe if he untied the moorings and really floated free for a moment – would that satisfy them?

Perhaps those cotton sails would hold and he could get across the channel. France or Holland. Start again there. He knew it was impossible; he had so much to do before he would be ready. If he could just speak to someone in authority, he felt sure they would understand.

He was pacing around his room. He noticed it had been cleaned. The pile of dirty, paint-covered clothes he had just taken off and dumped in the corner suddenly looked out of place.

There had been a warm spell of weather. He'd been working whenever there was daylight, laying decks and painting. And then the trip down here to London and the shock of this news in the post. He was exhausted. What could he do in four months? He curled up in his bed, dividing the days, the weeks, and the hours, and became aware of her smell – slightly soapy and faintly perfumed. She had been sleeping in his bed! Why? She had her own room! He didn't mind, as long as she was sleeping alone. He couldn't worry about that now – he was going to have to leave the country anyway. Then she could sleep in his bed with whomever she liked!

He wondered how he smelled right now, after two weeks with just the occasional swim in a grimy sea. He felt out of place, like his clothes.

Where was she anyway? On one of her secret missions somewhere. And where was Henry, her boy? Shouldn't he be in bed by now?

He woke up disorientated. He never slept well the first night off the boat. He missed the rocking, and kept waiting for the tide to come in.

He realised she was in the room when he heard a gentle sobbing. She was crouched down by the bed. Jesus! She'd been staring at him in his sleep! So why was she crying?

"I'm sorry," she whispered, "I didn't mean to wake you. I didn't know you were back."

"Where's Henry?" he said, and regretted the harshness of his tone as he saw her recoil. Then, in a softer tone, "I see you've cleaned the room. Thank you."

"Yes, I couldn't . . . He's away, staying with friends. I couldn't . . . I went out for a drink. I didn't know you were here."

She looked to him like a deer on ice, unsure whether to run or stand.

"I couldn't . . . I've been sleeping in here," she said, glancing at the bed.

"I know," he said, "it smells of you."

"Oh! I'm sorry."

"Oh no, it's nice. I'm the one who smells right now."

A pleasure disallowed crossed her face. "Can I . . . ? Could I . . . ?" She glanced down at the bed again.

"What are we whispering for?" He laughed. "There's no-one to hear us for a mile away. If I'm going to have company I'd better get clean and try to smell nice too."

He went over to the ruined fireplace and lit a fire, then filled the large coffee pot – one of his better foraging finds – and placed it over the flames. She sat on the bed watching as he soaped himself. He tipped the heated water into the tin bath pulled up before the fire. He sat in the bath, and started rinsing off.

And then she was there, running the warm water over him with her cupped hands, allowing her pale hair to cling in heavy tendrils across his back and chest.

They led each other over to the bed, too impatient to get dry. His cry of urgency was followed by hers as they entered the sheets and each other, the tide of their need moving all before it. He broke into her as if into a sea that closed over him without trace. Afterwards, they lay rocking together in the reflected light of the sulphurous London clouds.

# FRANCIS FALLER

*a poem*

## EVENING WITH A BACHELOR FRIEND

You cavil at the clarity of the wine: it's no surprise!
Me, too, you find obscure. What anxiety, what caprice
made you shake the bottle, turn it upside
down? You'll taste that leather tang of lees.

We've been too intimate tonight; you've carped
at marriage, at a cage, the bleakness of a customary vow.
(When I hint at a lover's breasts and thighs,
you substitute the plastic torso of a crowd.)

Something overwhelming's happened to my mouth:
words have poured but, lying on my tongue like stone,
discoveries! You wanted talk of love,
to prove me love's bitter sediment. And now
you're satisfied, a naked intellect, alone.
The bottle's drained. And look! your lips are stained.

# YVONNE KEMP

## *a story*

### ABIDE WITH ME

Aletta Jordaan had always been a devout believer in God. When she was seventeen and gave her virginity to the Scotsman with the long black hair and the Vespa scooter, it was many weeks before she could go into the church without her hands getting sweaty. Sooner or later the Pastor would surely find her out. God would show him the truth in a text which would spring up from the pages of the Bible, and he would lean over the pulpit and stab his finger at her. Or one of the Brethren would see her naked in her sin as she was before God and the Scotsman, and on Communion Sunday he would refuse to let her drink the thick sweet juice from the silver jug. It was one of the worst times of her life and she was very thankful, the day she married Jan Jordaan, that it was all behind her.

But it was the same when she first committed adultery, with the new Italian hairdresser. She was standing at the foot of his big double bed and taking off her stockings when the realisation came upon her. She said the word inside herself and saw it written across the sky in bright red letters. She looked at the Italian hairdresser to see how he felt about it. He was already in his underpants and how he was feeling was very clear. She thought if she did it quickly, maybe it wouldn't count. Even so, she expected the thunder to roll as she took off her panties, and as she opened her legs she thought now is the hour. Going up in the lift, afterwards, to her office, some leftover semen spilled a secret dampness into her panties and she thought they will all surely know, and look, and they will get out at the very next floor. And when nothing happened, then or later, Aletta knew that God was expecting her to make her own punishment for this sin that would not fade from her soul the way the damp patch had slowly dried from her panties.

So she telephoned the furniture removal people, and she visited her mother and they cried together. Then on Saturday she made bacon and eggs for breakfast. She prepared the meal with care. The bacon was pale brown and crisp, ready to be shattered between the teeth. She spooned hot butter over the yolks of the eggs until they were covered with a thin white film, and she toasted the bread on one side only, the way Jan liked it, with the butter melting into the soft side. She had made up her mind to tell Jan straight away, but the smell of bacon and eggs was too everyday for what she had to say, so she waited until they were drinking their coffee. She explained to him, then, about the furniture removal van that was going to come on Monday and how she would stay at her mother's until she found a flat. Jan said why now all of a sudden, and so she explained also about the adultery. She knew now, she said, that she couldn't go without sex for such a long time, especially not when Jan was busy with one of his girlfriends. She knew that it would be wrong to expect him to change anything, and so she could see already that she would go again to the Italian hairdresser. She loved Jan with all her heart, she said, but to carry on sinning like that would be too hard. So it was better to go.

Jan asked her many questions, all of which she answered, even the ones that made her ashamed. She did not want to tell him about the body of the Italian hairdresser, nor that she had enjoyed it although it was a bit quick, but she must just bear it. God obviously expected it of her. She felt very surprised when Jan's voice started to get deep and he got that look on his face. It was a funny time to want to make love to her, after all these months, but she had never said no before. Afterwards he told her to cancel the furniture removal van, so on Monday when she got to work she telephoned them and also her mother, who said she was glad they had sorted it all out.

Aletta wasn't so sure about that, but she did know that God was sending her some kind of a message. She felt quite puzzled about it at first, and she looked up the Ten Commandments to make sure she knew what God meant about adultery. She thought about the message the next time she took off her clothes for the Italian hairdresser, and she thought about it when she locked her legs around Jan's waist in the middle of the night. He liked it in the middle of the night, and she wasn't always sure, the next day, whether he thought he had dreamt it.

From time to time, Aletta asked God please to let her know if she was misunderstanding Him in some way. A few times, too, she thought that maybe she had got muddled and how all this time she could have been listening to the Devil. But Aletta didn't believe in the Devil the way she believed in God. And anyway, she had prayed to God and not to the Devil for Jan to love her and for her to be a good wife for him, and it was true that he loved her more, now. Also, when the Italian hairdresser moved to another town, she very soon met a farmer from Gatooma and it wasn't long before he was making regular visits to town. At first she didn't like going to the hotel, but Jan was just as interested in the farmer as he had been in the Italian hairdresser. He would ask her, does he make you feel like this, pulling at one of her nipples with his teeth, and she would laugh because that was what he liked her to do.

Even so, it took Aletta a long time before she could feel completely sure of what God was showing her she must do. She asked him once why He wanted her to live this way. It was in church, at Sakkie du Toit's wedding, and she had grown very angry with God while she listened to the Pastor talking about no man putting asunder what God had joined and so on and so forth. Why did He make it so difficult to understand? He kept telling her one thing in private and saying all kinds of other things in public. She was shocked to find that she could think this way, right in the middle of saying Praise the Lord, and she realised what a terrible blasphemy her disobedience could lead her into. She remembered how her mother had always told her that the worst sin of all was to question the ways of the Lord. So when she met Sakkie's best man at the reception, later, she said yes she would love to have some more champagne, and yes she would love to dance, and she relaxed her thighs against him, and moved her hips in just so, and let her belly go slack against the ridge of his heat spreading through them both.

By the time she met the French architect, she had grown more or less used to the whole thing. She knew straight away that he was available, but he was a bit older than any of the others. He had the kind of mouth she liked, full lips and quite red, although it was a bit loose and with wrinkles all along the top lip from smoking since before she was born. He had the kind of eyes that enjoyed looking at women's faces and bodies and, in the end, when he invited her to a cocktail party, she thought she would go. He took her to a caravan that he kept at a dam just outside town and, except for the first time, it was the quickest adultery she'd ever done. She thought maybe he was one of those who did it quickly once and then again, more slowly. But nothing else happened and they went back to the party. He telephoned a week later, and she agreed to go to his office in a few days' time. She didn't really feel like it, but she couldn't ignore God's will just because He sent her to such an old man. So she had a few drinks with the French architect, at his office, and she followed him to his house in one of those quiet streets where the shadows from the trees screen you from the hard white of lamplight and the moon mixed up together. This time the softness of his body didn't worry her so much, and the little plops inside her when he came felt quite nice.

She saw the note on her car before he did. She read it without at all understanding what it said. She noticed, when the French architect asked her what was wrong, from the way his eyes kept so still, that he was anxious so she said it was alright, it was just a note from Jan, her husband, and she would go home now. The French architect cleared his throat. He said oh, and then yes, well perhaps she should do that. Although she wanted to read the note again she got into her car and waved goodbye. The tyres of the car made a terrible noise every time she took a corner, but she didn't mind because the sooner she got home, the sooner she would understand what was in the note.

She stood right under the light in the sitting-room to see what it said, which wasn't much. "You never know where to draw the line. You always go too far." And then at the bottom, Jan Jordaan, but that she knew from the handwriting in any case. It didn't make sense. She had done, all along, what God's message told her to do and now this note made it all into rubbish. God hadn't said anything to her about going too far, and neither had Jan so how was she supposed to know. And what did it mean, too far?

Adultery was adultery, you couldn't go more far the twentieth time than you did the first.

She tried to explain this to Jan when he came home but it looked as if he didn't hear what she said. And while she was talking to him she remembered something he had told her a long time ago. How once, when he was little, his mother had made apple pie and all the time she was baking it in the oven he longed for the moment when it would be ready, and while he waited he could taste it, warm and sweet in his mouth. But when she took it out, she put it on the windowsill and went back to the fence to carry on talking to the woman next door. He followed her outside, but she just kept on saying yes, in a minute, and when she eventually cut a slice for him and put it on his special red plastic plate, he didn't want it any more. Jan said that was a lesson to him that when a thing was spoilt it was spoilt and it was no use to want it any more, because the moment when it would have been right was gone and you couldn't ever find it again. This was what Aletta thought of as she talked to Jan's face that said he didn't hear her.

She knew better than to cry, it just made your eyes swell up, so she went to bed and she didn't sleep much. The next day was Saturday, but she didn't get up to make bacon and eggs like the first time she woke up and thought about adultery. She waited in bed, pretending to be asleep, until she heard Jan leave the house. Then she got up and went to the bathroom. She didn't clean her teeth or wash her face, she just opened the cupboard on the wall and took out some bottles. She poured a glass of water and took it to the bedroom, with the bottles. She took another bottle out of the drawer on Jan's side of the bed, and she went to the dressing-table and looked in all the drawers until she found a few more. She stared at her face in the mirror, and she sat down and arranged the bottles in a row, next to the glass of water. She saw she had made a mistake with one of the bottles, it only had nail varnish inside, a bright pink that wasn't in fashion any more. She shook it so that she could see the little metal balls making the silver and pink parts streak through one another and slowly sink together into a paler new colour. Her mother-in-law had once watched her painting her toenails, carefully separating the toes with fluffs of cotton wool the way she'd seen them do it in that film, about that kid. Aletta opened the cupboard on the right-hand side of the dressing-table and took out a plastic bag full of pink and yellow and blue balls of cotton wool. Her mother-in-law had said, that day, that there was something about painting your toenails that was a bit wicked. She had smiled at Aletta as she said it, so Aletta had smiled back.

She squeezed the plastic bag, then she rearranged the row of bottles so that the tallest ones were at the front and the smallest at the back. She left out the bottle of nail varnish. The bottles were at right angles to the mirror, so that there was one line coming towards her and another line that went back into the mirror. She looked again at her face above the two lines. She took out a blue and pink ball from the plastic bag, and lifted her foot up onto the chair so that she could put the cotton wool between her big toe and the second toe. She smiled at her face, raising her eyebrows and making her lips thin until she was making the smile of her mother-in-law.

"Well. Fuck you," she thought, looking at the smile.

She took another ball of cotton wool, and this time she said it aloud as she put it between her second and third toes. "Fuck you." She started to laugh and when she tried to put the third ball of cotton wool in its place, the wad between her first two toes fell out. This made her laugh even more, and it took a while to get everything back into place.

She stopped when she got to the little toe, and looked up at the ceiling. "And you," she said. She made another smile, this time the kind that stretches your lips until they crack and your eyes begin to water. "Fuck you too."

She settled the last piece of cotton wool, and held out her foot with its toes all splayed out. She reached for the bottle of pink nail varnish, twisted the top off and began steadily to paint the nail of her big toe.

•

# GEOFFREY HARESNAPE

## *a poem*

**EXPEDITION**
*to a replica of a Padrão near the Cape of Storms which carries a misleading
inscription that an original was erected there in 1486*

Scholar
>   I'm wanting to see
>   where Diaz
>   raised up his cross.

Couple
>   We're at a loss
>   catering
>   for such old man's zeal.
>
>   and prefer the sleek, sliding feel
>   of the car
>   in our clamant mood.
>
>   Is it very rude
>   of us
>   to be having thoughts of bed
>
>   while he shakes his head
>   at the date
>   chiselled in by mistake?

Scholar
>   The fools did not take
>   account
>   of the long months' delay

in the wild and wind-driven way,
the voyage
from the Tagus to Cape.

Couple
We linger to gape
at Europe's
white phallus, erect

where two roads bisect
the blank veld;
a symbol of storms

in these restive forms –
this landscape,
his mind, and our hearts.

# HILLARY HAMBURGER

## *an interview with Lionel Abrahams*

*I first saw Lionel from the top of a Kensington tram when I was thirteen or fourteen years old. After school I would often take the tram to the centre of Johannesburg where my father owned a small tearoom, there to indulge in milkshakes and movie magazines. The customers, having a cup of coffee and a toasted cheese – working class people waiting for their buses, busdrivers themselves, their wives and children, pimps and prostitutes – showed me a different world from my own. Hungry to escape from the ghetto of my child-hood and adolescence, I found my imagination fed by this world of the Loveday Tearoom.*

*My school, Jeppe High School for Girls, was two blocks away from 87 Roberts Avenue, which I learnt much later was the Abrahams's home. There was a tram stop outside it. The first time I saw Lionel my eye was caught by the sight of a strangely uncoordinated man, heaving and pulling himself up the steps that ascended from the front gate to street level. I watched from the top of the tram with both curiosity and shock. That night at the supper table I described what I had seen. "Ah," said my mother in a knowing and sombre voice, "that must be the Abrahams boy. He's been spastic from birth. What a tragedy!" After that I remained somewhat curious but no longer shocked when I saw Lionel labouring his way along the pavement or climbing onto the tram. He had, in my mind, become a neighbourhood fixture.*

*When I finished school I went to the University of the Witwatersrand on a Transvaal Education Department loan. No one in my family had ever been to university. For all my excited anticipation, I was terrified by the strangeness of the place. I didn't know a soul. And how lost I was as I entered the first his-tory of fine arts lecture. I looked around for an empty seat, anxious to find a place to put myself. Then I saw Lionel – a comforting familiar anchor in a sea of uncertainty. And the seat next to him was free. I made for it.*

*He smiled as I sat down. "Hello, I'm Lionel Abrahams."*

*"I know," I answered "I've seen you from the top of the tram. I also live in Kensington."*

*After the lecture we talked over coffee. That was in 1954, Lionel's second stint at Wits. We've been talking ever since. But what I couldn't have known then was how much his powerful intellect and abundantly generous spirit were to enrich my life.*

## REALITY IS THE RICHEST SOURCE:
## AN INTERVIEW WITH A FRIEND

*HILLARY HAMBURGER: Your parents were Jewish Lithuanian immigrants. You were an only son, the eldest of three. Your sister Rae was born two years after you, and Carmel two years after her. You went to school at the Hope Home and Damelin College. You went to Wits in 1949 and dropped out the following year. That must have been round about the time I saw you from the top of the tram. What were you and your world about at that time?*

LIONEL ABRAHAMS: I must have been catching the tram to university. Being accepted for university was a huge test. Herman Charles Bosman had entered my life by this time – my father had hired him to coach me in creative writing. Bosman had done two things for me. He had made me critical of the academic world on the one hand while encouraging me on the other to go to university to acquire a background. I was ready for that. I was hungry – and uncertain. Uncertain about whether I was going to enjoy the things I wanted.

*HH: I know that trams were important in your life. In 'A Right Time For Trams' – one of my favourite stories – you describe Felix catching one for the first time at the age of nineteen. Was that autobiographical? And if so what was its significance?*

LA: I'm always reluctant to confess that my stories are autobiographical. But yes, becoming able to mount a tram was very important to me – a huge extension of my independence. It enabled me to get to know and enjoy the city. This had a special significance for me because Bosman had implanted in me the thought that I was a Johannesburg writer. He imparted some of his own feeling for Johannesburg to me. And then of course the ability to ride trams – and buses – made it possible for me to go to university. I wouldn't even have met you if I hadn't made that conquest. Tram riding also freed me to explore relationships and collect my library. So in many ways tram riding was a genuine liberation.

*HH: What did being Jewish mean to you?*

LA: My parents were powerfully conscious of being Jewish. My mother was not religious and my father was observant but not strictly so. When I went to the Hope Home my Jewishness became a mark of difference. It became something not altogether easy to live with. There was a fair amount of anti-Semitism around. I suppose to compensate for the uncomfortableness of that I got into the way of squeezing whatever bits of pride I could out of bible studies at school. On the other hand at one stage I decided to convert to Christianity and I even tried to convert my mother. But for all that, my experience of the Hope Home left me with a romantic expectation that I would find special warmth with Jewish friends. I had to learn that that was a simplification. By the way, because of being at the Home I never had a Barmitzvah. As a result I remained uneducated in things Jewish compared to other boys. But my father encouraged me and my sisters to join a Zionist youth group and for some years of my adolescence I was a passionate right-wing Zionist. Goodness knows what sort of bigotry might have set in if I hadn't come under the influence of George Gemmel (a supervisor at the Hope Home), Bosman, and others. In the course of time I learnt that being Jewish was simply interesting in a way comparable to being a South African or a Johannesburger.

*HH: Your creative gifts have found many outlets. Among your writings are a novel,* The Celibacy of Felix Greenspan, *essays and criticism, and four volumes of poetry. And you've done much work as an editor, publisher and teacher. Where does it all begin?*

LA: I always knew I wanted to be a writer. But there was more to it. Whenever there was an indication that I had got something right, that I had produced some writing that had engaged or amused someone, I felt gratified. The opposite was true as well. When I did not get it right I was miserable. But I never took it for granted that I manifested any particular talent. There is a contradiction – I do not think I have ever linked the two things – because I was also horribly ambitious, hugely romantic in my aspirations as a child and adolescent. I had to get over my sense of being special, a genius waiting to be discovered. I do not know if it was a question of growing up or Herman Charles Bosman's dictum about humility that gave me a realistic and decent balance. I wasn't always humble. I had to learn how to be humble. (Laughs.)

Before I met Bosman I thought that anything worth writing had to be invented, made up out of your imagination. Bosman opened my eyes to reality as the richest source of material, which is very interesting as a sidelight on Bosman, because one does not think of him as a realist. I now began to discover stories in my own experience.

*HH: Yet* Felix Greenspan *is not written as autobiography or memoir.*

LA: That's so. I was dipping into my experience to write short stories. After many years I put *Felix Greenspan* together but I thought of it as a collection of short stories. When I wrote the stories originally, some were written in the first person, some used different names. I edited them to make them agree with each other but I still thought of them as a collection of stories. Then Patrick Cullinan, my publisher, identified it as a novel.

*HH: In 1952 a little collection of short stories called* Twenty *was published. How did it come about?*

LA: *Twenty* was a home-made book. It was called *Twenty* for two reasons. It contained twenty stories. And all the contributors were in their early twenties, except me. I was twenty-five.

The collaboration came about because the four writers and the two illustrators all lived in Kensington and were friends. The four writers were Barney Simon, Peggy Marks, Myrna Blumberg and myself. The two illustrators were Harold Rubin and my namesake Lionel Abrams.

*HH: But how did it all happen?*

LA: I had founded and edited the children's magazine at the Hope Training Home. It was called *The Pepper Pot*. It was roneoed so I knew about that kind of thing. Later Bosman instilled an interest in me in local writing and I think my three friends shared this kind of interest. There weren't many openings for publications. Barney and I had each had a story published in *Trek*. (Bosman was *Trek*'s literary editor at the time.) So *Twenty* grew naturally out of our interest and circumstances. It was Barney's idea to bring in Harold and Lionel. The process of actually producing it was an enormous effort. Various people allowed us the use of their offices and duplicating machines on weekends. All sorts of things went wrong. It went on for weeks. Barney carried the main burden. Once the pages were printed, we would bring them to my house and set them on the dining-room table. There they stayed for a long time and whoever was available would be asked to walk around the table, pick up pages and collate copies. We invented what we called collating parties, which we went on holding in the early days of *The Purple Renoster*.

In the end we managed to put together about 250 complete copies and we sent it all to a printer to print a cover and bind them. We then gave copies to the newspaper book reviewers and offered copies to the bookshops. To our surprise it cornered a lot of attention. We had several enthusiastic reviews. Barney in fact attracted the greatest attention with his powerful stories, and some of Harold Rubin's illustrations stick in my mind to this day.

*HH: I know that Barney was an important person in your life. Why?*

LA: Barney and I were originally drawn together by writing. Each of us was nourished by the other's receptivity. I had not been particularly good at friendship before. Barney was an altogether new kind of friend – enthusiastic about the same things as I was. He got into the habit of arriving at my house late at night, which was when I often did my writing in those days. I'm talking about 1949/1950. He would call from the garden below my high bedroom window. I would go round and let him in. And we'd talk and talk and talk.

Though Barney was four years younger than me he had at least as much to teach me as I had to teach him – at least as many books, ideas, interests and experiences to talk about. We always had our own individual approach to things. Theatre of course was Barney's special interest. But out of that friendship came *Twenty* and *The Purple Renoster*. It might even be true to say that without Barney in my life, without the confidence he nourished in me at the beginning, not only might *Twenty* not have happened but also *The Purple Renoster*, Renoster Books, Bateleur Press and *Sesame*.

*HH: You mentioned that you and Barney had each had a story published in* Trek. *I think Nadine Gordimer was a contributor as well. Did you know her then?*

LA: No, not then. But I noticed a story of Nadine's in *Trek* which I particularly liked. Philip Stein, a friend and bookseller, encouraged me to write and tell her. My letter to her began "Dear Miss Gordimer, this is fan mail . . ." Many years later when the gagging clause was enforced, I mentioned to Nadine that writers might get round that law by publishing anonymously. Out of that remark grew the idea of an anthology of South African writing which would ignore the gagging clause. Nadine interested Penguin Books in the project and we collaborated on it. This was published as *South African Writing Today*. In the end the idea of pseudonyms fell away, so of course the book was banned in South Africa.

*HH: You moved from being a short-story writer to being a critic?*

LA: I came to Wits and won the short-story Arts Festival Competition. That was very thrilling. One year I won first and second prize. Another year I won first prize. I remember an evening in the Great Hall when there was a reading of my story and a prize-giving and me sitting there feeling very excited – actually sniggering with excitement. I did not accept acceptance in a complacent way.

I had already come under the influence of Bosman and had my first story published in *Trek*. Bosman was enormously encouraging. He would react with excitement to some of my writing and made me excited about my own possibilities. When I came out of Bosman's hands, there was no sign of a critic in me. That grew gradually out of English at Wits, out of the essays I wrote. How did I come to be asked for that first book review? I can't remember. It now seems so natural to write about writers, writing, and the other arts. In the early days there was always something being asked for. I had to give so much time to criticism that it got in the way of creative writing. But I did get a lot of value out of doing particular articles. Once I'd started *The Purple Renoster* there was a lot of critical writing to do.

*HH: I know that your creative-writing class has been a source of inspiration to many people. This book marking your seventieth birthday bears witness to that.*

LA: The workshop has been going for twenty years. But I was doing that kind of thing in a less formal way for many years before it started. One uses the word teacher as a convenient label but it is actually a misnomer for me. It is vaguer than that – a mixture that includes subeditor, receiver, listener, encourager and critic. If you ask me what I have taught, I'd be hard pressed to say. I have encouraged people who have wanted to write. The workshop has kept itself going for so long that it looks as if it has produced only successes. What is hidden are the failures. People who came once or twice and then dropped out outnumbered those who stayed. And I am afraid that some that pulled out after a few sessions showed bruises. There have been some bad failures. In some cases it was because what they were looking for was therapy, some kind of comfort. I did not see that. I proceeded with my literary concerns. Looking back, if I had understood I may have been able to say, "I can't help you." But without knowing what was being asked for I could only say bluntly, "This is not working as a poem." I was looking for art and communication and here was someone bleeding. I only learnt that afterwards.

*HH: If people came for the wrong reasons, that surely was their responsibility. Having said that, perhaps I can admit to you now that I regard myself as one of your failures. But this book is testimony to your successes.*

LA: (Laughs.) I'm sorry about you. But it's beautiful that there is something to show. I didn't make the successes happen; rather I helped a little to allow them to happen. I initiated the workshop but it is the interaction between everyone there and the spirit in which it happens that encourages creativity.

*HH: I have heard it said that one of your strengths as a teacher is to make an aspirant writer feel excited about his or her own work. I know that Bosman did that for you. Perhaps as a teacher his mantle has fallen on your shoulders?*

LA: (Laughs.) No comment!

*HH: 'Poetry, the most intimate, truthful and heroic employment of language, must penetrate the cataclysm, its ironies, its paradoxes, must articulate the inwardness of disaster, and thus triumph over it – that is to say, convey our humanity through and beyond it.'*

*Wonderful words! You should recognise them because I am quoting you. How did you come to poetry?*

LA: My very first attempt at writing as a child was making up rhymes and jingles. Pure ego rather than a poetic imagination. I wanted to show how clever I was. I had no idea of what poetry was in my final year at school. Later when I wrote verse, I still did not dare think of it as real poetry. I did not take myself seriously as a poet until after I met that marvellous poet Ruth Miller. I was about thirty years old. She took my poetry seriously and it was only then that I could begin to do so as well.

*HH: She seems to have played an important role?*

LA: Once we had met and got to know each other, she, and her husband, liked having me as a visitor. Our contact involved her testing her poems on me and my submitting mine to her. She responded with serious interest and even though I often found myself arguing with her criticism, I was both instructed and encouraged.

*HH: Stephen Spender called the concentrated effort of writing poetry a spiritual compulsion that disembodies the poet. He writes of poets having to anchor themselves in the physical world. Schiller liked to have rotten apples around; Walter de la Mare had to smoke when writing. Auden drank endless cups of tea.*

LA: That is very interesting but it is not my experience. I cannot get away from the feeling that I am an accidental poet. Spender is talking about people for whom being a poet involves them in being a different sort of human being. That is a very high level of specialisation. There are lower levels of specialisation, taking the form of well worked-out theories of poetic technique. People have a very conscious grasp of their poetics. I am not even on that level. I am an accidental time-to-time kind of poet. I don't keep it up. It is not a vocation. It happens when it happens and that is not too often.

*HH: (Laughing.) Well, often enough to have got four volumes of poetry published.*

LA: I'm amazed at that!

*HH: What about your publishing career?*

LA: It is something I am especially proud of. In a number of cases my choices for publishing have been so marvellously justified. I'm referring not only to books I published but also to books I edited, having spotted, or discovered the writers. How can I feel anything but proud when I think of Oswald Mtshali, Wally Serote, Modikwe Dikobe, Herman Charles Bosman, Barney Simon, Ruth Miller? Sometimes when I am tempted to gloat about this I have to remind myself that there were several writers to whom I gave the thumbs down who afterwards did very well.

*HH: How did* The Purple Renoster *come about?*

LA: With *The Pepper Pot* and *Twenty* in the background, I could think of myself as doing something about publishing. When *Trek* folded, Barney, others and I had a sense that there was no outlet for our stories. The idea of a new magazine of our own was very natural. And we found a lot of enthusiasm for it among other friends. We took it for granted that we would roneo it so that it wouldn't cost very much. My father was willing to help so it all happened. In the course of years it changed from being a domestic and ivory-towerish sort of venture into something much more socially open and generally South African. Those changes weren't a matter of policy but rather of evolution as the magazine came to be more widely recognised.

*HH: Did* Renoster Books *evolve from* The Purple Renoster?

LA: In a sense it grew out of *The Purple Renoster* because over those years in dealing with writers and publishing in that small way, I nursed the idea of branching into book publishing. When we had come across Oswald Mtshali and he had accumulated a good body of poems, it came to me that this might be a good book to begin with. Please note this was not because I expected it to do well in the market but because I thought it was new and different. The book became a possibility through the enthusiasm of Robert Royston and Eva Bezwoda. They were assisting me on *The Purple Renoster*. I had introduced them to Alec Natas when he had asked me to recommend an editor for some of his own writing. They told him about my dream of publishing books. He simply presented me with the R1 000 it took to bring out *Sounds of a Cowhide Drum*. The rest, as they say, is history.

*HH: How did Bateleur Press fit into that picture?*

LA: Robert and Eva were my partners in Renoster Books and, in 1972, by the time we had published four volumes, they decided to emigrate to England. I didn't feel up to running Renoster Books on my own. Barney introduced me to Patrick Cullinan, who also cherished a dream of publishing. We formed a partnership under the name preferred by Patrick, namely Bateleur Press. During our seven or eight years, we brought out a good handful of well-received books — Barney's *Joburg, Sis!*, first poetry collections by David Farrell and Peter

Strauss. Three editions of *Bateleur Poets*, which included people like Mike Kirkwood, Robert Greig, and Walter Saunders.

*HH: And* Sesame?

LA: *Sesame* was my last literary magazine. It, and its internet descendant, *Electronic Sesame*, grew out of my writing workshop.

*HH: How does it feel looking back now that you are turning seventy?*

LA: That's not simple. I have been lucky to have been given a life that I find very interesting. I have been endowed with enough of a brain to make interesting connections. I have been thrown into circumstances that I did not always enjoy but which turned out to be enriching and extending.

I have found myself living in an interesting city that has engaged me and I have encountered marvellous people who have added and added and added to my life.

But I am not totally pleased with the way I have lived it. I have a sense of a number of challenges I failed to meet. Reading is one of my deepest sources of satisfaction and yet I have read relatively little. There are so many valuable things that I ought to have learnt about in my own fields of interest. There are huge gaps of ignorance. I have wasted a lot of my time on rubbish. Some failure has to do with laziness and some has to do with fear.

*HH: Fear?*

LA: Obviously fear of exposing myself to dangers, fear of exposing my ideas to too much challenge. In certain respects I have been too soft, in the sense of acting in order to be liked, instead of refusing some request in order to get on with what I thought was important.

*HH: So many of your early stories deal with frustration or pain in your love relationships. Yet your obvious happiness in your marriage to Jane seems not often to be reflected in current work.*

LA: I think it is true to say that in those early stories there is often a quality of twistedness in a particular situation or relationship. There is irony, difficulty, or tension. That's why there is a story to tell.

Another thought – what distance is there between experience and writing? My experience of – and with – Jane is very close to me. I don't seem to have the kind of perspective on experience that makes for that kind of story telling. But for all that, the way Jane has come to me is a marvellous story and is one more story in a life of marvellous stories. And that reinforces the idea that there is a tale to be told. What I have done so far is highly selective. So much has been left out. Now my mind is turning to autobiography.

*HH: In your Olive Schreiner Prize acceptance speech you said, "I want to belong to South Africa; I want to serve the ends of liberal humanism." You have been labelled a liberal. What does that mean to you?*

LA: I have to go back to a time when I remember myself reacting with irritation to gestures which were called liberal. They had to do with two elements. The one was an early form of affirmative action or tokenism where people would do a bending over backwards in a way that distorted the reality of what was right under their noses. The other part was a political identification with 'our side'. When did I begin to feel differently about that label? When liberalism began to get a bad name I began to change my mind because I thought it was getting a bad name for behaviours I approved of. That is when I began to think of myself as a liberal.

*HH: But were you taking a political position?*

LA: I suppose so. There was my anger with different kinds of censorship.

*HH: Do you remember I came to you after the Rivonia arrests in 1963. I was looking for safe houses to hide people. Your parents were away on holiday. This made it possible for you to hide someone the police were after. You readily agreed. Were you not taking a more radical step with that action?*

LA: I also allowed Ruth First to hold a meeting at my house although I made a condition that no violence was to be discussed. I was prepared to accommodate them because I felt that these people were being treated unfairly – because of bannings, gagging, ninety-day detentions. Particular things appalled me. I remained a particularist.

*HH: When I think of the things that appalled me I think of the things that affected the ordinary lives of ordinary people – the uprooting and relocation of communities, the pass laws, and arrests, group areas, job reservation, Bantu education, the immorality act, censorship laws – it goes on and on. I identified with people whose lives were devastated by those laws. I always assumed that you were equally appalled?*

LA: I wouldn't have used the word 'appalled' then. A year or two before I met you I was working in my dad's timber yard. I became friends with Jim. He was the 'boss-boy', an older man, bright. I would talk to him about the South African situation and the injustice of it. One day he came to visit me at home. He must have been with me for an hour and I never invited him to sit down.

I feel lousy remembering. If anyone had challenged me I would have been deeply ashamed. But I might have been caught up in my parents' attitude. I wonder though whether my inhibition came from a silly assumption on my part. They may well have treated Jim better than I did. But I remember many quarrels with them about what seemed like their unfairness. On the other hand when Nadine Gordimer was writing about the need for identification with the oppressed, I felt uneasily challenged – wondering why I had never imagined such a possibility.

At the beginning of Nadine's career, her writing had the effect of bringing South African reality into literature in a new way that was exciting. Suddenly we could see our recognisable world in books. That hadn't been quite the case before. At the peak of her marvellously sustained career you could say that she took South African literature into the world in a new way. That's the symbolic meaning of her Nobel Prize.

*HH: But did you not identify with black oppression, black impotence, black outrage? When you delivered your Hoernlé lecture, 'The Democratic Chorus and Individual Choice', you equated Barend Strydom with Robert McBride. Strydom was a right-winger who gunned down six black civilians in Pretoria. McBride was an ANC operative who planted a bomb that killed three white civilians in a beachfront bar in Durban. Your equating these two distressed me.*

LA: I look at the deed and not the cause. My stand is, to hell with murderous methods. I don't know what methods I thought ought to be used. If you are asking me for some kind of philosophical justification for my position, I can't give it to you. I know though that I did not sympathise with the armed struggle.

*HH: Do you think that your lack of interest in politics or rather your suspicion of politics has to do with the difficulties caused by your physical handicap? Did your childhood development with your own personal struggle leave no room for identification with political struggle?*

LA: No, I don't think so. I hope not. That sounds as if I was so involved with my own survival that I had nothing left over for other people. But I don't think that is the case. Why did I form any kind of friendship with Jim? Why did I talk about the unfairness of things? I stayed with the editing of *The Marabi Dance*. I made a friend and protégé of the author, Marks Rammitloa. I supported the use of a nom de plume, Modikwe Dikobe, to get round the gagging clause and kept that nom de plume secret. I helped him with the education of his children. Why did I get involved with PEN? Why was I so eager to make friends with black writers? Why was I so frustrated when the political situation blocked that contact? Why did I run a workshop in Alex in 1985 when few whites were going in there? Why did I find joy in discovering and promoting Oswald Mtshali and Wally Serote?

*HH: Were all those acts informed by a political consciousness?*

LA: In *my* sense of the word they are not political acts. Thinking back to my early association with Wally, we were in a reading circle together. It was quite a long time before I saw things in his writing that I liked. And only then did I involve myself in promoting him and eventually publishing his first book.

By the time he was on to his third or fourth book, the work had lost some of its subtlety and complexity. By that time he had become an important figure. I had a sense that the people who were promoting him were operating in political terms. Some people who were deeply involved in literature were deserting their critical standards. I was unhappy about that. There was plenty of politics in Wally's first book *Yakhal'inkomo*. But it had the subtlety, complexity and originality that made it important poetry.

*HH: How do you reconcile your self-definition as a liberal while at the same time claiming your need to stand outside political debate and, even more drastically, political concerns per se?*

LA: It is not quite a matter of self-definition. I would prefer not to have a label attached to me because I don't like labels. It's a question of what I like and what I don't like. I prefer acting individually. I dislike organisational discipline. I distrust activism. When it becomes violent the evil of the method is easy to define but not the virtue of the cause. That is something we can never absolutely establish. There are always contradictory causes also claiming virtue. I distrust most kinds of idealism, especially social – impersonal – idealism. I distrust intensified morality. Naughtiness is often good for a laugh.

I'm not always tolerant but believe I should be. I like certain kinds of order and tradition, but dislike conformism.

My politics is the politics of defending myself against political interference.

*HH: Can we turn from the temporal to the sublime – from politics to God?*

LA: I do find myself thinking more and more about that sort of thing. The sublime? Spirituality? God? What to call it is a problem. I want rationality. In some ways I mistrust mysticism as much as politics. I've had the thought that often it is only unclear explanations that give rise to mystical ideas.

Growing older I find myself less and less comfortable about aspects of contemporary life – things to do with morals, language, artistic styles. There's an ugliness that seems to spring from a lack of connectedness. Obviously not the kind we see in conformity and mass demonstrations of sentiment – there's no lack of that. I'm talking about the connectedness that involves the individual's sense of identity with humankind across space and time.

That's what I often feel to be lacking in today's world. Too many new things affect me as disgusting, perplexing and frightening, so that sometimes I feel quite alien and under threat of extinction in more than just a personal sense. To protect myself against this negativity I try to hold in mind the tradition of human values embodied in literature and the other arts, in science and philosophy, and – despite all the horrors and muddle – even in history. I mean values involving intelligence, sympathy, the consciousness of beauty, the idea of sacredness in man and nature, which tend to connect us all into one entity. These values are most of what I mean by spirituality. If they survive, then, because I feel identified with the human race they define, my own individual spirit also, in a sense, survives beyond my life.

Incidentally, I now begin to understand that this may have been what Bosman was pointing to when he used to declare to me that: 'Art and life and God are one.'

*HH: You've spent a great deal of time editing, publishing, reviewing and supporting other people's writing. Do you think you did this at the expense of your own creative writing?*

LA: Yes, I'm pretty sure I would have done more of my own writing. But I chose all those activities and I don't regret them. They have been rewarded on a scale I didn't expect. I do sometimes have regrets about my own writing. But then I have to ask myself why I did it that way? I don't know.

*HH: I've always thought that your doing it 'that way' grew out of your generativity. It's a concept that includes creativity and productivity, but goes beyond that to nurturing and guiding the next generation. It's got something to do with a knowledge of the inevitability and necessity of the continuity of life.*

LA: What I have to say is this – my satisfaction in having helped others bring their talents to fruit is real. I can't explain it! Do I have to?

# ACKNOWLEDGEMENTS

The Editors would like to thank the following people for their kind assistance: Lionel Abrahams, Martin Bliden, Claudia Braude, JM Coetzee, Patrick Cullinan, Charl Durand, Juan Els, Gus Ferguson, Jane Fox, Chantal Friedman, Michael Gardiner, Mark Gevisser, Hillary Hamburger, Michelle Handler Shimansky, Charl Hattingh, Es'kia Mphahlele, Pat Schwartz, Arik Shimansky, Nicky Stubbs, Adrian Tyghe, Stu Woolman, the members of the Lionel Abrahams Writers' Workshop and, of course, all our contributors and other members of the South African writing community for their universally warm response to this project.

A big thanks to William Kentridge for allowing us to use his artwork on the cover, and to Kim Segel for helping with, amongst other things, the notes on contributors. Much appreciation is also due to our publisher and editor, David Philip, for embracing this book so enthusiastically. We especially want to thank Matthew and David Friedman for putting up with our commandeering of the dining-room table, and Tracey Segel, for being our part-time 'boss' and helping us – with ideas and administration – to get this book off the ground, and for keeping us going with her wonderful meals.

The Editors and Publishers have made every effort to trace copyright holders and publishers. Where this has proved impossible, we would be very interested to hear from anyone who might have any information to convey. We undertake to amend any omissions in the event of a reprint. We wish to express our gratitude to the contributors for allowing us to publish their work, and to acknowledge the following publications, where some of the pieces have previously appeared:

*Carapace*; *New Contrast*; *Ophir*; *Sesame*; *UCT Poetry Web* (http://www.uct.ac.za/projects/poetry); *Electronic Sesame* (http://www.pix.za/barefoot.press/esesame/esesame.htm); *Barefoot Press Free Poetry Pages* (http://www.pix.za/barefoot.press); *A Very Far Place* by Eleanor Anderson (Snailpress, Cape Town, 1995); *South African Writing Today* edited by Nadine Gordimer & Lionel Abrahams (Penguin, Harmondsworth, 1967); *One Hundred and Three Poems* by Eva Royston (Bezwoda)

(Renoster Books, Johannesburg, 1973); *Unto Dust* by HC Bosman (Human & Rousseau, 1991); *The Paperbook of South African English Poetry* edited by Michael Chapman (Ad. Donker, Johannesburg, 1986); *Lionel Abrahams: A Reader* edited by Patrick Cullinan (Ad. Donker, Johannesburg, 1988); *The Marabi Dance* by Modikwe Dikobe (Heinemann Educational Books Ltd, London, 1973); *The King of Hearts and Other Stories* by Ahmed Essop (Ravan Press, Randburg, 1997); *Carpe Diem* by Gus Ferguson (Carrefour, Cape Town, 1992); *Snail Morning* by Gus Ferguson (Ad. Donker, Johannesburg, 1979); *The Dancer and Other Poems* by Jane Fox (Snailpress, Cape Town, 1992); *Jump* by Nadine Gordimer (David Philip, Cape Town, 1991); *In the Provinces* by Robert Greig (Justified Press, Rivonia, 1991); *New-Born Images* by Geoffrey Haresnape (Justified Press, Rivonia, 1991); *A World of Their Own: Southern African Poets of the Seventies* edited by Stephen Gray (Ad. Donker, Johannesburg, 1976); *I Must Show You My Clippings* by Wopko Jensma (Ravan Press, Johannesburg, 1977); *The Anvil's Undertone* by Douglas Livingstone (Ad. Donker, Johannesburg, 1978); *Solstice* by Don Maclennan (Snailpress/Scottish Cultural Press, Cape Town, 1997); *Ugogo* by E M Macphail (Hond, Pretoria, 1994); *Ruth Miller: Poems, Prose, Plays* edited by Lionel Abrahams (The Carrefour Press, Cape Town, 1990); *earth-stepper/the ocean is very shallow* by Seitlhamo Motsapi (Deep South/ISEA, Grahamstown, 1995); *In the Land of Plenty* edited by Roy Blumenthal & Robert Berold (Barefoot Press, Johannesburg, 1994); *Down Second Avenue* by Ezekiel Mphahlele (Faber and Faber, London, 1971); *Sounds of a Cowhide Drum* by Oswald Joseph Mtshali (Renoster Books, Johannesburg, 1971); *The World of Nat Nakasa* edited by Essop Patel (Ravan Press/Bateleur Press, Johannesburg, 1975); *The Return of the Amasi Bird: Black South African Poetry 1891–1981* edited by Tim Couzens & Essop Patel (Ravan Press, Johannesburg, 1982); *Fire Dance* by Robert Royston (Renoster Books, Johannesburg, 1973); *Surfer* by Riva Rubin (Moriah Publishers, Tel Aviv, 1996); *Hurry Up To It!* by Sydney Sipho Sepamla (Ad. Donker, Johannesburg, 1975); *Yakhal'inkomo* by Mongane Wally Serote (Renoster Books, Johannesburg, 1972); *Tsetlo* by Mongane Wally Serote (Ad. Donker, Johannesburg, 1974); *Joburg, Sis!* by Barney Simon (Bateleur Press, Johannesburg, 1974); *The Conversation* (Bernard Stone & Raymond Danowski. The Turret Bookshop, London, 1992); *Missing Persons* by Ivan Vladislavić (David Philip, Cape Town, 1991); *Presence of the Earth: New Poems* by Stephen Watson (David Philip, Cape Town, 1995); *Last Walk in Naryshkin Park* by Rose Zwi (Witwatersrand University Press, Johannesburg/Spinifex Press, North Melbourne, 1997)

# CONTRIBUTORS

**TATAMKHULU AFRIKA** was born in Egypt, published a novel at age seventeen but did not write again until 1987 after having been banned and imprisoned for anti-apartheid activities. Since then he has published several poetry collections (including *Nine Lives* and *Turning Points*), two novels (*The Innocents* and *Broken Earth*), and a collection of four novellas (*Tightrope*). His poetry prizes include the CNA Debut Prize (1991), the Olive Schreiner Prize (1992) and the Sanlam Literary Award (1994). He lives in a little wooden hut on the grounds of a house in Cape Town's Bo-Kaap. **MIKE ALFRED** has earned his living as a technical writer for some years, having moved from the field of Human Resource management. He has published poetry, short fiction and travel articles. He and his wife live in Johannesburg. **ELEANOR ANDERSON** was born in a small British Columbia town. Love brought her to live on a goldmine in South Africa in 1941. She published short stories and poems and, for the *Star* in the sixties and early seventies, social commentary about the absurdities of apartheid. A collection of stories and poems, *A Very Far Place*, was published six months before she died in December 1995. **FAROUK ASVAT** is a medical doctor living in Johannesburg. He was banned from 1973 to 1978. He has published two collections of poetry. **JILLIAN BECKER** has been acclaimed internationally as a writer of novels (*The Keep, The Union, The Virgins*) and non-fiction (*Hitler's Children* has been translated into eight languages and was a *Newsweek* Book of the Year choice). She won a Pushcart Prize (USA) for a short story. She became the Director of the Institute for the Study of Terrorism in 1986. South African born, she has lived in London since 1960. She has three daughters. **EVA BEZWODA** was an editor and director of Renoster Books, and assisted Lionel with *The Purple Renoster*. She published a great deal of poetry in literary journals in South Africa and abroad. Her collection, *One Hundred and Three Poems*, was published in 1973. She left to live in England in 1972 and committed suicide on 1 January 1976 shortly after a visit to South Africa. **ROY BLUMENTHAL**'s poems have appeared in *Sesame, New Coin, Carapace, Botsotso, Staffrider* and other journals. He has performed his poetry on national television and radio, and in venues around South Africa. His collections include *Brutal Syrup, Blur, The Music Next Door, Portraits of an African Landscape* and *Sweatland*. 'Hanging On', a screenplay he co-wrote with Jeremy Handler, is a finalist in the international Channel 4 Short & Curlies short film competition. He runs an internet marketing company, and Barefoot Press, a publishing house which publishes literary fiction and distributes free poetry pamphlets. He is completing his first novel. **HERMAN CHARLES BOSMAN** was born in Kuils River, near Cape Town, in 1905. He went to the University of the Witwatersrand, qualified as a teacher, and worked in the Marico district of the then Western Transvaal before turning to journalism (he worked for six years on Fleet Street). In his early twenties he killed his step-brother with a hunting rifle and was given the death sentence, later commuted to eight years with hard labour. He served just under four years at Pretoria Central Prison, an experience he turned to good effect in *Cold Stone Jug*. Probably South Africa's most enduring and beloved short-story writer, his other works include *Mafeking Road*, *Unto Dust*, *A Bekkersdal Marathon*, a volume of poetry, *The Earth is Waiting*, and a novel, *Jacaranda in the Night*. He died in 1951. **SANDRA LEE BRAUDE** was born in Johannesburg. She lectured in English for seventeen years before becoming Assistant Administrator and Editor for COSAW. She has published stories, poems and articles in local journals, and two books, *Windswept Plains: Poems and Stories* and *Mpho's Search*. She won First Prize in the Storytelling Conference, Budapest, 1992. She is the editor of *herStoriA: South African Women's Journal*. **GUY BUTLER** was raised in Cradock in the Eastern Cape. He is Emeritus Professor of English at Rhodes University, and was Department Head from 1952 to 1980. His poetry collections include *Selected Poems*, which won the CNA Literary Award. He has written plays and edited various works, including *A Book of South African Verse*, and has published three volumes of autobiography. **PAUL CHRISTELIS** is a psychotherapist. He has written plays, poetry, song lyrics and has hosted a radio show. *Rabbit Season*, a novel, is under consideration by Barefoot Press. He is pursuing a career in film and writing in the United Kingdom. **PATRICK CULLINAN** was born in Pretoria in 1932. After his education, mostly abroad, he farmed and ran a sawmill in Mpumalanga. Apart from a lifelong commitment to poetry, he has also been a headhunter, publisher (with Lionel Abrahams), magazine editor and university lecturer. His stories, poems and articles have appeared widely in South Africa and overseas. He has published four collections of poetry, an historical biography and an anthology of Lionel Abrahams's work. He is presently writing a novel. **JULIA CUMES** was born in Alice in the Eastern Cape in 1972. She was educated in Johannesburg, Honolulu (having moved to Hawaii in 1987), and on the US mainland. She has a Masters in Fine Arts (Poetry and Fiction) from Cornell University, where she teaches creative writing and a course on South African literature. **MODIKWE DIKOBE** (Marks Rammitloa) was born in 1913 at Seabe in the then Northern Transvaal. He went to Johannesburg at the age of ten, left school after standard six, and thereafter led a varied life as a newspaper vendor, a hawker, a clerk, a book-keeper, a trade unionist, and a night watchman. In the forties he was prominent in the Alexandra Squatters movement. *The Marabi Dance*, written after a three-month detention in the 1960s, was published under a nom de plume because he was banned. *Dispossessed*, his poetry collection, was published in 1983. **ALISTAIR DREDGE** has an honours degree in philosophy from Wits. He lives in Braamfontein and works as a computer programmer. His poetry has been published in *Electronic Sesame* and in the *Star*. **SHIRLEY ESKAPA**'s bestselling novels include *Scales of Passion* and *Blood Relations*. Her non-fiction study of wives and mistresses, *Woman versus Woman*, was translated into nine languages. She has made a number of television appearances, including guest spots on the Oprah Winfrey Show. She has lived in Johannesburg, Geneva, Monte Carlo and Palm Beach, and now lives in London. **AHMED ESSOP** was born in 1931 in Dabhel, India. He has a BA degree and has taught at schools in Fordsburg, Lenasia, and Eldorado Park. In between, he worked in commerce. In 1986 he left teaching to devote himself to full-time writing. His work includes *The Hajji and Other Stories*, two novels, *The Visitation* and *The Emperor*, and his latest book, *The King of Hearts and Other Stories*. **FRANCIS FALLER** has, for nearly twenty years, been involved in teacher education at the Johannesburg College of Education. He has published two volumes of poetry, *Weather Words,* an AA Vita Poetry Award winner, and *Verse-Over*, a Sanlam Literary Award winner. **DAVID FARRELL** was born in London in 1941 but arrived in South Africa at the age of six. He went to London in 1982 and stayed 13 years before returning to settle in Cape Town. His poetry has been published in various South African magazines, including *The Purple Renoster, Contrast, The Classic, Izwi* and *Wurm*, as well as in numerous anthologies. A collection of poems, *The Charlie Manson False Bay Talking Rock Blues* appeared in 1974. He now lives in Fish Hoek and works as a sub-editor on the *Cape Argus*. He has a daughter and two granddaughters. **PNINA FENSTER** is the editor of *Marie Claire* magazine. Prior to that, she wrote for a variety of international and South African publications, and was a columnist for the *Sunday Times*, and a features writer for *Sunday Magazine* and *Fair Lady*. Her journalism has won several awards and her short stories have appeared in anthologies of contemporary writing. **GUS FERGUSON** was born in Scotland in 1940 and came to South Africa at the age of 10. He is a cartoonist and poet. His books include *Snail Morning, Doggerel Day, Carpe Diem*, and *Light Verse at the End of the Tunnel*. He lives in Cape Town where he works as a pharmacist and edits the poetry magazine *Carapace*. He has published many poets under the Snailpress and Firfield Press imprints. **JANE FOX** immigrated to South Africa in her early twenties and is currently Thames & Hudson's trade representative in Johannesburg. She has three children and three grandchildren and lives in Rivonia with her husband, Lionel Abrahams. Best known as a short-story writer, her work has appeared in *Sesame*, the *English Academy Review*, and *Hippogriff New Writing*. A collection of poetry, *The Dancer and Other Poems*, appeared in 1992. David Philip will be publishing her novel, *The Killing Bottle*. **GRAEME FRIEDMAN** works as a psychotherapist in Johannesburg where he lives with his wife and two sons. He has published academic papers on torture and apartheid's political trials. In 1994 he won second prize in the Macmillan Boleswa/Pace Writers' Competition for a novel which was based on his experiences as an expert witness for the defence in trials of ANC cadres and other activists. His short stories appear in two anthologies of South African literature. In 1996 he won first prize in the *herStoriA* Short Story Competition. He has just completed *The Fossil Artist*, his second novel. **MICHAEL GARDINER** has published articles on the writing of Pauline Smith, Wopko Jensma and on a number of linguistic and educational topics. He was awarded a British Council Fellowship in 1988 to research 'People's Education'. He is currently co-ordinator of the Cultural Studies Research Programme at Vista University, Soweto. **MARK GEVISSER** is a free-lance journalist living in Johannesburg. His *Mail & Guardian* profiles were collected into a book called *Portraits of Power*. He is the co-editor of *Defiant Desire: Gay and Lesbian Lives in South Africa*. He is the South African correspondent of the *New York Nation* and has also written for the *New York Times*, the *Guardian*, *Vogue* and other magazines. He was educated in the United States. **MARC GLASER** was born in 1936 in Johannesburg. He studied for periods at the Michaelis Art School in Cape Town and at the University of the Witwatersrand. He has had exhibitions in Cape Town, Johannesburg and Pretoria and his stories, poems and drawings have appeared in various journals including *Sesame*, *Staffrider* and *New Coin*. *The Unquiet Love*, a collection of short stories, was published in 1993. **NADINE GORDIMER** was born in Springs. Her short-story collections include *Some Monday for Sure* and *Jump*. Amongst her numerous novels are her first, *The Lying Days*, *The Conservationist* (joint winner of the Booker Prize), *A Guest of Honour* (James Tait Black Prize), and her latest, *The House Gun*. Her collections of essays include *Writing and Being*. She won the Nobel Prize for Literature in 1991. **ROBERT GREIG** was first published, when he was a schoolboy, by Lionel Abrahams in *The Purple Renoster*. Since then he has published two collections, *In the Provinces* and *Talking Bull*, which won the Olive Schreiner Prize for poetry. He is arts editor of the *Sunday Independent*. **HILLARY HAMBURGER** was born and raised in Johannesburg. She worked as a high-school teacher before taking on her vocation as a psychotherapist. **GEOFFREY HARESNAPE** was born in Durban and now teaches South African poetry and creative writing at the University of Cape Town. He has published a novel, *Testimony*, and three books of poetry: *Drive of the Tide*, *New-Born Images* and *Mulberries in Autumn*. His poems and short stories have appeared in numerous magazines and anthologies. He has won several literary prizes including the Sanlam Literary Award, the Heinemann/Weekly Mail Literary Award, and the Arthur Nortje Memorial Award. **ABRAM HLABATAU** lives in Alexandra, where he attended Lionel's workshops. He was a contributor to *Sesame*. **CHRISTOPHER HOPE** was born in Johannesburg in 1944 and now lives in France. He has published novels, poetry, plays, non-fiction and children's books. His prizes include the Whitbread Prize for Fiction (for *Kruger's Alp*) and the CNA Literary Award (for the non-fiction *White Boy Running*). His novel, *Serenity House*, was shortlisted for the 1992 Booker Prize. **FRANCES HUNTER** spent twenty-six years in Johannesburg where she worked as a social worker and as a journalist. She now lives in the USA, the land of her birth, where two of her four children have emigrated. Her stories and poems have been published in various literary journals and anthologies, including *The Vita Anthology of New South African Short Fiction*. **FLOSS M JAY** is a psychotherapist living in Pietermarizburg. Her poems and short stories have appeared in various anthologies, including *LIP from Southern African Women*, and literary journals including *Contrast*, *New Coin*, *Sesame* and *Staffrider*. **CUZ JEPPE** is a worker in wood and glass. He built a sea-faring boat which took him around the world and was hijacked by pirates. He speaks of himself as a 'sometime learner writer' who is 'more travelled than learned'. **WOPKO JENSMA** published three volumes of poetry: *Sing for Our Execution (Poems and Woodcuts)*, *Where White is the Colour Where Black is the Number* and *i must show you my clippings*. **LEON JOFFE** trained as an electronics engineer at Wits. He started out by designing concert hall acoustics, and moved on to weapons design. He is now trying to make ploughshares as well as swords. He is married to Pitta Joffe, the foremost authority on South African indigenous plants. **ANNE KELLAS**'s poems have been published in a variety of magazines in South Africa, the United States, and Australia. Her work has appeared in a special Columbia Magazine issue on South African writers, and in the anthology, *Like a House on Fire: South African Women's Art and Writing*. Her poetry collection, *Poems from Mt Moono*, was published in 1989. She now lives in Tasmania, where she is an editor for the literary journal, *Famous Reporter*, and co-edits *The Write Stuff*, an internet book review publication. **YVONNE KEMP** was born in Cape Town in 1944, and is the head of the editorial department at UNISA. Her stories have appeared in *The Vita Anthology of New South African Short Fiction* and in *Sesame*, where she won two Eleanor Anderson Awards. **MAJA KRIEL** was born in Johannesburg, but thanks to the restless urges of a vagrant father, spent her childhood years in the lower reaches of New York City. She is now a determined Johannesburg *bittereinder*. Her short stories have been published here and abroad in literary journals. *Original Sin*, a collection of short stories, was published in 1993. She has also written an unpublished novel, 'Rings in A Tree'. **DEBBY LAPIDOS** was born in 1961. She completed a BA majoring in English, taught privately in Spain, and then did the H.Dip.Ed. diploma at Wits. She was an English teacher for three years and presently works as an education consultant and yoga instructor. **HUGH LEWIN** was born in Lydenburg, schooled in Johannesburg, and went to university at Rhodes. He collected the material for his first book (*Bandiet: Seven Years in a South African Prison*) by way of a political sentence in Pretoria in 1964. Thereafter he spent two decades in exile, first in London, then Harare, which also produced his children's books, including the Jafta Family series. Other books include *Community of Clowns*, a history of the Urban Rural Mission for the WCC in Geneva. His latest book is a Heinemann title for teenagers, *Follow the Crow*. His poems have appeared in *Sesame* and in several anthologies. **DOUGLAS LIVINGSTONE** was one of South Africa's foremost English-speaking poets. He was born in Kuala Lumpur in 1932 and worked as a marine biologist. He won major international and local awards for his poetry, including the CNA Literary Award for *Selected Poems*. Other works include *Eyes Closed Against the Sun*, *A Rosary of Bone* and *A Littoral Zone*. **DON MACLENNAN** was born in London and came to South Africa when he was nine years old. He has taught at the University of the Witwatersrand, the University of Cape Town and Rhodes University. He has published a number of plays, short stories, six collections of poems (including *Letters* and *The Poetry Lesson*) and a handful of scholarly works. **E M MACPHAIL** was born on a farm not far from where Soweto is today. She has lived in isolated parts of the bushveld and in small towns in the Transvaal. She now lives in Johannesburg with her husband. Her first novel, *Phoebe & Nio*, won the CNA Literary Award, and her second, *Mrs Chud's Place*, garnered the Sanlam Literary Award. She started creative writing when she joined Lionel Abrahams's workshop in 1977. She has published several collections of short stories. **DAVID MEDALIE** studied English at Oxford University and the University of the Witwatersrand, where he is currently teaching in the English Department. A collection of short stories, *The Shooting of the Christmas Cows*, was published in 1990. 'Recognition', a short story, won the Sanlam Literary Award in the unpublished category in 1996. He is the editor of *Encounters: An Anthology of South African Short Stories*, published in 1998. **RUTH MILLER** was born in Uitenhage in the Cape, in 1919, and spent her childhood in the northern Transvaal. Her writings have been included in numerous journals and anthologies here and abroad, and two collections of her poems have been published. The first, *Floating Island*, earned her the inaugural Ingrid Jonker Prize. The second, *Selected Poems*, was accepted by Cecil Day Lewis for the Phoenix Living Poets series, and appeared in 1968, a few months before her death. She is widely recognised as one of South Africa's best poets. **BENJAMIN MOLEFI** was homeless when he attended Lionel's workshops in Alexandra. It was in this forum that he honed his poem, 'Sleeping in the Church'. His work has been published in *Sesame*. **JONATHAN MORGAN** is a freelance writer and a regular contributor to *Sidelines* and *Cosmopolitan*. He is also a psychotherapist in private practice, runs Rocket Language School with his Japanese wife, and has created Gener8, a post-modern singles club for those allergic to inhospitable venues devoid of intelligent life. **ROSE MOSS** was born in Johannesburg and taught at Roma, the University of Natal and Unisa before emigrating to the United States. She has published two novels, one non-fiction book, and many stories and articles. She now teaches writing at Harvard University and works as a management consultant. **SEITLHAMO MOTSAPI** grew up in Bela-Bela, near Warmbaths in the Transvaal. He has degrees from the University of the Witwatersrand and the University of the North, where he now lectures in English. He has published poetry in literary journals, and his first volume, *earthstepper/the ocean is very deep*, was published in 1994. **ES'KIA MPHAHLELE** was born and raised in Marabastad, Pretoria, the setting for his first autobiography, *Down Second Avenue*. He earned his PhD in English at Denver University in the US. He was the first Professor of African Literature at the University of the Witwatersrand, and retired in 1987. He has also taught in Paris, Nairobi, Denver, Lusaka and Philadelphia. He now lives in the Northern Province. His works include short stories, a novella, critical essays, several novels, a sequel to his autobiography and *Exiles and Homecomings*, an experimental documentary. **OSWALD MTSHALI** was born in 1940 in Vryheid. He was awarded the Olive Schreiner Prize for *Sounds of a Cowhide Drum*. On his return from Columbia University in 1980, *Fireflames* was published. **LIONEL MURCOTT** has studied and taught in Natal, Cape Town and Johannesburg. He was born in the Transvaal, and lives in Johannesburg, where he teaches art at a high school. His poems have appeared in *My Drum 1* and *2*, and in various literary periodicals in South Africa and abroad. His drawings, paintings and ceramics have been included in many group exhibitions, and he is listed in *A Dictionary of SA Painters and Sculptors*. His most recent publications include the Barefoot Press poetry pamphlet, *Tuis*, and the introduction to Roger Ballin's latest book of photographs, *Cette Afrique Là: Photographs*. **NAT NAKASA** was a regular contributor to *Drum* and *Golden City Post*, and later joined the *Rand Daily Mail* as its first black journalist. He founded and edited *The Classic* (named after a shebeen), whose objective was to encourage black writing. He was awarded a Niemann Fellowship to read journalism at Harvard and was refused a passport. He left on an exit permit, unable to return to South Africa. He had started contributing to the *New York Times* and American journals, when, on 14 July 1965, he committed suicide in New York City. He was twenty-eight. **NJABULO S NDEBELE** has degrees from Cambridge and Denver. His awards include the Thomas Pringle Prize and the Noma Award for his collection *Fools and Other Stories*. He was a lecturer and the vice-rector at Roma University in Lesotho, head of the African Languages Department at Wits, the vice-rector of the University of the Western Cape, and the rector of Turfloop. He is chairperson of the National Arts Initiative. **KAIZER M NYATSUMBA** was born at White River in the Eastern Transvaal in 1936. He was educated at the University of Zululand, and Georgetown University in Washington. He works as the Deputy Editor of *The Mercury* in Durban. He has authored two books of poetry, two short-story collections and a book on South African politics. His work has also appeared in *Staffrider*, *The Classic*, and *The Vita Anthology of New South African Short Fiction*. **ZACHARIAH RAPOLA** lives in Johannesburg, and works as a director and screen writer. He recently won a fellowship to attend film school in Denmark. His poetry has appeared in various publications, including *Tribute*. **ETHELWYN REBELO** is a divorced mother of three children. She works as a psychologist at the Hillbrow Hospital and at the Family Life Centre in Parkview. **ROBERT ROYSTON** has published poems in literary magazines such as *The Classic* and *The Purple Renoster*. With his wife Eva Bezwoda, and Lionel Abrahams, he started the publishing company Renoster Books. He has worked as a journalist and as an editor. His volume of poetry, *Fire Dance*, was published in 1973, shortly before he emigrated to England. He has lived there since, and now works as a psychoanalytic psychotherapist. His play, *The Struggle*, was performed at The Gate Theatre in London in 1989. His second play, *Home Time*, was shortlisted for the Verity Bargle Award. He has written two novels and has had stories published in *London Magazine*. **RIVA RUBIN**, poet, translator, editor and teacher, was born in South Africa and has lived in Israel since 1963. Her publications include five books of poetry. Her work has appeared in anthologies in most English-speaking countries and has been widely translated into Hebrew as well as into Spanish and Rumanian. She has won several literary awards including the Dulzin Prize. She served on the Executive Board of the Israel Chapter of PEN for five years, and edited its 1993 English language anthology of Israeli writers. **WALTER SAUNDERS** has lectured in English at UNISA and at the University of Venda. He has recently moved to Normandy, France, where he is devoting himself to writing. With Peter Horn, he co-founded *Ophir*. He was the founding editor of *Quarry*. His poetry is widely published and includes *Masks, Faces, Animae*, and the tribute, *For Douglas Livingstone: A Reminiscence*. **SIPHO SEPAMLA** was born near Krugersdorp in the Transvaal. He at present lives with his wife and family in Wattville near Benoni. He trained as a teacher and taught secondary school English and Mathematics. He has promoted theatrical arts in Johannesburg and was the director of the Federated Union of Black Arts (FUBA). He was the editor of *New Classic* and *S'ketsh*. His poetry collections include *Hurry Up To It*, *The Blues Is You In Me* and *The Soweto I Love*. Many of his poems and short stories have appeared in anthologies and literary journals. **MONGANE WALLY SEROTE** was born in Sophiatown. As a Fulbright Scholar he completed a Master of Fine Arts degree in 1977 at the University of Columbia. His published works include a novel, a book of essays, and several volumes of poetry, one of which, *Third World Express*, won the Noma Award. He has lived in Botswana and in London, where he was head of the ANC Cultural Desk. After returning to South Africa he headed the ANC Department of Arts and Culture. He is now a Member of Parliament. **ARIK SHIMANSKY** is currently sharing his time between doing a PhD in physical chemistry, running a successful internet marketing business, writing poetry and fiction, and, with his wife, raising his first child. **BARNEY SIMON** took over the editorship of *The Classic* after Nat Nakasa left the country in the mid-sixties. He wrote TV and film scripts, song lyrics, and published a collection of short stories, *Joburg, Sis!* During the seventies and early eighties he was involved with health education projects in Winterveld, KwaZulu, and the Transkei. Best known for his theatre work, he was the artistic director of the Market Theatre Company, where he was a much-loved nurturer of actors and writers. He directed, amongst many other plays, *Born in the RSA* and *Woza Albert!* He died of a heart attack in 1995. **LILIAN SIMON** is married and has three children. She has taught Latin most of her life, after starting off as an English teacher. Her writing has appeared in *New Coin, herStoriA, The Bloody Horse, Sesame, Jewish Affairs, Firetalk, Hippogriff New Writing* and *25/25 English South African Poetry. Inyanga* was published by Justified Press. **DOUGLAS REID SKINNER**, born in Upington in the northern Cape, now lives in London. He was the editor of *New Contrast, Upstream,* and *The South African Literary Review,* and was a director of the Carrefour Press. He has published four books of poems: *Reassembling World, The House in Pella District, The Unspoken* and *The Middle Years.* He is the joint winner of the 1995/6 British Comparative Literature Association translation competition for his renderings from the Italian of poems by Marco Fazzini. **CATHERINE STEWART** is a film writer and director. She has lived in Argentina, Uruguay, the United States and Spain, and currently lives in South Africa. Her poem, 'At Three in Her Morning', recently received the Deon Hofmeyr Creative Writing Prize. She has a Master of Fine Arts in film writing and directing from Columbia University. She lectures in screen writing and directing at Wits University and is also completing a Masters in African Literature. **TONY ULLYATT** was born in England and has travelled widely. He is currently Professor of English at the University of the Free State. His poems have been published in Australia, Canada, America, New Zealand, and South Africa. **IVAN VLADISLAVIĆ** was born in Pretoria. After studying at the University of the Witwatersrand, he worked as an editor at Ravan Press. He was assistant editor of *Staffrider* magazine, and co-edited the commemorative anthology, *Ten Years of Staffrider.* He now works as a freelance editor. His work has appeared in many journals, including *Grand Street, New Contrast, Revue Noire, Sesame, Soho Square, Staffrider, TriQuarterly* and *World Literature Today,* and has been translated into French, German and Swedish. He has won several awards, including the Olive Schreiner Prize and the CNA Literary Award. He has published a novel (*The Folly*) and two collections of stories (*Missing Persons* and *Propaganda by Monuments*). **STEPHEN WATSON** was born in Cape

Town. He is an Associate Professor of English at the University of Cape Town. He has published four books of poems, including *Return of the Moon* and *Presence of the Earth*. His latest book is *A Writer's Diary*. **PETER WILHELM** was born in Cape Town and spent his early life on a mission station in the Transkei with his grandparents. He now works in Cape Town as a financial journalist. His most recent novel, *The Mask of Freedom*, won the Sanlam Literary Award in 1995. He is at work on a selection of his short stories. **ROSE ZWI** was born in Mexico, lived in London and Israel, but has spent most of her life in South Africa. She now lives in Australia. An author of five novels, she has won several prizes for her work, including the 1994 Human Rights Award for her novel *Safe Houses* and the 1982 Olive Schreiner Prize for *Another Year in Africa*. Her other books include *The Inverted Pyramid, Exiles, The Umbrella Tree* and *Last Walk in Naryshkin Park*.